STAR BREAKER

AMANDA BOUCHET

MIX
Paper from
responsible sources
FSC
FSC® C104740

Piatkus
An imprint of
Little, Brown Book Group
Carmelite House
50 Victoria Embankment
London EC4Y 0DZ

An Hachette UK Company
www.hachette.co.uk

PIATKUS

PIATKUS

First published in the US in 2020 by Sourcebooks, Inc.
First published in Great Britain in 2020 by Piatkus
This paperback edition published in 2020 by Piatkus

1 3 5 7 9 10 8 6 4 2

Copyright © 2020 by Amanda Bouchet

The moral right of the author has been asserted.

A CIP catalogue record for this book is available from the British Library.

ISBN 978-0-349-42091-2

Printed and bound in Great Britain by Clays Ltd, Elcograf S.p.A.

Papers used by Piatkus are from well-managed forests
and other responsible sources.

www.littlebrown.co.uk

For Callie,
Our chances of meeting were slim, so I'm pretty sure
the universe gave us to each other on purpose.
Thank you for being my friend.

CHAPTER

1

TESS

WHERE'S DANIEL AHERN?

My leg bounced under the table as I discreetly scanned the crowded restaurant for the hundredth time. Our contact wasn't here. Fashionably late crashed and burned a good forty minutes ago, and I was ready to take care of my own business now instead of his.

"Ahern's not going to show," I muttered tightly into my com.

"We don't know that." Shade's deep voice rumbled softly from his wristband into my earpiece. My eyes flicked over to where he sat, meeting his honey-brown gaze from across a sea of heads and indistinct chatter. "Sit tight."

I took a deep breath, trying to settle my jangling nerves. Movement blurred in my peripheral vision. My lungs squeezed as I darted a look at the door. A soberly dressed unsmiling trio walked in. Not who I was waiting for.

"You look like you're about to jump out of your skin," Shade murmured. "Act normal. Eat your soup."

I scowled. My lunch had a better chance of landing on Shade's head than in my stomach if he told me to eat again.

"I can't." My necklace picked up my almost inaudible whisper, transmitting it not only to Shade but to Jax and Fiona, who were somewhere outside, and to Merrick, who'd stayed on the ship. "We shouldn't even be on this mission."

Shade's soft grunt of agreement didn't change the fact that we were stuck. "Can't say it seemed as though we had much of a choice."

No, and that was just one of the weird things about it. We weren't spies. The *Endeavor* wasn't a ship housing soldiers and moles. We were Nightchasers on a big old cargo cruiser, rebels who brought food, medicine, and other supplies to people who needed it around the galaxy. This wasn't a mission for us. So why did the head of the rebel council suddenly decide that *we* were the ones who needed to go meet some guy about freeing his incarcerated wife from the Dark Watch?

I toyed with my soup to look busy, little surges of adrenaline spiking inside me and keeping me on edge. I'd been here for an hour and had worked up a sweat and lost my appetite—the opposite of what you wanted in a restaurant where the food smelled so freaking good.

While Shade polished off his lunch, I used my spoon to poke at a few recognizable vegetables and what the menu called beef. *Steak* and *beef* were just generic terms for red meat these days. I didn't know what kind of cattle—another generic term—they raised on Korabon for food. I'd never been here before, had never planned on coming. *Shouldn't* be here now. Time was running out.

I set the spoon back in the bowl. A glance toward the basket of thickly sliced trigrain bread made my stomach flip over, rejecting even that. Anxiety killed my appetite as fast as a Dark Watch patrol showing up and barking out "Background checks!" to everyone in the room.

Shade sighed. "Baby, it's more suspicious *not* to eat."

I sighed back at him. "It'll make the return trip if I try." The few bites I'd managed weren't sitting well. "Do you really want a soupatastrophe on your hands?"

His quick smile blazed across the room. It ignited a little flame in my chest that helped ease some of the tightness there. "Given the choice, there are other things I'd rather have in my hands."

"I didn't say *in*, I said *on*. There's quite a distinction."

"Ah. My mistake." He wiped his mouth with his napkin, probably hiding a grin.

I mashed my lips together and forgot to be nervous for a second. I even managed a bite. Just one, though.

Shade took a moment to look at me hard. I got the message he couldn't say out loud over the coms. *Eat. Keep your strength up.* He and I were the only ones who knew I'd drawn more of my unique A1 blood.

Or maybe it wasn't that unique. Maybe these Mornavail I'd heard about were out there somewhere, healing faster and never getting sick. Like me—an evolutionary step up. And also like me, hiding from the Galactic Overseer, who wanted our blood to create an army of super soldiers.

Fun times across the eighteen Sectors. My grimace had nothing to do with my soup this time.

"My picture was just all over a database for bounty hunters. Now, *you* have my enormous bounty on *your* head. How can you eat?" We should be lying low and delivering the food we still had for the Outer Zones, not sitting in a restaurant on a highly monitored rock.

"I may be new to life in the Dark, but I'm a fast learner. Fresh food only comes around so often in a space rat's life. It's tragic to waste it."

"Shade's right," Fiona whispered over the coms. "Eat the damn soup," she hissed.

"Shhhh!" Jax scolded quietly.

A laugh churned inside me. Briefly, my eyes collided with Shade's again. It was hard not to focus on him. A handsome man treating me to a meal in a not entirely shabby establishment had never happened before today. Too bad we couldn't sit together and only one of us had an appetite.

"Fine." I steeled myself and took a bite so that everyone would stop hounding me. "Happy?"

Shade huffed, evidently unconvinced.

I forced down another mouthful, chewing and swallowing carefully. At least my battle with the soup got my mind off Ahern. And the food would do me good. The six bags of blood I'd taken from my own veins in as many days hadn't totally wiped me out, but I hadn't been able to completely shake it off yet, either. Beef—or whatever this was—would help.

The two women occupying the table next to Shade's threw him flirty glances and leaned over to ask him a question about desserts. The waitress immediately joined in, having already attempted to draw Shade into conversation twice. I got it. It wasn't often that tall, dark, and smoldering sat alone in a restaurant.

They finally left him alone after deciding on a choco seed dessert loaf to share. The waitress went to get it.

"Wow, you really are a wanted man," I grumbled, a hint of tartness in my voice.

Shade's small snort vibrated over the com, tickling my eardrum. "I want their dessert."

"You *are* their dessert." He was six foot two of solid yumminess with a healthy appetite, broad shoulders, a square jaw, and scarred knuckles that said *I can protect you with my bare hands*. I'd even bitten him and knew for a fact he tasted good. "But trust me, neither wants to share."

Humor sparked in his eyes, and for the first time in an hour, I forgot why we were here.

The happy lapse didn't last. My heart kicked when the door opened again. An older couple walked in, and the waitress for my corner threw me a dirty look, clearly wanting me to get lost so she could give my table to someone who might actually eat something.

I'd love to, I growled inside my head. *If Daniel Ahern would just show up*.

If Ahern wanted us to rescue his scientist wife from her extended stay in the imperial prison system, he needed to get his rebel butt in here and give me his new intel before a Dark Watch patrol spotted two of the galaxy's Most Wanted through the floor-to-ceiling windows, stormed in, and Shade and I were toast.

I chewed my lower lip, wondering what was really going on. "Why the short notice? Why us?" I murmured. We only just found out about this mission, giving us barely enough time to wrap up the ship improvements Shade had been working on in the Fold, make the jump to Korabon, dig out the old coms I kept aboard the *Endeavor*, and get a few hours of sleep. We'd arrived in the dead of night here and couldn't do much else.

"Been asking myself the same questions, starshine." Shade's low curse told me he was still livid about not having more time to prepare. "Giving us this little to work with feels like we're being set up to fail."

"I don't believe that." I *couldn't*.

The sudden attention from Loralie Harris and her rebel council didn't surprise me, even if the last-minute nature of this odd assignment did. We'd just managed the coup of the century, stealing Overseer Novalight's entire supply of super-soldier serum and bringing it to the rebel leaders in the Fold. We'd dealt the biggest blow in living memory to the tyrant I used to call Dad, and now we were apparently special enough to get "the good missions"—just when I needed to be left alone.

Still, that didn't explain the lack of information or support tech. All we got from the rebel council was a picture of Ahern and a meeting place. No handy gadgets. Nothing about Korabon or the Dark Watch here. Maybe it didn't matter. We weren't tourists, and the military on Korabon would be like anywhere else: all over the place.

Right now, I was more worried about bounty hunters coming after my boyfriend. I probably wasn't all that recognizable outside of Shade's ex-circle of elite hunters. Images of the Overseer's supposedly long-dead daughter popping up on screens across the galaxy would raise questions that even a *shut up or blow up* dictator might have trouble answering. But Nathaniel Bridgebane, top Dark Watch general and the Overseer's right-hand man, had threatened to go after Shade with a vengeance—and my uncle always did what he said.

I stole a look through the windows but didn't see Jaxon or Fiona. They'd hunkered down somewhere discreet and weren't muddying up the coms with unnecessary chatter like we were.

My mouth puckered. I was more than ready for all of us to get back to the *Endeavor*.

To hell with it. There had to be a time limit on waiting for informants. I couldn't sit here anymore, stewing in my own fear about getting where I needed to go with those six bags of blood by tomorrow, universal time, or I'd lose one of the most important people in my life. I was done here.

I wiggled a hand into my back pocket and grabbed some of the currency units Shade had handed me earlier to cover the restaurant charges. I was broke after paying for repairs on the *Endeavor*. Paying Shade, actually. But he was finding ways to give the money back, such as buying and installing top-notch hot-water tanks for the *Endeavor*'s kitchen and bathrooms and getting my room a bigger bed.

Four nights together—that was all we'd had since I decided to give Shade a second chance.

Bringing cat toys to Bonk had helped melt some of my lingering reservations after Shade nearly cashed me in to the Dark Watch. On our first day in the Fold, he'd come back from hardware shopping with a pair of rodent-shaped mechanical playthings that did tight little flips. Bonk kept presenting the now half-mangled fuzzy gray robots to me like gifts.

I caught Shade's eye again, murmuring, "Five more minutes and I'm done." The coins I'd counted out hit the table with a clink. I put what was left back in my pocket.

Merrick's voice came through for the first time along with a faint crackle of static. My coms were shit—a hodgepodge of old pieces we'd connected to the same signal. "Something must've held Ahern up. You can't leave until he shows."

I shook my head in silent rejection. I could, and I would. Either Mareeka's or Surral's life hung in the balance while I sat in a restaurant in Koralight Crown, one of the ten most disliked cities in the galaxy—or so I'd read during my negative two seconds of prep for this.

"Easy, partner. You've got this." Crazy as it seemed, Jaxon's voice helped. I still couldn't see him—he might be a block away or five—but I could feel him inside me, reassuring me and untangling some of the knots in my stomach. We'd been partners in prison. We were partners on the *Endeavor*. There was no one I trusted more than Jax.

"Just sit tight, Tess. A little longer, that's all." His voice lowered to the soothing tones I remembered from when I was nineteen, terrified for my life, and tossed down a mine shaft on top of him. Keeping me safe on Hourglass Mile, both above and below ground, had been the only thing that stopped Jax from totally disintegrating in the face of his grief after just having lost his wife and children. "Fi and I can see you through the windows now. We've got your back."

After a slight hesitation, I gave a quick nod. It mirrored the one Shade gave me from across the restaurant, reinforcing what Jax said.

As much as I wanted to give up on Ahern, they were right. I couldn't bail on the first job the rebel leaders had specifically assigned to my crew, even if interrupting a prison transfer was an odd choice of tasks for us. Nightchasers weren't part of the rebel forces. More like the rebel periphery. We pursued our own missions, mostly scouring the galaxy for food and medicine. We believed in a more equitable distribution of both, even if that meant theft. We also believed in training and prep work, so being slapped with our first spy mission only hours ago and just when I needed to be somewhere else really sucked.

Shade wasn't impressed. I'd heard him mutter earlier that poor planning and shitty gear were how alive people turned up dead.

I wiped my clammy palms on my lap. The need to move

spidered down my spine and into my legs. The thought of missing my clandestine—and frankly treasonous—blood exchange with my asshole uncle was eating a hole in my hide.

How much longer do I have to wait? I didn't want to ask. Everyone would just tell me to stay put.

Merrick would be so much better at this. He'd done some spy work for the rebellion, but then he got caught, shot up against his will with the Overseer's experimental enhancer, and turned into a seven-and-a-half-foot-tall, faster-than-the-eye-can-blink, barrel-chested, muscle-banded super soldier who'd escaped the Dark Watch. The big black man didn't exactly blend in.

Soft and low, Shade's voice whispered over the com again. "You're on, starshine."

My head whipped up—the exact opposite of playing it cool. Daniel Ahern walked in, or a man I was ninety-nine percent sure was him. Adrenaline ripped through me. I'd been waiting for this, just wanting it to be over, but now, I didn't feel ready in the least.

This guy fit the picture Loralie Harris had shown us in the Fold. Tall and slim, with a head of thick silver hair, a long face, and green eyes. Eyes the color of grass, according to the rebel leader. Grass colors varied from planet to planet, and a lot of places didn't have a single blade, but when people said something like that, they meant green. Generalizations always went back to Earth. It was our one common denominator after generations of expansion across the stars.

Ahern swept a casual glance around the restaurant. Only two people dined alone. His eyes lighted on Shade first but didn't stop. They got to me and locked on. Someone must have told him to look for a woman.

What else does he know? More than we did wouldn't be a stretch.

He headed straight toward me, and I took him in as he walked. He was about sixty years old, distinguished-looking, and sharply but conventionally dressed. His brown suit and stiff white shirt matched the plain colors the Overseer favored, but he'd folded a rebellious red handkerchief into his breast pocket. It just peeked out and looked like a blood-stain on his chest.

I swallowed. Logically, there was no reason to fear this meeting—this wasn't the hard part—but nerves still gripped my throat in a stranglehold.

Had someone followed him here? Could he have made a dirty deal to exchange *me* for his wife? What if he wasn't who I thought, or who he said, or a friend at all? Could it all be lies? It wasn't as though *that* hadn't happened before.

I glanced at Shade, a sharp jerk yanking at my heart. I trusted only a handful of people or let them anywhere near my personal space, and Shade—the man I fell for with the speed and recklessness of a meteor on a collision course—had messed with that. In the end, he'd saved my life and was trying to make up for his deception, but sometimes, the hurt and betrayal came roaring back and knocked the air from my lungs.

The silver-haired man stopped beside my table and peered down at me with a pointed look. "It should be a fine night for stargazing."

Considering I could barely breathe, the required response slid surprisingly easily from my tongue. "The city lights are too bright. You'd have better luck at the Mercury Tides Planetarium. I hear they have a great show."

He nodded and pulled out a chair. "I'll try that," he said, sitting down across from me. "Thanks."

I exhaled slowly and unclenched my fists, flexing my fingers under the table. *I can do this.*

The waitress appeared, flashing a welcoming smile at Ahern as she brought up the menu on a lightweight portable screen. He ordered a coffee, and she left with a frown. The corner table in the back wouldn't be a profitable one for her this afternoon.

"Are you who I think you are?" Ahern asked.

That depended. Who did he think I was? "Tess Bailey," I answered. I'd been using the name for eighteen years. I certainly wasn't going to say Quintessa Novalight and open that whole can of worms.

Sitting back, Ahern folded his arms across his chest. "Captain of the *Endeavor*, right?"

He'd heard of me? And my ship? I might have blushed.

"She's old and beat up but gets us where we need to go," I confirmed with a nod.

The corners of his mouth lifted, a smile that didn't quite reach his eyes. "I understand the Demeter Terre refugees can thank you for feeding them."

In our four-and-a-half-minute briefing with the rebel leaders, we'd learned that Daniel Ahern and his wife, Reena, were DT natives. There weren't that many left. Ahern and his wife had gone farther afield and risen in the rebel ranks, but most survivors of the Demeter Terre massacre had stuck close to their ruined home and colonized its nearby moons.

"We're not the only ones," I said. Plenty of Nightchasers brought food and supplies to the barely inhabitable rocks orbiting the ex-agricultural giant of Sector 18. From what I understood, Reena Ahern was the only scientist in the galaxy who'd come anywhere close to figuring out how to decontaminate Demeter Terre after the Overseer poisoned the atmosphere.

"Did you know that Sector 18 lost ninety percent of its population?" Ahern asked.

I nodded. I was too young to have lived through the final Sambian War, but I knew my history. When the imperial hammer pounded down with extreme violence and a total disregard for human life, it obliterated the strongest resistance to military rule. Sectors 17 and 18 finally fell, and the Overseer—a.k.a. thank-the-Powers-that-man-wasn't-my-father-after-all—only stopped when my mother bargained her future and her body away for the safety of what was left of the Outer Zones.

Ahern wasn't the only one who wanted his wife back. If Demeter Terre could produce again, Sector 18 could repopulate.

The waitress arrived with Ahern's coffee, and we kept silent while she set it in front of him with a couple of compacted sugar disks and a self-heating tube of milk—luxuries we couldn't afford aboard the *Endeavor*.

Well, maybe Shade could, but sweetening and creaming my coffee with Dark Watch earnings might ruin my favorite drink.

Ahern picked up a spoon and stirred in a bit of both milk and sugar.

He smiled at me again, seeming to sense my anxiety and wanting to put me at ease, but a bleakness remained in his features, somehow etched in. I knew enough about the DT survivors to know they didn't sing lullabies to their children. They sang songs of revenge. But while I relished the idea of the Overseer toppling from his imperial throne probably more than just about anyone in the galaxy, I hated the idea of another generation drowning in bloodshed. That reservation had made it very hard to turn over the lab full of enhancers to the rebel leaders, despite wanting to give my friends and allies an edge in this seemingly endless fight.

"How's the soup?" Ahern asked.

I frowned at the bowl of congealing food. What a mundane question. It seemed out of place. "Cold."

He chuckled, erasing a decade from his face. "I apologize for being late."

"It's fine." It totally wasn't. I was a nervous wreck.

He tipped his head to one side, studying me. "My sister has three children. They're alive thanks to you."

My brows drew together in question. "I'm sorry … I don't know what you mean."

Ahern leaned forward, lowering his voice until the din of the restaurant nearly swallowed up his words. "That first haul you brought in? About five years ago? You had a few dozen cure-alls, too. You passed them over to the food coordinator on Mooncamp 1 along with a huge supply of canned goods. Said to give the shots to whoever needed them most. Said you were sorry you didn't have more."

I nodded. I remembered. Who forgot their first heist? It was a big one. The DT Mooncampers couldn't believe their eyes when the never-before-seen *Endeavor* suddenly showed up with three cargo holds' worth of food. With that delivery, we became Nightchasers in more than just name. I had a ship, a crew, and a purpose—everything I'd dreamed about while hacking unstable minerals from the disgusting bowels of a prison mine.

"The kids were in bad shape. My sister, too. Some kind of lung infection had gone around the DT moons and hit their household harder than most. Those vaccines saved them. Four people are still in my life thanks to you."

The shock of heat that seared my eyes from behind took

me by surprise. I blinked away the burn. I didn't know what to say, but I was glad Jax and Fiona could hear this. "I've got a great crew. It's a team effort—every time."

Ahern acknowledged my words with a slight dip of his chin. "Then you can thank them for me also."

A white-hot stab of grief speared me. If only I could. Half my crew was gone. Miko and Shiori weren't listening in from the ship. Miko would never hear anything again, and we had no idea where the Overseer had locked up Shiori, or if she even lived.

I inhaled and exhaled with deliberate evenness. Emotion in. Carbon dioxide out. We needed to get to the point of all this. "I hear I can maybe help you again."

Ahern's cautious green gaze darted around the restaurant. No one was paying attention to us, but his voice stayed barely audible in pitch. "It's not a transfer, like I thought. That already happened days ago, and I just found out. That's why I was late. But I know where she's being held. I've got someone on the inside who can help."

A bad feeling sank through me. Interrupting a transfer would be easier than breaking into a prison. There was potential chaos in movement. It didn't require sneaking into a lion's den. "Where?"

His features tensed. Lines bracketed his mouth. "Starbase 12. Somewhere on the lower prison levels."

I felt the blood drain from my face. He couldn't be serious.

In my ear, the tiny com transmitted someone's soft curse. Jax's maybe. Shade's eyes met mine for a startled split second. Both of us looked away fast. Reena Ahern was in the most secure place in the known universe. This was an impossible task. A death sentence. No one broke into Imperial Headquarters and *lived*.

I'd been there before. Of course I had. It orbited my birth planet, and the Overseer had shuttled us back and forth between Alpha Sambian and Starbase 12 all the time. Mom had hated it—said the place stank like doom. At the time, I didn't understand what she meant. I'd liked the trips up. They got me out of our prison of a home with the basement lab where the man who was supposed to love and protect me strapped me down and stole my blood.

A boulder of sheer dread pinned me to my chair. For the first time in about eighty minutes, I stopped fidgeting and stared. "We're supposed to break her out. How?"

Ahern drifted closer, his crisp white shirt nearly hitting the rim of his untouched coffee mug. He drummed long fingers against the table—a sound that went straight to my nervous system and exploded there. "Ten days from now, my contact will deactivate the plasma shield alarm on Landing Platform 7 at nineteen hundred hours, universal time. Slip in, slip out. The alarm will reactivate three hours later. Be out, or you're done for."

I gaped at him. We ran stolen food around the Dark. We pilfered cure-all vaccines from the military to give to children. Sometimes, I stole books. We'd rescued a few rebel prisoners from the Dark Watch, but that had mostly been dumb luck!

Panic surged up with an acid burn of half-digested soup. I'd made the decision to bring the enhancers to the Fold. I'd spouted off about free will and choices, trying to make sure the rebel leaders didn't force the body-altering serum on anyone like the Overseer had. A few days later, they handed us a suicide mission. *What the fuck?*

My voice shook. "There must be a crew more qualified for this."

"You're here. I'm here." Daniel Ahern dropped a few coins on the table for his coffee and stood. "Someone chose you, and I'm counting on you to get my wife back."

I stared at him in utter shock. Had I condemned us all? Were the people I'd believed shared my values and ideals really no better than Simon Novalight? Ready to flatten any bump in their road without a second thought?

Ahern adjusted his suit jacket, his back to the room, his voice hushed, and his grass-green eyes cutting into me like chips of glass. "Break into Starbase 12. Bring Reena back to me. She'll save Demeter Terre, and the Outer Zones will be free again."

With that bold statement, he turned and strode out the door while I choked on my own dry throat and my heart pounded like the drums of war.

CHAPTER

2

SHADE

I WALKED ACROSS THE CROWDED RESTAURANT TOWARD a shell-shocked Tess. Her pale face reflected the stiff, cold panic echoing in my chest. Could Nightchasers say no to missions, or was the rebellion like the Dark Watch—you took your orders and shut up?

When I reached her side, I held out my hand. Tess slipped her fingers into mine. "Time to go."

She gave a jerky nod as I drew her up, her blue eyes huge and haunted. From day one, everything about her had struck me as younger than her twenty-six years—her faint freckles, her heart-shaped face, her stubborn hope that justice still existed—except for those eyes. They'd seen too much to stay innocent.

The restaurant staff threw us confused looks as we left. My almost-too-friendly waitress narrowed her eyes at me over the top of her menu tablet, and the women still sitting at the table next to mine glared at Tess.

A quick pause at the door revealed no obvious danger

outside the restaurant. Jax and Fiona were already on their way back to the *Endeavor*. Their presence had been a precaution, just in case the meeting with Ahern turned into something we weren't expecting. We headed out a little behind them.

The moment we hit the street, sunlight beat down on us from two stars, one redder than the other. Tess squinted and angled her face away from the heat. Not me. I liked it. Air as thick and heavy as the inside of a steam sauna clung to my skin, making perspiration pop out and bead along my hairline. The sweltering humidity reminded me of the full-blown summer I'd left behind for the Dark, although Albion City rarely got this hot.

My nostrils flared on a breath that smelled of baked pavement and mild pollution. The atmosphere back home was better. It didn't leave this chalky aftertaste.

Images of Albion 5 flashed through my head, so vivid and intense I could almost reach out and touch them. A hollow feeling spread through me, and I bit down hard, stopping it. Missing a place I could never return to didn't help me any more than thinking about my dead parents, or regretting the questionable choices I'd made over the last ten years—all for nothing.

My docking towers were gone. I'd lost them, and now there was no buying them back. I'd wanted Tess safe and hopefully with me more than I'd wanted the urban empire my family had built from the ground up. People were more important than buildings. The sorry state of the whole fucking galaxy was more important than buildings. Once I figured that out, there was no going back. Now, I was a rebel, an outlaw. The only thing I truly had left was universal currency, and sometimes, when Tess looked at me with wary eyes that couldn't quite let go of the past, I wished I didn't even have that.

She glanced at me, no smile on her lips.

"Relax, starshine. We're almost done." The empty words left a bad taste in my mouth.

"Almost done?" Tess let out a soft snort, keeping her voice low. Her gaze cut to mine, bright blue and sharp. "This is the easy part. How can we possibly do what he asked?"

I squeezed her hand. "One thing at a time." We had to take care of Bridgebane and the blood exchange first. "We'll figure it out."

Her *Yeah, right* expression told me I could shove my platitudes up my ass. At least her annoyance was better than her wide-eyed trust and misplaced faith in me that had torn me up day and night on Albion 5.

Tess remained on edge, gripping my hand harder than she probably realized. Our palms sweated. Our fingers stuck. But I'd take any contact that bound us together. I'd had her underneath me last night. She'd been on top this morning. She was trusting me with her body again, but I couldn't tell if her head and her heart were really following.

I looked over at the woman who'd turned my life upside down in the best way possible. The worried crinkle between her eyebrows was deeper than usual. I increased the pressure on her fingers, hoping the weight of my hand would show her she wasn't in this alone—unless she chose to be. So far, I'd been lucky. She'd kept me around despite my bounty-hunting past and decade-long ties to the Dark Watch.

I scanned the neighborhood as we walked, my eyes peeled for danger and my ears cocked for the sound of a military patrol. We'd paid for a platform on a docking tower near the meeting point with Ahern, trying to avoid using the crowded, tubelike shuttles racing all over the place. The multilevel network ran both above and below ground and was huge and complex. A twenty-minute walk through the grid-patterned city center had seemed easier, but now I was thinking it might've been a mistake. The walk to the restaurant had already seemed strangely quiet, and from what we were seeing again now, Koralight Crowners didn't stay on the streets. They either went inside or got in a tube, funneling toward the frequent shuttle stops at a quick pace.

We'd only had a few daylight hours to observe the city, and things had looked different from two hundred and fifty-two levels up. If I'd had more time to prepare, I would've known the people here didn't go anywhere on foot; they took the damn shuttles. The fact that Tess and I had just walked by two stops was already suspicious.

Seeing a cross street that looked mainly residential, I guided us off the main avenue toward a neighborhood I hoped had fewer obvious transportation hubs.

While they'd been acting as lookouts and watching over us, Jax and Fiona had instinctively headed inside, rotating between the several shops and large food emporium in the area around the restaurant. I increasingly understood their urge to take cover as we made our way back to the *Endeavor*. Outside just didn't feel right.

They hadn't checked in for a few minutes, which meant they were on track to get back to the ship soon. We'd all gone mostly silent after Ahern dropped his bomb, blasting to smithereens what little safety we thought we'd gained after passing off the enhancers to the rebel leaders in the Fold.

The Fold. I still couldn't quite wrap my head around that place. Untraceable except for a big, dark gravity field. Constantly moving around the Outer Zones. Expanding to fit whatever was inside it—right now, an entire rebel base. It hurt like hell going in and just as badly on the way out. Somehow, it knew friend from foe. Unfortunately, the Overseer's serum made any enhanced soldier able to cross the barrier without suffering from the aneurysm that usually took out enemies on their way into the rebel stronghold.

They'd have to find it first, though. As far as I could tell, the Fold was the best-kept secret in the galaxy. Being inexplicable probably helped. If you weren't born there or brought there, the human mind just wouldn't conjure up an alternate pocket in space like that.

I lifted Tess's hand and brushed my lips against her knuckles. It was only partly an excuse to talk into my piece-of-shit wristband. I kissed her every chance I got.

"Coms still on?" I asked quietly. The silence was eerie when we were supposed to be connected.

Two masculine voices immediately answered with "Check." Jax and Merrick.

"Fungi!" Fiona said, her tone enthusiastic but hushed.

A small laugh bubbled out of Tess. It was just a little huff, but it loosened her shoulders. Her stride lengthened, less tense. The *Endeavor*'s botanist had accomplished what I hadn't all day: a real smile from Tess.

Moments like this drove home how new I was to this group, still finding my place. Merrick was new, too, but it was different. He'd been a rebel all along, and he'd never set out to deceive the crew of the *Endeavor*. Lies, subterfuge, and near-betrayal—that was all me. They hadn't kicked me out on my ass, but real trust didn't come back fast, if ever.

"Where are you guys?" Tess's softly spoken question echoed through my earpiece a fraction of a second after I heard it in real time. I frowned, wanting to bury this material back in the dark ages where it belonged.

"We veered off to blend in with some people," Jax answered. "They all stopped at the first shuttle entrance, though. Now, we're alone."

"Us too." Tess freed her hand from mine and pushed a tiny hinge on her bracelet. The polished green stone slid aside, revealing a flat, dark surface. She pressed another button, and a gridgram linked to our coms sprang up in front of us.

Shit, that's huge. The equipment I'd kept below my shop in Albion City was a hundred times more sophisticated than the things the crew of the *Endeavor* could afford. I'd spent ten years accumulating the best gadgets on the market so I could be discreet and efficient, and now here I was, walking down the street next to a holographic map twice the size of my head.

Wariness pricked the back of my neck as I glanced from side to side. The deserted street didn't help assuage the cold unease growing inside me.

Two dots advanced together a couple of blocks ahead of us on the neon-green gridgram. Merrick's speck remained stationary on the ship. The whole thing blinked in and out like a beacon, especially in the shadowed alley. I was two seconds from covering Tess's wrist with my hand when she flicked her bracelet closed, cutting off the ginormous pyramid of light.

"You're a lot closer to the ship than we are." She tucked her loose hair behind her ears and started moving faster. "Merrick, can you power up? ETA is fifteen minutes."

"Will do," Merrick answered.

"Eight for us," Jax said.

"Wait... Is that purple clawberry?" Excitement electrified Fiona's whisper. "Most people don't know the fruit is edible and just use the bush for shrubbery. I need a cutting. This is too good to pass up."

She needs a plant? Tess's gaze snapped to mine. Through her lightweight but long-sleeved shirt, she tapped her still needle-marked inner elbow twice and then flapped her hands like a bird, not making a sound her necklace would pick up.

I nodded. I got it. We had to fly away fast and bring her A1 blood to Reaginine by tomorrow or her uncle—a fucking Dark Watch general *and* my ex-boss—would arrest one of the two women Tess considered a mother. Mareeka or Surral. Nathaniel Bridgebane would take one of them to Hourglass Mile if Tess didn't deliver the six bags of blood that were currently hidden in a cooling unit on my little star cruiser, and I was pretty sure the safety and well-being of the Starway 8 orphanage, the kids in it, and the two women who ran it meant more to Tess than anything else in the entire universe.

We still hadn't come up with a good excuse for the two of us taking off on our own to the Grand Temple on Reaginine. Announcing that we had to go hand over a cooler full of the base ingredient for the Overseer's super-soldier serum wasn't going to cut it. I could say I needed to pray at the home of the Church of the Great Star, but needing to pray *right now* was kind of ridiculous. And everyone knew Tess was firmly agnostic. The fact was, she'd stolen the Overseer's supply of enhancers, and Bridgebane had blackmailed her into giving some back—or at least the means to make several new batches.

Now, I just had to make sure she didn't get caught—by

her Dark Watch enemies *or* her rebel friends. Either would be disastrous.

With a questioning shrug, I held up five fingers and mouthed *Five minutes?* It wouldn't make a difference at this point, and Jax and Fiona were already ahead of us on the walk back to the ship.

Tess bit her lip and then said, "Sure. But be quick, Fi. People don't seem to hang around outside in this place. Jax, watch her back."

"Always, partner," Jax said.

"I can't quite reach it from the street," Fiona muttered a few seconds later. "There's a high fence. I have to go into the park for it."

"Park?" Tess hesitated midstep before letting her long strides eat up the pavement again. "There could be surveillance."

"It's empty," Fiona assured us over the coms. "Not a soul in sight."

A bad thought suddenly ignited like gunpowder in the back of my mind. The ambiance on Korabon—the crowded restaurant but the empty streets, the swarming shuttle system but no real pedestrian traffic—was starting to scratch at something in my memory, something from one of my early hunts. I tried to remember... Could Korabon be on parole?

Tess caught my brooding look. "What is it?"

"Do you think this place enforces any AGLs?" I asked.

Her eyes widened. Worry shot through her expression, and she immediately spoke, low and urgent. "Fiona, I think you should stop. Merrick, check my tablet. Have any additional galactic laws been imposed on Korabon? Something that would explain why people keep off the streets?"

"They're not common, but I'll check," Merrick answered.

I swore under my breath. This was the shit that happened when you went in blind.

"I'll be quick," Fiona said.

"Leave it, Fi." Tess turned toward where we knew the others were, despite it not being our best route back to the ship.

I followed, matching her rapid pace and letting my limbs loosen and my body warm up. Something told me we'd be running before we finished this walk.

Paroled planets generally kept a low profile, trying not to attract anyone's attention, let alone the Overseer's. I'd studied up on a lot of places for different jobs, but I didn't know the situation of every rock in the Dark. Nearly a decade ago, I'd followed a prize to a planet required by the Overseer to prove good behavior for a fifteen-year period in order to benefit from galactic financial and medical assistance again. Now that I thought about it, the unnerving emptiness I'd encountered outdoors there had felt a lot like this.

"I'm seeing incident reports," Merrick relayed from the *Endeavor*. "Riots and uprisings in Koralight Crown about twelve years ago ... Iridium deposits around and underneath the city ... Nonviolent sanctions to preserve the continued exploitation of the element ... "

Ir? I'd worked with it once. "Iridium is used in the manufacture of hyperdrives." My engineering studies didn't feel like a lifetime ago, even though in some ways, they were. I'd expected to use them again, just not like this. "It's expensive and difficult to shape but extremely durable. Even at two thousand degrees Celsius, it won't corrode or melt. A hyperdrive reactor lined with iridium lasts on average three times longer than one that's not." Essentially, the silvery-white metal was one of the only things able to withstand some of the severest conditions technology or nature could create.

Tess looked at me, her mouth pressed flat. I nodded, furious also. With just a little more time to prepare, to ask ourselves the right questions, we would've known this. Better yet, someone in the Fold could've handed us a fucking file with the information we needed. Even Ahern might've mentioned it.

"This has AGL written all over it." Tess nearly broke into a jog and checked herself at the last second. "Everyone to the ship. No stops."

"It's okay to steal when it follows your agenda?" Fiona snapped. "We take risks every day for orphans and the Outer Zones, but I see a fruit-bearing plant and I can't have it?"

"*Of course* I want you to have it," Tess ground out. "But AGLs don't pop up in cursory searches, and we didn't have time for anything else. If there are additional galactic laws here, the Dark Watch will be twice as nasty as everywhere else. It's free rein to terrorize people. Fines. Imprisonment."

"Oh, you mean a regular day in the galaxy," Fiona shot back.

"No, I mean *worse*."

"Fruit, Tess. Fresh fruit on board. Think about it."

"*If* you can make it grow," Tess said.

Fiona scoffed. Tess let out a tight breath.

I stayed out of it. I understood the allure of a berry bush for a space-rat botanist. Hell, I'd only been living like a Nightchaser for a matter of days, and I already missed the food, fresh air, sunshine, and comforts of planet-dwelling life. But Tess was right. The Overseer didn't want his draconian AGLs headlining as anything unusual on the rocks he'd imposed them on. For the citizens of Korabon, these laws were simply the norm, and outsiders just shouldn't come here.

The thing was, we hadn't come. We'd been *sent*—and someone should've warned us.

I ground my teeth in frustration. So far, the rebel leadership seemed as full of assholes as the Dark Watch.

"I'm almost there." Fiona's stubbornness didn't surprise me. It seemed an automatic extension of her perpetually swinging ponytail.

"Jax!" Tess didn't say more. One word was enough.

"Let's go, Fi," Jax said.

"Not without my plant."

"Now." Steel laced Jaxon's voice.

"Ow!" Fiona sucked in a sharp breath.

Tess's pace turned furious. "What?"

"I forgot it had thorns. Cut myself," Fiona said.

"Someone's coming," Jax warned.

Shit. I broke into a run, my heart boom-booming with a surge of adrenaline. Tess didn't run; she sprinted. I stretched my legs to keep up.

"Oh no, they're here." Fiona's quiet horror made my hair stand on end.

"Sit on a bench. Hold hands. Look natural," Merrick said from the ship.

We turned a corner and caught sight of the park. An eight-foot-tall spiked fence closed it off from the street. I didn't see a gate.

Reaching out, I gripped Tess's wrist and pulled her to a stop. Silently, I signaled for her to wait. She twisted out of my grasp with a scowl. I shook my head. If we barreled in, we could make things worse. I tapped my ear, telling her to listen to what they said. She nodded but continued toward the park at a determined walk.

"There are no benches!" Fiona's hushed voice rose in pitch.

"Then hold hands walking around," Merrick said.

"I'm not armed," Jax mumbled.

None of us were. It was a risk we'd all taken. Guns weren't illegal, but they were the height of suspicious. Getting caught with one meant an automatic interrogation for anyone without clear ties to the Dark Watch.

"Are you bleeding?" Tess asked.

"A little. Jax is hiding my hand in his." Fiona's almost inaudible response faded into a mere hint of sound as a whistle blew in the background. Its shrillness shot me through with tension. Tess flinched but didn't slow down.

A masculine voice replaced the screeching whistle. "Loitering is prohibited under AGL, Regulation 19."

"Isn't this a public park?" Fiona asked.

"Are you talking back?"

Typical Dark Watch. Even asking a question was a risk.

"We're new to Korabon," Jax said after a beat of silence. "Are parks off-limits?"

"I guess you should've read the Citizen's Code if you moved here. The only place it's legal to gather outdoors is at the shuttle gates."

"But we're not gathering," Fiona said.

"I see two people," a woman sneered. "That's a gathering."

Tess's head swiveled my way, her jaw dropping in silent protest.

"She giving you attitude, Drake?" a different male voice asked. "The captain told you loitering's prohibited. That's a fine."

"Three hundred units." The captain again, Drake. "Pay up and we'll walk away. Pretend we never saw you."

"I want to see this code," Jax grated. "And the fines by regulation."

The goons all murmured. Someone snickered.

"More attitude," the female said with an audible sniff. "That'll be six hundred units, since there are two of you... *loitering.*"

"Six hundred!" Fiona cried. "That's ridiculous!"

"You bleeding?" one of them asked. That was a fourth voice, another man. The Dark Watch rarely went anywhere with fewer than three goons if they were on duty. The typical foot patrol was a unit of five.

"I tripped and cut myself." Fiona's carefully even tone only highlighted her hostility. "Accidentally broke a branch." I pictured her holding out a thorny stick to show them.

"Disorderly behavior," someone barked. "Misdemeanor, a night in jail, and full background checks."

"This is harassment," Jax ground out.

They laughed. Of course it was. That was the point.

Tess was done listening. She started running again. I took off alongside her, looking for a way in.

Fiona suddenly gasped. "Jax!" she cried out.

"Don't. Touch. Her." Pure volcanic fury boiled in Jax's voice.

"Or what?" one of the men asked.

"Or you'll find out," Jax growled.

Tess and I shot through a stretch of fraught silence. Light steps. Pounding breath. *The gate!*

"Eight hundred, and I forget I just heard that threat," the captain snarled.

"Extortion!" Fiona fumed.

"Big word, bitch. We charge extra for those." The captain and his goons all grunted and snorted like animals. The Dark Watch really was the devolution of humankind. "That's a thousand now, or we drag you both off."

"Try." The word rumbled from Jax like a landslide.

"Five of us. Two of you—and she obviously doesn't count for much." The captain paused. "You wanna say that again?"

Jax didn't bother. A crack I'd recognize anywhere snapped over the audio, the bone-crunching sound of fist to face.

A quick and angry uproar followed. The hum of shock wands sent a buzz of electricity into my ear. Shock wands hurt like a bitch and could incapacitate. Having them probably meant this group wasn't carrying guns.

Tess and I whipped through the gate and sprinted into the park together. Five goons surrounded Fiona and Jax.

Two turned, sensing new prey. They started toward us. One had the gall to smile, all teeth and confidence. A blue-white current sizzled at the top of his two-and-a-half-foot-long club. The second soldier widened his stance and lit up his stick also.

They had a lesson coming if they thought being armed meant victory. Jax was a solid wall of muscle, Tess was comet-fast and ferocious, even if she lacked fighting finesse, and I was willing to water this nice grass with Dark Watch blood if it meant getting all of us to safety and away from this parody of peace the Overseer had created.

I smiled back, all teeth and disgust. *This* was Novalight's grand galactic gift? The calm we should all be so grateful for? The last ten years of my life suddenly made me so sick that I wanted to kick the shit out of these goons and make them pay for my regrets.

Tess didn't slow down at all. She rocketed toward the

closest soldier like a missile with coordinates locked in. He raised his shock wand, either to attack or defend. It didn't matter. She went low, sliding in underneath it to knock him down. He hit the ground with a harsh grunt of surprise. Tess wrenched the shock wand from his hand, tossed it to me, and pounced like she was going to eat that goon alive.

Who's the animal now, asshole?

Narrowing my eyes, I lit up the stick and slashed it at the other goon who'd come at us. He parried with his own, and for a second, we stayed locked in place, weapons crossed, both of us pushing hard. Hot light crackled in my face. The searing energy made my hair vibrate. He was strong, and I was done with this. I spun out of the deadlock, shifted my weight, and kicked him in the gut. He doubled over, exhaling.

I glanced at Tess. She was still on the ground, behind the goon now with her arm in a tight V around his neck. Her other arm pushed his head down as she increased the pressure on his arteries. He flopped but couldn't shake her. In seconds, her sleeper hold knocked him out without even touching his windpipe.

"Cuff him!" I shouted. He'd wake up almost as fast as she'd put him under.

Tess dug zip ties from a pouch on the goon's belt while my guy lunged at me. I weaved, avoiding his fist. He blocked my jab and I spun into a kick, knocking him back a step. I pressed my advantage just as Jax roared like a monster. I looked over to see him taking a jolt in the chest to protect Fiona.

In the second I turned my head, the goon got me in the hip with his stick. The zap of electricity numbed my right leg to the ankle. Leaning into my left side, I threw a punch that split my knuckles and cracked his lip. He reeled backward.

Tess trussed her goon up, hands first and then feet when he came back to himself and tried to kick her.

Jax fought like a madman to keep the other three away from Fiona, all fists and growls until the Dark Watch captain sent him to one knee with another violent thump of volts. Jax's shirt smoldered. He'd have burns on his chest. I needed to reach him.

The patrolman I was fighting popped up in front of me again, his face bleeding. *Good. Let's end this.* I sidestepped his attack, grabbed him, and rammed my knee into his groin. He folded in half, and I brought my elbow down hard between his shoulder blades. He fell flat and coughed into the grass. Crouching, I struck the vulnerable spot in his neck that would knock him out. He didn't move again. I found his own restraints and cuffed him.

With Tess beside me, I sprang toward the trio still trying to get the best of Jax and Fiona. From his knees, Jax threw up a thick arm to shield the scientist. In the big man's shadow, Fiona didn't even pretend to fight; she was fishing something from her vest pocket. The female goon suddenly hauled off and cracked Jax over the head with her stick. Already shocked into a stupor, Jax swayed and almost toppled. His lips pulled back in a grimace.

Pure rage ignited in Fiona's face. Tess grabbed my sleeve and jerked me to a halt just when I would've jumped in to defend Jax. Before I could wonder why she stopped me, Fiona shot her hand out over Jax's head and squirted something into the woman's face.

The woman shrieked, a bloodcurdling scream that cut through the heat of battle. Pain. Fury. *Fear.* She stumbled back, swiping at her skin. Her fingers smoked. She dropped her hands, still screaming. Blistering face. Bubbling eyes.

Fiona yelled like a banshee and whipped a thin branch across the woman's burning face, taking off a chunk of her disintegrating nose with it. Fiona didn't miss a beat, bringing her arm back around to slash the branch at the two men. They scrambled back, trying to avoid the thorny weapon.

Jax groaned, and Fiona stood protectively over him. In a flash, she squirted a second dose of acid and melted Drake's face. He screamed like a baby.

"Tetrafumicfullerbehrenheim acid." Fiona leaped in front of Jax and kicked the yowling man away from him. "There's another big word—bitch." Her ponytail flew as she twisted and clocked the last man over the head with her berry branch. She wouldn't grow anything with that one. It was fucking magnificent.

The final goon yelped and started running. Jax lunged and grabbed the shithead's ankle. He held on tight and I moved in. My kick might've cracked the guy's skull. His eyes rolled back, and he hit the ground with a thud that echoed through me.

A hush descended. Breathing hard, I looked around me. *Holy shit*. That was the most savage fight I'd ever been in. No rules. At least two people dead. And here I'd thought my former colleagues Solan and Raquel fought dirty.

Something deep inside me recognized that *this* was the turning point. Or maybe the point of no return.

Before this, I'd just been living. Now, survival was a *goal*. I really was a rebel.

Tess's goon was conscious but keeping damn quiet after all the face melting. I strode over and knocked him out again with a well-placed strike to his temple. He slumped in his cuffs, unmoving.

"We need to get going." Tess looked worriedly at Jaxon,

who struggled to his knees again. "Merrick, be ready for us. We take off the instant we reach the *Endeavor*."

"No." I grabbed Tess's elbow, craning my neck to look over the park bushes. There were no new goons in sight, but there was no way one of these hadn't pushed a panic button. Every Dark Watch soldier had one on their belt. Even I'd had one. "They'll be scanning the docks for heat signatures. Power down the ship."

"It's already hot," Merrick said. "They'll see it even if I turn off the engines. Better to go if we can."

Is it? "They'll come at us with real firepower. Crowd us so we can't jump out of here."

A change came over Tess's face, and I knew an idea had sparked. She looked at me hard. "We'll hold them off in your cruiser. You and me. We'll distract them while the *Endeavor* jumps away from here."

Great Powers, she was a genius. I nodded, vowing to never underestimate this woman. She'd just given us our trip alone to Reaginine and a viable way off Korabon for everyone.

If we made it to the ship.

"We'll rendezvous at the Mooncamp food drop-off in three days," I said. "That way, we can all blur our trail from the Dark Watch before meeting up again."

Tess nodded back at me, her face somber. Plan made. Now, to execute it.

Fiona helped Jax sit up straighter. She feathered her fingers just below the lump at his hairline, murmuring, "Thank you. I'll fix you up."

For just a second, he leaned into her, his eyes closing. Then he heaved a sigh and staggered upright. Fiona rose also. She turned, walked over to what must be the purple clawberry bush, and carefully snapped off another branch to work with.

I glanced left and right to make sure we still didn't have unwanted company. It was a nice park. Too bad no one could use it without risking harassment, fines, and worse.

I slid a shoulder under Jax's arm and helped him toward the gate. Tess and Fiona strode beside us, watchful and ready. Regret didn't shadow their faces. Only determination. Fight for each other. Fight for what you believe in. One day at a time. Keep going.

That was my life now, except I had a feeling existence was going to be minute by minute until we escaped Korabon.

"Hovercrafts are already moving toward the docks in this area." Urgency sharpened the usual low rumble of Merrick's voice into a hard bark over the com units. "Get here fast, or we're not getting out this time."

CHAPTER

3

TESS

BOTH ICE AND FIRE POUNDED THROUGH MY VEINS AS WE left the park and headed toward the *Endeavor*. We'd just killed people. I'd never killed anyone before, although I knew Jax and Fiona had. I didn't know about Shade. I was certain he'd turned over people to the Dark Watch who'd never been heard from again, so wasn't that the same?

I glanced at my hands. Dirty but not bloody. A reflection of reality, I supposed.

"Take your next left," Merrick ordered over the coms.

We all veered left, hurrying Jaxon along.

"Now right!"

We did as Merrick instructed, trusting him and the gridgram he must have up to give us the best route back to the ship. As a group, our feet made too much noise. Koralight Crowners peeked out at us from behind partially closed blinds, their brows lowered in frowns. Conscious of my grass-stained hands, I curled my fingers into fists and kept walking, trying not to make eye contact with anyone.

"Got any more of that acid, Fi?" Jax's mumble-slurred words matched his stumbling footsteps.

"One more." She glanced over at him. "Why?"

He cocked an ear. "We might need it."

I heard the faint rumble of incoming hovercrafts, too. Jax's body might have taken an electrical trouncing, but his hearing was just fine.

Shade looked around, scanning above and behind us. Fiona did the same with narrowed eyes. The street was empty. Anyone watching us was doing it from inside.

"Even that acid won't take down a whole hovercraft." Fiona focused forward again. "Not in the quantity I have."

The soldiers' screams in the park echoed in my head again, and my stomach cramped at the carnage we'd left behind us. Those Dark Watch goons were power-abusing bastards, but I couldn't quite bridge the gap in my head between knowing they were assholes and thinking they deserved *that*.

"Left," Merrick directed, "then straight for two blocks, cross the big avenue, and you're at the base of the tower."

We turned left and had to walk by a shuttle stop at the next intersection. The few Koralight Crowners who remained outside because of the long line looked at us with curiosity when we didn't move to join them. Their expressions turned wary and then accusing as we walked on without pause.

I watched them out of the corner of my eye. *Yup—we're the jerks who are about to get your parole extended.* What an awful thought. Another how-many years of living inside or underground all the time? Poor people. I couldn't wait to get off this oppressive and lifeless planet. There weren't even any ships in the sky.

A man near the back of the shuttle line took out a personal camshot device and followed us with his gaze. The line shuffled forward, but he stayed put. *Shit.* The guy had informant written all over him from head to foot.

One of the hovercrafts we'd heard earlier appeared behind us and zoomed overhead in our direction. Hot air billowed beneath it, lifting grit from the street that pinged against my cheeks. Hair swirled in my face, and I ducked, panic wrapping its icy fists around my lungs. We were just far enough from that shuttle stop—and going *away* from it—to look incredibly suspicious.

I waited, tense and holding my breath. The hovercraft didn't swing back around. It kept going toward the nearby docks. I breathed again.

Our luck didn't hold. The guy with the camshot ran forward and pointed his device right at us. I had just enough time to block his view of Shade and Jax and turn so he got the back of my head. A stride in front of me, Fiona was right in his line of sight.

"Hurry!" I kept my face averted. "Fi, I think you just got tagged. Some jackass with a camshot."

"Won't be the first time." The tension in her voice shot to hell her cavalier response.

A metallic whine buzzed toward us. "Do you hear that?" My brows snapped together. We all went quiet and listened.

"Drone!" Shade warned a second before a Red Beam military drone swooped down and nearly clipped our heads. The little craft swung around in front of us and sent out a crimson laser that scanned us all from head to foot.

"Shade Brian Ganavan. Wanted. Halt." A tinny robotic voice barked out orders, and it was no secret that if you didn't obey, the Red Beam would shoot. "Fiona Anne Winterly. Wanted. Halt. Jaxon Mitchell Boudreau..."

"Can you run?" Shade asked, glancing at Jax.

Jax nodded, pale but steadier on his feet now. Jax could always run. He'd die running, I had no doubt.

"...Wanted. Halt. Tess Bailey, captain of the *Endeavor*. Wanted. Halt."

I have a title? Classy. And still attaching that name to this face in the Dark Watch system, even after last week's showdown with my uncle and the Overseer, meant that someone in charge really didn't want my true identity getting out.

That didn't mean the drone wouldn't shoot me. A stun blast from a Red Beam could incapacitate the hell out of a person and make those patrol-grade shock wands look like jokes.

"Go. Go. Go!" I urged the others as I took off at a sprint and jumped, catching the Red Beam by the snout. It was arming the stun blaster, and the gathering energy zapped a sharp yelp from me. A numbing heat ricocheted up my arm as I pulled down hard, slamming the drone into the pavement. The people who still couldn't fit inside the underground shuttle stop gasped and scuttled back, not wanting to be implicated in any of this. That was the tricky thing about revolution—if no one stood up to fight, you just had a few fools causing mayhem and running for their lives.

My hand burned and throbbed. I didn't even look at it as we raced for our docking tower. There was no point in trying to be inconspicuous now. Next to me, Shade shook his head, his mouth flat, his brown eyes like stones.

"I got rid of the drone!" I snapped in my defense.

"You could've lost a hand!" he snapped back.

"Then I'd have made myself a hook!" Tess Bailey: pirate. Sailing the galactic seas, stealing shit, and pissing off the authorities. All true.

"You think you're funny?" Shade growled as we barreled into the arched bottom level of our tower. It was open to the outside with a set of six elevator tubes in the center.

Three hovercrafts converged on the lower part of the building just as we made it to cover. We skidded to a stop in front of the lifts. Jax slammed his hand down on a button.

I pushed a button on the opposite side in case it came faster, urgently rattling the little lighted square with my fingertip. "You think I'm not? *Brian*?"

Shade's eyes narrowed. "The Red Beam didn't name you. Not really."

Of course not. The Overseer didn't want to have to explain me to the galaxy, and Bridgebane didn't want me getting hauled in before I handed over the blood he needed. Quintessa Novalight would probably spark one hell of a manhunt across the Sectors whereas Tess Bailey was just some rebel nobody stirring up trouble in random places. Red Beam facial recognition was unparalleled, so yeah—for the moment, no one wanted to correct my name in the system.

"Comeoncomeoncomeon!" Fiona hopped in place while we waited for an elevator to swoop down and rescue us from the invasion that was about to happen. Boots thudded outside—no doubt soldiers fast-roping it down from the low-flying hovercrafts.

I glanced at the emergency stairwell to the left of the bank of elevators. Two hundred and fifty-two flights of stairs weren't an option. No way. No thanks.

Shade took hold of my hand and turned it palm up. The skin was red. There were two blisters. All in all, it looked better than I thought it would, but I already knew that superficial wounds healed quickly thanks to my A1 blood.

Footsteps scuffed and churned behind us. I looked over

my shoulder, and fear spiked inside me as a team of goons spread out, blocking our exit.

"Stop! Stay where you are!" someone shouted.

Jax's lift opened. We swept inside and flattened ourselves against the walls. The second we moved, the Dark Watch opened fire. Bullets slammed into the mirror behind us. Glass shattered, crumpling our images. Shards flooded the floor like water. I shot out a hand and pressed the button for our docking level. Sparks flew off metal, and I curled into the corner. Shade covered me with his body.

Shooting and shouting, soldiers sprinted toward us as the doors began closing. Tension locked me in place. Would the panels latch before they reached us?

A dozen goons bore down like a black cloud of destruction. My heart clenched so hard it nearly folded inward. A woman at the front lunged, her hostile gaze clashing with mine for an awful split second before the doors met in the middle. She thumped hard against them.

We started moving. Yelling snuck through the cracks in the elevator. I exhaled in a gust, my heart exploding back into beating. The voices faded, but the sudden quiet blew like an eerie wind around us, untrustworthy. Fear and gun smoke stung the back of my throat as I waited for the lift to lurch. To stop. To drag us down again.

I looked at Shade, trying to hide the volcanic terror inside me. He looked back, and I knew he saw it anyway. The hard set of his jaw turned his sweat-slicked face even grimmer. Short brown hair spiked in places, damp from exertion. Eyes that were always warm when he looked at me now blazed like bonfires. He lifted his hand to the back of my neck and kept it there, gently squeezing. I closed my eyes and leaned against him. We continued rising, thank the Powers.

"Everyone okay?" Merrick asked tentatively. I'd fear the worst, too, after hearing all that gunfire.

I opened my eyes and straightened. I hadn't seen any injuries, but I took careful stock of my companions before answering.

"Yeah. Miraculously, no one's bleeding." My pulse still rioted as I watched the levels crawl by. *Fifteen. Sixteen. Seventeen.* We had a hellishly long ride ahead of us, and this had to be the slowest elevator in existence.

"I'm surrounded now," Merrick said tightly. "This tower's mostly empty platforms. They locked on to our hot engine almost instantly. Three hovercrafts are blocking our exit."

I cursed softly. "We're going to have to either plow or blow our way out. Shade?"

He kicked some broken glass away from me. "I've got firepower on my cruiser, and I set some pressure-sensitive charges this morning that should keep the hovercrafts away from the dock. They try to land, they go boom. And if we have to, we'll set them off."

"You set explosives? When? Before I woke up?"

"Yeah." He looked at me like rigging bombs at the crack of dawn was par for the course. "Just in case."

"We could've stepped on them," I said in shock.

Shade shook his head. "You'd have seen them if you went anywhere near the edge of the dock. And I didn't activate them until we were all off the tower this morning. I told Merrick. He knew to watch out."

I frowned. We didn't do large-scale damage. Then again, we didn't melt faces, either. Apparently, today was a day for firsts. "Okay." If it meant getting off the platform, I'd blow it up myself.

"Merrick, can you somehow cover us while we run to the

ship?" Battering our way off the dock required *getting* to the battering ram first.

"I've got six Grayhawks loaded and on me," Merrick answered. "But it depends on the guns they've got aboard those hovercrafts."

I glanced at the digital readout showing our position on the tower. *Eighty-two. Eighty-three. Eighty-four.* The painfully slow progress made me want to light a rocket under the elevator.

"Can you do something super-soldiery?" I asked.

"Well, I can't fly, and I'm not bulletproof," Merrick grumbled. "I'm open to suggestions, though."

"Sorry," I muttered, squeezing my eyes shut.

"S'okay." Something clanged over the coms, and Merrick grunted. "I'm thinking."

"Me too." Unfortunately, I wasn't coming up with a safe way to cross the distance between the elevator tubes and the *Endeavor*.

Three floors higher, shots banged in our eardrums. My lungs squeezed tight, and I touched my necklace. "Merrick?"

He didn't answer, and my heart beat harder.

"Are you okay?" Fiona crunched over broken glass, pacing the small area. "Merrick!"

"Yeah, I'm here. Just keeping 'em back." More loud pops nearly drowned out Merrick's answer.

I shifted nervously. Back was good, but the Dark Watch could still shoot from a distance. Running across the no-man's-land of the dock couldn't possibly end well for us.

I swung my gaze to where Jax leaned against the opposite wall of the lift from me, his complexion ashen. Fat beads of sweat pearled on his brow and slid down his temples. A bloodshot sheen brightened his brown eyes to something feverish and lacking focus.

I darted a worried glance at Fiona. She immediately sidled closer to Jax. He didn't react, even when her hand brushed his knuckles. Her fingers almost curled around his. With a little encouragement, they might have.

A deep ache wrenched through me as I looked across the shattered glass sea of the elevator at them. Jax would have held my hand. He would have let me comfort and help him. Why wouldn't he give himself that from Fiona?

Because it's not the same. My heart whispered the truth inside me. Jax was family to me. A little bit brother. A little bit father. A bit of everything, really. A hulking tower of strength, protection, and reassurance. A home that traveled with me. But I never looked at him like I wanted him to kiss me until I couldn't breathe or think or feel anything but him around me, and that was exactly what scared the shit out of him with Fiona.

Jax's previous life got burned to the ground, and he was so afraid of losing people again that he kept his distance from everyone except for me. I'd thought time might heal him. Or maybe Fiona. Maybe nothing could. Or maybe he'd snap awake one day and finally take a step forward.

Two hundred. Two hundred and one. Two hundred and two … I watched the numbers climb, my anxiety rising along with them.

"We're almost there," Shade told Merrick.

Freaking finally. But what happened when we arrived?

Shade took my uninjured hand in his and brushed his thumb across the inside of my wrist, a slow swipe that sent a shiver through me. "Stay safe. Stay with me."

I nodded. "You too." I squeezed his hand back.

A muscle flexed in his jaw. His mouth flattened, and he dropped my hand as we came up on the two hundred and fifties.

"What's the status out there, Merrick?" Shade asked.

"Still surrounded. Four hovercrafts now—and some combat cruisers in the area, according to the radar."

Shade swore. I winced. Fiona looked worriedly at Jaxon, who didn't react. He stared straight ahead as though no one had spoken.

Fear churned in my gut. One-man fighter ships were bad news on the best of days, and today was already terrible.

I peeked at the digital display again. Just one more level. I braced for the doors to open, hoping Merrick had come up with a plan to get us out of the elevator.

The lights blinked out. The lift jerked to a standstill. My heart jackhammered in the darkness, and then an emergency light flickered on in the top corner.

"Merrick?" The others stood stock-still, all bathed in a faint orange glow and as wide-eyed as I was. "We stopped with one floor to go. What happened?"

"Power just went out in the whole tower," he answered. "They shut it down. Can you get out through the ceiling?" *Bang. Bang.* Gunshots rang outside again.

We all studied the top of the elevator, taking stock of the person-sized emergency exit.

Shade turned to me. "On my back, starshine." He cleared broken glass out of the way and bent down, bracing one knee and a hand against the bottom of the elevator.

"Fi's smaller." I pulled her over and helped her sit on Shade's shoulders. She got her balance and he stood, putting her high enough to reach the safety hatch above us. Shade braced her legs with his arms, and Fiona yanked on the lever. It didn't move. With a grunt, she pushed harder.

"I can't...*get it*." Grinding her teeth, Fiona put all her weight behind it. She shook her head. "It's no good. I'm not strong enough."

Fiona slid off Shade's back, crushing glass into dust as she landed behind him. I was about to try when Jax nudged Shade aside and took his spot on one knee, his other leg bent and braced in front of him. He tapped his thigh and nodded. Without waiting for more of an invitation, Shade stepped onto Jax's big thigh, reached up, and grabbed the lever. He pulled hard, and the seal broke with a suction pop of rubber. He flipped the hatch open, leaving a dark hole in the ceiling.

Shade hopped down and turned to Fiona. "Climb." He lowered his center of gravity and laced his hands in front of him.

Jax stood and helped steady Fiona as she stepped onto Shade's foothold, her hand on Jax's shoulder for balance. Shade lifted as she reached up and grabbed the edges of the opening. He sent her partway through, and Fiona wiggled the rest of her way out of the hatch. On top of the elevator, she turned and reached for me.

I did the same, using Shade as a stepping stool and Jax for balance. Fiona helped pull me through and someone pushed on my feet from below, making the climb easier.

I sat up and glanced around, trying to adjust my eyesight to the dimness. It was even darker in the shaft but just bright enough to see the ominous outlines of gears and wires pressing in on us. It reminded me of some of the tighter, darker mining tunnels below Hourglass Mile.

I burst out in goose bumps and looked over my shoulder, half expecting to see a guard with a whip looming over me, his arm cocked back, the threat obvious. But only the doors to our platform sneered down at me—a tight-lipped vertical barrier next to a rung ladder that ran the entire length of the elevator tube. There wasn't a crack of daylight. Where was Merrick?

I swung my gaze back around and peered through the hatch. Shade was down on one knee and offering up his thigh as a step stool the way Jax had earlier.

"I'm too heavy," Jax mumbled.

"Stop stalling." Shade's tone brooked no argument. He looked at Jax expectantly.

Irritation flared in Jax's expression—the first sign of life in a while. Scowling, he set his foot on Shade's thigh and hefted himself partway through the hatch. Fiona and I helped haul him the rest of the way up, although the men did most of the work on that one. We were all breathing hard by the time Shade jumped, grabbed the rim of the hole with both hands, and heaved himself up to join us.

He stood, taking my hand and tugging me up with him.

"Impressive." The muscles in Shade's arms and shoulders were something to look at. I'd admire them very thoroughly if we lived through this.

He leaned forward and kissed me. The quick, hard contact shot warmth from my lips to my toes. My hands curled in his shirt, holding on for a second. Our eyes locked and then Shade stepped back, checking on Jax and Fiona.

I checked on Merrick. "Hey, Big Guy, can you make it to the lift and pry the doors open? We're climbing out of here."

"Gimme a minute." A door whooshed in the background. The sound of Merrick's running feet reached us. "There are six elevator tubes. Which do I open?"

"Middle shaft, inner side," I answered, gripping the cold

metallic rung in front of me. Before I lifted my boot to the ladder, I glanced at Jaxon.

He rolled to his knees and staggered upright. The way he creaked told me every movement cost him. Running around and climbing and jumping definitely weren't doctor recommended after taking a violent shocking.

My throat thick with worry, I turned back around and started climbing. "We're on our way up, Merrick. Get ready."

A harsh grunt chuffed over the audio connection followed by what sounded like ripping metal.

What in the galaxy? I frowned down at Shade. Through the shadows, his eyes met mine in mutual question.

"Merrick?" Shade followed me up the ladder.

"On my way." Pounding feet. A door whooshed again. More gunfire.

"You go first, Fi." Jax sounded so tired. I glanced down again, uneasy.

"Not a chance." Fiona planted herself like one of her bushes. "You go first, or I'm not moving."

Jax stuck out an arm and herded Fiona toward the ladder. She dug in her heels, skidding over the top of the elevator.

"Don't be stubborn," Jax grated. "Just go."

"No," she growled.

"Come on, Fi!" I snapped down at her. "Merrick's coming. Let's not give the Dark Watch *more* time to get into position to kill us." At least four hovercrafts waited outside with armed soldiers just itching to shoot the blood and guts out of us. At this point, we only stood a chance because Merrick was a super soldier and Shade had wisely set explosives.

"If we're all out, I'm afraid he'll just sit down and give up!" Scowling, Fiona tried to shove Jax forward. "You first."

"Quit it, or I'll fucking carry you up," Jax snarled.

"Fine." She stepped right up to him, challenging Jax to do just that. They stood toe-to-toe, glaring at each other.

"Jax isn't a quitter," I said. "Now move it. Both of you."

Unfortunately, a tiny part of me wondered if Fiona was right. Sometimes, when Jax shut down and got that misery-clouded far-off look in his eyes, I worried there was a chance he wouldn't fight so hard to make it out of some bad situation the next time. I knew for a fact he would have walked straight into a toxic explosion seven years ago on Hourglass Mile if a terrified nineteen-year-old girl hadn't literally been dumped on his head as a prison partner. Keeping me safe had kept him alive. But now, I had Shade in my corner. Would that make a difference to Jax?

I sure as hell hoped not.

"Fiona, get on the ladder. Jax will follow when there's room." Right now, we couldn't move anyway. I was at the top, Shade was behind me, and Fiona could barely fit a foot on.

A stab of daylight suddenly appeared, piercing my eyes with brightness. I blinked as huge hands gripped the edges of the doors like claws, prying the panels apart with a crunch of metal. Merrick's shiny black face appeared, dripping sweat and grinning when he saw us. Some kind of shield protected his back and now me from a constant barrage of gunfire.

"What *is* that?" I slipped through the crack and stood in the shelter of Merrick's big rectangular shadow. He'd strapped a huge metal panel to his back with cargo belts and bungee cords from the *Endeavor*. Shade came out behind me.

"Your kitchen door." Merrick gathered us close and covered all three of us as we ran in a cluster toward the ship's open entrance. Bullets pinged off the shield. Sparks flew, streaks of orange in my peripheral vision.

"My door?" Shock gave way to admitting it was good thinking. The panel was taller and wider than Merrick and made of the same space-worthy armored metal as the rest of the ship. I grinned. "Who needs privacy in a kitchen?" It was a communal space anyway.

Merrick cracked a smile as he scooted forward at a side shuffle, shielding us. The bottom of the door grated against the platform, adding to the almost deafening cacophony of automatic weapons, engines, and megaphones blaring orders we were never going to listen to.

"Genius," Shade yelled, keeping his head low and his feet moving.

Something more powerful than a bullet slammed into the door panel. Merrick lurched, just barely keeping his balance and nearly knocking Shade and me over. An explosion boiled around us, sudden and searing. We huddled behind the shield. I gasped, squeezing my eyes shut until the blaze subsided.

"Go!" Merrick urged us onward. At the open starboard air lock, he angled his armored back toward the hovercrafts as Shade and I vaulted up into the ship and scrambled behind opposite sides of the doorframe. Three Grayhawks waited in my corner. I slid two toward Shade and picked up the other. We both flattened ourselves against the walls and hammered off shots at the Dark Watch. Merrick hurried back toward Jax and Fiona at a loping side step, his shield gouging the tarmac.

"You take the ones on the left. I've got the right," Shade shouted over utter chaos. I nodded and kept shooting, my hearing dulled by the roar of gunfire.

"Good thinking with the explosives!" I could see them now that I was looking in the right direction, mines of some kind dotting the outer section of the platform. "What are they?"

"Incendio charges," Shade answered.

"Never heard of them," I hollered back.

"Big noise. Big fire. Not a huge range of actual destruction but intense at the source. Not a good idea to land on them."

I nodded. Shade's forward thinking was the only reason the hovercrafts hadn't touched down and goons weren't swarming the dock right now.

"That's my whole supply. Was hoping to get them back." Shade tossed me a roguish smile that curled around my racing heart and steadied it. "Not looking so good."

No, but the incendios had saved our butts so far—along with Merrick. "Those won't stop them from fast-roping it down." While discreet, the explosives were visible and avoidable to feet, even if a whole hovercraft couldn't wiggle a landing spot around them.

"Then keep shooting, starshine. They're not going to pop over the sides and slide down with us aiming at them."

Probably not. Goons were well known for their highly developed sense of self-preservation. It almost rivaled their penchant for abusing power. The two likely went together.

A new sound punched my ears like bad music—the whine and thump of more sophisticated engines. The individual cruisers Merrick had picked up earlier on the radar buzzed our tower. A group of them raced over the city skyline before swinging back around, noses—and weapons—pointed toward us.

Dread cramped hard in my stomach. Shade and I glanced at each other. Those cruisers would have firepower the *Endeavor*'s outer armor couldn't deflect as easily as bullets.

My gaze flicked toward the elevator tubes. Jax and Fiona were out. A small missile exploded against the shield, and I cried out in fear for them. Merrick nearly buckled, but Jax helped prop him up while Fiona burrowed into Jax's chest, hiding her face from the blast. Grimacing against the heat, Jax used his free arm to protect the back of Fiona's head.

I quickly scanned the hovercrafts, found the source of the missile, aimed, and fired. My bullet sparked off the launcher and the soldier wielding it ducked behind the armored wall of the hovercraft. Merrick and the others started running again. I unloaded bullets toward the same spot and didn't let up until my gun clicked, empty.

"Shade! The missile launcher!" I pointed.

Shade kept the goon down with his second Grayhawk until the others made it to the ship. I threw my empty gun behind me and reached for Fiona. She clambered up while Shade covered Jax and Merrick. Merrick half lifted Jax inside and then leaped up after him. The huge door on his back forced Shade and me away from the opening. Without turning, Merrick slapped his palm down on the door control. The panels slid shut, and everything went totally silent. For a moment, my own heartbeat was the loudest thing in the air lock. Then I sprang into action.

"Let's go! Shade, get to your cruiser and power up. Jax, you're Captain of the *Endeavor* until I get back. Merrick, you're the navigator."

"Go. I'll catch up." Merrick went to work on the buckles keeping the door on his back.

We turned and ran. A moment later, I heard the heavy panel drop and the safety door to the air lock close behind Merrick. He caught up in a flash.

"I have my cruiser," he said. "I'll help fight them off so the *Endeavor* can get out. I'll stick with you guys instead."

"No." I nixed Merrick's idea for several reasons, including one I couldn't admit to. "Fiona can't fly or navigate, and Jax can't do it alone." He'd just been electrocuted and hit over the head. The *Endeavor* needed a backup pilot, and Fiona wasn't it.

"The ship needs a recharge on the way to Mooncamp 1." Shade slid a small square detonator box from his cargo-pants pocket as he ran. "The Outer Zones couldn't be farther from here, and we used a lot of energy to get to Korabon fast."

I'd planned on the *Endeavor* sticking around here for a few days to recharge. *Guess not.*

"Make it a two-jump journey." I turned to Jax. "What's your plan, partner?"

"We'll go to Maylewatch," he answered. "Stay in high orbit and recharge from their sun. When the core's up to full power again, we'll head to the DT Mooncamps."

I nodded. "Sounds good." Maylewatch was about halfway there, quiet and out of the way, and had a nice bright sun to shine on our solar panels. "Like Shade said before, we can all lie low for a couple of days and then meet on day three to finally drop that food off." We'd been carting a huge haul around for weeks—since before I found the enhancers or met Shade.

Jax confirmed with a bob of his chin. I watched him out of the corner of my eye, looking for signs of concussion or weakness. "Might as well feed some people before we all die trying to break into Starbase 12," he said.

I snorted. Gallows humor was still humor, and Jax was holding up.

Shade veered toward the main cargo hold and his cruiser, his tread light and fast. There were both agility and danger in every step he took. I saw it in the way his mind worked, too. It made me glad he was on my side now.

I turned right with the others and ran toward the bridge. I had to make sure they were all set and say goodbye to Bonk.

The *Endeavor* quaked. Jax and I looked at each other. "Bullets can't do that."

Jax shook his head. "But those fighter cruisers can."

They'd looked about double the size of Shade's star cruiser. We'd be more maneuverable, but their phasers would pack twice the punch.

"Brace yourselves," Shade said over the coms. "I'm detonating some of the charges. It'll give us a smoke screen and keep them back."

A second later, a roar erupted and the whole platform shook. Even with Shade's warning, I nearly lost my footing and banged hard against the wall. The rumble quieted. The *Endeavor* didn't shudder again.

We burst onto the bridge. A wary Bonk ran like a streak from under my console and jumped on me. I caught him midair and screeched to a halt, holding him against my chest. He climbed higher, his claws pricking my neck. Whiskers tickled my jaw. He didn't purr, and his ears lay flat. Bonk hated loud noises, and I was pretty sure shaking the whole damn ship didn't help.

I dug little cat nails out of my neck and bent to deposit Bonk on Jax's old, crumpled-up sweater. He sat. His tail swished, and greenish-yellow eyes accused me of setting him down unfairly and way too fast.

"I gotta go, Bonk. You take care of my people." I kissed his gray-and-black-striped head and rubbed my fingers under his chin just enough to get him to angle up and give me better access. "Eat. Play. Live." I gave him a final pat. "I'll be back."

"Take him with you." Jax looked over his shoulder as he set himself up at my console. He flipped switches, opening the main cargo bay. I had to book it to Shade's cruiser. We'd fly out and create a distraction while the *Endeavor* got away.

"No time to get his stuff." I popped up and gave Jax a fierce hug, whether he wanted it or not. "Take care of him, partner."

Jax squeezed me back. "He'll have food and water. I might even let him sleep on my pillow."

That's it! I pulled back, my eyes widening. "You need a pet, Jax."

"Bonk's enough." He shooed me toward the door, shaking his head.

I shuffled backward, my heart firmly planted on the bridge. Was I really about to leave the *Endeavor*? Watch her fly off? "His litter's in my closet."

"I know." Jax turned back to the controls when the whole ship trembled again. I shifted my balance. The Dark Watch was back at it with guns we couldn't ignore.

Fiona reached out and gripped my wrist as I met her in the doorway. Leaning forward, she whispered, "I'll take care of him."

Emotion welled in my throat. Jax would be in good hands, even if they weren't mine. "Thank you."

She nodded. I swallowed.

"Merrick!" I called across the bridge. "You're the best Big Guy around!"

"See you in three days, Tess." Merrick smiled and waved me off from the navigator's chair, a green grid of coordinates flashing out a confirmation behind him. All set for Maylewatch.

Biting my lip, I backed off the bridge. This was it. I had to go.

Another blast rattled the ship, finally spurring me into turning and sprinting toward the main cargo hold. My burned palm was already better, thanks to my accelerated healing, but the new beating didn't help as I bounced off walls and careened around corners. An explosion growled. Alarms wailed out warnings. The lights flickered, and I ran even faster.

"I'm ready to go, Tess. Door's open." Shade's words hit my earpiece, clipped and urgent. The sound of his engine and gunfire blasted down the corridor.

"I'm almost there!" I raced into the central cargo bay and straight into hell. Engine heat blew my hair back. Noise screamed over me. I pushed through beating air, deafening pops, and gritty smoke and lunged, reaching for the hand Shade held out to me. His fingers latched around my wrist. He pulled and I leaped across him, sprawling shoulder first into the passenger's seat.

Scrambling around, I righted myself and reached for my harness. As I strapped in, Shade took off.

"We're out!" he called, flying straight toward the hover-crafts. Neither of us flinched. They should be afraid of us, not the other way around. The one-man cruisers were a different story.

"Look out!" I cried.

Shade banked hard, narrowly avoiding a bright-blue energy blast from one of the fighter pilots. It hit the dock, and an explosion rolled upward, licking at the bottom of our cruiser.

I glanced over my shoulder, my heart banging against my ribs. The *Endeavor*'s cargo door finished closing just as a great ball of fire slammed against it. The flames died out. A hole gaped in the platform.

I turned back around, blowing out a quick breath. *Okay then.*

Shade flew with the skill of a military pilot, but that didn't keep me from gripping the edges of my seat until my fingers cramped. He went vertical, straight up the tower, drawing fire and getting the Dark Watch cruisers to follow, and then dove hard, speeding back down and forcing the hovercrafts to scatter.

Our front console flashed out damage warnings—minor for the moment. So far, we'd avoided any direct hits, but we couldn't keep this up forever. Maybe I should have let Merrick help us. Fiona was good at math. She could have set the freaking coordinates and handled the bridge with Jax.

A warning blared. Shade barreled into a roll to keep a fighter cruiser from targeting us. Buildings. Sky. Ground! A scream rose in my throat. I choked it down when Shade straightened and pulled up hard. He zoomed back toward our platform and challenged the two hovercrafts blocking the *Endeavor*'s exit to a game of do-or-die chicken that had me curling into my seat, my eyes half closed.

I braced for impact just as both hovercrafts suddenly dropped, avoiding our charge only to ram into each other. One's engine exploded and blew a hole through the side of the other. They spiraled toward the ground, a mess of smoke and fire. Soldiers abandoned ship, leaping over the sides and activating the gliders on their backs to take them down to street level.

"Holy shit." I glanced at Shade. His mouth was set in a grim line of concentration.

More hovercrafts moved in to block the *Endeavor*.

"Fuckers won't get…the way," Jax muttered, interference chopping at his voice midsentence. "Should I ram them?"

He could bully the remaining hovercrafts out of the way, but those one-man cruisers had firepower that could ground the *Endeavor*. We had to get the ship out *now*. The crew needed to get to safety, and this was my one chance to get to Reaginine with the blood bags before my uncle dragged either Mareeka or Surral off to prison.

"How many incendio charges can we still blow?" I asked Shade.

Wordlessly, he put the multidetonator box in my hand. Three out of five buttons still jutted out, waiting to be activated.

"Brace yourselves," I warned. "You're about to lose half that platform."

"We're ready to fly, Tess. Do it." Jax knew the *Endeavor* could take a roasting. It was high-intensity electromagnetic radiation we had to worry about. Phasers burned holes through metal, messed with systems, left ships dead or limping.

Steeling myself, I pressed all three buttons. One hell of a conflagration erupted, throwing a thundering arm of fire out from the platform. I winced away from the burning wave, and even though the cruiser's outer armor protected us from the heat, we bumped and rattled like particles in a reactor. I grabbed the handle above my window panel, my teeth clacking. On my right, goons dove for cover behind the chest-high walls of the open hovercrafts. Their pilots kicked it into reverse and then banked away from the inferno, emptying the area of the hulking obstructions.

"We're up and clear," Jax announced. "Leaving."

I craned my neck to watch the *Endeavor* emerge from utter chaos, her gray metal wavering in a heat mirage of engine fever and explosion fire. She lifted away from the jagged edge of the dock, sending loose bits of platform flying. Debris pinged against our front panel, and both Shade and I jerked. The flames died down, but black smoke billowed, climbing up and out and everywhere. As soon as the *Endeavor* cleared the tower, Jax tilted her nose toward the spheres and punched up the power.

In front of us, a ragged blister glared at me from where Platform 252 used to be. I could almost smell the ignition fuel, feel the sting of smoke in my eyes, and taste the melting tar on my tongue. I swallowed, fear of the whole tower crumbling to the ground spreading through me like battery acid and biting into me hard.

"I put the incendios where they'd chew the hell out of one side of the platform but not cause major structural damage."

I looked at Shade. Was I that obvious?

Clearing my throat, I murmured, "Thank you." If I could trust anyone to know how sturdy a docking tower was, it was Shade. And I was relieved to know he chose not to go any further than necessary with potential damage.

Our radar beeped. Once. Twice. Faster. We turned our eyes to the sky. Several one-man fighters came at us. Shade evaded, but we took a glancing blow and lost altitude. I gasped, gripping my harness. Shade's hands flew over the controls, steadying his cruiser and quieting the warnings. He launched a counterattack that sent some of the Dark Watch fighters scattering. The rest stayed on us.

Shade accelerated and rolled in a dizzying spiral down a huge avenue, towers hemming us in on both sides and shots chasing us until we swung hard around another building. Heavy g-forces dragged at my body, and I held on tight, holding my breath, too.

We came back around to ... *nothing*?

"What the hell?" I leaned forward, then swiveled my head around. My eyes flicked up. "They're after the *Endeavor*!"

With a well-placed tap, Shade coaxed our sputtering visual-aid system back into working order and zoomed off in pursuit. "Time to show them what we've got, starshine."

"They could ground her." Or worse. I wouldn't voice *worse* out loud, though.

"They won't." Shade pushed a button, and a panel opened in front of me. Automatically, I reached for the joystick that emerged from inside the front console, my thumb already hovering over the little red button. A target monitor lit up behind it.

"Shoot 'em out of the sky if you have to," Shade told me.

I nodded, doing my best to ignore my cramping stomach. I hadn't shot anything but bullets before. And I'd never shot to kill.

As we came up on the Dark Watch cruisers, a few of the fighters swung around to engage us while others stayed hot on the tail of the *Endeavor*. I picked one and tracked its movements, my fingers tensing around my control column. It was getting closer to us. Too close. It shot off an energy blast that sizzled down our left side and caused a damage warning. *Shit*. I couldn't just sit here. I clenched my jaw and fired.

A beam shot from our weapons system and engulfed the Dark Watch cruiser. The goon's scorched and pockmarked craft went dead in the air and dropped. The pilot ejected, spiraling backward.

"Whoa!" My eyes widened. I looked down. The cruiser exploded below us. "It's a good thing no one walks around outside here!"

"I might've souped that phaser up a bit," Shade said, grinning.

"You think?" I swung the megaweapon toward an incoming cruiser. The Dark Watch pilot got the hell out of my line of fire.

Another fighter closed in on our right, spitting shots that left our ship shaken and blaring alarms at us. Shade fired back but only managed to destabilize it. Watching my monitor, I adjusted my aim, locked on, and fired. The pilot ejected, popping up and out before what was left of his cruiser crashed and burned on the empty avenue alongside the other.

I whooped. Adrenaline pumped through me as I scanned for my next target. "My gun is bigger than your gun," I teased, a little smirk in my voice.

Shade rattled off more shots with his itty-bitty phaser. "I'm steering *and* shooting. That shows talent."

"Being able to multitask doesn't make up for size."

He flashed a quick smile as two incoming cruisers banked away from us. "Watch this. You might reevaluate."

Shade accelerated like a fiend. My whole body pressed into my seat, and I couldn't move a muscle. He came up between the *Endeavor* and the two remaining Dark Watch cruisers, leveled out so fast my stomach flipped over, and started shooting. The fighters veered off in separate directions. We waited, blocking their path to the *Endeavor*. After a moment, it was clear they weren't coming back again.

I sank into my seat with a heavy exhale and then caught a spark of sunlight off gray metal. I looked over my shoulder. The *Endeavor* hadn't jumped yet. She picked up speed, racing spaceward and getting smaller and smaller. She made her way toward freedom, and my heart lurched after her. My hands fell from the joystick. I stared up at the shrinking dot, unblinking. The second she leaped into warp speed, I'd be out of contact.

Watching her go, I felt suddenly lost, untethered. Static already droned in my ear, the distance growing too great for our outdated communication system.

"Jax?" Tears stung my eyes with abrupt intensity. He was my home. I was his. We'd built each other for seven years now.

My hands crunched down on my knees, squeezing so hard I'd leave bruises. "Partner?"

"I'm here, Tess." Increased interference didn't hide the strain in Jaxon's voice. It equaled mine. Was maybe greater.

I started shaking and gripped my legs harder as Shade rose quickly, following the *Endeavor* out of Korabon's atmosphere. We jiggled from the force of the climb, and my skin pulled back against my bones again, flattening. Hot and cold flip-flopped inside me with sickening volatility, and my vision went spotty as blind panic took over.

I made a noise—something between a whimper and a choking swallow. How had I ever thought this would be okay? Jax and I didn't *separate*. We hadn't been apart for longer than eight hours since the day we met on Hourglass Mile. Prison created bonds, a pressure cooker that fucking fused people.

"Jax!" My scream flew out before I could stop it. My breath came short. I pounded my hands against my window. I couldn't help it.

Shade looked over, frowning. Was I scaring him? Well, I was scared shitless.

"You're a fucking badass rebel capt…" Jax's words garbled and then cut off completely at the nearly broken connection. "I'll see you in three da…partner."

A bright spot in the distance glowed hot and then winked out—the *Endeavor* jumping away from us.

Vomit rose hard and fast in my esophagus. I held my breath and swallowed. Emotion punched up and I punched it back down, squeezing my eyes shut until I could breathe without stomach acid hurtling up my throat again.

I shook. The hot-cold sensation wouldn't leave me. It gathered, pooling in places that felt deep and empty and afraid inside me.

Shade reached across the middle of the cruiser and squeezed my knee. "We did it. We got them out. Brace yourself now. We're jumping."

I nodded, closing my eyes again. I swallowed convulsively. Seconds later, we jumped the hell out of there—and likely straight into our next disaster.

CHAPTER

4

SHADE

TESS FINALLY SPOKE FOR THE FIRST TIME SINCE WE popped out of warp speed within sighting distance of the green and blue planet. People called Reaginine earthlike. As if they'd ever been to Earth. I knew I hadn't.

"Reaginine is pretty," she said numbly, watching out her window as we approached the Temple Lands after a long cruise over the jungle-covered southern continent. I'd wanted to arrive somewhere with next-to-no air traffic to make sure we hadn't been followed before flying into this busier area.

I glanced over at her. She looked nauseous, which normally I'd blame on the long jump—my stomach still felt a bit twisted up also—but she'd looked sick *before* the trip through hyperspace. Leaving Jax was the problem.

"You've never been here?" I asked, hoping to distract her.

"Dad—I mean, the Overseer—never let Mom and me come. We celebrated Emergence on Alpha Sambian, when it was actually autumn on our part of the planet." She shrugged.

"Better than the dead of winter, like in Albion City. The cold made it hard to pray all day outside under Her rays of sunlight—metaphorically, anyway." I winked, dragging a weak smile from Tess.

When it was midsummer at the Grand Temple on Reaginine, it was Emergence. It didn't matter where you were in the galaxy—on a planet, in the Dark, whatever season on your rock or not—the citizens of the eighteen Sectors celebrated the birth of the Sky Mother on the summer solstice here on Reaginine. The Great Star was here, shining on us right now. And the heart of the Church of the Great Star rose before us in the form of pyramidal temples. My current destination was a hidden gem several kilometers beyond them.

"On Starway 8, it didn't matter. There are no seasons on a spacedock, and we followed the universal calendar. It was just another date to me anyway, except we made cookies and didn't have lessons."

"That sounds better than freezing my ass off on a rooftop to get as close as possible to Her far-off rays of holiness."

A fuller smile quirked Tess's lips. "Careful, you're sounding blasphemous."

"Nah. My Sky Mother is concerned with the bigger picture."

Tess snorted. I didn't pick a fight. I got where she was coming from. The bigger picture didn't look great.

She turned back to the jungle after only a cursory glance at the temples. "Do you think they have flervers here?"

I held back my amusement. The conflict in her was obvious, just like it had been on Albion 5. Cautious but curious. Nature scared her. She also loved the adventure of it. She'd face down an armed city goon with only her fists and feet for weapons, but she'd run screaming if an animal came near her.

Not that she was wrong. Some of the animals here could gobble up a human in one bite.

"I think flervers are a Sector 2 thing. I've never seen them anywhere else—although they do have snakes here." And other things Tess didn't need to hear about right now.

Her head thumped the back of her seat as she looked straight ahead again. "Great."

I reached over and twined my fingers through hers. "The biggest snake might be your uncle. According to my watch, we have sixteen hours before meeting day starts."

She sighed, her gaze straying back to the crowded temples. "Let's find a place to dock, then."

"I have that covered." I let go of her hand and, with a swipe of my fingers, woke up my new com unit. I baptized it with a call to the automated reservation service on Reaginine. "Aisé Lodges. Private bungalow for two. Two nights total," I ordered.

SEARCHING scrolled across the screen in green block letters.

Tess shot me a wary look. "Whatever that is, it sounds expensive. I can't afford that."

"I can." The only thing I had left from my pre-outlaw life was currency. Might as well use it.

"Money can run out," Tess said.

"Don't worry, starshine. Unless I need to finance the entire rebellion on my own, the money's not going to run out."

Her lips puckered. The huge stash of universal currency I'd amassed to try to buy back my docks from Scarabin White obviously left a sour taste in her mouth. Her chin lifted. Her eyes hardened to blue ice, and my gut sank. I should've known better.

Here was the reckoning. I could feel it coming on at warp speed. It wasn't the money itself that bothered Tess. It was how I'd made it. I'd wanted to treat her to something special. Instead, I was about to get a fight—one I'd had coming for a while.

She turned away, her hands curling into fists in her lap. They drummed against her thighs with light, steady beats. The rest of her stayed stony and silent.

Fuck. "Say it."

She glanced over with a crisp turn of her head. "Say what, Shade?"

"Say what's on your mind."

Her frosty gaze dropped the temperature inside the cruiser to subzero. Would she refuse to talk and pretend everything was fine? Or would she finally spit out all the hurt and anger and disappointment that had been festering like a sore between us since Albion 5?

"Fine." Anger suddenly charged the air around us, replacing the chill with something fury-hot and fierce. "You want me to say it? How's this?" Tess's nostrils flared, and I braced myself, every muscle inside me tensing. "How *could* you? What were you *thinking*? How could you *live* like that? How could you live with *yourself*? Do you have any idea how many people you've hurt? The damage you might have done to the rebellion? To my friends? To the whole freaking galaxy?" Her voice rose. Her eyes spit fire, nothing icy in her expression now. She growled at me. Literally growled, her teeth clamped together and her face all flushed.

"You're right." Call me stupid, but Tess's angry outburst sat a lot better with me than the frigid distance she'd tried to put between us. That didn't stop cold from worming its way into my chest and freezing my lungs solid with how deeply I'd failed everyone who'd ever counted on me. I was done failing, and I'd apologize to Tess as many times as she needed me to. "I'm sorry. For things I've done. For lying to you. I would change so much if I could."

Her eyes squeezed shut, clamping so tight her nose scrunched up. "I know." When she opened her eyes again, the light inside them was different, softer somehow. "And then I think: what's done is done. He's made a new choice. Changed. He's helping. He's helping *me*. And he's *mine* now, so just move on."

Mine. The word electrified my heart, heating it up and making it beat too hard. I wasn't even sure Tess understood how true that was. I'd been bone-deep devoted to getting my docks back, no matter the cost to myself or anyone else—until that cost had been the woman next to me.

Bone-deep devotion to *her* now thickened my throat, giving me a sandpaper voice that scratched out in a low, rough rasp. "I hated what I did. Hunting people down for the Dark Watch? That's not something I ever wanted. I did it because I backed myself into a corner of epic proportions, and it was either give up my family's docks forever, work for Bridgebane, or start hacking banks." I looked at her, willing her to at least try to understand. "There are some sums that are just...astronomical. There's no way to make that kind of money through regular means."

Her eyes narrowed.

"It's not an excuse," I blurted out. "It's an explanation." And it sounded weak to my ears.

"So explain. How does one become my uncle's top bounty hunter for the Dark Watch?"

I tapped my fingers against my knee, remembering how fast it had happened. Maybe I hadn't wanted to give myself time to think. "The opportunity just presented itself one day when Bridgebane needed a quick repair on something. I was at the base of Nuthatch, moping around my lost docks, as usual. He asked me who in the area could fix a finicky cruiser. I could, so I did. Figured I'd tinker with an engine and earn a little money."

She frowned. "Uncle Nate was on Albion 5?"

I had no idea why, but he'd definitely been in Albion City not long after life as I knew it fell apart. "About ten years ago. After I got his cruiser up and running, he offered me a one-time job to test me out. It turned out I was good at bounty hunting. Jobs kept coming in. I advanced to his elite force. Currency piled up, and I put it all aside to buy back the docks as soon as I could. It was only ever a job to me. A means to an end. I didn't do it for fun."

"But you did it anyway." Bitter disgust from my girlfriend made me feel like shit, especially when I deserved every ounce of her outrage and could add my own self-loathing to it.

"Yeah, I did it anyway. But now I've stopped. Because of you, Tess, I changed my life."

Something more brittle, like hurt, jerked across her expression. "So it's my fault you lost everything?"

"No!" *Shit.* I ran a hand through my short hair, gripping the back of my neck. "Changed my life for the better. I met you, got to know you, and I realized you were the kind of person I wanted to be. I didn't like who I'd become, but I liked you, and I wanted to like myself again."

Tess digested that in silence, mashing her lips back and forth. Finally, "Do you—"

A robotic voice coming from the cruiser's com unit interrupted whatever she was about to say. "Bungalow 39. Two-night reservation. Please proceed to these coordinates."

I didn't bother looking at the numbers that popped up on the screen. I could walk the Temple Lands of Reaginine with my eyes closed and had been stomping around the nearby jungle and taking ill-advised dips in the Gano River since I was a kid. One Aisé bungalow or another had been my own personal paradise for three weeks of every year of my life until a little more than a decade ago. When my parents died, I stopped coming. I didn't want to be here alone. Praying could be done anywhere, and honestly, I didn't do it that often. Now that I was back, though, something *did* feel holier here. More sacred. But this place equated family to me, and I didn't have one anymore.

Or if I was lucky, maybe I did. I glanced at Tess. It didn't matter to me that she was skeptical about the church. Reaginine had more to offer than the Sky Mother and a place to worship.

I slowly dropped in altitude and headed for the riverside resort nestled in the heart of the Gano Jungle. The weight on my chest wouldn't let up, but I didn't know if that was because Tess was mad at me for things I couldn't change or because the last time I was here, I was a university student who'd gone fishing with his dad and read out loud to his mother. She always said that poetry sounded better when you could just close your eyes, sit back, and enjoy it.

Tess sighed and scrubbed both hands over her face. "I'm sorry."

"You have nothing to be sorry about." I was the one with bad decisions darkening my soul in every corner.

"Sometimes, I can't get out of this cycle. In my head, you

know? Thinking about things. Replaying them. Good and bad. Over and over. I guess that's why people talk about love–hate relationships."

I arched a brow in her direction. "You hate me?"

"No." She laughed a little. "But I hate things you've done, even though I know you had good reasons. And I know you want to do things differently from now on. I guess it all just boiled up a minute ago, like some messed-up accusation soup spiced with...I don't know..." She shook her head. "Lust and rage?"

"The rage is justified." I slid her a slow smile. "I can work with lust."

Her lips twitching, she swatted me with a soft backhand across the chest.

"And light slapping," I added.

Tess laughed. The fading light didn't hide the electric-blue spark of interest in her eyes when they met mine across the center aisle.

"Who gets to do the slapping?" She looked eager as hell, and I grinned as I flew us over the hazy dark-green jungle, relieved we were done arguing.

"I'm a firm believer in equality. I say we take turns."

She nodded. "Where do you like to be slapped?" she asked, utterly serious.

I chuckled, that heaviness finally lifting from my chest. I breathed deeply for the first time in what felt like hours. I loved the way Tess just said things like "I'm fully vaccinated and on birth control" or "Where do you like to be slapped?" She was worth every second of the agonizing decision I'd had to make on Albion 5. Not to mention this whole bounty-on-my-head, run-for-your-lives, suicide-mission thing we had going on now. I'd do it all again in a heartbeat.

I threw her a heated look. "Slap me anywhere you want, starshine. I'm up for it."

"*Anywhere*?" Her eyes dipped to my lap. "*Up* for it?"

"Well, let's avoid some places, right? Or it might cut the fun short."

She grinned. Then the thickening jungle caught her eye, and she leaned toward the window again. "It's beautiful! So lush and green." She watched the treetops go by, and I lowered us even more, making sure she got the best look possible without disturbing the birds and other creatures living in the forest.

"What's that?" she asked, pointing down. "It's like the trees are connected by something. Woven together."

"Vines. They're as thick as my arm in places, sometimes thicker. And little creatures run across them, going from tree to tree."

"Like monkeys?"

Her uncle had called her *monkey*. They were long extinct, too sensitive to have survived the downfall of Earth, but she must've read a book about them. "Something like that. Here, they're called ganokos." I tilted my head toward the rolling blanket of textured greens. Pockets of mist hung in clearings and swirled around leaves. "All that, as far as you can see, is the Gano Jungle. And see that river? The Gano. It's full of terrifying things. Fish with teeth the size of your hand. Reptiles. Snakes. Creatures that belong in nightmares."

Tess slowly pulled away from the window, still peering down.

"But there are places where it's safe enough to be on the banks. For fishing. Hiking. Maybe a swim, if you're really careful." I hadn't always been careful. Kids did stupid shit, and I was surprised I'd come back in one piece—or at all—from some of my jungle adventures. A close call when I was sixteen helped me realize I wasn't indestructible. As an adult, I had to wonder what the hell my parents were thinking, letting me run wild along the river.

"I know of a few safe spots to take a dip." I glanced at Tess, a smile pulling at my lips. "And the water's warm here—unlike in *some* places."

She laughed. "The beach on Albion 5 or my old shower?"

"Both." I shuddered. "Either."

She watched the tropical forest go by, her curious eyes seeming to gobble up every detail and color. The subtle tilt to her spine still angled her body away from the window, but the excitement on her face and the way her hand pressed against the clear panel said she was ready to brave the jungle. "I can't swim," she murmured.

"I know. But I bet you're a quick learner."

Her wide, giddy smile snuffed every crazy and heart-wrenching moment of the last few weeks out like a candle. I didn't give a damn about the past anymore. My only concern was the future.

"You'll do great." I smiled back at her, my chest lurching with the privilege of getting to be the one to bring exciting firsts into Tess's life from now on, hopefully starting with skinny-dipping.

"Do you think we'll have time?" she asked. "To swim, I mean?"

I took us down lower as the first of the bungalows appeared by the river. "We don't meet your uncle until tomorrow, universal time. Daylight here is ahead of that clock by several hours. We'll have all morning before he'll even technically start looking for us."

"He didn't give an exact time, so who knows when he'll

even show up," she said. "Hour one, hour twelve, hour twenty-three ... We could be waiting for ages."

"Hour one. Bridgebane's always on time."

Tess stopped fidgeting, her sudden stillness making me look over. She frowned at her lap. "You know him better than I do. I guess I'll take your word for it."

I didn't like the hurt in her voice—or the fact that she tried to cover her pain with notes of bitterness. "I might know him, but he was still willing to shoot me and put a huge bounty on my head. *You*, he won't touch."

"I can't imagine why." She sniffed and looked out the window again, avoiding my gaze.

Couldn't she? Whatever Bridgebane's crimes in Tess's eyes, he'd spared her life twice, *against* orders. Her uncle obviously cared about her.

She exhaled, definitely closing the subject with the long breath she let out. "Isn't this kind of far from the Grand Temple? There's plenty of docking space for personal cruisers around the Holy Hollow, and people usually just sleep in their transportation units. Shouldn't we stay closer to tomorrow's meeting spot?"

"Sleeping in this cruiser is for contortionists only, and I had enough of it during those first days on board the *Endeavor*. It's not that far, and the Aisé Resort runs a private shuttle to the Temple Lands on a regular basis, if you prefer that to the cruiser tomorrow." The resort shuttle would be more anonymous, although I trusted Bridgebane to come alone and didn't think anyone else would be looking for us on Reaginine right now.

Tess went back to watching the scenery. The river snaked through the darkening green like a rainbow serpent, reflecting the sunset colors. Purple, pink, yellow. A splash of red faded into dull orange. The fiery sky made a feral backdrop for the even wilder jungle.

I rubbed my jaw, the pads of my fingers scratching over light stubble. I'd missed this place. Or maybe I just missed my parents. Memories flooded back as though carried on the muddy rapids of the Gano. Some made me want to smile. Others made my heart twist. A few were on the tip of my tongue to share with Tess, but I didn't trust my voice to come out as anything other than thick and hoarse.

When the main lodge of the resort came into view, I finally looked at the exact coordinates and located Bungalow 39. The private cottage was on the small side, but it was just Tess and me, so I didn't mind. The landing pad was spacious and unshaded by the thick vegetation cutting us off from any sign of other people. The cruiser would recharge nicely starting at sunrise. I popped out all the delicate solar panels before powering down and getting out. My first breath of humid Reaginine air came within a hairsbreadth of choking me up. I blinked and cleared my throat.

Tess hopped down on her side as I rounded the cruiser. She shivered, looking around. "I've never felt so isolated in my entire life."

That sounded ideal to me, but I didn't want Tess feeling marooned on a strange planet. I wrapped an arm around her shoulders.

"Listen." Opening my ears to the jungle's chorus, I tilted my face up to the first stars. Night fell slowly here. It was only dusk, but silver dots still splashed across the deepening sky like diamonds tossed up to the heavens in a careless handful.

Tess cocked her head. At first, only a breeze seemed to whisper through the trees. Then the chirping of insects began to fill the spaces between warm gusts that smelled of jungle mist, rich earth, and foliage. The soft, gurgling music beneath the other sounds was the swiftly moving water of the Gano.

"Is that the river?" She looked downhill in the right direction.

I nodded. She shivered again, even though she pulled her sleeves up. Goose bumps peppered her arms.

"How can you be cold in this heat?" I tucked her closer to me.

"I'm not cold. I'm freaking terrified." With another shudder, Tess leaned into my side. "I'm absolutely certain a horde of flervers is about to jump on me."

Don't laugh. Don't do it. "Flervers are solitary creatures. And in Sector 2, like I said before."

"Nope. They travel the galaxy in hordes and eat space rats for dinner."

"And you got this from what source of information?" I asked, my smile two seconds from bursting.

"From my overactive imagination. It's very helpful."

I grinned. "Try to rein in thoughts of death and destruction by flerver. Seriously, they're like beavers."

"I don't like beavers, either."

"Have you ever seen a beaver?"

"No." Tess huffed. "They're extinct. You know that as well as I do."

I smiled against Tess's long bangs that were always slipping forward and kissed her temple. "Okay. Let's go inside before a Sector-hopping horde of hungry flervers smells your fear and zeroes in on us from across the galaxy."

"Don't make fun of me."

I put my hand over my heart. "I would never."

Tess's scowl didn't fool me. The humor in her eyes told the real story. "They'll eat you first. More muscle."

"If it keeps you alive, I'm happy to sacrifice my biceps."

"Good. Plenty to gnaw on." She nodded in apparent satisfaction. "But really, you should just stop siccing flervers on me."

Laughter bubbled in my chest. My steps more buoyant than in years, I urged her toward the bungalow. "I'm your navigator, but I still might need a map to show me exactly how the conversation got to this point."

Tess slapped her arm. Grimacing, she brushed away a crushed bug, leaving a big smear of red near her elbow. "I'll draw you one inside with the blood of my enemies. Sound good?"

"Sounds hot."

She rolled her eyes at me.

"Come on. Your safe haven awaits." Or maybe it was my safe haven. How had I ever stayed away this long?

I strode forward and opened the decorative shutters hiding the console next to the bungalow's front door. With the code from my least used bank account, I transferred the required currency units for a two-night stay. A key card emerged once the payment went through. I swiped it in front of the lock, opening the door for Tess. She stepped past me and went inside.

Soft lighting automatically clicked on, even though it wasn't truly dark out yet. Tess stopped dead. "It's open." She looked from side to side, taking in the two-and-a-half walls and partial roof above us. "It's amazing. But open."

"Netting covers the whole patio and attaches to the house. It's sheer but electrified. Nothing gets through uninvited, big or small. I promise. No bugs. No critters."

She moved farther in to examine the large landscaped area with flowers, shrubs, a pool, and plush outdoor furniture. "What if it rains?"

"The netting is waterproof, partially UV-blocking, and totally impenetrable to wildlife." It even blended seamlessly into the environment, held up by tall posts made to look like trees with branches and vines connecting them. "It's not just draped against the ground, either. It's buried deep and pinned down. You're perfectly safe inside the house and patio area. I've seen a cyclodile try to break through and make zero progress."

Tess's head snapped around. "What's a cyclodile?"

"A one-eyed reptile." I nodded down the manicured lawn, which sloped toward the river below us. "From the Gano over there."

Absently chewing her bottom lip, Tess left the open-plan "indoor" area and started exploring the patio. She poked her nose into a few of the flowering plants, dipped her fingers in the pool and swirled them, and then sat in the center of the decadent U-shaped couch, facing nature head-on like I knew she'd rarely had the chance to do in her lifetime.

I came up beside her. Her hair hung past her shoulders in a dark wave, the shorter bits near her neck curling in the humidity. Her usually space-pale complexion reflected the warm glow of the dying sunset colors, almost making her look tan against the white cushions. She smiled up at me and patted the couch next to her. I sank down with a muffled groan of contentment, tossing my feet up on the coffee table and crossing them at the ankles. I leaned my head back. Perfection. This was it. I could stay here forever.

Tess laid her hand on my thigh. "It's beautiful. I've never seen anything like this. The house, the view, the jungle..."

"Does that mean you like it?" I sprawled my arm over the top of the couch. The way Tess automatically curled into me made my chest muscles tighten while I waited for her answer. I'd missed this place. The Gano Jungle was home to me almost as much as Albion City. I'd lost that home. Maybe I could still have this one.

My heart pounded as I curled my hand around her shoulder, waiting for a final judgment.

"I'm torn." With a sigh, Tess started drawing light circles on the top of my knee that tickled a little. She watched her slowly moving fingers. "I'm torn between thinking it's wonderful and hating where you got the money to pay for something like this."

My mouth flattened. Her answer was about what I was expecting, and maybe more generous than I deserved. "If I could take back the last ten years and start over, I would. But that path also brought me to you, which is something I can't regret. So I guess I'm torn, too. Giving away the money wouldn't help either of us at this point. We might need it. Or not." I shrugged. "We don't have to spend it on stuff like this again if you don't want to. We're safe for now. The *Endeavor* and everyone on it should be, too. Maybe let's just try to enjoy tonight and tomorrow morning before we face whatever the meeting with Bridgebane brings."

Tess didn't respond. Tension built inside me at her silence. I shifted and looked around. Stars shined brighter now, still framed by the hazy outline of jungle shadows. The wide belt of the river faded, darkness swallowing up the view down the lawn in increments. It was probably a good thing. The snapper jaws and cyclodiles stalking the banks for their dinner wouldn't help Tess settle in at the bungalow. The worst predators were known to gather upriver from here during the daytime, which meant it was more or less safe to walk the banks near the bungalows except at mealtimes.

Tess looked over her shoulder, checking out the softly

glowing interior again. The only closed-off room was the bathroom. Privacy had certain benefits. There would also be a shower I could really use—with Tess, if she was willing. But I could feel her pulling away by the second, and I had no idea how to bring her back again.

I'd been a fool to bring her here and flaunt my bounty-hunting earnings, even if that hadn't been my intention. The Aisé Resort was one of my favorite places in the galaxy, all wrapped up in family memories and the faded joy of youth. I'd wanted to share it with Tess, but that was just one more mistake in a long line of them. I should've docked at the Holy Hollow and been done with it.

Tess sank deeper into the couch, leaning into the crook of my arm again. Her eyes focused on things beyond the netting, even though it was getting pretty dark out there. "I can hear all the jungle noises. It makes me want to find out what's in the trees, see the animals. The bungalow in the middle of it all is ... really special." She glanced over her shoulder again. "And that bed over there could fit about ten people."

A chuckle forced me to stop holding my breath. Maybe she didn't hate it. "Do you want me to go find eight others, or are you good with just me?"

Her mouth quirked. "You'll do." Her tense shoulders dropped an inch or two, but she was still uncomfortable. I could tell. Tess had spent most of her life inside one metal container or another. This had to be nature overload. Along with her other objections, it was too much.

"We can go. If this isn't right for you, we can find something else." I lifted my arm from around her. "I'll look into some options."

Tess gripped my leg, stopping me. "I don't want to go.

I want to see what's in that ginormous refrigerator and eat my weight in fruit, if I'm lucky. I want to swim in the pool, because I'm pretty sure you won't let me drown. I want to sleep in that massive bed and watch the sun rise from your arms before I walk down to the river and try to spot a cyclodile—preferably from a distance."

"Yeah?" Relief swelled my heart so big my ribs ached from the pressure.

"Yeah." She took a deep breath. "But I have to tell you something first."

Tess looked at her hands. She laced and unlaced her fingers and then sat there, seeming unsure. When her eyes finally rose, meeting mine, a chill prickled up my spine and shot little icy darts of worry through me. She looked so nervous that there was no way in hell this could be good news. My relief forgotten, I got colder and colder the longer she took to talk.

"What is it?" I rasped, my stomach tying itself in knots. "Baby, just tell me." Could it really be worse than the things we'd already faced, both alone and together?

She swallowed. Cosmic-blue eyes hit me square on. "Before you risk yourself any further with me, *for* me, I think you should know… I'm going to inherit Starway 8."

I stared, having expected… I wasn't sure what. Not that. "You can't inherit an orphanage."

"I can. It's private. The Dark Watch regulates Starway 8 to a certain extent, just like it regulates everything—I guess under the supervision of Bridgebane—but despite most people's assumption, it's not a galactic entity. Mareeka is full owner of the orphanage, and I'm her heir. It's in the paperwork."

"But you're wanted." I frowned. "On the run."

"Well, it's not going to happen tomorrow or anything, and who knows what'll happen between now and then. If I have to, I'll find a way to change my appearance and take a different name. But when the time comes, and Mareeka and Surral want to retire, I'm going to run the orphanage."

"That's a huge obligation." I squeezed the back of my neck, trying to wrap my head around Tess being responsible for that whole place—for thousands of children, their food, clothes, health, education. Everything.

It took me all of two seconds to realize it was perfect for her. And if nothing changed in the galaxy, she'd churn out little rebels as fast and furtively as her beloved Mareeka did.

"It's not an obligation. It's a gift." Her voice thickened, dropping. "But it's an important and difficult gift. Lives will be in my hands. People's health and safety and education. And not just schooling—a sense of duty, justice, ethics. Starway 8 is a city, and I'll have to run it. Make decisions. Deal with problems. Make sure supplies are coming in and repairs are made and security's up to scratch. Hire employees, caretakers, nurses, and teachers when there are openings. There'll never be a day off. Never a day when multiple people won't need me. It's what I want, but it's also a commitment of epic proportions." Her eyes flicked to mine before skating away again. "I'd love to have help—I'll need it—but I also realize that not everyone's looking for that kind of responsibility."

She looked off in the distance, as if expecting that to be the end of us. Did she think there was even a nanoparticle chance of that? All her words did was yank up everything I'd thought about constantly over the last ten years with a violence that left me reeling. I'd practically sold my soul to try to do *exactly* what she was describing. The Albion 5 docking district should have been *my* city. The dozens of towering buildings my responsibility to maintain. The employees mine to organize, help, and protect.

"Why are you telling me this now? Tonight?" I practically shook from the rush of adrenaline in my blood.

Tess took what seemed like a fortifying breath. "My uncle put a huge price on your head. Coming with me tomorrow, staying with me in general—it's going to put you in danger. You don't have to be a Nightchaser. You can come up with a new identity and find a nice rock out there where no one'll look for you or bother you again. Starway 8 is my future—if I live long enough to inherit. It's the only thing I've ever wanted. Well"—her gaze tipped skyward—"besides the Overseer's timely and gruesome death, I suppose."

I smiled. My lips just did it, involuntary.

Tess smiled, too, our eyes meeting for a quick shot of shared humor before she turned serious again. "I've known since I was a teenager. Mareeka watched and understood. She saw me take any responsibility offered to the older kids. I wouldn't stop, kept wanting more, so she groomed me. She taught me about running Starway 8. I could go back tomorrow and take an administrative position, but they don't need me yet. Not really. And right now, I'm a danger to them. I don't think I should go back for a while."

Maybe not, but she sure sounded like she wanted to. So, this was why Tess hadn't shown any interest in moving up the rebel ranks. With the enhancers as leverage, she could've demanded pretty much anything, even a spot on the council. But Tess didn't want to change her future. She just wanted to live long enough to embrace it.

I took her fidgety hand in mine, squeezing so she'd hold still and look at me. "It would cut you to the bone and crush you if you could never go back there."

She nodded. "I *will* go back—unless it's not what's best for the orphanage. I have to know, Shade. I realize it's still early in…everything. And we've had issues…" She glanced away, her gaze roaming the patio and landing on anything but me. "But if you can't at all see yourself there someday, with me, with those kids, then there's no point in going to the Grand Temple with me tomorrow. There's no point in putting yourself in danger again."

I replayed her words in my head, not answering right away. There wasn't a single thing she'd just said that I shouldn't take very seriously. Part of it smarted. Tess had been my first choice, but I wasn't hers—at least not yet. But none of this felt like an ultimatum, either.

Her gaze dropped to the patio floor. She angled away from me.

"Where are you going?" I slid my hand around the back of her neck, stopping her. "Don't you want an answer to what you just told me?"

Her eyes flicked up, the mix of hope and fear in them making me want to rip out my own beating heart and hand it to her like some kind of fucked-up savage. "I don't want you to *ever* have to give up something you love that much. Not for me. Not for anyone. The only thing that should possibly keep you away from Starway 8 is knowing its occupants are safer without you. And even then, I know you'd keep protecting it from afar. Providing and defending."

Moisture rushed to her eyes, making them glisten in the low lamplight. I pulled her in until our foreheads touched. Tess's breath sped across my cheek, and my pulse thudded heavily. This woman's absolute dedication to things bigger than herself was why I loved her.

I held her gaze. The whisper of air between us began to

simmer with heat and the best kind of tension. "I want you, whether you come with no kids, or five thousand."

Her little gasp was the most satisfying sound I'd heard in ages. "More like seven thousand."

All right. "The more the merrier."

"Are you being sarcastic?" She pulled back, her eyes narrowing. Already getting her ruff up over those kids. Who better to guard them?

"Not at all, starshine." My heart took up a fierce beat inside me, galloping toward a finish line I could finally see again. This was my second chance. There was no way in hell I was wasting it.

"If I'd been able to buy back my docks from Scarabin White, I would've been responsible for thousands of employees on two planets, for managing managers, for bookkeeping, safety regulations, building maintenance, contracts, deliveries, and about a million other things that aren't all fun or fascinating but that would've been part of a whole that was *mine*. Mine to build, to protect, to take care of. I wanted that—the whole package. I understood the scope of the job from watching my father do it. And I understand the kind of commitment it would take to be at the head of that orphanage. It doesn't scare me to think about helping you with that. Granted, the newborn to eighteen-years-old age group and everything that comes with it is a new element, but I can adapt." I searched her eyes, willing her to understand. "Don't you see? You're offering me everything I thought I'd lost, including you in my future."

Tess looked completely stunned, so I kissed her. It took her a second, but she kissed me back, going from hesitant and a little unsure to hungry and eager like she had a hyperdrive switch and had just thrown it. Satisfaction gusted through me the moment she ignited. Tess always exploded like a bomb in skin. Her sexy little whimper melted into my mouth and turned my cock rock-hard in seconds.

A low sound rumbled inside me as I slipped my hands into her hair and angled us closer. Tess gripped my sides, holding on as if she thought I might evaporate. I wasn't going anywhere. Not willingly. I kissed her long and deep to prove it. She swept her hands under my shirt, stroking bare skin. My abdomen tightened, and the air around us blazed ten degrees hotter with each light, questing brush of her fingertips.

Her hands flared out, smoothed, pressed. My senses narrowed to her touch as she slowly ran her palm down my torso to my lap and closed her hand around the bulge in my pants. Volcanic desire shot to the surface and made me want to pounce. Instead, I held as still as possible and used my mouth and tongue to show Tess just how deeply I wanted to get inside her, and not just physically. She gave back twofold, wiggling all over the place to get closer, stroking me through my clothes, and cranking up my need like a furnace.

Breathing like I'd just run a race, I clasped her head in my hands and separated us. Tess looked at me with hazy eyes, her parted lips plump and shiny from my kisses. My heavy pulse drowned out everything except for the words forming with perfect clarity in my head.

Her hand stayed on my cock. She squeezed as she watched me, dragging her bottom lip between her teeth. I groaned and pressed into her hand, lust ripping through me like a lightning bolt.

Fuck, I liked clear signals. And I wanted her more than I wanted my next breath. But I wasn't done talking yet. Maybe

I was going too far, too fast, but my chest was bursting with words that wanted out.

Hardly recognizing my own deep rasp, I said, "And maybe someday, a few of the kids running around that place will be ours, playing with the other little space rats."

Her breath hitched. "Shade?"

I kissed her again, kissed her until she could barely breathe and clung to me for balance. Needing her even closer, I lifted her to straddle me. Tess came willingly, getting up on her knees to rub against me, our mouths fused, our tongues taking and giving, no air between us. My hands tightened on her hips. She rolled her ass like she loved the hard pressure. With a guttural sound, I sank my fingers into soft flesh and rocked her.

Just as the firestorm was starting to blind me to everything else, Tess drew back. I stared at her through a dense, want-thick fog. It cleared the second I saw the worried crease slash between her eyebrows.

"What, baby?" I half stood, getting ready to set her behind me. Had she heard something?

"No, wait." Tess dug her nails into my shoulders, stopping me. "It's just… You're thinking clearly, right? You're not making decisions based on"—she glanced down at where our bodies met and blazing-hot need electrified everything—"want?"

The heat in my groin pounded, intense and insistent. Despite that, I shook my head. "No. Not now, and not before. My head and my heart warred over you a lot on Albion 5, but nothing below the belt got a vote—hard as it tried."

Her dark brows winged up, erasing the troubled frown from her forehead. "Hard?"

I held back a snort. "Really? You're going there?"

Tess giggled. Little laugh lines fanned out from her eyes,

and her teeth flashed in the rising moonlight. "You walked right into that. Admit it."

Growling, I dove in to kiss where her neck met her shoulder. Actually, I devoured it. Between nibbles and sucks, I said, "One more false accusation and I'll call you 'sugar.'"

Tess gasped. "You wouldn't."

"Try me." I swatted her backside.

Her eyes lit up. "Oh, good! The slapping's started already."

Grinning, she tried to swat me back and couldn't. Laughing, I got her again. Tess shrieked a happy sound I wanted to bottle for later and shot off the couch, running toward the huge, high bed. She hopped up, pulling off her shoes and tossing them aside as she turned back to me. Smiling, she kneeled on the edge of the bed and watched me from across the room. I'd never seen anything so inviting.

I got up and prowled over, kicking off my boots as I went. When I reached her, she lifted a hand and braced it against my chest. Could she feel the pounding thud of my heart? Did she know it beat for her now?

Tess leaned forward and licked me from collarbone to ear, flicking her tongue over the shell of it. I tensed all over, igniting, and caught her hips in a firm grasp. I pulled us roughly together.

She tilted her head back, her eyes heavy with desire. "How do you want me, Shade? What's in that mind of yours?"

My cock pulsed at her husky whisper. Images flashed through my mind. Possibilities.

She nipped my earlobe, sending a bullet of sensation down my back and into my legs. My chest rose and fell, brushing hers with every breath. Tess was offering to explore fantasies. I'd take her up on some of mine soon enough, but right now, I just needed to make love to her.

"I want to cover you." *Protect you. Shelter you. Lose myself in you.* "I want you under me." I slid my hand between her legs. She scalded my fingers already, even with her clothes on. Tess rocked into my grip, her hips rolling in a sultry motion.

She reached down and tore her shirt over her head, her hair flying in every direction. It looked brighter in this lighting, some of the redder strands standing out from the brown. I brushed a lock over her shoulder. She shivered, her lips parting on a sweet sound.

Tess dropped her shirt on the floor and leaned her forehead against my jaw, breathing raggedly. My arms came around her, my heart thumping like a hammer. She seemed suddenly vulnerable, half-dressed and balanced against me, and my heavy pulse echoed with all the worries and hopes we'd just confessed to each other. How had I ever contemplated turning her over to the Dark Watch? It would've been like carving open my own chest and tearing out my vital organs.

I'd made my intentions clear—I was in this, with her, for the long run. I wanted to say more. I wanted to tell her how I felt about us, about *her*, but Tess's breath fanned my neck in fast, warm pants, and the words grew too big and clogged in my throat, sticking there.

I nudged her down and undressed us both. Words wouldn't come, so I used my body to show her. And if she didn't understand that I loved her, then I'd show her again tomorrow.

CHAPTER

5

TESS

THE SUN ROSE IN SPECTACULAR FASHION, POURING WARM splashes of dawn-pink light into the open side of the bungalow. Watching the jungle-thick air brighten and change from Shade's arms and the hot-blooded sex that followed made me wish we were here for more than just two days—and for an actual vacation. Getting out of bed early wasn't even hard when the stocked kitchen provided fruit, juice, sweet trigrain rolls with chocolate centers, and fresh-ground coffee complete with cream and sugar. A delicious three-course breakfast magically—well, *robotically*—appeared at our doorstep only a few minutes after we pushed selection buttons on a wall-mounted menu. The Aisé Resort was heaven.

The Gano River, however, was hell.

Shade kept us well back from the bank until the lumbering-on-land-but-deadly-in-the-water cyclodiles mostly cleared out and went back to their den or burrow or mud pocket or whatever it was they had upriver. A few lingered, their knobbly backs breaking the surface like prehistoric monsters before disappearing again under the eddying ripples.

A multicolored flutter caught my eye. "Shit!" I flapped my arms wildly, but the graceful long-necked bird swooped down from the treetops and landed in the middle of the river anyway. Two seconds later, it disappeared in a thrashing of foam and feathers. A bit of pink, yellow, and white plumage popped back up and swirled downriver on a blood-soaked current.

I made a face. "Awesome date, Shade. You took me to murder highway."

He shrugged. "Predators. Prey. It's just the natural way of things."

"Says someone who's only been a predator."

He went quiet, and I instantly regretted my words. I hadn't meant to bring up his bounty-hunting days and ruin our morning together.

"Mostly," he finally said, "but not always. I'm pretty sure I was easy prey for Scarabin White when he was holding my father's gambling debts over my head."

I tightened my ponytail, getting my hair off my sweaty neck. "You were young and grieving. Anyone might have made the same mistakes."

He looked away and then back at me, a small self-critical smile flattening his mouth. "Maybe."

"If you'd won that bet White offered, it all would've worked out. You'd have had your docks, debt-free. We all make choices, and only hindsight can tell us if they're good or bad. I'm choosing to protect Mareeka and Surral and Starway 8, even if it means the Overseer getting some enhancers from my blood."

Shade took my hand in his and led me toward what

looked like a bridge, although I was kind of hoping the long, narrow, vine-hung contraption wasn't our next destination. The cyclodiles were already terrifying enough.

"I hope you don't live to regret your decision, like I regret mine," he said.

"I don't regret your decision." I swung our joined hands a little. "It's selfish, but I don't."

Shade rubbed the back of his neck, his gaze firmly trained on the river. The hand that held mine squeezed. "You know what? Maybe I don't regret it anymore, either."

My heart leaped, the hard beat rocketing heat through my whole body in one quick rush of blood. Grinning, I ducked my head.

"Careful now." Shade snagged me around the waist and whirled me away from the riverbank. As we spun, I saw a flash of teeth. Heard the snap of jaws. I yelped, getting ready to run. Shade clamped a hand around my arm.

"Shh. Hold still. They're attracted to sudden movement and noises." His voice just a hint of words in my ear, he added, "Having one eye means their hearing is well-developed."

I didn't move a muscle, not even to breathe. The beast turned and slipped back into the water with a scaly twist, the tip of its ridged tail disappearing last.

Quietly, I dragged in a shaky breath. "I thought they were done with their breakfast."

Shade wrapped his arms around me and nuzzled my neck. "Mmm. You *are* tasty. Can you really blame them?"

"Yes!" I shoved away from him, his warm kisses not enough to distract me from the remnants of total terror. "And I'll blame you when I'm dead, mauled and eaten by cyclodiles."

He chuckled, as though that *weren't* a genuine possibility

right now. "Let's cross the bridge. We climb up and away from the river on the other side."

I eyed the bridge, getting my first good look at it now that we were closer. "Yeah, I don't think so. Ropes? Wooden slats? Hung between two trees? *That*, Mr. SRP, is a hazard to humanity."

"Where's your sense of adventure, Captain Bailey? Besides, I wouldn't be a Space Rogue Phenom if I didn't know which jungle bridges were safe in the galaxy."

I huffed. "It might be rotten in the middle. We'll fall straight into a monster's gaping maw, landing whole inside its huge belly to be slowly digested by stomach acid along with a flock of shredded birds."

He cracked up. "You *do* have an overactive imagination."

"Like I said, it's very helpful. *In keeping me alive.*"

"The bridge is perfectly safe. The resort maintains it."

I narrowed my eyes. At him. At the bridge. At the now-undisturbed water. "Can cyclodiles jump?" I searched the river for signs of impending doom. "Where is that thing? Lying in wait? Licking its chops? Planning something gruesome?"

Grinning, Shade held my hand and tugged me in the direction of obvious disaster. "Cyclodiles can't jump, but they can run, even if it's awkward. We'd be safer on the bridge than here, and the far bank is even safer." He continued toward the jungle walkway that looked like something people had stopped building about a bazillion years ago—for good reason.

Half-heartedly dragging my feet, I eyeballed the whole construction. There were at least six-inch gaps in between each of the planks across the wide, lazily moving river. You had to climb a huge old tree to get onto the bridge and climb down a huge old tree on the other side to get off it. The only way up or down was a freaking rope ladder.

Excitement rose inside me nevertheless. No way was I missing out on this. "Is encouraging guests to face possible death just for fun and resort ambiance?"

"That's what I've always assumed. Really livens the place up." Shade winked at me, handsome and cocky enough to pull even that off without seeming ridiculous. "But seriously, who would come here if they couldn't take a little kick of adrenaline?"

"Someone who's being led around blind and doesn't know what she's getting into," I answered dryly.

Playful challenge charged his expression with little sparks of humor that lit up his brown eyes. "Tess Bailey: the galaxy's Most Wanted. Can jump into a black hole but won't cross a river?"

"I didn't plan on surviving that trip. *This one*, I rather hope to come out of."

"And you will." Shade grabbed the bottom of the rope ladder and gave it a few hard tugs to show me it was sturdy. "See? Nothing wrong with it."

"Ow!" I slapped an insect from my wrist. *Crap*. Too late. My sixth itchy red welt of the day rose, puffing into a lump right under a freckle like a bull's-eye for the next vicious little biter. "Damn it. If I don't get attacked by a hungry one-eyed reptile or fall off the rickety bridge, I'm probably going to keel over from some weird Reaginine venom."

Shade's lips jumped up. He pressed his mouth flat. It popped back up again.

"Don't laugh," I muttered. "They're not eating you—which is totally unfair, by the way."

"I told you you were tasty."

I scratched the new bite. "Compliments don't work on me when they involve bloodsucking whatsits."

"Scratching makes it worse." Shade removed my scraping fingers from my wrist. "And I think you're grumbling so much because you secretly love this."

I scowled.

"See? It's obvious," he said in response to my scrunched-up face.

I hmphed. It was almost a laugh, and Shade knew it. His eyes practically glittered in triumph.

"Are you trying to get rid of me?" I asked. "There are easier methods than death by bugs, monsters, or hazardous walkways."

Shade placed both my hands on the rope ladder. "You're just stalling. You won't fall off unless you throw yourself over the railing."

"Well, don't make idiotic suggestions."

Giving me a stink eye that barely contained his laughter, Shade gripped the ladder to hold it steady. "If you keep hopping around on the bank and making noise, every predator in the Gano is going to head over, and I'll be forced to shoot something."

I grimaced. *No thanks.* There was enough killing going on here already. We both carried holstered weapons, though, just in case things in the jungle got too crazy. We'd drop them off at the bungalow before meeting with Bridgebane. Guns weren't permitted in the temples, even for the Dark Watch.

I glanced back in the direction of the house, suddenly overwhelmed by our real reason for being on Reaginine. Not that I'd forgotten for a second, but Shade made it easy to think about other things. "I don't want to be late for our meeting. Maybe we should just go to the Grand Temple and wait."

"It's not technically meeting day yet, and even here, it's still early. Better to blend in with the bigger crowds later today—like we already decided."

I nodded. We had a plan and should stick to it. I took a first hesitant step up the rope ladder. Uncle Nate wouldn't be here yet—or at least not checking his watch for us. Shade was right; we should enjoy our morning. With the Ahern mission looming, who knew if we'd even still be alive ten days from now, or free, or together.

A painful burst of memory jolted through me. Was I repeating a pattern? Seven years ago, my boyfriend Gabe and I had been in a good place, happy together, looking for a crew to join after leaving the orphanage. But we took on a job out of our league that went bad so fast we didn't know what hit us. The Dark Watch showed up. We ran and got separated. They caught me and hauled me off to prison. I didn't know what happened to Gabe. I probably never would, and now it could happen all over again with Shade.

I lifted my chin, did my best to shake off those thoughts, and climbed the damn ladder. It swayed, even with Shade holding it. I didn't mind the movement. Or the height. Or the setting. I was mostly complaining for the fun of it, and because I liked how happy it seemed to make Shade to reassure me and guide me through this place.

Sure, the Gano Jungle and this scratchy rope ladder were slightly terrifying, but life without any unexpected zaps to the nervous system didn't seem worth living. And Shade and I were making memories together. Good ones. I wanted that with him.

Almost to the top, I looked over my shoulder. Honey-brown eyes met mine. The sexy curve of Shade's lips sent a zing of heat through my belly.

I climbed the final few rungs, transferred my weight onto the platform, and tested it with a couple of hops before letting go of the ladder. Shade started up after me.

As he scaled the tree, I ventured out onto the narrow walkway. It rocked beneath me, lifting and rolling in a way that made my stomach roll, too. It squeaked and bounced higher with every step I took away from the anchor of the tree. Fear hit my bloodstream like a flare of solar energy. My heart punched against my ribs, and I froze, my hands gripping the thick rope railings for balance.

Turning carefully, I waited for Shade to catch up, my breath coming short from the way my pulse pounded. "Don't you think it's weird the Overseer didn't mess with universal time? I'm surprised he didn't switch it to match Alpha Sambian or something."

"Are you trying to distract yourself?" Shade asked from below me.

"Yes." *Don't look at the river.* "Go with it."

"Novalight's megalomaniac enough to do it," he agreed, three quarters of the way up now. "Give him time. Maybe he just hasn't thought of it."

"Or gotten around to it." The Overseer was too busy making sure he and his Dark Watch controlled everyone's lives down to the thoughts we allowed ourselves, the books we read, and the color of our clothing. If it wasn't restrained, dull, and limited, he didn't like it. If his endgame was to anesthetize the entire population with a mixture of fear and boredom, it was working.

Shade swung a foot onto the platform. "He's too busy spinning the oppressive shit he does as necessary to our well-being—and making sure people either buy into it, or shut up about it."

That about summed up life as we knew it on every planet, spacedock, and ship across the galaxy. But our rebellion worked against him, and it was powerful enough to turn *resist* into a dirty word for the Overseer.

I glanced at my watch as Shade took in the view from the platform, double-checking that my alarm would go off the second we hit the day we were supposed to meet Bridgebane. I moved around so much that my watch only showed universal time. I'd never bought anything fancier or that required multiple dials. Shade's had two: the date and time in Albion City, and the date and time on Earth, at some place called Greenwich.

"Greenwich," I muttered aloud as I verified the time there, pronouncing it like *sandwich*, which Mareeka insisted was wrong. It looked like Green Witch to me, though. I liked the way it sounded—and the idea that some ancient witch dressed in green had imposed her notion of time on all of humankind.

The earliest galactic government had established universal dates and time based on Earth's orbit around her sun. That had still meant something to them at the time and had proved useful in the long run. Some planets had seasons, others didn't. On some, a day was short and spent in half darkness. On others, it was bright and interminable. An orbital year was four universal months on the fast-moving Greera but took thirty-two universal months on a slow giant like Capita Leo. Every inhabited planet kept its own calendar right alongside Greenwich mean time, which was used to calculate age, among other things. Spread out as we were now, with some of us living in the Dark most of the time, it was one of the ways for humanity to maintain something in common. Certain things would never change. We all needed to eat, drink, and breathe. And apparently, grow old on the same schedule. In any case, universal time gave a useful reference point for all the space rats who zigzagged across the galaxy.

Shade's hand shielded his eyes from the bright light of

the Great Star as he surveyed the jungle from the platform. He looked perfectly at home here, as though he could just as easily have been an archeologist, a naturalist, or an explorer instead of an engineer, navigator, and bounty hunter. He was even still tan from summertime on Albion 5, although life in the Dark was starting to chip away at that. There didn't appear to be a drop of sweat on him, which just proved he was in his element. I was blazing hot and dripping.

He turned, lowering his hand. Finding me watching him, he smiled as he stepped onto the bridge. It jiggled under his weight, and I held on for dear life until he joined me. Shade gave me a peck on the lips before slipping past me, his hands skimming the weather-smoothed railings without really gripping them. When I didn't immediately follow, he looked over his shoulder. "Come on, starshine. You can do it. One foot in front of the other."

Cautiously, I trailed after him. The river rushed beneath us, a low and constant rumble. The long bridge bobbed and swayed, moving up and down and back and forth, which was frankly a little too much unpredictable movement for my liking. Shade slowed down so that I could just shuffle along behind him, absorbing sights and sounds I'd never imagined seeing even in my most vivid daydreams.

A pair of ice-blue birds with fancy white crests and four crimson-tipped wings swooped back and forth across the river, bringing bits and pieces to a large nest they were building. A smaller species crowded several entire trees, singing to each other from the branches, their calls operatic and their feathers an explosion of different shades that defied my knowledge of colors. On the opposite bank, not far from the rope ladder, a squat little creature with creamy-white fur and fuzzy ears clung to the side of a tree and tapped at a spiky purple pouch stuck to the bark. The orange stripe down its back matched the long nails it used to pound on the thorny ball like a hammer.

"An orange spearback," Shade said quietly, nodding toward the animal in the tree. He stopped and held out an arm to keep me behind him.

I peered past him, watching the small round-bottomed creature work industriously. It seemed almost cuddly, about the size of Bonk. "The name sounds more dangerous than it looks."

"That orange stripe down its back is made of hard plates with pointed tips that are lying down right now. Threaten it, and it'll raise them up like armor. Really piss it off, and it'll shoot them at you hard enough to do some damage."

"Like lose an eye?"

"Like sever a jugular."

Okay then, not like Bonk. "Let's stay here, shall we?"

Shade's low chuckle made me ridiculously happy. I wrapped my arms around him from behind. His hands covered mine on his abdomen.

"It's almost done. It'll take off after it gets what it wants." Shade watched the banging process as avidly as I did. I couldn't wait to see what happened.

The purple shell finally split open. Something fat, gray, and shiny slithered in a viscous goo. The little animal scarfed it up like a gourmet meal. After, it lapped up the goo.

"Ick." I grimaced.

"Yeah, I wouldn't eat that, either."

I buried my laughter in Shade's back, trying not to disturb the animal.

The orange spearback licked its paws and whiskers, looking very pleased with itself. After a quick glance around, it scuttled down the tree headfirst and disappeared into the jungle. Shade continued across the bridge once we couldn't see the spearback anymore.

My SRP boyfriend's clear competence here helped me fear the jungle less and enjoy it more. He really was a Space Rogue Phenom. My insides almost fluttered at the idea of what he might prove he could do next. Slay cyclodiles? Swing on vines? Start fire from sticks?

My smile so big I was probably catching gnats in my teeth, I listened to myriad unseen things call, chitter, buzz, and rattle. The shady-hot air filled my lungs with extra oxygen. Trees everywhere—giving life and air and cover to all the exotic and spectacular things here. Who'd have guessed? Tess Bailey, Space Rat, right in the middle of an untamed rain forest. The vibrant heartbeat of the jungle pulsed through me, wild and electric. I was sure that every time I closed my eyes for the rest of my life, I would hear it echo again inside me.

Shade stopped, leaning his elbows on the thick rope railing. I did the same. It was impossible to hurry past the open views from the bridge. They were too remarkable and demanded attention.

"Earth had tropical forests like this." Because our abandoned motherland was our common history, we all studied it. Galactic schoolchildren spent an entire universal year on Earth's geography, climate, animals, noteworthy history, and famous figures. It was how I knew what beavers were but not flervers. It made no sense that we hadn't moved on more definitively yet, but I was glad we hadn't. That had been my favorite school year. "It must have been amazing."

"Earth had everything. It was the universe's chosen planet—the start of humanity and civilization." Shade finished crossing the bridge and stepped onto the wide platform.

I followed him toward the rope ladder that would bring us down again. "Then why do you think it hasn't attracted all that many returners?" Hitting the solid wood of the platform threw me off-balance, and I swayed a little. I must have gained my bridge legs during the crossing.

"Because it's a cesspit."

I burst out laughing, startling a bird that took off abruptly from the tree next to us. "Not really. Not anymore." Time cured everything, even radiation and plastic. "That one little planet still affects our lives after all this time, and yet hardly anyone actually wants to go back there. I mean, I don't give a crap what time it is on any of the rocks I've been to recently, or even on this one, really. I care what time the clock says it is on Earth, a barely populated planet across the galaxy."

Instead of starting down to the forest floor, Shade hopped up on the platform railing, looking pensive. "I suppose it's because we need constants, and we can all trace ourselves back there. Earth was home to all of humanity for a lot longer than anywhere else ever has been."

"True... But don't you think it's strange? How hard we hold on to things that shouldn't have any meaning for us? My favorite books are all mostly pre-exodus, talking about places and animals and ways of life that don't even exist anymore." Although right here didn't feel all that different from some of the locations I'd read about.

"Pre-exodus books are hard to find these days."

"The Overseer's book purge." I sighed in disgust. "Too many thoughts out there that weren't his own."

"Or that didn't serve his purpose."

Shade swung his legs, a slow *tick-tock* as he answered my

earlier question. "I think we hold on to the past because we haven't changed. Sure, we have more sophisticated tech and things our ancestors could only dream of, but otherwise, what's really different about us?"

"We're all lorded over by an asshole?"

Shade flashed a quick smile. "As if that's never happened before."

"There are *more* of us being lorded over by an asshole?"

He chuckled, gently rocking on the railing.

I itched to reach out and make him stop moving up there. "You're right. Things external to people have changed, but inside, we're still the same as always. Hopes, fears, dreams, love, family... You could stick Jax, Fiona, or me on an exodus ship, and we'd fit right in with all those terrified, fleeing Earthlings." We spent most of our time terrified and fleeing, anyway. "And stop leaning backward. You're freaking me out."

"Because I might fall?" Shade held up his hands and wiggled.

"Shade!" I lunged forward and grabbed him. "Men are such jerks!"

He laughed and jumped down. "Happy?"

"No." I scowled, the rampaging heartbeat in my throat nearly choking me.

He gave me a quick kiss to try to mollify me. It didn't work, and I turned my nose up at his attempt to placate.

Looking almost contrite, Shade started down the ladder. "As for the slow repopulation, I don't know. Earth's perfectly habitable again." He gave me a questioning look. "Would you ever go back?"

"*Back* isn't the right word because I've never been there, but no, not to live. Why would I?"

"I don't know. Roots? Nostalgia?"

I saw the exact moment his playfulness evaporated, likely dried up by thoughts of his roots on Albion 5—and the fact that he could never go back there.

An ache hatched in my chest, the muscles cramping uncomfortably.

Should I feel guilty?

No.

Did I?

Kind of…

The rawness inside me grew as I watched Shade move down the ladder. He'd given up more than his docks for me, hadn't he? Home wasn't something that could be quantified in buildings or wealth. It was so much more than that. He wouldn't want me feeling guilty, though. If anyone took responsibility for his decisions, good or bad, it was Shade.

I breathed in deeply, expanding my lungs. "I think moving to Earth would feel like living in a cemetery—walking on bones and seeing ghosts."

"I guess so." He didn't sound convinced, probably because he was used to walking beside the ghosts of his parents and watching the docking empire his family had built fall apart in the hands of Scarabin White. "Besides, there isn't room on Earth for even a fraction of the population of a place like Sector 12, let alone the rest of the galaxy."

"Well, I prefer the *Endeavor*. Or wherever Bonk is."

He grinned up at me. "Miss your kitty?"

"Yes."

"Me too," I heard him say as he jumped off the ladder.

I rubbed my chest. That sudden burst of heat may or may not have been my heart melting. I chose not to analyze.

Shade held the ladder steady for me. I followed him to the ground, turned in triumph—I'd just successfully completed jungle obstacle number one, after all—and leaped to hug him a split second before a hard-coated insect bashed me in the head.

Screaming, I batted my arms and reeled back. Fast-moving wings hit my hand with a stinging thud. The insect buzzed louder and stayed in my face. Gold. Blue. Eyes all over its head! I swerved. It swerved. I ducked. It dropped. *What the hell?* It didn't fly away. It banged straight into my head again because tangling in my hair was *so* smart.

"Shade!" I yelled.

"Hold still." He reached out with both hands and grabbed it. My hair clung to furry legs—*multiple* legs—and Shade had to tug and detangle as I screeched in panic. He finally tossed the fist-sized insect skyward. It got the right idea this time and buzzed away from us in an upward spiral.

"What was that?" Frantically, I scrubbed my hands all over my face and head, trying to erase the feeling of fuzz and stick and flutter.

"Just a draakwing. Harmless. And dumb as shit, or it wouldn't fly toward predators."

"I'm not a predator."

"To it, you are." He waggled his eyebrows. "They're tasty."

"What? Ack! How do you know all these things?"

He smoothed back my hair, tucking the sweat-dampened strands toward my ponytail again. "I used to spend a lot of time here. I came every year with my parents for as long as I can remember. We'd stay at the resort for a few weeks— one of those Aisé bungalows. Until they died in that shuttle crash. I haven't been here since then. Until now."

"Every year?" My heart fumbled its next beat. "Why didn't you tell me?" The memories must be tearing him up inside. But he loved it here—I could tell. That was the part he'd been showing me since yesterday.

He shrugged. "I didn't want you to feel obligated to like it."

"I love it." My throat thickened. *I love* ... I swallowed and bit my lip. "Did you come here for prayer at the temples?"

Shade nodded and moved up the bank. I followed him away from the river. A sign in the shape of an odd, pot-bellied animal with bushy eyebrows and a long black-and-white mustache pointed us uphill through the jungle.

"More for the outdoors but, yeah, prayer, too." He held back an overgrown branch for me.

Ducking around it, I couldn't hide my skepticism. "Why? What has the Sky Mother ever done for you? Where are her Powers? I mean, look at the state of the galaxy. I don't see any evidence of positive and balancing forces at work."

"Don't you?" Shade glanced at me, his brow drawing down. "On the one hand, there's the Overseer and his Dark Watch. On the other, there's a whole rebellion, places like Starway 8 and the Fold, and people like you, Jax, Merrick, and Fiona."

"That's not balance. That's a minority trying—and mostly failing—to make a difference."

"It has to start somewhere."

I hiked in Shade's footsteps, watching for pits and snakes. "As pessimistically optimistic as that sounds, I still think that's people and their choices, not some big star supposedly sending out rays of light that change our lives on a daily basis."

He turned back to me. "Can you imagine living in total darkness?"

A shiver rippled through me at the velvet hitch in his voice that hinted at true believing. "I'm thinking in terms of science—a big ball of hot gas giving off light and heat and radiation. You're speaking metaphorically. And no one has real answers. It's like with any religion throughout the ages, the *eons* of mankind. There's never any proof. Or maybe there is, but only after you're dead, so who knows?"

"Faith—throughout the *eons*—is believing without proof. I'd rather have certain beliefs to comfort me when things seem too dark than nothing at all to brighten the horizon."

Part of me wanted to gape at Shade like he was a total stranger. The other part of me knew to respect other people's choices in religion.

I thought about the handwritten text Susan, the bookshop owner on Albion 5, had given me. It purported that the Sky Mother had provided us with the Mornavail, a sort of second children to spread her light into the gathering darkness. Now, it seemed the Mornavail were like me—human, but with a more evolved immune system. I was basically a walking cure-all, with blood that could be chemically modified into enhancers. I'd yet to meet another like me, though—and most people who'd heard of the Mornavail thought they were a myth.

Good. Stay hidden.

The Overseer had sniffed me out, and I'd spent half my childhood strapped to a chair with needles shoved into my veins. The result was an entire floating space lab filled with super-soldier serum partially concocted from my blood.

Serum I'd stolen away from the Overseer and given to the rebel leaders.

Serum that had led me to Shade—and lost me Miko and Shiori.

Serum the Overseer could engineer again after I handed over six bags of my blood to his right-hand goon in just a few hours.

Shit. What a mess. At least we had more enhancers than he did.

But how many super soldiers had the Overseer already created?

"I could use a little Sky Mother help after all," I muttered.

"What's that?" Shade asked, glancing back at me.

"Nothing." I scrambled up a steep, rocky incline, sweat gluing my clothes to me. "People pray and pray, and there's zero concrete feedback. No proof, and not much reward, in my opinion. I don't understand how you can maintain faith when you've lost everything."

Shade held a finger to his lips instead of answering. He tilted his gaze upward, leading mine to the nearby branches. Small brown creatures with butter-yellow heads, liquid-dark eyes, tufty ears, and black button noses watched us, cocking their heads in curiosity and munching on things they held in their tiny humanlike hands with five fingers.

Awe burst inside me like fireworks. "Those are the cutest little things I've ever seen."

"Ganokos," Shade said softly.

Holding hands, we watched them in fascination until the pack moved on, looking for the next tree with fruit or nuts to nibble on. Once they were out of sight, I felt as though a piece of me went missing. I was beginning to understand Shade's attachment to the jungle, how it got under your skin and became a part of you.

"Come on. I've got something even better to show you." He led the way again, the hike getting steeper and more difficult by the minute. I didn't press him for an answer about maintaining faith. It wasn't a discussion we needed to have any more than it was an argument one of us needed to win. I just enjoyed hearing his perspective on things.

About a half hour later, Shade heaved himself onto a wide lip of rock that jutted out from the mountainside. Pivoting on his knees, he turned back to me with an outstretched hand and pulled me up to join him.

My jaw dropped in wonder as we stood together. Birds called, insects chirped, and the jungle rustled on a humid breeze that propelled me farther out onto the flat shelf suspended high above the Gano River. A waterfall cut down the cliffside beside us, crashing into a large pool and throwing rainbow spray through the air like ribbons. I reached out to touch the shimmering moisture. "Shade, this is amazing."

"I love this swimming hole." He crouched down and circled his fingers in water so transparent I could see every glistening stone on the pool's bottom.

Big-leafed vegetation teemed with exotic birds all singing to different tunes and making a striking chorus. Warbling calls. Sharp chirps. Squawks from somewhere. Colorful blossoms grew from cracks in the slippery cliffside. Vines tumbled down from above, twisting and curling through the flowers. "I've never seen a place so … flamboyant." I looked around, stunned and reverent.

Shade smiled at me, shaking drops of water from his fingertips. He stood again and turned to look out over the vista. There was something almost pained in his expression, as though this place stripped back layers of skin and arrowed straight into the heart of him.

The water called to me, if only to stick my feet in, but first, I joined Shade in admiring the view in the distance. The bungalows and manicured lawns of the Aisé Resort dotted the far bank like little pockets of civilization just daring enough to dip a toe into the wilderness. Beyond that, small from here despite their grandness, the five temples of the Holy Hollow formed a star around the inner gardens and main temple—the one where we would meet my uncle.

"Thank you." Overwhelmed by everything we'd shared last night, this morning, and now *this*, I felt tears threaten.

Shade stood beside me, just our knuckles brushing. "This is my favorite place in the galaxy."

The knot in my throat tightened, my eyes prickled, and I got the same feeling as when I rounded a corner on Starway 8 and suddenly came face-to-face with the bright, swirling colors of the Rafini Nebula. Reverence. Amazement. Fascination. And maybe, just possibly, the stirring of belief in something *other*.

"What we were talking about earlier? Faith?" Shade turned to me. "I've been thinking. I've lost things, but I haven't lost everything." His eyes met mine, his dark-amber gaze more open than I'd ever seen it. "And maybe, I've gained more than I ever thought possible."

Emotion charred a pathway to my heart, incinerating all defenses. "I've never, ever been in a place that stirred me the way Starway 8 does. But this … " I trailed off on a shuddering breath. "Who would have thought that a jungle on Reaginine might reinvent me?"

A soft smile curved Shade's lips as he looked out over the vista again, his eyes seeming fixed on the golden tip of the Grand Temple. At midsummer on this part of Reaginine, light from the Great Star pointed straight down through the hole in the top of the temple, lighting up Her image carved into the floor and kicking off the galaxy-wide festival of Emergence—the supposed birth of the celestial being. Believers across the eighteen Sectors took that day to rejoice, no matter the season where they were, or how seasonless their home in the Dark might be. I'd never bought into it, but right now, I couldn't deny feeling *something*.

"I'll never try to make you believe one thing or another, but I look around me"—Shade's eyes lighted on the temples, the jungle, the waterfall and swimming hole—"especially here, and I can't help thinking there's something that makes all of this more than just random."

Under the warm rays of the Great Star, I almost started to understand the faithful and their devotion. Maybe it was just the moment, the beauty, and looking out over a place that people flocked to because they believed so hard in something they couldn't see or touch or prove existed. We'd abandoned our old God for this one. Somewhere down the line, we'd abandon the Sky Mother for the next *whatever* in a long line of them. Maybe they were all one and the same, so it didn't matter what we called them. Or maybe there was no greater power, nothing except for what the collision of imperfectly balanced matter and antimatter had given us.

"I might start my own church," I said, suddenly desperate to lighten the mood again. "The Church of the Big Bang has a nice ring to it."

A chuckle ghosted past Shade's lips. "Will you worship photons?"

"Well, and gravity. And subatomic particles. I might throw in some quarks as my Powers."

"Should you have been a physicist instead of a thieving rebel?" He arched his brows, sounding impressed. Too bad I had to burst his bubble.

"No. I pretty much just exhausted my knowledge."

He grinned and reached for me, pulling me against him and settling his hands on my waist. "You know what quarks do when they're together?"

We stood toe-to-toe. I draped my arms around his neck. "I'm afraid I missed that lesson. Mareeka was always making me clean the air ducts on Starway 8 because I kept skipping out on math and sciences."

"Quarks latch on to one another." Shade tugged us even closer, demonstrating. I angled my hips forward, warmth spreading through me. He pressed back a little. "And the harder you try to separate them, the harder they hold on to each other."

I looked at him through my lashes. "Are you asking me to be your quark, Shade Ganavan?"

"Baby, you're my quark and then some." He dipped his head and kissed me.

My eyes fluttered closed, and a lavalike heat rose in my blood faster than I'd have thought possible. Shade kissed my jaw, my neck. My breathing accelerated. My bones grew heavy. He dragged his lips down the column of my throat. I tilted my head for him. At the hollow of my neck, he opened his mouth against my skin and thrust his tongue against me.

I gasped, the muscles between my legs heating and clenching. Arousal blazed inside me, urging me to move against him. Shade's heavy hands anchored me, keeping me still. Our lips fused again for a kiss that only made me more desperate for friction. Our mouths and tongues didn't satisfy the need building and throbbing like a primitive drumbeat deep inside my body. Tearing off my clothes, clutching Shade's shoulders, and climbing up him had just moved to the top of my priority list.

I broke away. "Jungle sex," I panted.

"Let's go swimming," Shade said at the same time.

We stared at each other. He grinned like a loon. I blinked and then grinned also.

"I like the way you think, starshine." Desire was a bright lick of flame in his eyes, and I knew I could convince him. I also knew he wanted to get in that beautiful clear pool for the first time in more than a decade.

"We'll finish this later?" The pressure between my thighs protested the decision, but the rest of me thought swimming sounded fantastic.

The promise burning in Shade's expression flipped my belly inside out. "I wouldn't miss it," he vowed.

I glanced at the pool. "I might have to punish you for teasing me like this."

He hummed low under his breath. "I'll look forward to that."

"You won't like it." I'd grown up in an orphanage with thousands of kids. I was pretty inventive when it came to payback.

His eyes smoldered, somehow growing in intensity, and they'd already been melting me on the spot. "We'll see about that."

Curiosity leaped inside me. Leave it to Shade to make punishment sound like something I might want to open my horizons to—you know, time permitting.

"I don't have a bathing suit," I hedged, suddenly nervous about how deep the pool might be. Clear water could be deceiving.

"Jungle swimming is always naked."

I'd have to take his word for it. Shade was the expert. "Are there *things* in that water?"

"There shouldn't be. It's pretty hard to get to."

Hmm. Not a hard no, but I'd accept it. "Can I stand?"

"It'll come up to your shoulders."

"What if there's quicksand?" I'd read about that. It sounded awful. A bit like death by floating, only slower. And dirtier. Really, the only thing they might have in common was me ending up without air, which I wanted to avoid wherever.

"There's not. Don't worry about that. I know this place, and I won't let you drown. I promise."

"We don't have towels." I didn't even want to avoid swimming. Excuses kept popping out anyway.

Shade set down the pack he'd brought. I'd only seen him put in water, but he pulled out two towels and a picnic lunch and turned back to me with a smile. "A good Space Rogue Phenom never goes anywhere without provisions and equipment."

I grinned. He'd thought of everything.

Shade undressed in record time and jumped into the pool feet first at the deeper end. He reemerged and shook water from his head. Droplets sprayed around me. His wet shoulders glistened in the heavy tropical sunlight, a ripple of tanned skin, broad bones, and hard muscle. The water reached his pectorals, lapping at his chest in a way I wanted to follow with my lips and fingers.

Shade held out his hand to me. "Let's teach you to swim while we can. We've only got a few hours until we have to deal with Bridgebane and all hell might break loose again."

I tossed aside my clothing and reached for him. Shade eased me into the pool, our bodies touching and tangling under the pleasantly warm water. My heart soared in spite of the uncertain remainder of the day ahead of us. Right now, I was Tess-the-Fucking-Jungle-Queen, and I was ready for anything.

CHAPTER

6

SHADE

TESS WAS A NATURAL AT PRETTY MUCH EVERYTHING—
except for swimming. By the end of our lesson, she could
float—mostly—and blow bubbles underwater. That was
already something, but throw in waves, cold temperatures,
or anything stressful, and I had a feeling she'd sink like a
meteor.

None of that mattered, though, because she had *fun*.
Seeing her smile was all I wanted. I doubted it would last
long. Nathaniel Bridgebane could be on Reaginine right
now, waiting for his clock to hit day ten after we'd struck this
messed-up bargain with him. Technically, we had the entire
day to make contact, but I knew he'd be there at hour one.

Good. The sooner we gave him Tess's A1 blood in
exchange for the safety of the Starway 8 women, the better.
Then Tess could stop worrying about them, and we could
go meet the *Endeavor* on time—and worry about a metric
ton of other things.

We rounded the corner of Bungalow 39, our hair still wet

from swimming. Tess's damp shirt clung to her, teasing me with the long, lean lines of her torso and the subtle curves of her body. I slid my hand up her spine, palming the back of her neck and lightly gripping. Her lips parted, her eyelids grew heavy, and she leaned into my hand, her shoulders softening.

I smiled. Maybe we had a few minutes.

"What do you think about a hot show—" I stopped and swiveled my head from side to side, my eyes narrowing. Silence. But I'd just heard a click.

I pushed Tess into the hollow of the doorframe and stood in front of her.

"What?" she whispered.

"A gun just cocked." Adrenaline pumped through me as I scanned the landing pad around the cruiser. Empty. And there was nothing along the visible side of the building. Whoever was out there had either skulked around the corner or was hiding in the bushes.

"Show yourself," I demanded, shielding Tess with my body.

The greenery to our right rustled, and Solan's glistening bald head appeared, black as midnight. Dark glasses on and muscled body easing forward with coiled menace, he stepped out from behind a tall fern that shaded one corner of the bungalow. Moving toward the open docking area, the bounty hunter lifted his arm and pointed a Redline at me.

My lips pulled back in a snarl. That same gun had sliced a shot through Tess's side just ten days ago.

"What the fuck, Solan? How'd you find us?" I'd searched my cruiser inside and out for tracking bugs. I'd changed all my clothes before leaving to find Tess. I'd left nearly everything I owned behind. I'd ditched my cruiser's small portable com unit somewhere in the Outer Zones and bought a new one in the Fold to replace it. My accounts were all coded. I was thorough and careful. There was *nothing* to lead them here. So what the hell happened?

Solan didn't answer. He just shook his head, his gun leveled on my chest. Keeping one eye on him, I looked around for Raquel. She'd pop up soon enough with her utility belt, tranquilizer gun, steel-tipped boots, and lightning-fast feet ready to do some damage.

Solan tilted his head in Tess's direction, his eyes unreadable behind his reflective sunglasses. "Her megabounty's on your head now, buddy. Come quietly, and we'll leave her out of this."

Raquel finally sauntered out of the bushes, her ambling gait doing fuck-all to disguise her lethal agility and hard edges. "I know you were unhappy, but seriously, Shade. *This? Her?* Cashing her in was the better option."

Of course the ice queen of bounty hunting would think so. "How do you live with no heart in your chest? Are you *actually* a machine, or do you just act like one?"

Apparently considering that a compliment, Raquel smiled in that panther-like way of hers. She fit right into the jungle, a feline hunter at the apex of the food chain and not doubting for one second her ability to catch her dinner. I'd thought she was pretty when I first met her, a confident medium-height brunette with golden-brown eyes and a nice smile. Now, all I saw were the claws and teeth of an expert predator.

"How. Did. You. Find. Me," I ground out.

"We chipped you," Solan answered. "When your rebel girlfriend left you behind on the Squirrel Tree, Raquel tranqued you, and we chipped you before you woke up."

My jaw spasmed. "Where is it?" I ran my hands up and down my forearms, even though there was no way I'd feel a tiny microchip underneath the muscle. And it could be anywhere. My legs, my back, my torso.

"As if we'd tell you." Raquel hooked her thumbs in her belt, which was no doubt filled with illegal weapons. "Don't give us trouble, and Little Miss Rebel of the Year can go back to being a pain in everyone's ass and we'll try to forget about her—as long as we get our money."

Rage pounded through me like the punches I wanted to land in both their faces. "I've known you for ten years. Ten *fucking* years," I growled. "Why am I even surprised you're this mercenary?"

Solan's mouth flattened, intractable. "That's our deal. Take it or leave it."

"We choose 'leave it.'" Tess brought her arm up next to me from behind and cocked her Grayhawk, pointing it at Raquel. "Surral can find it and take it out of you," she whispered.

I wasn't sure we'd make it to that point. These two were vicious.

I reached for my gun, just a twitch of my fingers, and Solan took a menacing step forward.

"Don't even think about it," he threatened, "or you won't make it out of this."

"Touch him, and I shoot her," Tess informed the bounty hunter coldly. "I don't care about your frenemy issues or how long you've known each other. I care about Shade, so back the fuck off, asshole."

"Feisty!" Raquel laughed. "I'm starting to like her." Her eyes said otherwise. They hardened.

I had a choice. Let all of this happen, or take a risk. Raquel didn't have a gun out yet. And would Solan really shoot me? My money was on no, even though it was his money also.

I lunged, leaving Tess partially sheltered in the doorway. "Shade!" Her voice rang with shock.

I didn't look back. She had a Grayhawk trained on Raquel and knew how to use it. It was unlikely Tess would aim for anything vital. Raquel could draw fast but didn't usually shoot bullets.

Solan's wide brow flew up in surprise. He stood his ground, his gun level. His jawline hardened. I ran. One step, two steps, three. He stood there and didn't pull the trigger.

I crashed into him and we wrestled for the weapon. He had height and pounds on me, but I was quicker. I ducked a punch, twisted, and grabbed the top of the gun, pointing it downward as I cracked my fist into Solan's forearm. He dropped it.

There was no time to reach for either of our weapons before he tackled me and sent us both flying. I landed hard on my side, Solan on top of me. We grappled. I kneed him. We rolled, hot pavement searing my bare arms and grit grinding into me. I came out on top after a brutal struggle and reached for his neck. His big fist drove into my face. Pain exploded across my cheekbone. The world turned upside down, spinning. Ground became sky. Solan lifted my shoulders and slammed me hard into the blacktop. My skull thudded. The breath flew from my lungs like a thunderclap.

I blinked, wheezing and seeing nothing but darkness for a second. In that sudden void, I reevaluated. We might kill each other after all. Chest-clenching disappointment bit into my rage as I ripped off his sunglasses and went for his eyes, ramming my thumbs into the sockets.

Solan roared away from me. I twisted out from under him,

and my feet came back around like a hammer. He flew over backward. I sprang up. He rolled to one knee and crouched, facing me. His eyes watered. He squinted.

We stared at each other across the scorching asphalt, our chests heaving. My cheek throbbed. Solan thumped his big hand against the ground and growled in what seemed like frustration.

What did he expect? He'd never gotten the best of me in a fistfight. Only Raquel had. Solan was usually making off with my target while she and I beat the shit out of each other until she pulled some underhanded stunt that gave her the advantage.

"Had enough, *friend*?" I taunted.

"I need this," he grated, rising.

"So I should just forfeit my freedom and go with you because you *need* this?" I scoffed. Solan and Raquel were rolling in bounty money—almost as much as I was. "Never gonna happen."

Solan moved in a slow circle, looking for an opening.

"How 'bout we both put down our weapons?" I heard Raquel offer. She must've drawn something while I wasn't looking. "We can do this hand-to-hand, the old-fashioned way. The way the men are."

"No!" I shouted. Raquel would wipe the floor with Tess, and she'd fight dirty.

"Fine," Tess answered. "But you first."

"You think I'm stupid?" They could probably hear the sneer in Raquel's voice three planets over.

"Same time, then," Tess said.

I whirled. "Tess!" Lowering her weapon would be a mistake. She had no idea who she was dealing with.

Solan came in fast and hard, a shadow-flash in my side vision. I barely evaded, my concentration broken.

Fuck hand-to-hand. I was done fighting fairly. I freed my gun but wasn't sure who to aim it at. Probably Raquel. She was the greater danger.

The hesitation cost me. Solan kicked the Grayhawk from my hand, and I went numb from wrist to fingers. He plowed into me, toppling me over again. I kept my head up this time, but the backs of my arms scraped along the landing pad surface. Ignoring the pain, I threw my legs up and wrapped them around his neck while his balance was pitched forward. Twisting, I brought him down hard on one shoulder and sat on him. My fist barreled toward his face with a decade of fury and frustration behind it. Pain flared in my hand, but it was the near-knockout punch I needed. Solan blinked at me, limp and groaning.

I shifted my weight to pin him better. "Back off, call off your harpy, and we can go our separate ways again."

"Can't," he said thickly, his eyes unfocused. "Need the money."

Compressed air popped with a burst of pressure. Tess grunted. My heart seized, and I whipped around to find her.

Raquel sprang forward and grabbed Tess in the doorway. The bounty hunter propped Tess against the front of her body, keeping her upright as Tess's knees sagged and a heaviness I knew all too well overtook her body. Terror burst in Tess's eyes two seconds before her features began to slacken.

"Shadey Poo, I've got your girlfriend." Raquel's singsongy words filled my chest with poison. I doubted I'd have killed Solan. Her, I wasn't so sure about. I snarled.

Raquel smiled at me as Tess's expression glazed over. A tranquilizer dart poked out of her shoulder. Her jaw sagged, slowly falling open, and Raquel pushed her mouth closed by thrusting Tess's Grayhawk up under her chin. Raquel's finger tightened on the trigger.

"No." A cold fist wrapped around my heart and squeezed out the hardest beat of my existence. "Don't."

Raquel smirked. She knew she had me. "Let my husband go, or I'll plug her with more than just a tranquilizer."

I slowly put my hands up.

"Do little rebels survive bullets to the brain?" Raquel wiggled Tess's limp body. "I wonder."

I jumped off Solan, a bitter taste flooding the back of my mouth like acid. I backed away from the bounty hunter. "Let her go."

"No." Tess formed the word with difficulty. She shook her head, trying to fight off the sedative. "Run, Shade."

Run? As if that would fucking happen.

Raquel gripped her harder. Tess stopped moving. Her head lolled, but then she straightened it and forced her eyes open.

"Tie him up." Raquel nodded to Solan. "We're just wasting time now."

Solan rose with a groan, moving slowly. After a hard blink, he grabbed my wrists and forced them behind me. A cord circled them, cold hard plastic. He drew the single cuff tight with a yank that jarred my shoulders.

"So much for a decade of not-quite-friendship." I rounded on him in disgust. "I guess I was right to never really trust you two. You always do something to screw me over."

Solan shoved me toward Raquel, muttering, "I didn't want to."

"That didn't fucking stop you!" I hadn't even begun to think about being court-martialed, or spending life in prison, or whatever the hell was about to happen to me. I only knew these assholes had just ripped my first happiness in years away from me.

Solan refused to look at me, his expression stony.

"Take the key card from my pocket and give it to Tess. And *don't* touch her." They had me. As promised, they'd better leave her out of this.

"Shade…" Tess's weak croak made me want to set fire to the universe—and then burn it down a second time. Raw pain ripped through me. This couldn't be over.

"Tess!" My end wouldn't be hers. I'd make sure of it. "498721BVR—that'll turn on the cruiser. Do what you need to do and get out of here."

She moaned, her eyelids drooping.

"Baby! 498721BVR," I shouted again, trying to penetrate the fog she was in. "You gotta remember the ignition numbers!"

If she didn't, she'd be stranded here. The crew might think she didn't make it. She didn't even have her tablet to contact them. They had one device, and it was on the *Endeavor*. She'd never get into mine unless she had expert hacking skills I didn't know about. The thought of Tess alone halfway across the galaxy from her crew with no ship, no money, and Nathaniel Bridgebane as her only possible point of contact sent me into a blind panic.

"Tess!" I bellowed.

Raquel rolled her eyes and dropped Tess in a way that could've been disfiguring if she'd gone over face-first. I jerked against my restraints—an automatic impulse to catch her. But I was too far away and fucking *tied up*. I howled. Tess lay on her side, breathing shallowly, her eyes half-open and on me.

I glared at Raquel, white-hot fury consuming me. How

had I ever had a normal conversation with this woman? Sat at her table? Shared meals with her and Solan? "You're such a bitch. Just wait until you find out that payback is an even bigger one."

Raquel smirked. "Good luck with that—from life in prison."

Oh, she had no idea. If the Dark Watch killed me, I'd haunt Solan and Raquel across the galaxy until I had my revenge for this, but I wasn't thinking about me. I was thinking about Tess and her friends. If Tess asked them to, they'd find the bounty hunters and fuck them up in ways these two couldn't even imagine. If Fiona had her say in it, it might involve tetrafumic acid.

Raquel took a pen from her utility belt and wrote the cruiser's ignition numbers on the inside of Tess's forearm. She scowled at me. "Happy?"

"No. Not ever again in this lifetime."

Her chin went up, her expression brittle. "Let's go." Her eyes flicked to Solan. "We have to get back to Maya."

My eyes narrowed. They loved their daughter—the little girl was probably the only thing they loved besides each other—but I'd never heard one of them say *that* before, especially when a hunt had been this fast and easy.

I refused to move, even when Solan pushed me. "What about Maya?" As far as I knew, the five-year-old was home in Sector 6, as usual.

Raquel's face lost some of its habitual callousness. For the first time in ages, she looked almost human. Actually, she looked like her daughter, with big mahogany eyes, heavy dark lashes, and wavy hair down to her elbows. Maya's long hair was blacker and springier, which she got from her father.

A visible anxiety I'd never seen before in her crept into

Raquel's features. "Why do you think it took us ten days to come after you?" She shook her head like I was the idiot and the asshole, when they were the ones who'd just ambushed us, captured me, and drugged my girlfriend.

"I don't know. You tell me," I ground out.

"Even though we chipped you, we didn't pursue you ourselves or tell any of the other bounty hunters where you were because we chose *not* to." Raquel seemed to regret that decision wholeheartedly in retrospect. "In spite of her two hundred *million* units being transferred to *your* head." She pointed back and forth between Tess and me, as if I needed the visual cues to know exactly who she was talking about.

Did she want me to thank them? Fuck that. "What changed?" I asked.

She clamped her mouth shut, so I glared at Solan.

He scrubbed a hand over his shaved head, grimacing. "Maya got sick."

"What?" My brow slammed down. "What kind of sick? What happened?"

"Everything was normal at first," he answered. "After your asinine behavior on the Squirrel Tree, we went home and kept tabs on you. We watched you go to Starway 8 for some reason, then you zigzagged around the Outer Zones with no logical direction, then you disappeared. We thought you'd been blown up or something. There was no trace of you anywhere. Then Maya collapsed the other day."

Solan took a deep breath. He glanced at his wife. She stared straight ahead at nothing. "She was playing normally. Then she started complaining about feeling dizzy. 'Spots in my eyes,' she said. We gave her a snack and thought she was okay again. A few hours later, she just dropped, folded like her strength fell out from under her. She couldn't get back up. She's in a clinic now. They say it's an aggressive new blood disease, and they don't know how to treat it." His next words choked him. "They say she won't make it."

"Shit. I'm sorry." I was sorry, despite the rest of this. Then anger reared up. "And you ditched her in a clinic to go hunt down the one person who might actually care about her besides you two?"

They both flinched, which was unprecedented. I'd only seen Maya here and there, a couple of times a year, on average. She wasn't the easiest kid in the galaxy—hell, look at her parents—but I usually got her to come around to games that didn't involve setting things on fire or beating the crap out of something. And I knew where Solan and Raquel kept the paperwork. The paperwork that fucking named *me* as Maya's guardian if the two of them bit it somewhere.

"We didn't ditch her," Raquel said stiffly, not sounding like herself either as she moved closer to me and Solan. "We put out feelers. There's a black-market dealer who says he's got a cure-all like nothing anyone's ever seen before. He swears it'll fix anything, even this, but he's only got one. He'll sell it."

"Let me guess," I bit out. "For two hundred million."

"*Three* hundred million." Solan actually looked sorry, like this wasn't how he wanted things to end between us. "You popped up on Korabon—alive, apparently—so we told him we could get the money for his cure-all. We tracked you here in the meantime." He shrugged. "The rest is history."

Black-market dealers were greedy fuckers, but still... "That's a hell of a lot of currency."

"It'll wipe us out," Solan said. "But at least we'll have Maya."

"There's no guarantee of that." They'd never acted like

they were born yesterday. Why start now? "This guy could be pulling a fast one on you. He could take your money, hand you a useless saline solution, and disappear into the Dark forever."

"You're just trying to save yourself," Raquel spat out, livid—probably because she feared exactly what I just said. She reached out, twisted her hand in the neck of my T-shirt, and pulled. "Our cruiser's over at the next lodge. Start walking."

Tess laughed from the ground. Little huffs and giggles leaked from her as she shoved herself up and sat against the wall of the bungalow. She blinked like her vision was fuzzy. I couldn't believe she was even conscious. Was her A1 blood helping her?

Raquel let go of me and whirled on Tess, practically foaming at the mouth as she stomped back toward her. "You think this is funny?"

Tess laughed again. Raquel pointed the Grayhawk at her. Cocked it. I leaped forward, but Solan jerked me back, growling.

"Don't!" I shouted, my heart banging in my throat. "You promised."

Raquel's lip curled. She lowered the Grayhawk.

"Not funny," Tess mumbled. She squeezed her eyes shut and shook her head. "Your drug is making me loopy." She wrinkled her nose and blinked some more, looking owlish. "I can help."

"Come again?" Raquel stared at her, so hostile I tensed. I'd seen her kick in someone's teeth when they were down, and I had no doubt she'd do it again.

"I can help your daughter," Tess said more clearly. "And I won't even charge you three hundred million units in universal currency." She pointed at me, her hand wavering. "I want *him* in exchange." Her hand dropped, thunking into her lap again.

Raquel whipped back around, her laser-sharp gaze zeroing in on me. "Is she for real?"

"Shade, man, what the hell's she talking about?" Solan sounded half pissed-off and half anxious with hope. Poor bastard.

I laughed. I threw back my head and laughed, just like Tess had. This was so fucking perfect.

"Yeah, she can help you. Assholes." I strained against the cuff biting into my wrists. It didn't budge. "And we both would've helped Maya if you'd just fucking asked. I have no hope of buying my docks back now. But I would've bought her life with that cure-all if you'd just told me—instead of this."

Neither of them would look at me. Did that mean they were capable of guilt?

"Let him go," Tess said.

"Not a chance, bit—" Raquel stopped, swallowed the rest of her insult, and tried again. "Tess. Show us what you've got and then we'll decide."

Tess struggled to her feet. She swayed and slid back down the wall, her hair clinging to the fake wood and falling in slow motion around her shoulders. She closed her eyes. Giggled. Took a few deep breaths. "You got an antidote for this stuff?"

Huffing like a dragon, Raquel tucked Tess's Grayhawk into her belt, pulled out a small pistol, and shot Tess.

Tess gasped. Her eyes popped open, and her leg jerked up, a blue-tipped dart jutting from her thigh. The red-tipped one was still in her shoulder.

"You're unbelievable!" I snarled. Raquel shrugged.

Tess blinked a few more times, scrunching up her face. She stood and ripped the darts from her leg and shoulder. "Wow. That works fast." She looked at me and managed an odd smile. "See you in a few minutes."

I nodded, some of the tightness in my chest easing now that she was up, steady, and moving again. Tess walked to the cruiser. Since we'd been doing essentially the same thing for Bridgebane in the privacy of my little ship, we had everything she needed to draw her own blood and pass if off as a surprisingly red cure-all.

Tess climbed into the pilot's seat and looked out through the clear panel at me. She sat there for a moment, staring. Solan's grip on my shoulder hardened until it hurt. "She's gonna leave without you and screw us all over."

My stomach dropped. She could lock up the cruiser. Ignite the engine. Meet Bridgebane. Go to Demeter Terre. All without me. "No."

"She did before." Solan didn't need to remind me. Raquel murmured in agreement, her eyes fixed on Tess in the cockpit.

"That was then. This is now." *Right, baby?*

Tess glanced at her arm, clearly looking at the ignition numbers. Ice-cold panic pierced my chest.

"She's about to take off. Fuck," Solan muttered. "Never trust a rebel."

My pulse went haywire. "Just give her a minute. Then you can get the hell out of here and help Maya."

Tess bent down. I lost sight of her below the clear panel and stopped breathing. Was she setting coordinates?

She straightened, and I braced for the engine to fire up. For my heart to shatter. For my life to be over. The highest-earning bounty hunter in the galaxy brought in for the biggest bounty ever offered. The irony was almost poetic.

Tess stood and moved toward the back of the cruiser. Relief hit me like an asteroid. She wasn't leaving.

I breathed again. I breathed until I didn't feel broken.

"Huh." Solan grunted in surprise. Then his brow furrowed. "She wouldn't do something bad? Something to hurt Maya?"

"You mean something scheming, untrustworthy, and unprincipled?" My blistering tone hopefully scathed both of them to the bone.

"You're no better than we are," Raquel snapped.

Solan was smart enough not to agree with that.

Tess's tall form flitted across the open central area of the cruiser and then disappeared again. "The woman in there is the most compassionate person you'll ever meet. She would never hurt a child, and she's going to save yours."

"How?" Raquel asked.

"How doesn't matter." I hit her with a rock-hard stare. "Just don't ever forget what she's doing for you."

"She's doing it for you, not us." Solan slanted me a curious look. "So why were you so worried?"

Worried? I was fucking terrified. My back stiffened. "I wasn't."

"Sure you were." Raquel—helpful, as always.

Solan offered up his thoughts when I didn't answer. "You need her more than she needs you. It's obvious."

"What are you talking about?" I balled my hands into fists behind me. For the last year and a half, all I'd wanted was for these two to leave me alone, but they kept showing up, uninvited. Tracking me. Calling me with offers to work together. Messing up my hunts. Ambushing me and stealing my targets. To top it all off, now they were giving opinions about my love life? My jaw flexed.

"You dumped everything for her." Solan's dark eyes were a little too perceptive and penetrating. "Why? Her bounty was your docks back. The prize money would've finished off the sum you needed, and Scarabin White would've been obligated to take your offer. She was your life back— everything you'd been working toward *forever*."

Did he think I hadn't agonized over the decision? That it hadn't been hell? My own personal nightmare?

"Because he's stupid," Raquel said in disgust.

I clamped down on the burning urge to crank my forehead into the Wicked Witch of the Galaxy's nose. "You just know, don't you? You meet someone, and that's it. There's life before them, and there's life after." I shrugged as best I could with my hands cinched behind my back. Tess once told me it was do or die. She'd been talking about other stuff, missions probably, but her words had hit home. I'd understood the consequences. "I made a choice. I chose her. I don't regret it."

Raquel heaved a sigh that made me wonder if a small part of her actually did care about my well-being. "You screwed yourself out of everything."

I disagreed entirely. "I got what I wanted most."

That shut them both up. *Finally*.

Tess appeared again at the front of the cruiser, her dark hair swinging as she moved around the confined space and wiggled into her cropped leather jacket. It would cover any bruises or needle marks but would also leave her suffocated and sweating.

"Didn't you guys know?" I asked, watching Tess through the window. She gathered what she needed and turned to the door. "When you met. Love at first sight or something?"

Raquel's snort was telling.

Solan chuckled. "Hell no," he answered with feeling.

"No?" Frowning, I threw a quick glance at each of them in turn. Raquel looked put together, despite the hot and sticky weather. There wasn't a smudge or a scratch on her. Unsurprising, since she hadn't brawled like we had. She'd obviously conned Tess into thinking they'd have a fair fight without weapons. Solan had a swollen eye, a bruised cheek, and a split lip. *Good. He deserved it.*

"It took us a while," Solan admitted. He tipped his head toward his wife. "She's mean."

Raquel's eye twitched. It was entirely possible she was contemplating the best way to carve up his balls and serve them to him for dinner.

Suddenly, they were smiling at each other, surprising the shit out of me. I shook my head, my lips curving also. In an instant, it was as if the last two years got shaved off our rocky partnership. We used to work better together, without all the sneaking around, stealing targets, and trading insults.

Tess hopped down from the cruiser and shut the door behind her. She looked perfectly steady. Three capped-off test tubes filled with dark-crimson liquid dangled from her fingertips.

"Dump all the bullets out of your guns," she said, holding up the vials and gently swinging them. Her threat was implicit: *Do as I say, or I drop them.* "Tranquilizers, too. Then toss aside the weapons. We're keeping them."

Solan and Raquel dumped their bullets and darts out on the hot landing-pad surface. They threw their weapons into the bushes just to be pains in the ass and make us search for them.

"That's my Grayhawk," Tess snapped before Raquel could heave it into the ferns. "I want it back."

Without a word, Raquel threw the weapon toward the doorstep.

Tess narrowed her eyes, seeming to search for tricks or hidden gadgets. Raquel didn't go for anything in her belt, which was always filled with illegal shit no one was expecting.

"Give up your belt," I told her. I wasn't taking any chances.

"Oh, come on!" Raquel complained.

"You want to help Maya?" I asked.

Her nostrils flaring, Raquel unbuckled her utility belt and flung it toward the bungalow. After that, she didn't move a muscle. Neither did Solan.

Tess glanced at me, her blue eyes a silent question. I dipped my chin in answer. I was as satisfied as I could be that they wouldn't spring anything else on us.

"Free Shade. Unbind his wrists," she ordered.

"I want those cure-alls first," Raquel said.

"You think *I'm* stupid? You got me once with your *Let's have a fair fight* crap. I'm over that. You do as *I* say now." Tess separated one of the vials from the other two and held it out over the pavement. "I want Shade, or I drop this."

"Wait." Wariness spiked in Solan's hasty plea. Tess was a wild card he didn't know how to deal with. "We don't have a bargain yet. What are those? What's in them, and where did you get them?"

"First, answer this." Tess swung the vial like a pendulum. "What did your black-market dealer say about his cure-all?"

Solan glanced at Raquel. She nodded.

"That it would do more than just heal the body," he answered. "That it would increase height, strength, speed, and overall immunity. He also said there might be negative side-effects, like increased aggressiveness and anger. Possibly lifelong hallucinations."

Tess's eyes bored into mine. The dealer had obviously gotten ahold of one of the Overseer's enhancers. Merrick definitely had the increased height, strength, speed, and healing. I hadn't seen any evidence of hallucinations or anger issues, but there would almost certainly have been different test batches and experiments. Merrick had only gotten captured and shot up recently, possibly as a test subject for the final product. This black-market "cure-all" could be an older version of the serum.

"He also said that administering it would be incredibly painful for the subject," Raquel added, looking at the ground for a moment.

Tess stopped dangling the test tube. "I know what he has, and this is different."

"How do you know?" Raquel's gaze shot back to her, suspicious.

"That's none of your business," Tess said. "But I know this is a hell of a lot better and a hell of a lot safer. I truly believe it will heal your daughter and cause her no pain or harmful side effects. One might be enough, but I'm offering you three because no child should have to suffer. I'd administer them intravenously with two days in between and monitor Maya's progress. This will attack the bad blood cells and then gradually leave her system. Keep it cool in the meantime, and I wouldn't waste any on tests or experiments."

Solan stepped forward, his hand outstretched for the cure-alls. Tess shook her head along with the test tubes in a double negative that made him stop dead in his tracks.

"I don't think so. Not yet. Untie Shade and unchip him. Then swear on your daughter's life that you won't tell anyone where we are, where we have been, or anything about this"— she tilted her head toward the vials—"*ever*. Not family. Not friends. Not other bounty hunters. Not the Dark Watch. No one. Even if the price stays on Shade's head forever, you *will not* come after him again. Or me, for that matter."

Neither of them immediately took her up on that offer.

"Too bad." Tess shrugged and tossed one of the test tubes into the air.

"Wait!" Raquel cried.

Tess caught it. She arched her brows, waiting.

"Fucking unchip him!" Raquel snarled to Solan, throwing an impatient hand in my direction.

Solan took a thumb-sized remote from his pocket, squatted, and swept it over my right calf. It beeped, and he hit the flashing button. A small pain flared in my leg, almost like the jab of a needle. The remote went dark and quiet. Solan dropped it on the ground and stepped on it. He left the broken remains on the blacktop. "The chip's still in there, but I destroyed it. We all set now?"

"No," Tess answered. "Swear on your daughter's life. Both of you. Agree to my terms, or I smash these." The test tubes glinted in the sunlight, the liquid inside a shocking bright-red against Tess's black jacket.

Solan and Raquel quickly agreed this time, swearing on Maya's health and safety. Solan cut through the cuff, freeing my wrists from the plastic binding and shoving me forward. I turned, facing them as I walked backward. I rolled my shoulders and rubbed my wrists, trying to work the kinks out of them. I gave them both a frosty once-over.

Tess met me halfway and placed her blood on the ground. We both backed away from the vials. "You got a cooler?" she asked.

Solan nodded. "What if it doesn't work?" He moved forward to retrieve what he thought were cure-alls.

"If that doesn't work, then nothing will cure your daughter." Tess offered them a smile they didn't deserve from her. "I hope she lives. And when she does, tell her the Incorruptible have helped her."

Raquel took the vials from Solan's hands and carefully put them in her pockets. "The Incorruptible?"

Solan frowned in my direction, as if I had answers. I was as clueless as he was—and didn't like it.

"Let's go," Tess said, looking at her watch. The alarm she'd set ten days ago would beep any second.

"I want to see them take off." I hoped their priority was getting the cure-alls to Maya, and they'd given Tess their word to leave us alone after this. They'd also proven to be underhanded people, and I didn't want them following us.

Tess nodded and waited beside me. If she was impatient, she didn't show it.

Gruffly, I said, "I hope Maya gets better." I'd probably never know one way or the other, which left an ache inside me.

Solan and Raquel both just looked at me before walking away without a backward glance. No goodbye. No thank-you. No have a nice life, or don't get killed. Nothing. The ache grew, surprising me. We hadn't been exactly friends lately, but we'd still been something.

The meeting-day alarm went off. Tess stopped it after three beeps and didn't pressure me to leave yet.

A cruiser I recognized finally took off in the distance, heading straight up into the atmosphere. And that was that. The last chunk of my old life—gone.

Briskly, I turned to Tess. "First things first. Let's pick up those weapons and sweep the cruiser for bugs."

We gathered Raquel's belt and the discarded guns and bullets. I pulled two search wands from my utility chest, and

Tess checked the inside of the cruiser for tracking bugs while I covered the exterior of the ship. Neither of us got a hit. We swept each other for good measure and came up clean.

Satisfied, I fired up the cruiser and we took off, heading for the Grand Temple. Neither of us suggested the resort shuttle at this point. We had another unfortunate meeting to get through today—and we might already be late.

CHAPTER

7

TESS

AS IF THE MORNING HADN'T ALREADY BEEN TERRIFYING enough. Cyclodiles having their breakfast. Suspended bridges over murky rivers. Draakwings that couldn't fly *away* from human heads. A sneak attack by a pair of nasty bounty hunters. I had to face my uncle now? *Great*.

It took us a while to find him. The sanctuary was huge and not well lit except for intermittent spotlights shining down on garish relics. The constant throng of people filtering in and out of the different sections didn't help. A tall man with broad shoulders finally caught my attention, mainly because he wasn't shuffling along with the rest of the slow-moving crowd.

Nathaniel Bridgebane stood under a representation of the Sky Mother suspended in an alcove near the east entrance. The Great Star hovered above him, her five points forming an abstract human figure, the arms and legs outstretched and her elongated head rising from them. Several rotating rings of smaller stars orbited her in gyroscopic circles. A soft radiance emanated from somewhere within the statue and reflected off the smaller stars—Her Powers.

The alcove's lighting threw Bridgebane into alternating patterns of brightness and shadow, making him harder to spot than he already would have been in the dimly lit temple. He also wasn't in uniform and looked a lot like everyone else here, dressed in predominantly dark colors. My uncle wasn't alone, which violated our deal. Then again, neither was I. Shade was with me. A black woman I didn't recognize stood beside Bridgebane. She wasn't in uniform, either, but I could tell she was military just from the way she held herself, alert and fighting ready.

In a low voice, I pointed them out to Shade. We veered in their direction. They hadn't seen us yet, and Bridgebane's hand tapped against his thigh, his posture stiff and his searching gaze impatient.

Coming at them from an angle gave me a chance to study my uncle in a way I hadn't gotten to during our previous encounter. Towering, strong, fit, and handsome, he looked a decade or more younger than his actual age of sixty. The silver strands glinting in his short dark hair were his only outward sign of aging. Piercing blue eyes, a long, straight nose, and a firm jawline made him striking in a severe fashion. He didn't look like he smiled much—if ever. Life as the Overseer's right-hand man was clearly a barrel of laughs. All that fun hunting down and enforcing.

All in all, I couldn't find the entertaining, generous, smiling man I remembered from my childhood anywhere in the person we were approaching. Nathaniel Bridgebane had obviously buried whatever humor and integrity he had left in him deep in my mother's grave on Alpha Sambian eighteen years ago, right alongside her.

Bridgebane's restless, scowling face blanked the moment he saw me. While he appeared to experience an emotional shutdown, an explosion of feelings detonated in me. Heat. Fury. Incomprehension. His eyes narrowed to blue slits when he saw Shade—the one man the Dark Watch general had called for backup when he cornered me on Starway 8. That hadn't worked out as expected.

So here we were, all of us betraying the people and ideals we fought for.

I took in my uncle's companion as we came to a standstill—although *standoff* might have been the better word for it. I couldn't tell if she was curious or suspicious. I only knew that her intense stare seemed to penetrate straight through to my internal organs, which wasn't a sensation I cared for.

Bridgebane looked Shade up and down as if he were a piece of space garbage. Shade wasn't his favorite flunky anymore. My uncle liked skilled, intelligent people—unless they turned on him.

"*He's* still alive?" Impressive. Bridgebane could say something so tightly his mouth barely moved.

"No, he's the Ghost of Bounty Hunters Past," I shot back, certain Uncle Nate would remember the crumbling book we'd read together. Only now, *he* was the coldhearted bastard who needed to wake up and see the error of his ways.

That scraped the contempt off his face. He definitely remembered those parchment-like pages with illustrations that made little sense to us and references to things we could only guess at. We'd had fun trying to figure them out. The rest was easy. It was a story about people and how they could change.

Too bad my uncle hadn't changed for the better.

Bridgebane rallied, forcing out a clipped "Maybe I should double his bounty."

"Or maybe you should cancel it. We're late because we had to avoid complications—complications that almost got *me* captured." That wasn't a lie exactly. Raquel *had* captured me. And if my uncle understood that he was hurting me by trying to hurt Shade, it might solve one of our major problems.

Bridgebane ran a critical eye over Shade's scratched jaw and swollen cheekbone. A bruise blossomed like a purple and blue flower around his left eye, which no longer fully opened. Shade was a mess, and I was still slightly nauseated from the tranquilizer and its antidote in quick succession. I'd had to sit in the cruiser and fight the urge to vomit before I could even think about preparing those "cure-alls" for the bounty hunters. I'd been stupid to lower my weapon. Raquel had put hers down, too. I just didn't know she had another.

Crossing my arms, I stared at my uncle. "Well? Are you going to call off the bounty, or are you going to continue putting me in danger?"

Bridgebane had one hell of a poker face. He looked like a wax statue, stiff and emotionless. Something in his eyes still gave him away this time, at least to me. In them, I saw the man who'd tried to keep me out of a black hole, who'd shot at Shade but not once at me, who'd pointed a gun at his own head—because he wanted my forgiveness.

I knew I'd won before my uncle realized it. The unclenching in my stomach told me so.

Scowling, Bridgebane turned to his companion. "Lieutenant Mwende. My tablet, please."

My mouth puckered. "I thought we agreed: no goons."

His eyes cut back to me. "She's my personal bodyguard.

There's no one else with me." He swept a dismissive glance over Shade. "You obviously brought your guard also, although he doesn't look very effective."

"We're here, aren't we?" Shade sounded prickly. Did my uncle's opinion matter to him?

"My niece doesn't have a scratch on her, so I'm assuming she came to your rescue."

"She did." Shade's flat answer seemed to startle Bridgebane. "But she wouldn't have needed to if you weren't pissed off that we're together."

"It was a mutual rescuing," I corrected. "And you should be *happy* I have Shade looking out for me. Wasn't he your favorite? The best of the best? The guy you called when you wanted something accomplished?"

"That's the problem, Quin," Bridgebane ground out. "He has no conscience. He turned on me; he'll turn on you. He's bagged people without asking a single question."

"On *your* orders," I flung back. "Any dirt on Shade is shit-layered mud on you, *General Bridgebane*."

I was expecting my uncle's expression to deaden again, to shut like a door in my face. Instead, his color rose.

"I would die before I turned on Tess." Shade glanced at a passing couple and lowered his voice. "I had no idea you were related. Or protecting her—in your way, at least. I betrayed you *for* her. Don't you get that?"

Bridgebane was listening, but he was hard to read. So was Lieutenant Mwende, who stood beside him holding a small tablet. She didn't take her midnight stare off us. An angular chin, high forehead, and wide, prominent cheekbones gave her an elegant, almost diamond-shaped face. She'd slicked her black hair into a tight bun. If charisma and deadliness were to be mixed into one person, I had a feeling she was it. I wanted to look at her almost as much as I wanted to study my uncle. No part of her was soft or gave the impression she could be molded by anyone's design but her own. Tall and poised, she exuded command. She also looked like a sleek, gleaming bullet marked for a precise target. You wouldn't see her coming until you were already bleeding out and done.

My uncle finally took the tablet. "Thank you, Sanaa." His politeness with her made me wonder how he could be so awful to everyone else.

A moment later, Bridgebane flashed the tablet at us, showing us some kind of database with listings on it. He tapped a line, calling up Shade's description, picture, and astronomical bounty. A header reading DEAD OR ALIVE prefaced the whole thing in big block letters and scared the crap out of me. My uncle scrolled to the button that said Cancel and pressed it.

Shade and I looked at each other. *Could it really be this easy?* One click, and we were free of the bounty?

The page refreshed to show the database menu again. Bridgebane handed the tablet back to Mwende. "I don't approve of your association, but I don't want it putting my niece in additional danger, either."

"First of all, I don't give a damn about your approval," I announced, incredulous. "Second, how about *your* choice of associates? You know, that mass murderer?" Grief surged up my throat so fast I choked on it. "The one who killed my friend? Who killed my mother?" My breath hitched, and I clamped my mouth shut.

Bridgebane went back to looking like a rock-faced asshole. "I've given you something you wanted—something that wasn't even part of the deal. Now, do you have what I need for the Overseer?"

"Yeah, I've got what you need." I jerked my pack off my shoulder and swung it in front of me. Unzipping it, I pulled out the insulated carrier case inside. I unzipped that also and showed him the six full bags of A1 blood.

"How do I know it's yours?" he asked.

"Do you really think I'd risk them?" He'd threatened to haul either Mareeka or Surral off to prison, leaving Starway 8 with half its leadership missing and everyone's hearts in tatters. If he tested this blood and it wasn't what he wanted, he would make good on his dark promise. I knew that. I shoved the bag at him.

He didn't touch it. "Give it to Lieutenant Mwende."

"Whatever." I handed her the cooler and then zipped my pack closed again, shouldering it. "Are we done here?"

A muscle in Bridgebane's jaw tightened. "Do you have any questions you want to ask me?"

I frowned. I'd just handed over enough of my blood to make dozens of enhancers. I had plenty of questions, but I hadn't expected him to offer—or be willing—to share information. "Yeah. How badly is that going to come back to haunt me?" I glanced at the bag Mwende was closing.

"That's not the kind of question I meant." Bridgebane pinched his forehead as though he had a headache. Or was maybe frustrated.

I scoffed. "Oh, is this the moment when you tell me 'everything'? Like you offered on Starway 8 if I came with you and let the Overseer use me as a science experiment for the rest of my life? I thought that deal was off, and this was the replacement."

"Quin—"

"Tess," I hissed. "Quin died in space, after being floated from *your* air lock, *Uncle Nate*."

Shit. I glanced at Mwende. Her ebony features didn't

change at all, so she was either unshockable or she already knew everything—and probably a lot more than I did.

"And I know he's not my father," I added. "He told me."

That got a reaction from Bridgebane. He paled, his eyes shining an almost inhuman azure in a face suddenly gone as gray as ash. "He's hunting you. You're in danger."

I laughed. Some temple-goer walking nearby shushed me, and I brought down the volume. The alcove was secluded, but we weren't alone by any stretch. "If that's your big information, it's old news. About eight years out of date."

His nostrils flared. "I'm trying to help you."

"Fuck you," I said. It just popped out, surprising me as much as him. Bridgebane's eyes widened. He didn't look angry. More … sad, and the stab of guilt that needled straight into my heart enraged me as much as the rest of this did.

Sanaa Mwende didn't move, but lightning-hot fury boiled in the fixed stare she leveled on me. If my uncle said the word, I had zero doubt she'd grind my face into the temple floor and thoroughly enjoy it.

"This is your chance," Bridgebane said with surprising evenness. "Use it wisely."

I wanted to be as distant and icy as he'd been in the months leading up to Mom's death and my faked floating. I wanted to give him the cold shoulder. Walk away, because I didn't need him. His lies. Or truths. Or whatever bullshit he was going to feed me.

"Why do you protect Starway 8?" I blurted out.

His eyes shuttered. His whole face shut down like I'd just hit a nerve that paralyzed him. "Not that one."

Why do I even bother? "Don't offer info and then say no, asshole."

"Don't speak to me that way, young lady."

My jaw dropped. "What the fuck?"

His eyes flared. "Your mother would have a heart attack if she heard your language."

"Mom's dead and you abandoned me."

"I left you in the one place you'd be happy!"

Pilgrims and tourists alike glared and shushed us. I didn't care. My eyes burned and my heart was doing backflips. I didn't understand how we were still family, this man and I, after all these years and despite everything. Only family could get under my skin this way—and we didn't even technically share a common ancestor.

My mother's stepbrother abruptly turned and stormed out of the alcove. I didn't get the feeling he was ditching me, so I followed, Shade and Mwende right behind us. Bridgebane exited the temple at an angry clip, his military bearing unmistakable now. Outside, sunlight hit my eyeballs like hot little daggers. Sweat burst from my pores. Grumbling under my breath, I handed my bag to Shade and ripped off my jacket. *Oof. Better.* I tied it around my waist, cinching it tight with impatient jerks.

I hardly noticed the wide paths and sprawling lawns of the inner gardens. They weren't overcrowded now that the temples were open. There was room to breathe, even if the humid air was as thick as honey. Bridgebane headed for trees—thank the Powers.

Shade walked beside me. Lieutenant Mwende took a few quick steps to join Bridgebane in front of us. She was alert to everything, coiled, controlled, and ready. Not outwardly aggressive, but still damn scary. She obviously knew what she was doing on the bodyguarding front. Where had she been the last time I'd seen my uncle? He'd been alone on Starway 8—until Shade showed up.

My stomach wound itself tighter and tighter as I followed them through the Holy Hollow. Nathaniel Bridgebane tied me up in knots, and this was only the second time I'd seen him in eighteen years. Time obviously didn't heal all things—or erase all betrayals. Right now, I still felt like that grieving eight-year-old girl he'd dumped in an orphanage. The one person left alive that I'd loved had held me back from him at arm's length, looked me in the eyes, and told me to change my name and never cross his radar again, or he'd kill me, just as the Overseer had ordered.

Bridgebane whirled once we were under the shade of a flat-leafed tree with conical clusters of nuts dangling from it. I almost ran into him and had to pull up short. We were too close. I flinched back, bumping into Shade instead. Shade put a hand on my lower back to steady me. My heart pounded, and Bridgebane stared at me. I glanced away, avoiding his fierce gaze by finding the tree immensely fascinating.

"It's a kimmery," he said mechanically, his tonelessness at odds with the sudden intensity in his expression. "Native to the Outer Zones. They've been brought here."

I grunted. I liked trees. Trees were awesome. Trees didn't rip out your heart, stomp on it, disappear for eighteen years, blow holes in your ship, try to arrest you, and then tell you it was all for your own good—to protect you and the whole damn galaxy. I touched the ridged bark with my fingertip, pressing hard to stop my visible shaking.

"Your mother liked crushed kimmery nuts sprinkled over vanilla frosting."

My hand fell. I swallowed. If there was one thing I remembered, it was how Mom had always looked at Uncle Nate—like he was her hero, and always had been.

"Dad let her eat that? I mean…the Overseer."

He shook his head. "As you know, that was a dessertless household. It was before we got there."

What had it been like for him, suddenly having a fourteen-year-old girl move into his house with her mother? He'd been sixteen, but as far as I knew, the stepsiblings had quickly become thick as thieves, mainly because my mother flatly refused to be left out of Uncle Nate's adventures.

"What else did she like?" I hardly remembered. Not details like that, especially because I didn't think she had anything she liked or wanted after she married the Overseer.

"Colors," he answered. "The brighter the better. And novels. And protecting others, even at the expense of herself. You're more like Caitrin than you realize."

He sounded as if that were a bad thing. Probably because Mom's choices had gotten her killed. I figured mine would, too—someday. I just hoped for later rather than sooner.

He cleared his throat. "I should get back to Alpha Sambian."

I waved a dismissive hand, instantly doused in bitterness again. "By all means, go back to being an evil minion of the empire."

"You understand *nothing*," Mwende hissed.

I took a step back, my hand flying to my heart. "She speaks!"

Mwende's dark eyes narrowed at my sarcasm. "I have a lot of words for you, Daraja."

"Daraja?" *What does that mean?*

"Take care of yourself," Bridgebane said stiffly.

"Wait." There was one question he'd better answer. "Where's Shiori Takashi?"

My uncle's mouth flattened, reluctance to tell me written in the tight seam of his lips. My heart started the painful *thud, thud* of being sure horrible news was coming. Was she dead?

Suddenly, on a quick gust of breath... "Starbase 12," Bridgebane said. "You'll never reach her."

"Starbase 12?" My eyes widened. Despair, hope, and impossible rebel missions crashed inside me like a cyclone. Breaking Reena Ahern out of Imperial Headquarters already seemed impossible. Getting Shiori out would only make it harder. But could we do both? I wouldn't go in for Ahern and not try to save Shiori.

"Is she okay?" I steeled myself for any answer.

"She's sedated. She bit through her own wrists in an attempted suicide. I believe it was to eliminate any incentive to come after her."

The bottom of my stomach dropped out with a heaving rush that left me reeling. I stumbled back from the harsh slap of his words, unsteady.

Shade was suddenly there, propping me upright. His furious gaze drilled into Bridgebane. "You couldn't have softened that up a bit?" he growled.

I breathed hard, set loose with no gravity. The image of Shiori—teeth red, wrists open—seared my eyes like the tears that built behind them. Nothing I knew about her made me think that was a falsehood.

"She's stable now," Bridgebane added more gently.

Shiori's screamed "Don't come for me! I forbid it!" rang in my head, an echo I heard daily. *Hourly.* She'd known I wouldn't listen. That I'd make plans to free her. Did that make this my fault? Gray hair stained crimson. Papery skin draining of color. Eyes that had been sightless for years, now wide open and waiting for Miko.

I inhaled, loud and shaky.

My uncle reached for me, his brow creasing. It was the weirdest thing when he wrapped a big, warm hand around my bare elbow and squeezed. It didn't feel...awful.

"She's my grandmother," I whispered. "Can you protect her?"

He looked at me oddly. "Your grandmother died when you were six. You never knew Caitrin's mother."

No. The Overseer wouldn't let Mom's family anywhere near us. Only Nathaniel Bridgebane had done something, said something, to get himself into the inner circle.

"She is." My voice cracked, nearly breaking me. "She's my family, and I love her." A tear spilled from my eye. I felt it track down my cheek and swatted it away, blinking rapidly.

My uncle let go of my arm and stared at me, clearly horrified. Did any sign of weakness appall him? Well, too bad. We couldn't all be dead-eyed jerks who deserted the people who needed them.

Shade tucked me closer, offering the comfort I needed. I tried to shake off the lingering feel of Bridgebane's hand on my elbow. Shade had the right to touch me. My uncle didn't.

"What about a hint?" Shade asked. "Something to go on—if we decide to try something stupid."

I stood up straighter, a tiny seed of hope wanting to take root inside me. If Bridgebane helped us, it could mean the key to two cages.

"Don't try. It's impossible. You'll end up captured. Or dead." Bridgebane looked at each of us in turn, forgetting to treat Shade as though he didn't exist anymore. "I might not be able to help you."

"We won't ask you to." Possibilities started to shoot through my mind like missiles—a chaotic barrage of risk versus potential reward. "But help us now. You must know something."

My uncle's face twisted. A low growl rumbled out from between his clenched teeth. "I shouldn't have told you. You're just like Caitrin. Too stubborn."

"Then help me." I wasn't above pleading. Part of me couldn't believe Nathaniel Bridgebane and I were having an almost normal, almost civil conversation. Another part of me didn't even feel the distance of years and desertion between us, or the fact that he was a Dark Watch general and I was a rebel Nightchaser. All I knew was that he brought out a deep ache inside me—made worse by fear for Shiori—and that the more we talked, the rawer and more uncertain I felt about everything.

Bridgebane shook his head. "I don't want you getting hurt."

I scoffed, the sound as dirty and icy as a comet.

"*More* hurt," he said, his jaw flexing.

"Starbase 12," I encouraged. "I remember my way around. I know how to get to the three incarceration levels through the back stairwells. I remember the U-shaped cellblocks. I even know where the cameras are located."

He glared at me, silent, his blue eyes burning. He believed me. He'd shown me all that when I was a kid. Anything to get me away from the Overseer, even if that meant wandering Imperial Headquarters from top to bottom and front to back.

"I won't give up," I vowed. "Contrary to you, I'd rather die than abandon my family."

Sanaa Mwende sliced a knife through the air so fast it whistled. The blade landed under my jaw before I could blink. I froze. Shade sucked in a breath, tensing. I had no idea where the weapon had come from, or how she'd produced it so quickly. None of us moved. My pulse beat against the sharp, hard metal. The lieutenant's expression promised all kinds of retribution for my cutting words.

"You shoot your mouth off about things you don't understand. I don't like it." She had a slight accent I hadn't noticed before with how little she'd spoken, enunciating her words very precisely.

I breathed shallowly. My eyes darted to my uncle.

"Stand down, Sanaa." Bridgebane uttered a world-weary sound that might almost have made sympathy crack open inside me if I didn't have a knife to my throat.

The blade pricked like a bee sting. I didn't dare swallow.

"She's disrespectful." Mwende didn't lower her weapon, which directly defied my uncle's order.

"Have I given her any reason to respect me?" he asked.

The question caught me off guard. Frowning, I eased back for some breathing room between my neck and Sanaa and her knife skills. I'd loved my mother unconditionally, but Uncle Nate had been the person I'd respected most in the whole galaxy—until he'd bought into the Overseer's crap and dumped Mom and me.

Mwende finally stepped back, sheathing her blade in one smooth motion. "People cannot know what you do not tell them."

Well, don't be cryptic or anything. I scowled. The lieutenant's chin lifted, her assessing once-over carrying a hint of challenge. If she thought I was going to ask, she was mistaken. Whatever explanations Bridgebane had for his behavior toward me or anyone else in the galaxy were going to have to die with these two, because I didn't give two fucks.

Maybe one fuck, but not two.

My lips tightening, I touched my neck and glanced at my fingers. No blood. Mwende hadn't even broken the skin, despite the quick jab toward my jugular. "Now that we're done waving knives around, can we please get back to Shiori? A code? A guard shift schedule? Anything? I know you don't want me to die—thanks, by the way"—my uncle's eyes narrowed at my tone—"so a hint would be really helpful."

He glanced at his lieutenant, as if she had a say in his decisions. She gave him a *What the hell are you waiting for* kind of look, as though she couldn't fathom why he was still just standing there like an idiot.

Apparently, she *did* have a say. Interesting. I'd never imagined him having a ... partner? For some reason, the idea made me like them both just a little bit better. Nothing about the way they interacted led me to believe they were lovers, but there was definitely something between them. Trust. Maybe friendship.

Bridgebane hovered in what looked like a state of indecision, shocking me. I couldn't claim to know my uncle well anymore, but I'd never seen him hesitate. Mwende took the next step for him, shocking me even further. She produced the small tablet again, shoved it into his chest, and let go. Bridgebane grabbed it before it fell. He glowered at her.

"There is a secure location where she could pick up information." Mwende clearly hinted at something they both knew about. "Just print out a key card. Give her the address. Unlock the door, General."

I wanted to scream, "What door?" but didn't. It took considerable effort to stay quiet and let them work out whatever this was between them.

My uncle clenched his free hand into a fist against his thigh and started tapping it. He looked at the sky. He looked down. He looked at the tablet. His mouth puckered, flattened. His feet shifted. *What the hell is wrong with him?*

"Fine." The word shot from him like a bullet. He glared at Mwende. "But this is on you if it backfires."

She nodded, accepting the consequences. Were they talking about something other than just the colossal danger of us trying to get in and out of Starbase 12 undetected? It felt like more than that, but I couldn't figure out the second layer of their conversation.

Bridgebane's hand flew over the screen, which he hid from me. His tapping was hard and precise, almost aggressive. He jabbed his finger down a final time and then waited. A moment later, a key card began slowly emerging from the side slot, the internal printer almost silent. He caught it when the tablet spit it out and rubbed his thumb over the raised dots of the encoded data. I reached for it, but he lifted it away from me, his grip so hard his fingers whitened.

"If I come up with something to help you recover Shiori Takashi, I'll leave it here in five days. Will that be sufficient?"

Sufficient? To be honest, I was flabbergasted. Who was this man? He knew Shiori's name, where she was, and what condition she was in? He must have found out for *me*, for our meeting today. How had Bridgebane gone from telling me he would kill me if he ever saw me again to helping me? How could the same person threaten Mareeka and Surral, take my blood for the Overseer, and still do something decent?

Confusion tied me up in knots as I held out my hand for the key card again. "Where's 'here'?" I asked, because there was no way in hell I was asking any of the other questions I wanted to blurt out.

"Sanaa knows the address." He handed the key card to his lieutenant.

What? "What?" I said aloud this time. My eyes widening, my head swiveled first to her and then back to my uncle. I stared at him blankly. "She's not coming with us."

"No way," Shade said, shaking his head along with me.

Sanaa Mwende barked out a laugh that could have cut diamonds. She looked at the key card in her hand and then at Bridgebane. Two seconds later, she went off on him in a language I didn't recognize, treating him to a one-sided tirade he didn't appear to understand, either, but listened to with stony patience, not interrupting.

My ears automatically perked to the unfamiliar sounds pouring from her mouth on livid syllables. With her high, proud forehead, starless-night eyes, unmistakable fierceness, and clear devotion to my uncle, this woman got more interesting by the second. Only a generously calculated one percent of the galaxy's population still spoke something other than the universal language, imposed on all at the start of the exodus for sheer convenience in a time of danger. And Mwende wasn't using only a word or two, passed down like keepsakes. This was a whole outburst, only none of us could understand it.

She finally switched back to the universal tongue, seamlessly continuing her rant with words we could comprehend again. "You worry about her—day in and day out. For two weeks now, ever since you found her. 'Oh, the girl. We must protect her.' You send me with her? Then who protects *you* now?"

Bridgebane scowled. "I don't need protection."

Mwende snorted as if that were the stupidest thing she'd ever heard. "This?" She pointed the key card at herself. "Is not what I was suggesting."

"Yes, I understood that, Sanaa. Thank you for your input." Bridgebane pocketed the tablet instead of giving it back to her. He took the cooler with the blood bags also.

Mwende shoved the key card into the bag she still carried, muttering again in her own language.

"Protect me? For *two whole weeks*?" I rolled my eyes. "What a trial!"

The lieutenant's furious gaze blasted into me, ink-dark and wholly terrifying.

My uncle's back stiffened. "I did just erase footage of you wreaking havoc on Korabon," he quietly thundered. "Do you have any idea how difficult it is to sweep a major security incident on a *paroled* planet under the rug without anyone asking questions? I had to pass it off as a surprise training exercise only I knew about—which is incredibly suspicious."

My heart thumped in surprise and then constricted with sudden unexpected contrition. *He'd done that? For me?* "Thank you."

"You're welcome," he grumbled.

An uncomfortable tension crackled between us, hot and prickly and too filled with negative energy for me to let him off the hook like I almost wanted. "What about the eighteen years before now? What about the eight years of my life when you had no idea where I was and didn't give a shit?"

"Not knowing and not caring are two different things," Bridgebane said gruffly. "What would searching for you have accomplished other than drawing unwanted attention your way?"

"I don't know." I shook my head at him, totally incapable of understanding how he functioned. I used to worship this man. Now, it was as if we were two lines on parallel trajectories. We would *never* meet in the middle. "Maybe I wouldn't have thought you were such a huge bastard?" Sanaa growled. I growled back at her. To my uncle, I snapped, "Maybe you could have gotten me out of prison?"

Things I tried never to think about gripped my throat in a stranglehold I couldn't breathe around. Fumes in my eyes, inmates crying, the crack of a whip, the dreaded shudder of an explosion. The raw taste of fear on the back of my tongue like stale food and contaminated water. I swallowed.

"Keep your voice down, Tess," Shade warned. "People are watching."

I looked to the side. A tour group had stopped just beyond the stand of kimmery trees and was setting up a late-lunch picnic. They slanted us curious glances.

I slipped my arm through Shade's and smiled at him, his face a little blurry through the hot moisture gathering in my eyes. "You're right." I laughed—through clenched teeth. "Let's pretend everything's fantastic and that the second most powerful person in the galaxy *didn't* leave his niece and only living family to rot in a hard-labor prison mine."

Shade smiled back at me, handsome as hell despite his beat-up face and the seriousness in the one eye that still opened. "Forty-two percent of the people sent to Hourglass Mile die within the first year there. You're a survivor. You don't need him."

I glanced at Bridgebane. He didn't say anything. Nothing to excuse or defend himself. No apology for his actions. He'd turned into an emotionless statue again, which I was starting to hate more than anything. He blew hot and cold so much that I didn't know where the fucking wind was coming from. I only knew that it was likely to slam into me hard enough to cause permanent damage.

"Of course she needs him," Sanaa Mwende sliced in

with authority. She scowled at me. "And your blinders make you no better than a robot. You only see what's been programmed into you."

I scowled back at her. "That's bullshit. You don't know me."

"Then stop acting like we're the enemy."

"You are the enemy," I sputtered.

Mwende stepped forward. We were about the same height, close to six feet, but somehow, I felt as though she towered over me. "I've half a mind to pin your eyelids open until you *see*."

My brows rose. "As far as threats go, that's original."

"You'll find I'm full of surprises. You'll get to discover some of them—while I'm your bodyguard." She glared at my uncle. "I think we've stayed here long enough, don't you, General?"

Bridgebane must have agreed because he ushered us down another pathway in the direction of the cruiser docks closest to the Grand Temple. He obviously wasn't going to address the I-abandoned-my-niece-in-prison issue. I stomped along the garden road, disgusted. If there was *one* thing besides him turning all cold on Mom and me at the end that I wanted him to explain, it was how the hell he could have not known I'd been condemned to life in prison. Clearly, it only mattered to me. He must have figured I'd escaped, so who cared now?

"I'm going this way." Bridgebane stopped by an on/off point to the moving walkway that funneled people into the vegetation-hung Rogo Docks. We were slightly farther away, because money didn't buy everything. "Sanaa's with you. If I have something useful, you'll know in five days."

Looking impressively awkward about it, he reached out and put his hand on my shoulder. I almost shook him off but then didn't for some reason. He squeezed.

"Don't expect a miracle, Qui—Tess," he corrected. "Starbase 12 is heavily guarded."

I sucked up all my hostility, confusion, and heartache and said, "I'd be grateful for anything."

Bridgebane nodded. His whole body abruptly twitched forward, as though he wanted to hug me. I stiffened backward, my eyes widening. He froze, and we stared at each other. He was half my life, six brand-new bags of A1 blood, a chilling threat against Mareeka and Surral, and a bullet in Shade's leg too late for this kind of affection. Didn't he know that?

He dropped his hand and turned to Shade, suddenly asking, "How did you two even meet? It seems unlikely."

"You blew holes in her ship. I'm a mechanic." Shade shrugged. The rest was obvious.

"Of all the cities on all the planets?" Bridgebane said, incredulous.

"It was the Black Widow that decided. After you chased me into a *black hole*," I added.

"I tried to keep you out of it," Bridgebane grated.

"Yes, by 'disabling me,'" I said with sarcastic air quotes. "The patched-up hull of my unarmed cargo cruiser thanks you for that."

"The Black Widow decided…" Shade echoed thoughtfully.

I'd just added light-years of fuel to the engine for him believing in a higher power, hadn't I?

"And you chose Quintessa over the two million units?" Bridgebane asked. "Over the huge bonus you could have had?"

As usual, my full name was a jolt to the system. It burned through me like a meteor shower, leaving craters all over the place.

"Yeah." Shade cocked his head. "I guess I made a better choice than you did."

The curiosity flickering in Bridgebane's expression died, and his face shut down again like an android in need of a recharge. "You used to be effective, Ganavan. For Quintessa's sake, let's hope you still are. And here—" He pulled a small packet from his pocket and tossed it at Shade, who caught it. "That's a new med wipe about to go public. It reduces swelling and heals cuts and contusions. You're drawing attention to my niece. Try not to get trounced next time."

Shade huffed quietly under his breath, turning the package over in his hand. "Thanks?"

My brows slashed down. "Can you ever *not* be a jerk for one second?" I asked my uncle.

Bridgebane met my fuming gaze head-on, his face still washed of expression. "No. I lost that ability when that heartless despot murdered Caitrin, and I was forced to desert you for your own safety."

I stared in shock. I'd never heard him denigrate the Overseer out loud before. And forced? Had he truly wanted to keep me?

My chest clenched so hard it mashed my heart to pieces.

"Yes, I made a choice." Bridgebane spread his hands between us, palms up, and it was the first time I'd ever seen him look even remotely helpless. "You—or everything."

He didn't mean his power or position; I knew that instinctively. He'd retained those, but I thought I finally understood *why* better. That dead look in his eyes wasn't from lack of feeling. It was his default mode now, the countenance of a man used to giving orders and weighing horrible choices against one another, even when innocent lives, his only family, or his own future hung in the balance.

Had it changed him? Yes. Was he happy? No. Did he deserve my sympathy? My understanding? My forgiveness?

My eyes stung, and I bit my lip. Maybe.

Uncle Nate turned and left me—again—stepping onto the fast-moving walkway and leaving his lieutenant and possibly the only person he trusted behind him. With me. Through vision that burned and blurred, I watched him zoom toward the base of the docking tower. He didn't look back at me. But then again, he never had, had he?

I clamped my mouth flat against a tremble that built like an earthquake. Shade gripped my hand, and I held on to him. One last flash of dark hair and broad shoulders was all I got before my uncle disappeared, swallowed by the shadowed entrance of the hive-like building.

A terrible pressure ground down on me. Maybe I wanted that hug after all, now that it was too late, and I might not get another chance.

CHAPTER

8

SHADE

OUR SECOND NIGHT IN THE BUNGALOW WASN'T EXACTLY the evening I'd hoped for. It was anything but, with Lieutenant Mwende tracking us with her dark eyes and pitiless stare while she sharpened her knives on the patio. There wasn't a door to close in the whole damn place except for the bathroom. Our privacy had been annihilated, and if I'd known we were going to pick up an unexpected and pissed-off guest, I'd have requested a place with a different layout.

At least the blood exchange with Bridgebane had gone well. That didn't seem like the right word for it, although it could definitely have gone *worse*. The Overseer would get enhancers out of the deal, but maybe he wouldn't be so determined to go after Tess herself or to launch a galaxy-wide hunt for anyone carrying A1 blood. It felt like a stalling tactic on Bridgebane's part, and the whole thing left Tess in a funk I couldn't shake her out of. She just kept saying, "Mareeka and Surral are safe now. Starway 8's fine. We're fine. He didn't do anything."

Right. Nothing but fuck with Tess's head and saddle us with an unwanted and spitting-mad bodyguard.

Sanaa Mwende made everything uncomfortable, mainly because she didn't want to be stuck with us any more than we wanted to be stuck with her. Tension ran high, but not because we feared betrayal. That didn't seem to be on Bridgebane's shady agenda, and Mwende was an extension of Tess's uncle. We spent the rest of the day in our separate corners, watchful and wary like independent pets abruptly introduced into the same household. I'd seen it with cats. Inevitably, they learned to live together, often becoming friendly.

Somehow, that thought made this new situation feel like it had the potential to last a lot longer than the five days we already knew we were in for.

We ate dinner, listened to the chorus of insects without adding anything to their chirping, and went to bed, Tess and me tamely on one side of the bungalow and the lieutenant on the couch under the netting. Our paradise felt a lot like hell all of a sudden. I barely slept, and when I did, it was with one eye open in case my instincts were wrong about Bridgebane and Mwende.

Things were no different in the morning except that Tess barreled into efficient mode instead of staring off into space anymore. It was time to meet up with the crew again. Tess showered, packed up what little she had, and emptied the complimentary contents of the refrigerator into my cruiser's built-in cooler like she had two jet engines strapped to her back. She was ready to go just after sunrise, and she didn't even like getting up early.

I took one last look around the bungalow, wondering if I'd ever come back to the Aisé Resort, ever watch the muddy river wind through the jungle, see a group of curious ganokos, or hike up to the waterfall where Tess had fumbled through her first swimming lesson. This departure somehow felt more permanent than the last time I'd left here. Maybe that was because I knew my life was going to be different from now on. Then, I hadn't even imagined the unexpected and heartbreaking changes coming my way. At least this time, I'd chosen a direction rather than being blindsided by tragedy and letting everything spiral from there.

I shut the door, leaving the key card inside, and used the outdoor console to pay the final balance. Tess and Mwende waited in the cruiser, ready to go, but my feet dragged. Saying goodbye to the resort felt a little like saying goodbye to my parents. Only that was a goodbye I'd never actually gotten. It just happened. One day they were there. The next, gone.

I took a long, deep breath, let it out slowly, and went to the cruiser. There were *alive* people counting on us.

Four more days until possible intel on Shiori.

Seven days to finalize an operation to try to free the Demeter Terre scientist.

If luck was on our side, we could retrieve both of them at the same time. If it wasn't...

I shook my head. A lot could happen. Plans needed making—the sooner the better, although now it felt like we had to wait for Bridgebane's possible contribution to know how best to move forward.

We took off to join up with the *Endeavor* as the Great Star slanted warm rays of early morning sunshine over the jungle. The wide Gano River cut an unmistakable, winding path across the entire continent, and I watched it until we cleared the different spheres and left the long ribbon of water behind us. Fishing hadn't happened. I didn't show Tess half of what

I wanted to. The *I love you* hovering on the tip of my tongue was still there instead of where it should be, between us.

At least we'd accomplished what we came here to do. That was something.

With open space ahead of us and the coordinates set for just outside of Demeter Terre, I got ready to jump us to Mooncamp 1. Hopefully, the *Endeavor* was already there.

Settling into my seat, I asked, "Everyone strapped in?"

Beside me, Tess nodded. Mwende confirmed that she was ready from her seat just behind me in the back section of the cruiser.

"We're off, then." I pushed the button to engage the hyperdrive engine.

Faster-than-light travel gripped us in its narrow tunnel. Pressure sat on my lungs with the weight of a neutron star. I hated this part. I couldn't breathe. Up was down, down was up, and I just wanted it to be over. My mouth filled with saliva as my insides rose and dropped and tilted. Warp speed affected all but the sturdiest of stomachs, and mine was no exception. Darkness whirled and spun us into a tight, crushing cocoon, but instead of emerging as something else, we suddenly emerged elsewhere.

My navel crashed into my spine as we slowed, the shift leaving me hollowed out and dizzy. For a second, it felt as though we were traveling backward. I slowly exhaled. Blinked and swallowed. Demeter Terre dwarfed the smaller rock beside her. The huge harvest planet and her biggest moon filled most of our clear panel.

I let out a low whistle as my insides settled back into their correct positions. "Damn, that's pretty." Demeter Terre was vibrant, varied, and a giant of a planet with the unmistakable deep blues of vast bodies of water and the fertile greens of

croplands that rolled on forever. Too bad it was contaminated. As for the moon, it looked windswept and covered in
tundra. The two were like night and day, but looks could be
deceiving. One seemed welcoming, but the toxins in the air
would kill you. The other appeared hostile, but apparently,
human beings could breathe there.

"That's going to be a shock to the system after Reaginine,"
I said of the mostly tan and red moon with what appeared to
be large rocky or frozen areas. "No wonder they're starving
here. Those aren't exactly growing conditions."

"They have greenhouses around the Mooncamps," Tess
said. "And pockets of livestock. But it's not enough to feed
all the refugees."

"How many are there?"

"Moons?" she asked. "Six habitable DT moons—they
were terraformed ages ago to house the seasonal workers
who came for the harvests—and six principal Mooncamps."

"And population?" That'd been my actual question,
although I was interested in the rest.

She shrugged. "Maybe five hundred thousand."

I glanced at Demeter Terre again. *Five hundred thousand?*
Of the *millions* that had once inhabited that planet? The
queasiness making my stomach fold in on itself had less to
do with the jump now and more to do with general disgust.
I was a toddler at the time of the DT massacre, but I knew
what happened here. Why had I grown up and lived my life
just accepting it? Why did anyone? Tess hadn't. The fact
that I had—for thirty-two fucking years—suddenly seemed
unconscionable.

I stared at that lost world. Images had been banned to dull
public outrage, but I could still picture the way it went down
that day. The chemical weapons simultaneously detonating

over all four continents. People around the planet gasping for breath, going into convulsions, dying. The thousands of cruisers and ships shooting off DT in a panic with zero supplies and their human cargo often succumbing within minutes to the blood agents.

The poisonous cocktail the Overseer had used was slowly fading from the atmosphere, but it was still toxic enough to prevent repopulation. Still, why six Mooncamps?

"The refugees could consolidate on the largest moon. Wouldn't that be easier to manage?" I asked.

"Farmers were kings down there." Tess nodded to the big blue and green planet. Anger hardened her expression. "They already knew what happened to all the eggs in one basket. Then, they got to live it."

"It's been a generation since the Overseer attacked. My entire lifetime. Why don't they leave? Go somewhere more hospitable? Any number of planets could absorb that few people, even if they all wanted to stay together."

"A generation?" Tess's cutting laugh chilled the whole front section of the cruiser. "It doesn't matter if it's been *ten* generations. That's their home, and they want it back. You of all people should understand fighting for something you've lost."

My lower jaw jutted out. Yeah, I got that. Got it in spades, in fact.

"And where do you think most of that new generation's ended up?" she asked. "Wait—" She leaned forward to inspect the console, found the button that closed the door between the front and back portions of the cruiser, and pushed it. In my side monitor, I saw Sanaa Mwende throw the newly sealed divider between us and her a dirty look.

Tess glanced over her shoulder to make sure she'd closed us off from Mwende. "A lot of them are in the Fold, working to further the rebellion. Or they're part of crews, running missions for the rebel leaders. Or they're Nightchasers, like us. Don't picture the DT Mooncampers like a bunch of lazy birds waiting with open beaks for us to fly by and drop food down their throats."

I scrubbed a hand over my jaw, nodding. I was more curious by the minute to see Mooncamp 1 for myself. "Since we've got a moment without the lieutenant listening in, what are we going to do with her?"

"Lock her up," Tess said.

"The brig?" I asked.

She pursed her lips. "No need for that. I can reprogram the door to Miko and Shiori's room so that it only opens from the outside."

"She won't like it. Or go quietly," I added.

Tess smiled at me, a glint in her eyes I hadn't seen since our hike in the jungle. "I'm counting on Merrick to overpower her."

"Now there's a confrontation I'd like to see. I doubt Mwende's a graceful loser."

Tess grinned. "She's going to hate it. I can't wait."

Mwende banged on the door between us.

Tess laughed. "Honestly, though, she's growing on me."

"She's very direct."

"Understatement," Tess said heartily. She reached forward and opened the door panel again.

Mwende poked her head into the front. "Are we establishing orbit or actually going down there?" she asked with a scowl.

"Sorry, Sanaa." Tess glanced at me, her lower lip caught between her teeth as she smiled. "Okay. Let's find the *Endeavor*."

"Can you make contact with Mooncamp 1?" I asked my copilot. Tess would know what frequency to look for.

She reached for the com unit. "You think they're here already?"

I angled us toward the moon hovering at the edge of our clear panel. "We know they escaped Korabon. That was the hardest part. Their only goal after that was to stay under the radar, recharge, and get here."

"Yeah. No reason to think they'd run into trouble." She fiddled with the dials and then said in surprise, "This is brand new. The only history in here is the reservation service on Reaginine."

"I took out my old com after finding you on Starway 8 and installed this one when we were in the"—shit, Mwende was listening—"you know where." The Fold was one hell of a place. I'd had no idea of the extent and organization of rebel operations until Tess had taken me to their secret hideaway. And by secret, I meant an alternate dimension or something. Wherever the Fold was, it wasn't *here* exactly.

"Where's the old one?" she asked.

"Garbage compacted and floated, somewhere in the Outer Zones." Once Tess had taken me aboard the *Endeavor*, there'd been no way I was attracting unwanted company from a contact list that was a mile long and short on integrity.

"Smart. Although compacting *and* floating might have been overkill," she teased as she sent the new device on a search for nearby open channels. Several popped up immediately, but she waited for the list to expand, half her face lit in blue from the control panel and the other half in shadow. She was so intent and beautiful that my heart pulsed with a quick spasm.

"Do you have any contacts here?" I asked.

"Several. This is one of our places. Kind of like home." She smiled at me.

I smiled back, but the idea of *home* knotted in my chest, tying an ache into it.

"Got it!" DT MOONCAMP 1—OPEN CHANNEL scrolled across the small square screen in green block letters. Tess selected the frequency. "Mooncamp 1, this is..." She looked at me in question.

"*Queen Bee.*"

She grinned at the name I'd just given my cruiser. I shrugged, a smile tugging at my lips. I'd never bothered to name my transportation before, but Star Cruiser Model R16 seemed too boring now that Tess was on board. She loved Starway 8, and everyone knew the orphanage was famous for its rare apiary and honey making.

"...the *Queen Bee*, requesting information."

"Mooncamp 1, here," a male voice answered within seconds. "How can we help you, *Queen Bee*?"

"This is Captain Tess Bailey coming in to meet the *Endeavor*. Is she around here somewhere?"

A faint note of tension underscored Tess's words. With each second that ticked by, my gut tightened.

"The *Endeavor*'s in hangar 9, Captain Bailey. She has quite the load for us. We're grateful."

Relief and joy blazed across Tess's expression, so brilliant it put the stars to shame. "Happy to help our DT friends. We'll be there in a moment. Our transportation is a small personal star cruiser. Model..."—she checked the badge above the passenger-side window panel—"R16. There are three of us on it."

"Copy that. I've already got you on our scanner. You

know your way in. Welcome back, Captain Bailey." The line went silent.

"See? They're fine." I reached over and squeezed Tess's leg. "Nothing to worry about."

Smiling, she turned off the com unit. "You got them out, thanks to those incendio charges and this ship's firepower."

"Merrick's kitchen-door stunt helped." The moon got bigger as Demeter Terre slid out of view behind us. "And I have things to make up for. Things I'm sorry about."

Tess sat back stiffly, staring out the window. "Is that why you're here, Shade? Guilt?"

"There's guilt," I admitted, worried about the sudden change in her posture. "Shouldn't there be?"

"I guess so. But it shouldn't dictate"—she looked around, as if searching for the right words out in space somewhere—"life decisions."

"And what should?" I asked.

"I don't know." She shrugged.

I was pretty sure she *did* know.

"What you care about?" she finally suggested.

I stared at her. So this was what a bullet to the heart felt like. It fucking hurt. "If I didn't care, starshine, I wouldn't be here. And guilt wouldn't be an issue."

She nodded without looking at me.

"I *am* sorry, Tess. I'm sorry for deceiving you. For putting you in danger. For leading you to believe I wasn't a threat to you and your crew."

"You weren't, though." She frowned suddenly.

"Oh, I could've been." And just the idea of it made me sick. "But I'll do whatever it takes to make it up to you. And to them. I promise you that."

I wanted to say more, something more powerful, but I

wasn't about to spill my guts with Mwende in the back, listening. If we'd been alone, I'd have let the cruiser float in low orbit while I showed Tess exactly how much I cared about her and we experimented with how tangled up two people could get in small spaces. As it was, the lieutenant impatiently drummed her fingers against the back of my seat, annoying the shit out of me.

Putting a lid on my frustration, I reached for the navigation controls. "How about some directions to this Mooncamp of yours, Captain Bailey?"

Leaping on the change of subject, Tess rattled off a set of coordinates she'd probably memorized a long time ago. I programmed them into my system, grateful to have something useful to do with my hands. It helped dilute the awkwardness.

"That'll bring us to the hangars," Tess said as I put us on autopilot. "It's where visiting cargo ships come in, but the food will be distributed to different storehouses."

"And how does that happen?" I asked. We started to rattle. The star cruiser's sleek design offset a lot of the bumps and jolts of atmospheric entry, but it wasn't perfect or silent.

Tess gripped her armrests and spoke louder. "They'll send a big crew with hover crates and some transport vessels to help us. Probably tomorrow—the time to organize a distribution map. Jax will have given them our inventory, and the head food coordinator—Raz Romo—will decide where things need to go, depending on how current supplies look in each depot and around the six Mooncamps."

"Eggs in different baskets?"

She nodded. "You got it."

The cruiser settled as we dropped in altitude. There was nothing in sight besides endless rolling tundra. I punched up the power to get us to our coordinates faster. Soon, a sprawling community of low, boxlike structures set out in a grid pattern appeared on the horizon. Mooncamp 1 was a refugee city, through and through. Gray. Metallic. Flat. A few scraggly trees. I had no clue where their water supply was coming from. Underground, maybe. Nothing looked permanent. No edifice appeared higher than four or five stories, and a strong wind or the thumping gust from a low-flying cargo cruiser's engine could probably blow the roofs off half these buildings.

A chill crept down my arms and back, raising gooseflesh. This place looked miserable and downtrodden, but for some reason, I got a wholly different impression. *Resist* was practically written in blood-red letters down every single dust-blown alley and mixed into the rust staining the corrugated rooftops.

"No one's planning on staying here, are they?" The DT refugees weren't turning the moon into a home. They hadn't accepted their new reality. They weren't working with it as best they could. They were waiting.

"The air on Demeter Terre will eventually clean itself out. Then they'll go back and start over."

Which could happen a lot faster if Reena Ahern found the right combination of chemicals to counteract the poisons.

"The Outer Zones will have their breadbasket back," Tess said. "It's just a question of when now."

And wouldn't that be galvanizing? The two Sectors most known for resisting imperial rule repopulating? Maybe even thriving again? Posing a threat to the Overseer? We weren't in the middle of a long and bloody war anymore. In fact, Simon Novalight loved to brag about the "peace" he'd created for us, the prosperity we shared thanks to him. Would the galaxy really stand for another massacre? I wasn't so sure—and maybe the Overseer wouldn't be sure, either. Maybe it would finally be his turn to tread carefully. A man couldn't both brag of peace and kill indiscriminately.

I looked over at Tess. "Let's get her."

Her blue eyes ignited with the kind of fire that led whole worlds to victory. She knew I meant Reena Ahern.

As we closed in on the hangars and slowed, I reached over and gripped her hand. "Thank you."

"For what?" she asked, a startled lilt in her voice.

"For giving me a second chance." I squeezed her hand, and she squeezed back. It was more than just a second chance for us, though. I could live with myself again, and that was the greatest gift anyone had ever given me.

CHAPTER

9

TESS

I JUMPED OUT OF THE CRUISER THE SECOND SHADE
finished powering down. The big starboard door of the
Endeavor was open, airing out the ship. The crew must have
heard us coming, and Jax, Fiona, and Merrick all vaulted out
to meet us.

For a second, I couldn't breathe. Seeing everyone safe and
sound was like a punch to the gut, too visceral for anything
other than pain, even if my brain was sending me all happy
signals. The sight of Jax—intact, smiling, there like he should
be—kind of crossed my wires. All I felt was *zap, zap, zap*
inside me, a heart that faltered, and lungs that wouldn't fill
with oxygen. I ran to him.

Jax sprinted and met me halfway across the private
hangar. I launched myself at him, and he caught me in a hug
that crushed me in more ways than one. I crushed him back
just as fiercely.

"Thank the Powers," he choked out. "You're safe."

I squeezed him with all my might, shaking from the effort.

No, just shaking. I buried my face in his shoulder. *I* knew they'd made it off Korabon and away from the Dark Watch, but Jax hadn't been sure of the same thing of me, had he?

"I'm fine, partner," I whispered, although I didn't really sound it. I had a terrible time letting go of him. We didn't hug often, but we weren't usually separated, either. My shuddering breath told me I wasn't okay yet. Jax stepped back to get a better look at me. He touched my cheek, and I nearly lost it.

Jax abruptly turned from me, sucking down a huge breath. My eyes smarted, and I swallowed. Fiona moved in and linked arms with me. Our hips bumped, which was the closest we'd ever come to hugging. That was fine with me. I knew she loved me.

Smiling broadly, Merrick joined us halfway to Shade's cruiser. "Welcome back, Captain."

"Thanks, Big Guy." I grinned, immensely glad to have the rebel super soldier as our newest crewmember. He came with experience, strength that wasn't just physical, and a good head on his shoulders, not to mention an even temperament that had kept me steady more than once already. "You fix my kitchen door yet?"

He chuckled, the sound as rich and deep as unexplored corners of the galaxy. "I'm working on it."

Feet hit the gritty floor of the hangar behind me. I turned, and Merrick's gaze lifted, lighting on Shade and Sanaa Mwende as they exited the cruiser. I nodded in their direction.

"Do you recognize her?" I asked.

Merrick shook his head. He wasn't totally bald anymore after having shaved off the shaggy hair and neglected beard he'd gained during his months in captivity. His clean-shaven jaw cut a hard, precise line now, but a short layer of thick black hair covered his scalp again. "Never seen her before," he said.

Neither had Shade, despite his various dealings with Bridgebane, which meant that Sanaa either wasn't always with the Dark Watch general, or she knew how to keep a watchful distance.

Fiona hung back with me while Jax and Merrick went to help Shade with the fresh food I'd taken from the resort refrigerator. Sanaa offered a hand as well, surprising me.

"I brought you strawberries," I said.

Fiona's whole face slackened, melting into something practically orgasmic. "Tess. My hero. Seriously, that'll be the most pleasure I've had that wasn't self-induced in five years and counting. I could kiss you right now."

My mouth twitched. "Shade might object."

She shook her head, the dark ends of her ponytail dancing across her shoulders. "Are you kidding? In my experience, men are hot for women kissing."

"But neither you nor I are hot for women," I pointed out.

"Well, there is that," she agreed. "Speaking of men, Jax is always a nervous wreck when you're out of his sight, but this time, he was about two nail bites away from a total breakdown."

I looked over at Jax, my heart pinching. He was a part of my skeleton, helping to hold me upright and together. I had other bones, though. Starway 8 and Mareeka and Surral. Shade. Fiona. Coltin. I hoped Shiori, and even Merrick now.

"I wish he'd let someone else in enough to..." I trailed off, not sure what I really wanted to say. It wasn't a burden to me to be Jax's anchor, but if something happened to me, it would be like the DT massacre—all his eggs in one basket.

Except he already loved other people and had a family

that loved him back. He just wouldn't admit it, especially his attachment to Fiona, because admitting it made it real enough to break him if something terrible happened, like it had to Miko and Shiori.

"It's his dead wife he wants, even seven years later." Fiona's moss-green eyes deadened like her tone. Hearing her sound so dejected jarred a frown from me. She was a fighter, through and through.

"I don't believe that for a second. He wants you. He's just too scared of losing the people he loves again to admit he loves anyone."

She sighed. "We all know he loves you."

"It's different. I'm like his sister." The sister he'd lost also, along with his wife and children. The Dark Watch had only spared him to torture him with loss, grief, and prison. "But that's not what he needs. He's a man in his prime. He needs a partner."

Fiona snorted softly. "Try telling him that."

"Maybe I will." Maybe I should have a long time ago, instead of indulging him in his need to pine for things that were gone forever.

I watched the man in question walk back toward us with a set of coolers in his hands. Big, sturdy, strong, fucked-up Jax. He was everyone else's rock, even though he was a landslide waiting to happen.

What would be less destructive in the end? Setting him off and clearing the terrain? Or trying to shore him up and keep the dam from breaking?

"I guess there are no secrets between us." Fiona dragged her eyes from Jax to look at me again.

If only that were true. Six bags of A1 blood in Bridgebane's hands right now proved otherwise. But she was talking about her feelings for Jax—a subject we'd broached aloud exactly once: right now. "He saved your life. He ran through an actual hail of bullets for you—a total stranger to him at the time. What woman wouldn't fall for that?"

"It was actually after. Or maybe it started then. I'm not sure." She shrugged. "I must like the tortured, unattainable type."

I squeezed our linked arms and bumped her hip again. The others were almost within earshot, so I lowered my voice. "I think you like the kind, capable, desperately-needs-you type."

Her eyes brimmed with tears. She slammed her lids shut. "Shit. What's wrong with me?"

I stared at her in shock. Fiona. Did. Not. Cry.

She turned, hiding her face, and I jumped forward to intercept the others. I said something inane to Shade, which I didn't remember two seconds later, and then dove into Jax's cooler to slow him down. I rummaged for a food I recognized. "Oh! Melon! Excellent!" Triumphant, I held up the green and yellow ball as though it contained the keys to the universe.

Everyone looked at me as if I'd lost my marbles. Fiona cracked up behind me, which was all I needed. My mission accomplished, I slipped the hard-coated fruit back into Jax's container, careful not to bruise it.

Once they got over my fruitastic outburst, the group's attention inevitably turned to the stranger among us. Whisking out a hand, I introduced the tall, sure-footed woman carrying the final stash of complimentary goodies from the bungalow. "This is Sanaa Mwende. She's General Bridgebane's personal bodyguard."

Jax whirled on Sanaa with a scowl. "What the hell is she doing here?"

"How did this happen?" Fiona's question was more reasonable, although her eyes shot daggers that would rival the lieutenant's hidden arsenal.

Merrick set down his food cargo, instantly fighting ready.

"We ended up on Reaginine and ran into my uncle." We'd already warned Sanaa that the crew didn't know about the blood exchange. They only knew that Bridgebane hadn't harmed me on Starway 8 and that he seemed to want to protect me from the Overseer. "It went surprisingly well, all things considered."

Protests erupted, almost deafening as they echoed around the hangar only we occupied. I held up a hand for quiet. "Not only did he agree to drop the bounty on Shade, but he's trying to get us information about Shiori."

Jax whirled on me now, his eyes widening. "Where is she?"

"Starbase 12." The significance wouldn't be lost on any of them. Reena Ahern. Shiori. We had two prisoners in one location.

"Is she okay?" Fiona asked.

"He didn't indicate that anyone had harmed her." She'd harmed herself. I just couldn't bring myself to say it.

Fiona's eyes zeroed in on Shade's bruises. "If it went so well with Bridgebane, what happened to your face?" The med wipe had cleared up a lot of the damage, but it was no miracle sick-bay laser.

"It ran into a bounty hunter's fist." Shade lightly touched the still darkened skin beneath his left eye. The swelling was a quarter of what it had been. "The other guy looks worse."

Jax looked more freaked out by the second. He eyed Sanaa suspiciously. "But you just said he dropped the bounty. What happened?"

"Ambush," Shade answered. "And then Tess found a way for two shitheads to leave us alone forever."

"Did you kill them?" Fiona asked me.

"What? No." I frowned, taken aback. "Not necessary." She and I had different viewpoints when it came to fighting off enemies. My conscience wouldn't stop me from killing if it was the only way to defend myself or the people I cared about, but I couldn't do it with unapologetic flair like Fiona did. "We gave them something they needed in exchange for them forgetting all about us."

"Something they needed?" Merrick questioned, scrutinizing Sanaa as though she were a ticking bomb he might need to defuse in a hurry.

Sanaa lifted her brows, meeting his mistrustful inspection head-on. Merrick's eyes narrowed.

"A special newfangled 'cure-all' for their dying daughter," I answered.

Everyone knew that was code language for my blood, although there wasn't a single person here who didn't already know about my A1 anomalies.

"Since my uncle is suddenly all about helping me—he covered our butts on Korabon, by the way, and passed that whole battle off as a surprise training exercise—he decided to get over Shade betraying him to protect me and dropped the ridiculously huge bounty. Now, his hunters can go after some other prize, and we can concentrate on what we need to do." In other words: breaking into the most secure location in the galaxy.

Fiona swung a probing look at me before her focus shifted to Sanaa, whose ability to remain expressionless when she chose to almost rivaled my uncle's. "Did he erase footage? That Red Beam caught all our faces."

"I think so." I glanced at the person who would know for sure. "Sanaa?"

She nodded in confirmation.

"Why would he give you information on Shiori?" Merrick asked, seeming more skeptical of my uncle's motives than of the actual intel he'd provided.

It was a reasonable question, and perfectly reasonable to doubt. "Because I asked him to."

Merrick shook his head, his dark eyes hardening. "That's too simple. It makes no sense. Even if he helped you a few times, why would you believe anything he says?" He glared at Sanaa, clearly lumping her into the untrustworthy category.

I didn't take his hesitation lightly. I understood it all too well, in fact. But when I reached deep down, examining both my heart and my mind as well as my gut instinct, everything in me clamored that there was a lot more to my uncle than I'd wanted to believe in a very long time. That growing conviction made me speak freely in front of Sanaa.

"I don't think Uncle Nate is loyal to the Overseer. I think he's been walking a tightrope for years, making choices that no one should ever have to face." Emotion and a good bit of hesitation roughened my voice. Was I really ready to shift my thinking *this* drastically? "I'm starting to think he might be the only thing standing between a madman and the entire galaxy."

"Finally, Daraja sees." Sanaa Mwende looked at me in satisfaction, dropping the impassive mask to look smugly pleased.

"Yes, well, unfortunately for you, you won't have the pleasure of pinning my eyelids back," I said dryly.

She grinned, displaying a row of even white teeth except for one eyetooth that twisted a little.

"None of this explains her presence." Jax looked at Sanaa, still wary but less hostile.

I'd been dreading this moment and now felt slightly headachy after a fitful night's sleep and the accumulation of enough confusion, anxiety, and heartache to almost rival Jax's emotional baggage. "If Bridgebane gets any info that might help us retrieve Shiori, he's going to leave it in a secure location four days from now. He wouldn't tell me where. Sanaa's supposed to take me there."

"Over my dead body," Jax growled, clearly thunderstruck by the sheer what-the-fuckery. "Just *let* the Dark Watch soldier lead you to some unknown location? We'll never see you again!"

"No." I shook my head. "I honestly don't believe that."

Jax snorted, turning to Shade. "Do you?"

"My opinion's not good enough for you anymore, Jax?" I jumped in before Shade could answer.

"Your judgment is clouded," Jax shot back, rounding on me again. "You want your family back so badly, you'll believe anything."

"I don't want my old family back, Jax. You're the one who wants his family back so badly that you can't see you've already got one!"

Brick by brick, his expression walled up and stoned over. *Shit*. I rubbed my forehead.

"We'll do it together, okay? All of us," I offered.

Sanaa looked dubious. "I'm not sure you'll want that." She gave me a significant look I had no idea how to interpret.

"You're not helping," I ground out.

She shrugged. "Your choice, Daraja."

"What does that even mean?" I asked through clenched teeth.

"Bridge," she answered, not expanding on it.

Well, that clears things right up. I shoved my hair back in frustration.

Movement out of the corner of my eye caught my attention. Bonk emerged from inside the *Endeavor*, sashaying right through the tension by delicately picking his way across the grated metal flooring of the starboard air lock. I let out a noise that might have been a squeal and leaped over to the entrance, a huge smile on my face and my heartbeat notching up a level. His small black-and-gray-striped body rippled with each step he took toward the open doorway. Joy twisted in my chest, and I felt all wrung out with happiness. "Hey, kitty."

He stopped and sat halfway between the two open doors. His tail curled around him.

I called to him, grinning, my arms outstretched. I couldn't quite reach him. "Come on, Bonk. Come closer."

His chin lifted, showing off the white fluff on the underside of his neck. Greenish-yellow eyes stared at me, unblinking.

"What's wrong with him?" I felt dangerously close to bursting into tears, which was insane. I'd been elated two seconds ago. "Has he forgotten me?"

"In three days?" Shade shook his head. "Unlikely. But hell hath no fury like a feline abandoned."

Bonk looked down his whiskers at me. "I didn't abandon you," I told him.

"He'll realize that soon." Shade came over but didn't try to pat Bonk like I had. "He's expressing his ire. By tonight, he'll be sprawled across your pillow, purring his little heart out."

"His ire?" How did Shade know so much about cats?

"He's pissed off because he didn't know where you were. He'll get over it. Cat grudges don't last long."

"How do you know that?"

"My family had a pair of cats. Halley and Comet. I grew up with them."

"Halley and Comet?" I couldn't help smiling. I lowered my hands from the open doorway. As much as I wanted to cuddle Bonk and feel his little engine rev up with purring, my temperamental tabby could get over his kitty tantrum while I dealt with Sanaa Mwende.

I turned back to the lieutenant, sighing. "You do realize that I'm going to have to confine you for the next four days, right? Don't take it personally. It's just a precaution."

Sanaa cocked her head to one side. It was her only reaction.

"We have a room for you," I said. "You'll have everything you need. Food, clothing, etcetera. Then you'll be free to go after you bring us to wherever that key card my uncle gave you opens."

"I decline captivity. Thank you." Sanaa smiled curtly, as if a little forced politeness ended the discussion.

I grimaced. She wasn't getting it. "I'm not giving you the choice. We have plans to make, and prying eyes and ears can't be around for those conversations."

Her eyes narrowed. "I'm not a spy."

"Whether you are or aren't is irrelevant. I'm not risking it."

"Then make me." Her sliding-note accent resonated with challenge and even a hint of humor, which seemed odd, considering the situation. She set down the resort food she was still carrying and moved away from the group until there was more free space around her. She shifted into a fighter's stance, her fingers curling to coax me toward her. Her lips curled also. Definitely a smile. "If you can lock me up, I'll stay there. If not, we work together to plan whatever is in your future, Daraja."

My brows flew up like rockets. "Me? No thanks. You must think I downed a stupid pill this morning. Merrick can do the honors."

Merrick grinned and cracked his knuckles. "How rough are we getting?"

Sanaa laughed as if Merrick had just told a great joke and she loved it. "Rough doesn't bother me." She blew a kiss at Merrick.

His eyes flared. A flush wasn't visible on his dark skin, but I could have sworn his color heightened. He stalked forward, not smiling any longer.

We gathered the food and coolers and backed up against the *Endeavor*, clearing the space around them. As they faced off, I started to have second thoughts about this. It was only for four days. Couldn't we just avoid her?

"Seriously, Sanaa, we don't want to hurt you." I tried again to reason with her. She was clearly capable—a total badass, to be honest—but Merrick was a super soldier. "Just go to a room on the ship. In a few days, we'll take care of business, and you can go back to my uncle. End of story."

Sanaa Mwende's mirthless chuckle skimmed toward me on a chilly air current, raising goose bumps. She and Merrick started to circle. "Your uncle wants me to protect you. Until he calls me back to him, I'm your bodyguard. Deal with it."

"I don't need a bodyguard. Also, you don't have to do what he tells you."

"No, I don't *have* to." Her night-sky eyes briefly scraped

over me before jumping back to Merrick. "And that's exactly why I listen to him."

I let that sink in. Absorbed it. She listened because Nathaniel Bridgebane wasn't a tyrant like the Overseer, no matter what I'd believed for the last eighteen years. The relationship between Sanaa and Uncle Nate wasn't at all what I would have expected from the hardened general or this woman, who clearly didn't take shit from anyone.

Merrick lunged first and Sanaa dodged with incredible speed. My eyes sharpened, and I stood up straighter. So did Shade. We glanced at each other.

"You need all the help you can get, Daraja. Accept it gracefully." Sanaa danced out of Merrick's reach with an ease that left him frowning.

I took a step forward, my senses prickling.

Merrick studied his opponent more carefully, looking her over with dark-eyed concentration. After a lull that brought total silence to the hangar, he feinted so quickly I barely saw the movement, and then slid the other way just as fast, trying to catch Sanaa off guard and subdue her without violence. Sanaa avoided him neatly and delivered a spinning kick that knocked Merrick away from her.

My jaw slowly dropped open. Merrick recovered, moved in fast, and got down to business.

He jabbed. She blocked. He punched forward like a boxer and she slid, ducked, and countered like a ninja, finishing with an open-handed smack to the sternum that left Merrick gasping.

"Don't leave yourself open like that," Sanaa barked with a scowl, treating Merrick as though he were in training at some Dark Watch boot camp she was running. "Your throat was wide open. The same hit there, and you'd be dead." She tapped the front of her neck, her eyes flashing.

Merrick drew a tight breath through pinched nostrils. "What batch did they give you? I couldn't tell until you started moving. An upgrade? Something different?"

It was obvious: Sanaa Mwende was a super soldier. Shade, Jax, Fiona, and I exchanged worried glances.

Merrick charged in a blur, not waiting for her answer. In a blink, Sanaa got behind him. She kicked him in the small of the back, and he stumbled forward. Merrick turned with a growl, his jaw clenching.

She smiled, her ebony skin gleaming under the long tracks of industrial overhead lighting. Strength and vitality infused her. Sanaa had just powered herself up like a weapon and vibrated with enough energy to annihilate things. Her grin widened. "I've missed sparring. I don't get to play with the super soldiers, and everyone else just breaks too easily."

"We're not sparring," Merrick grated.

"Oh yes, we are, darling." She winked at him and looked Merrick up and down, both appraisal and appreciation in her sparkling-eyed perusal. "You're fast. You're big."

"Don't forget strong." He shot out a hand and gripped her forearm. One hard yank sent her airborne and fifteen feet across the hangar.

Sanaa spun in the air and landed in a low crouch, her smile only growing. "You must have Batch 4—the finished product. Trial 3 made people angry. Trial 2 created deformities. Trial 1 simply killed you."

"Then what are you?" Merrick asked, jerking his chin at her.

"I'm the one and only." Rising, she swept a hand down her bowstring-tight body. "No great height or bulging muscles, but I'm the weapon of our century."

"And this is supposed to make us trust you?" Merrick began circling again, closing in slowly. "You're a spy, the enemy, and a menace."

"I'm none of those things—unless you try to cage me." She pounced and Merrick barely got out of the way. She clipped his jaw with her elbow. His teeth clacked together.

They both started to get a look in their eyes that I recognized from situations I'd been lucky to get out of. Blood running high. Adrenaline pumping. It was a recipe for real injury.

"All right, that's enough," I said sharply. "We don't need this. We'll find another solution."

Suddenly, arms blurred, bodies spun, grunts came from everywhere, and the thud of hard hits echoed around the concrete and metal hangar. Merrick's head snapped to the side, blood spraying. It took a second for his eyes to focus, but it was still faster than Sanaa expected. The two of them collided like meteors, and Sanaa went flying. She landed hard on her back and slid across the floor, her hands squeaking on the gray painted surface. She dragged herself to a stop, flat on her back, her head raised. Merrick stalked toward her.

"Had enough?" he asked, looming over her.

She grinned. "Darling, this is just the foreplay." Rocket fast, she rolled onto her side, kicked him, and popped back up in one smooth motion.

Merrick folded in on the hip she'd just hammered. Sanaa swept his legs out from under him, and he hit the floor with a smack of skin that sounded painful. His arm lashed out, and he somehow dragged her down with him. They grappled. Sanaa came out on top, straddling him. Her powerful legs hugged his torso in a vise grip, and she jammed her forearm under his jaw, forcing his head back. "Just so you know, this is my favorite position."

Merrick's eyes blazed, and his lips pulled back in a snarl. He grabbed her hips and heaved her off him, tossing her headfirst over his shoulders. Sanaa tucked and rolled, coming up on her feet again. He leaped up. She spun, ready.

Kicks, blocks, punches, parries. Merrick's cross whistled through the air next to her head, missing by inches. He let out a grunt of frustration. Gliding back, Sanaa produced a knife, waved it around, and flung it aside. Merrick watched her cheerfully taunt him, his expression stony.

"Oh look! Here's another." She threw a second blade aside. Then a third. Then a fourth. *Where's she hiding all those?* "You would be dead by now if I wanted to kill you."

"Why don't you two just arm-wrestle and be done with it?" Fiona called out.

Jax stifled a laugh. I gave them both the stink eye, but something about watching Merrick and Sanaa go at each other without any real malice was oddly electrifying and almost arousing. I glanced at Shade, wondering if he was feeling the same heightened…*something*.

He gave me a knowing look. A hot smirk and a half wink that made my belly do a pleasant little flip-flop. Warmth stole over me.

Sanaa strode toward the *Endeavor*, de facto ending the contest before Merrick lost a tooth, an eye, his pride, or worse. Not a hair of her tight bun was out of place. There wasn't a scratch on her. And no bruising that I could see, although her dark skin might hide it. "I prefer my meals in the kitchen. Thank you for your hospitality."

"I prefer my meals without the Dark Watch," Merrick muttered, glowering at Sanaa as she passed him.

She tossed him a grin over her shoulder. "Darling, I'm many things. The Dark Watch is only one of them."

She hopped aboard the *Endeavor* as though she hadn't just brawled with a super soldier, crouched briefly to scratch the soft fur under Bonk's chin—*and he let her*—and then moved deeper into the ship. To poke around, presumably. Good thing I had nothing to hide. She already knew more about me than I did.

"Bring my knives, will you?" Sanaa called from around the corner.

I huffed, looking at my crew and taking in Merrick's sparking-mad eyes and split lip in the process. "Well, I guess that's settled."

Shade's low laugh followed me up into the *Endeavor*.

CHAPTER

10

SHADE

WE'D JUST FINISHED DINNER WHEN A HELL OF A RACKET kicked up at the entrance of the *Endeavor*. The starboard side was still wide open, along with all the interior doors, even though hangar air on Mooncamp 1 didn't seem any better than the ship's recycled oxygen. The shouts and pounding reached us in the kitchen and sent Bonk running for cover only a few minutes after he'd finally deigned to hop into Tess's lap. He took off like a gray streak, leaving her hand suspended in mid-pat.

She frowned after her cat but didn't seem worried about the hullabaloo coming down the hallway.

"What's this pile of nuts and bolts doing in my hangar?" a male voice called out.

"I knew it." Tess smiled. "That's Frank—or I'll eat everyone's disgusting leftovers."

"No bet." Jax shook his head and pushed his half-eaten plate of food away from him. "You'll win and make us do something awful."

I wasn't sure what could be more awful than that dinner. I'd had some revolting meals lately, but this one topped the list. The Mooncamp's head food coordinator, Raz Romo, had stopped by earlier with some kind of meat slop in unmarked cans with no expiration date. The small guy with a buzz cut and glasses didn't even blink at providing such dubious food for the *Endeavor*'s welcome-and-thanks-for-feeding-us dinner, and the crew of the *Endeavor* didn't even blink at accepting it. At least fresh bread and ripe fruit from the Aisé Resort had helped wash down the stomach acid the meal had churned up.

"Bailey!" the man at the entrance shouted. "I'm coming for you, you tall drink of water."

Tess snorted. "Definitely Frank."

Enthusiastic drumming echoed down the corridors along with more hoots and hollering.

Fiona got up first, grinning. She left the kitchen and half jogged toward the racket, her high ponytail swinging. We followed, our boots adding to the thumping that reverberated throughout the ship. A group of two men and three women stood just below us outside the starboard doorway. Fiona squealed and threw herself out at them with zero hesitation. The man at the front caught her and swung her around, laughing. He gave her a loud, smacking kiss on the lips before setting her down next to him and keeping one arm around her.

My focus automatically shifted to Jax. A now-familiar walled-off expression rose to mask whatever he was feeling, but there was no concealing the steel rod that replaced his spine or how stiff his shoulders looked. He'd never said a word to me about Fiona, but some things were obvious. He'd completely shut down when she'd been injured—no sleep, no food, that blank look giving away whatever he thought he was hiding. I didn't know what he was waiting for. If he didn't get his head in the game soon, she might find another player for herself.

Fiona pulled away from the tall blond guy with a laugh. He was undeniably good-looking, about thirty-five with fair coloring and electric blue eyes. She turned to the others with a big smile.

"Asher!" Fiona opened her arms. The second man shuffled forward and engulfed her in a hug that was as stout as he was. She disappeared for a couple of seconds before emerging again, flushed with happiness.

She hugged two of the women at once next—twins with the same light-brown hair and eyes, medium height, and sharp, angular features. They all bounced a little before launching into a secret handshake. It was the kind of thing kids do behind buildings before getting into trouble. Fiona looked different, genuinely lighter. A part of her was so often on edge, like a pot ready to boil over. I had a feeling a lot of that simmering was due to Jax—who did his own fair share of stewing.

Fiona turned to the third woman. "Nic! When did you join Frank's crew? I thought you were taking it easy for a while."

The final crewmember, Nic, smiled and hugged Fiona. She was striking and tall, with high, pronounced cheekbones, a wide mouth, straight black hair, brown skin, hazel eyes, and a jaw that was squarer than most. Her voice came out low and gravelly, hinting at damaged vocal cords. "About three universal months ago. Taking it easy got boring. Too much air traffic controlling and not enough blowing shit up and stealing."

"We've had plenty of that lately," Fiona said wryly.

"Then we'll follow you guys around for some action." Nic's face brightened, but her rusty-gear words triggered a shot of adrenaline inside me.

I tensed and looked at Tess. We were headed to Starbase 12. I sure as hell hoped they wouldn't follow us.

Tess grinned and didn't look worried. "*Your* hangar, Frank?" She hopped down from the *Endeavor* and tossed a light play punch into the blond guy's shoulder. She didn't give hugs, and no one seemed to expect it. She moved toward the stockier, brown-haired Asher, though, and gave him a special smile I couldn't interpret. He smiled back, his ruddy cheeks dimpling.

Jax, Merrick, Mwende, and I exited the ship after her. Jax offered handshakes and a wide but slightly strained smile, especially when it fell on the strapping captain.

Frank looked us over and then peered into the open, empty doorway of the *Endeavor*. He frowned, asking softly, "What happened to your crew, Bailey?"

Tess glanced down. It took her a second to answer. "Miko got hit. A bullet. She's gone. Shiori was captured. The Dark Watch has her."

Frank paled, his eyes widening. "I'm so sorry. Shit, I'm sorry." His hand moved to his chest, pressing like it hurt suddenly.

His crew echoed him. Every single one of them looked sick, shocked, and saddened. One of the twins took a shuddering breath. Asher sniffled.

Tess swallowed hard, squared her shoulders, and introduced us. "This is Shade: navigator and mechanic. Merrick Maddox: hard-core rebel and all-around badass. And this is Sanaa." Tess hesitated. "Personal security expert."

Tess hadn't outed Mwende, which meant she'd just given us all the signal to treat the lieutenant like anyone else here, like a rebel Nightchaser.

We all did some nodding and mumbling that felt pretty generic before Tess launched into the remaining introductions.

"This is Frank, Asher, Macey, Caeryssa, and Nic of the *Unholy Stench*."

My brows shot up. "You named your ship that?"

Frank nodded, humor glinting in his eyes again. "I named her after the state of the galaxy. If we ever get rid of the stink, I'll rename her."

I smiled, relaxing. Tess seemed comfortable with these people, and I trusted her judgment. "Sounds fair," I answered.

Asher turned to Tess. "Have you seen Coltin lately?"

"Yes!" She lit up like a firecracker, and something twisted in my chest. Her joy was magnificent, but the fact that I had no fucking idea who Coltin was stung hard and fast.

"Starway 8 just got hit by a big epidemic—a really nasty virus. We brought some cure-alls we'd managed to gather, and it was exactly what they needed." She sobered. "Coltin looked bad. He scared the crap out of me, but he came around. I saw him getting better before I left."

"Wow. That's a relief." Asher scrubbed a hand through his hair. Despite his words, worry still cramped his face.

Tess glanced at me. "Asher is Coltin's uncle. Coltin is this amazing kid on Starway 8, kind of like my little brother."

So a child, not one of the adults who worked at the orphanage. "How old is he?" He couldn't be too young if Tess had formed an attachment to him there. She'd been out of that place for eight years.

"Eleven," she answered. "Well, almost twelve." She brightened all over just thinking about this kid Coltin.

Until now, Starway 8 had only two names and faces for me: Mareeka and Surral. I'd barely noticed the administrators I hadn't been introduced to while I gritted my teeth against a throbbing gunshot wound and we all reeled from the confrontation with the Overseer.

Tess turned back to Asher. "I left a message for him to study his math, but I doubt he'll listen." Her freckles bunched together as she wrinkled her nose. "I think he likes numbers as much as I do."

Asher shook his head with a chuckle. "That's because you've filled his head with too many stories. Now, all he wants to do is read more books about treasure hunts across the galaxy and swashbuckling space pirates."

Her eyes sparkled. "Then he'll definitely join you on Frank's crew when he's older." Tess's broad smile landed on the blond captain, and I felt an annoying stab of jealousy.

"Or he'll join *you*," Asher said pointedly.

Tess nodded. The kid was eleven, though, and she had other plans for the future. We'd see what happened.

"Bailey always finds the best treasures." Frank winked at Tess, his compliment sending a hint of pink across her features.

I'd never seen her look flushed or shy with anyone but me before, and I honestly hated it. I liked Frank, though, and I could tell his esteem meant something to her.

Tess waved his praise away with a quick "Whatever," but her not-quite-hidden smile got bigger.

"What did you guys bring for the Mooncamps?" one of the twins, Macey, asked. She dragged her booted toe along the floor of the hangar, leaving a streak in the grit that coated this whole place from top to bottom.

"A fuckton of food," Fiona answered. "We've been carting it around for ages but couldn't get here. You?" she asked.

"Same, although I wouldn't call it a fuckton," Macey answered. "Still, it was worth the trip here so that we can reload with the new haul we're about to go after."

"Got a tip on a heist?" Tess asked. "We could double crew it."

"That would actually be really good," Frank answered thoughtfully. "But you've gotta be ready to go in twenty-four hours. Dark Watch supply ships just restocked the security hub orbiting Ewelock. They're preparing for a major personnel shift. According to the message we hacked into, new people are arriving to man the starbase tomorrow. There'll be a flood of people in. Others leaving. Ships all over the place. I say we redirect a few cargo attachments before they figure out who's actually supposed to be there."

"Your intel is correct," Mwende offered.

I stiffened, seeing the same slight hardening in Tess. How was Mwende going to explain knowing that? "I'm General Bridgebane's personal bodyguard" probably wouldn't go over well here—or anywhere full of Nightchasers.

"Ah, good. You heard the same thing?" Frank asked.

The lieutenant nodded. The prickly feeling of sitting on a mountain of hair-trigger explosives built inside me. But they didn't question her further, and nothing detonated.

A tightness that had nothing to do with anxiety tugged my ribs together. So, this was how it felt to be a part of something. A team. Almost an extended family. Sanaa Mwende was with the crew of the *Endeavor*. Frank and his group took her at face value, just like that. Tess was letting it happen, which told me exactly which side she'd come down on in terms of trusting her uncle. Tess was no believer, but she still knew how to take a leap of faith.

"Twenty-four hours? We can manage that." Tess didn't show any of the concern I was feeling about taking on a new mission before we'd even started planning the Starbase 12 rescues. Maybe she was more fly-by-the-seat-of-her-pants than I'd realized—and maybe I wasn't impulsive enough for this new life.

She turned to us. "What do you guys think?"

Both Jax and Fiona confirmed they were okay with it. Merrick rumbled something to the effect of "Finally getting some action around here," as though we hadn't just fought for our lives on Korabon. Mwende didn't comment. She just stood there, apparently ready for anything.

"Sounds okay." I shrugged, going along with the majority. The ship was at nearly full power. We had four days before we had to be anywhere, and planning the Starbase 12 break-in without knowing what Bridgebane had to offer, if anything, felt a lot like tossing ideas into a pot, stirring, and seeing what didn't sink to the bottom. We could do this Ewelock heist. I just hoped nothing prevented us from getting to Bridgebane's drop point. Or, worse, derailed us from the main mission.

"Do you guys have a plan?" I asked, directing my question at Frank.

He nodded. "We'll go over the details later, but in a nutshell, we're going to hit the spine of cargo holds crawling up the outside of the spacedock. Upper levels A through O are food containers." He glanced at Tess's ship. "We can vacuum seal any two onto the *Unholy Stench* and you can latch two onto the *Endeavor*. We'd have only gone for one attachment without you guys, but it'll go a lot faster with Tess working her lock magic. You float 'em, and we'll snatch 'em up from the outside. You up for that, Bailey?"

"Have I ever said no?" Tess asked in challenge.

"Not to *that*," Frank answered flirtatiously.

Tess's cheeks reddened, and I had to combat the urge to stake my claim to her. Wrapping my arm around her shoulders and hauling her against my side was both what I wanted to do and what I knew I shouldn't. She liked a little caveman possessive in bed, that hint of dominance, but I doubted she'd appreciate it anywhere else, and especially not when she was talking business.

Corralling my baser urges, I asked, "Lock magic?" Tess had told me once that she could override any lock. Maybe I'd finally know how.

"I'll show you." The quick smile she flashed me looked stiff around the edges. What could she possibly have to be nervous about? Especially with me?

Asher covered a belch with his hand. "Did Raz give you that unidentifiable shit for dinner?" He grimaced, looking suddenly green around the gills. Another burble rumbled in his gullet.

Fiona pretend-retched. "That was worse than usual. We bring them stuff, and they thank us by giving us the expired crap nobody wants anymore. Raz is going to be sorry when all the Nightchasers feeding his Mooncamps are dead from food poisoning."

"I swear it was regurgitated rubber coated in sludge." Asher laid a hand over the center of his chest, looking like his dinner was about to come back up.

"Don't think about it," Fiona said sharply. "Engines. Cocktails. Puppies!"

Asher frowned at her. "What are you shouting about, Fi?"

"Just trying to distract you." Fiona shrugged. "This hangar already stinks enough without you throwing up all over it."

"The hangar doesn't stink." Tess leaned forward and sniffed. "That's Frank."

Frank danced in on a boxer's shuffle and gave Tess a light shove. "I *am* captain of the *Unholy Stench*." He grinned at her. Tess laughed.

I held very still. It was an actual physical effort not to touch her myself after that, not to hold her hand or put my palm on the small of her back. Tess hadn't introduced me as anything other than her navigator and mechanic. I didn't know what she wanted her friends to think, and it wasn't my place to decide for her. Now, I just had to convince my male body of that when it was operating more on a *Club rival, claim mate* level.

"The stink comes from flying through the shit of the Overseer." Caeryssa's sharp features twisted in distaste. "He crapped out the Dark Watch, and now his excrement is literally all over the place."

"Speaking of *that* unholy stench," Frank said, "did you guys see Novalight's latest transmission?"

"No... When was it?" Tess's eyes filled with wariness. "We've been lying low and out of touch for the last few days."

"Yesterday, eighteen hundred hours, u-time." Frank pulled a hand-sized tablet from his pocket. "*Now* you can all get ready to vomit," he added with zero humor in his voice.

He went to his recordings and tapped on the latest entry. The Galactic Overseer's face filled the screen. Brown eyes in a square, unforgiving face stared straight out from the tablet at us. Short brown hair hugged his scalp like a helmet, accentuating the brutish cut of his chin and his unanimated, robotic appearance. Honestly, a well-made robot probably had more feeling than he did. All this man cared about was his own aggrandizement. And holding on to power.

"People of the eighteen Sectors," the Overseer began from what looked like his home office. I glanced at Tess as she watched. Her blue eyes had gone glacial, as cold and hard as an ice-coated planet. She crossed her arms. Her chin jutted forward.

"In a continued effort to protect you and keep this era of peace and prosperity thriving, I have decided on a new measure of human and family recognition. Never again will a kidnapped child be lost forever. An accident befalls you far from home? With my new program, your loved ones can always find you. You've forgotten your code to a little used bank account? A simple scan can verify your identity. From newborn to fourth age, every citizen of the galaxy is to be assigned a new galactic identification number. Your GIN will be encoded into a tiny microchip specifically designed to flow harmlessly through your bloodstream. It will be in constant motion inside you. No nefarious person will be able to lock on to it or cut it out of you."

"Unless they slit your throat and drain you," Fiona said with a snort.

"Only officially issued GIN scanners will be able to read your microchip or locate specific signals across the Sectors. This is your galactic government protecting you. From near or far, we can find you."

Tess's mouth popped open on a gasp. She glared at the screen in utter disgust, two hot spots of color flagging her cheeks with fire.

"No fucking way," Jax ground out. Merrick echoed that, his jaw ticking.

"That's what we've been saying since yesterday," Frank muttered.

I shook my head, not quite believing the Overseer's new

measure. It was the equivalent of branding the entire population of the galaxy. *For life.*

I glanced at Mwende. Shock blared from her expression, her eyes almost apocalyptic with anger. She obviously knew nothing about this, which meant the Overseer had gone rogue, setting a major scheme into motion without consulting Bridgebane.

"Over the next six universal months, your local Dark Watch will be rolling out a program to issue every galactic citizen their new GIN. This is not the same as your birth record or Sector ID number. Everyone must get their GIN. Anyone found without a GIN six months from now will be automatically arrested and imprisoned."

"That bastard, stinker, shit-faced... Argh!" Fiona growled. "Babies... Kids... They won't have a choice! They'll grow up and can literally *never* go off-grid."

"Your lifelong security is of the utmost importance to me. I will protect you from those trying to take this hard-won peace away from law-abiding galactic citizens like yourself. Anyone not willing to claim their GIN is a criminal. Those criminals will be found, incarcerated, and forcibly put to work for the greater good."

"Holy shit." Tess turned to me, anguish graying her face. "A needle into every vein in the galaxy. This whole thing is orchestrated to gather blood samples and track anyone who meets his criteria."

Fuck. She was so right. The Overseer was searching for A1 blood, and these new GINs would lead him straight to anyone who had it. Once his plan was in motion, it meant a staggering potential for super soldiers.

"Why would he want that many blood samples?" Nic asked.

Novalight started talking again before Tess could answer. The asshole loved to pause dramatically and stare at the camera, his dark eyes beady and menacing.

"Connect now to projectyournewgin.gxy to find your local GIN center and choose a convenient time slot for your injection. Parents and legal guardians must make appointments for their children and charges. Spacedocks will be provided with traveling GIN units. Anyone without a permanent residence is required by law to request an appointment at the location of their choosing. Select the Temporary Visitor option. You have exactly six universal months from this day forward to claim a galactic identification number. Anyone found to be noncompliant six months from now will be hunted and arrested."

"Where will he put everyone?" Tess whispered in horror.

"Nine Circles still has three entire underground levels that are empty," Mwende said. "The place is huge and could accommodate hundreds of thousands."

"Holy Sky Mother." Tess's too-wide eyes swung from Mwende back to the screen in Frank's hand. A tremor went through her. She already knew firsthand the kind of hell that waited for inmates on Hourglass Mile. Nine Circles was a descent into misery few people could imagine. Convicts didn't come out of that place intact, if they ever came out at all.

"Claim your GINs. Help our galaxy stay safe and prosperous. It is your duty to encourage your neighbors to fulfill this new galactic obligation. It is also your duty to report anyone who fails to comply. Outlaws will be punishable under AGL 1409, the GIN Standard."

The Overseer stood there for a moment, looking rigid and smug as he stared out at our entire galaxy from his big

undecorated office. He'd had the exact same look on his face
after he shot Miko and grabbed Shiori. It was his *I one-upped
you* smirk, and I couldn't help wondering if this one was
directed at Tess also.

"All newly issued GINs will be checked off against galactic birth and death records spanning the last century and a
quarter. We'll know who doesn't claim a number. And we
will find you."

On that ominous pronouncement, the screen went dark.
ProjectYourNewGin.gxy took the Overseer's place in
big white block letters. They flashed a few times to really get
the viewer's attention and then went static again, staring out
at us.

Frank powered down the tablet and slipped it back into
his pocket. "And there you have it. Pretty soon, the Dark
Watch will be able to scan people on the streets, and if you
don't pop up with a GIN, they'll fucking jump out and arrest
you."

"I'm going to kill him. Then kill him again," Tess
murmured.

"What's this about blood samples?" Nic asked a second
time.

Her features screwed up in fury, Tess told them about
the Overseer's super-soldier serum, how it was based on a
rare blood type that otherwise boosted healing, and how
she'd stolen his entire supply and turned it over to the rebel
leaders. She didn't mention having A1 blood herself or
knowing anything about where it came from. "So basically,
this is my fault," she finished hotly. "If I hadn't stolen his
whole batch of enhancers, he wouldn't be hunting for more
A1 blood, which seems to be the one thing he can bind his
chemical cocktail to."

"First of all"—Frank's hands dropped to his hips, and he looked fixedly at Tess—"nothing that tyrannical psychopath does is your fault. Second, what are Loralie and the rebel council doing with the enhancers?"

"I don't know." Tess scraped her hair back, twisting it into a knot that fell down again. "Hopefully nothing but keep it away from the Overseer."

"But they could potentially make rebel super soldiers?" Frank asked.

Tess nodded, her eyes haunted.

"How many?" The crew of the *Unholy Stench* echoed Frank's question.

"Thousands," Tess answered, a thin catch in her voice. "There were thousands of prepared injections in that lab."

"And what would be so bad about that?" Frank asked, his brow furrowing. "That sounds like just the boost we need to finally do something about that bastard."

"I know." Tess spread her hands, looking as conflicted as ever about the enhancers. "That's why I gave it to them instead of blowing it up. It's just... I brought the stuff to the rebel leaders. I'll feel responsible for whatever happens to anyone who uses it."

"Okay, as much as I love you, Bailey, you're not that important." Frank softened his words with another light punch to Tess's arm. I couldn't mind—not when it brought a reluctant smile to her lips. "Your choice was to hand it over. Whatever happens next is *not* your choice. It's Loralie's, or whoever decides to use that enhancer."

"Yeah. Yeah, you're right." Despite her quick agreement, worry still shadowed Tess's features. More than once, I'd caught her brooding over the idea of rebel soldiers being lied to about the enhancer's effects on their bodies, or being forced into it. She had that look again now. "If there's a bloodbath, though, I'll feel like I'm swimming in it. And now, there's this whole GIN thing to worry about."

"We're all outlaws anyway," Jax said.

Fiona glanced at him, scowling. "Yeah, but we couldn't get flagged on the street just for walking by without registering on some hidden scanner."

"That'll make missions a lot tougher," Jax admitted, scraping a hand down his jaw. His frown deepened.

"How will we go anywhere? Get supplies? Do *anything*?" Tess snarled.

Macey, who didn't seem to say much otherwise, came out with a humdinger. "We won't. And there won't be any new rebels to keep the fight going. He's putting a leash on the entire galaxy. We either end this—end *him*—before the GIN Project is final, or the rebellion dies forever."

CHAPTER

11

TESS

SHADE AND I WERE BOTH TOO KEYED UP AFTER LEARNING about the Overseer's GIN Project to go to bed. He grabbed some tools and went to look at the glitchy lighting in Cargo Bay 2, and I took my tablet from the bridge, scooped up Bonk from his bed on Jax's old sweater, and shut myself in my bedroom for some much-needed cat snuggles and news from Starway 8.

I wondered how Mareeka and Surral had taken the fact that all their kids were about to get branded. It enraged me, so for them, I imagined some forced meditation had been in order. And possibly a sedative—or three.

I should find them a cat. Bonk's purring was already doing wonders for my anxiety level.

I checked that my encryptions were all in place and opened up my messages, hoping to see something from Starway 8. I wanted to know how the children were recovering after the epidemic, especially Coltin.

I could still picture him perfectly as a baby and then as

a toddler: sandy-blond hair, beautiful blue eyes, pale, and sickly. His breathing had always been a problem, and I'd rocked him through more nights than I could count while he struggled and wheezed, not knowing if he'd be alive in the morning.

Coltin had been too sick when he was orphaned for his uncle Asher to take care of him. Surral had been the infant's best chance at survival, and I'd taken on the role of replacement mother. I'd never done that with any other child. He'd just seemed to need me, and as he got older, I became more of a sister to him. And then I'd left, knowing he was in the best place he could be, with the best possible people.

If only I'd known when he was a baby that some of my blood could have helped him. Then again, I didn't actually know if type A1 blood could fight intense asthma the way it fought diseases and infections.

I *did* know now that it could have saved my mother. But for what? For more unhappy years under the Overseer's watchful gaze, in his oppressive home, under his terrifying bootheel? His fists hadn't flown often, but when they had, they'd hit hard. To be honest, I'd been more scared of being dragged around, poked with needles, and shoved into stark rooms with the lock thrown behind me and no clue when I'd be let out again. Mom and I had both gotten away from him. Death had been our escape, although mine hadn't been a real one. Maybe my escape wasn't real, either.

Nathaniel Bridgebane had stripped me of my identity, abandoned me halfway across the galaxy from the only home I'd ever known, and scared the crap out of me in the process. He'd saved my life eighteen years ago. I'd hated him for his choices, for not being my Uncle Nate anymore, for choosing the Overseer's dark cave of tyranny and intolerance over staying the fun guy who'd let me ride on his shoulders and whose biggest smiles were always for me and my mother.

But the man who'd once been a rebel hadn't bought into autocratic evil when he'd followed his stepsister to Sector 12, had he? He'd been trying to control it.

There wasn't a message from Starway 8 waiting for me, so I wrote to Mareeka with a quick update and asked for news from the orphanage. After sending off my note, I curled up with Bonk and flipped through the pages of the book Susan had given me on the Mornavail from her bookshop on Albion 5, looking for clues as to who might have A1 blood like I did, and where in the galaxy they might be hiding.

Just as with the first time I'd read the fairly recent but archaically presented book, I didn't get much out of it. It could have been myth, history, or just some nutcase's handwritten ramblings. "They" were in the Fold. "They" were a light in the darkness. "They" were "Incorruptible"— which I now understood wasn't referring to morals or integrity but rather to the fact that their health couldn't be corrupted by the usual illnesses that plagued others. All in all, I still had more questions than answers after revisiting the flowery, long-winded text, which unfortunately hadn't magically become more fun to read since the last time I'd slogged through it.

Before we'd gone to Korabon, I'd asked Fiona why she thought a large increase in white blood cells would benefit my health rather than causing problems. Any internal imbalance was bad news, as far as I knew, but she'd insisted that I wasn't out of balance. I was simply built that way from the start.

"If someone were to experience a sudden increase in abnormal *white blood cells,"* she'd explained, *"that would cause problems.*

Potentially severe ones, even fatal. Your cells are healthy and normal. There's no bad crowding out the good. There's just more good, and it's always been that way. That's your internal design. That's the engine that keeps you running."

Whoever the Mornavail were—and I was starting to believe they were really out there—they were like me, with the same slightly different composition from everyone else. But where were they? Not in the Fold. I would know, wouldn't I?

My tablet dinged softly. I closed the book and shoved it under my bed, its frustrating obliqueness making me give it a hard push out of sight. I grabbed the tablet and checked my incoming messages, seeing Surral's name and a Starway 8 address.

Dearest Tess,

Mareeka and I are so relieved to hear from you and know that you're all right. With your recent losses, I know that "all right" isn't really what you are, but I'm glad to hear that you and your remaining crew are safe. Please know that we took care of Miko for you. She's a beautiful bright color in the Rafini Nebula now and will always help watch over the children for us.

Tears burst to my eyes, hot and sudden. My breath shuddered. I sniffed the tears down, blinking rapidly. My grip tightened on the tablet.

Mareeka needs to deal with some new deliveries, which is why I'm writing you back in her place. I'm finally able to breathe after clearing the last of the children from sick bay only yesterday. We suffered no more losses after you brought us your new cure-all. We're so grateful. We're so sorry, though, for what it cost you. I know that Miko and Shiori were your family as much as we are.

My eyes watered. I sniffed again, the top of my nose burning. Surral was staying vague and discreet in written correspondence, but I'd seen before leaving Starway 8 that she'd figured out that my blood was in those cure-alls. She'd understood that I was somehow connected to the Mornavail, whom she'd heard of but believed were legendary.

Supplies are coming in with a vengeance now that cargo ships aren't afraid of the virus anymore. Mareeka is being run off her feet, but the older children are helping out, as they do, and as they should. This leaves the middle children to help more with the little ones, which is always interesting. It keeps them out of the usual trouble they are wont to stumble into, but creates new...shall I say... challenges?

I smiled through a lingering blur of tears, imagining the fierce bickering, the dressing-up, the games, and the messes that would probably make even my hair curl. Coltin was a middle child. I hoped he was well enough already to be leading pirate raids and inventing magic spells.

I got a new supply of scrubs in for my nurses. They're electric orange and lemon yellow and light up our hallways fabulously. You'd love them.

My smile widened. Surral and her scrubs. I thought she got them from people she still knew in her native New India Conglomerate, although she'd never told me specifically. Electric orange wouldn't be my best color, but bright, bold tones went perfectly with Surral's bronze-hued skin, black hair, and deep-brown eyes. I'd never seen a color that didn't work on her. Mareeka wasn't so lucky. With her white-blonde hair, milk-toned complexion, and ice-blue eyes, plain dark clothing looked best on her. The differences between the two women always interested the children. Babies were especially fascinated, their early vision delighting in contrasts.

Mareeka and Surral had both worn wedding rings for as long as I'd known them, although they'd never technically married. The Overseer had banned gay marriage about thirty years ago, around the time he'd coerced my mother into tying herself to him in exchange for stopping a genocide.

My face scrunched up, the unholy stench of the Overseer reaching me even here. I continued reading.

And now for the news you've been waiting for. Coltin is fine. He's been quite heroic, helping out in the infirmary. He recovered much faster than the others, perhaps due to that double dose you gave him. (Yes! I saw that!)

I bit my lip. Mareeka had insisted we vaccinate ourselves against the highly contagious virus. I hadn't wanted to waste a shot on myself, so I secretly gave it to Coltin.

Or not so secretly. Surral had eyes like a hawk, and apparently, I wasn't that stealthy.

He was very disappointed that you had to leave so quickly, but I explained a bit about the situation, and he understood your urgency. I told him you *specifically* said to work on his math, and I must say, he's been applying himself. But now you'll have to tell him to work on his writing, because the better his calculations get, the worse his penmanship. I'm starting to wonder if there's an inverse relationship there that I should begin studying.

A laugh bubbled inside me. My penmanship was great, and my math stank. Surral was probably on to something.

Math, however, was more important than neat writing. How much had I handwritten after leaving the classroom? Or even in it? Next to nothing. A list here and there, if someone else was already using the tablet and I couldn't type it out directly.

But how many times had I wished my math was better? Several—especially when I found myself fumbling through navigation.

Reading, though, was essential.

Coltin is an eleven-year-old boy and therefore much too cool to say how much he loves you. If you were here, though, you would see it in his face and the way he talks about you. Mareeka and I also love and miss you. Please send news again when you can.

> May the Sky Mother and
> Her Powers bless you.
> Surral

I sighed at the end of her message, a happy-sad sound that made Bonk look over. Happy because things were okay at the orphanage. Sad because a part of me always wanted to be there. I powered down the tablet and put it in my bedside table, thinking about Surral's parting blessing. She was a believer. Mareeka wasn't. That was just another contrast between them. I fell on the side of Mareeka, but I was glad other people, like Shade, could find comfort in whatever they thought was out there.

I scratched lightly between Bonk's ears. "If they're right, and I'm wrong, won't I be sorry?"

His engine revved up, vibrating through his small body.

"Is there a kitty God? Some deity to keep all you felines on the straight and narrow?" My fingers glided under his chin, and Bonk lifted his head for more, his yellow-green eyes slitting blissfully. "Never mind. You're it. The Cat Lord."

He purred louder, which I took as his wholehearted agreement.

"Good thing you're with me. I could use the Cat Lord. You know, the next time we're about to be blown to smithereens by the nasty Dark Watch. Just keep it in mind, will you? Bonk the Almighty."

He agreed again. I was sure of it. His whole black-and-gray body rumbled like an earthquake. The soft white fur beneath his chin was irresistible, so I leaned in and kissed it. He tickled my nose with his whiskers and didn't look entirely happy that I'd stuck my face in his neck. Cats must not like that. It was too bad. I did. It was so fluffy, and his purring was like an auditory blessing.

Shade knocked before sticking his head into the room. "Hey, baby."

"You don't have to knock." I straightened, smiling at him. "This is your room, too."

He smiled back at me, slipped inside, and shut the door behind him. Bonk jumped off the bed and went to Shade, weaving between his legs. After sufficiently bumping his head and whiskers against Shade's ankles, Bonk looked at the door, waiting expectantly. Shade opened it, let him out, and then shut the door again, throwing the lock this time. He turned back to me with a slow, sexy smile that sent a thrill shivering through my body.

"Yes, please." I got up on my knees and reached for him before he'd even moved again.

In two strides, Shade was in front of me, his hands on my waist. I loved big hands. Shade's had scarred knuckles.

He gazed down at me, his brown eyes blazing. "You read my mind, starshine."

I slid my hands around his neck and looked up at him through my lashes. "It wasn't that hard, actually."

Shade's eyes dipped to my mouth, a wolfish hunger sharpening his features. In one smooth move, he flipped me onto my back. I gasped, then grinned. His ability to maneuver me with so little effort was impressive. It turned me on as much as his beat-up knuckles and wicked space-rogue smile did. Anticipation electrified my systems, taking my pulse to the next level.

Shade lowered his head and kissed my chest just above the line of my shirt. I was pretty sure he was aiming for the smattering of light freckles below my collarbone. He slowly unzipped my top, kissing every new inch of exposed skin. I squirmed, already craving more than the soft, brushing contact. When he reached my navel, he palmed my breasts. I arched into his touch and felt his smile on my abdomen.

He unfastened my bra and laid it open. While he teased one nipple into a peak with his fingertips, he licked the other, circling the bud and flicking his tongue over it. When the tip was beaded and aching, he took it into his mouth and sucked with a hot, hungry pull that made my mouth fall open. I speared my fingers into his hair and held on. The erotic tug on my breast echoed from my chest to my sex, and a ribbon of heat pulled taut between them. I tilted my head back and rubbed my thighs together. Shade moved one hand down my body, the unhurried but targeted progression ramping up the needy tension thrumming inside me. I made a low sound when he finally slid his fingers between my legs and pressed down, stroking.

I sought more pressure and lifted my hips as he shifted his focus to my other breast, leaving the first one tight and pebbled in what now felt like cold air after the intense heat of his mouth. Shade teased this side with just the tip of his tongue and then bit down softly on my nipple. I sucked in a breath, arousal flaring inside me.

"Good?" he asked against my skin.

"More," I rasped out, bright sparks of excitement following his every touch.

He nipped again, making me jerk and moan before he licked away the sting and scattered kisses up my chest and over my shoulder. His hand moved deeper between my legs. He skimmed a finger up and down the seam of my pants, and I shuddered in pleasure.

"You're so hot down here. Already burning up. Is this for me, baby? All this fire?" Shade cupped me with his whole hand, ground down with the base of his palm, and groaned as though he'd found a treasure.

I nodded, all my focus on Shade's body and hands and

deep, husky voice. Sensation washed down my spine. Tingles raced through me. Desire slicked me hot and wet under his fingers, and I spread my legs wider.

"Shade..." I shifted against him, ready for our bodies to line up and lock. I could barely stand the emptiness where he should be, moving inside me and filling me up.

"I want you. Need you. Fuck, Tess..." Shade's breath came heavy against my neck. He rocked up, gripped my head with both hands, and captured my mouth for a fevered kiss that stole my breath and wound its way so deep inside me that my soul got tangled up in the embrace.

I clutched his shoulders and devoured him back, need tightening every inch of me. But it was more than that. The distinct feeling of handing myself over to someone else— and not just physically—hit me in a startling rush. A wave of heat engulfed me, and I pulled back with an audible gasp.

Shade looked down at me, his eyes heavy-lidded and his heart pounding so hard that I felt each thudding beat. He pressed the pad of his thumb against my lower lip and gently dragged at it. I flicked my tongue across his finger, and his eyes darkened, a low sound rumbling in his chest.

His reactions thrilled me. That catch in his breath. The sudden hardening of muscles. The gaze that hazed over with desire, just like I knew mine did. Here, like this, I knew with absolute certainty he was honest.

"Too many clothes." My whisper surprised me when the rest of me was so thunderingly alive and on fire. "I want skin. Your skin." I gathered Shade's shirt and lifted.

He sat up and tore his shirt over his head. My mouth went dry at the sight of his lean, strong body, still sun-bronzed from life on Albion 5. He was a masterpiece, truly beautiful. I traced the sculpted indent near his hip, my eyes riveted to the line of muscle. "So warm and solid." It was as though he'd absorbed the summer heat from his home planet and brought it here for me to bask in.

"Believe me, that's not the only part of me that's hot and hard," he said wryly. His hands hovered at my waistline. "Skin for you, too, starshine?"

My lips kicked up at the corners. I was already halfway to naked, but I liked that he'd stopped to ask. "Wild, romping sex will be kind of hard with these pants on," I teased.

A laugh cracked out of Shade. "So, it's wild and romping you want, is it?" Smoldering promise lit his eyes, making my belly tighten.

I grinned as he peeled my pants down my legs and tossed my quickly removed underthings aside. I wiggled out of my open shirt and bra and shoved them off the bed without looking.

Shade stripped off the rest of his clothing, his shoulders and back rippling with each swift, concise movement. I watched in blatant appreciation, an eager flutter warming me. "You're sinfully gorgeous, you know. Like a warrior of old, worthy of songs and stories."

Shade chuckled, some incredulity sneaking into his expression. "You're the gorgeous one, but you can go ahead and sing my praises if you want to."

He stretched out next to me on his side, and my eyes dropped to where he placed one big warm hand on my stomach. I liked seeing it there. His fingers pressed a little, a possessive tightening that tugged hard at several fantasies inside me.

"Maybe later," I said. "Or if I get drunk. I'm not much of a singer otherwise."

"I can't picture you drunk at all." Shade slid his hand

around my rib cage and tipped me onto my side, facing him.

"It doesn't happen often." I let my gaze slowly roam over his naked body. I admired every inch of him that I could see, from the dusting of dark hair on his broad chest to his powerful, capable hands that seemed ready and able to fix anything, to the impressive erection that jutted between us.

I studied it, tilting my head a little. "I love the fact that I know what that big thing feels like. *Inside me.*"

Shade coughed out a laugh. "Baby"—he nudged my chin back up, and our eyes met—"I love the fact that you *let* me inside you." His face turned serious. "Sometimes, I think about it—us, together—and everything gets so tight and hot and wound up inside me that I can't breathe anymore."

I swallowed, knowing just what he meant. That hot burst of feeling, the excitement and memory and anticipation all converging into enough unstable energy to make every sensitive place on my body shiver and ache. It happened nearly every time Shade touched me. Or when our gazes locked unexpectedly. Or when I closed my eyes, and he filled my vision anyway.

My pulse drummed heavily in places I didn't usually feel it as I stroked my hand down his torso, touching him from shoulder to hip bone. Hard planes, warm skin, crisp hair, solid muscle. Shade's body tightened under my fingertips. His cock pulsed, and my heart skipped a beat. This man was an addiction.

Lowering my hand even farther, I gently wrapped my fingers around his erection. The warm weight of his arousal, rock-hard but velvety soft, sent a need-charged current of desire through me. I stroked him, loving how his lips parted and his breathing accelerated. His eyes grew unfocused.

Shade rocked into my touch, and I worked my hand over him faster. His breath hitched, a rasp in his throat. A bead of moisture appeared at the tip of his shaft. I swiped my thumb over it, spreading the slick warmth.

"You're the sexiest woman alive." He twisted his hand in my hair. His fist closed, tugging my head back. "The hunger on your face. What you do to me."

Shade angled my mouth so that he could feast on it. I didn't know who took and who gave, but the deep, consuming kisses left me panting and reaching both hands up to grip his shoulders as he rolled on top of me.

"Tell me," I whispered, his weight pressing me into the mattress. I brought my knees up, settling him more intimately against me. All he had to do was adjust the angle, thrust, and penetrate. Everything down low pulsed hard at the idea, needy and ready.

"Fuck, baby, I felt that." Shade's breath shuddered out.

I dragged an openmouthed kiss up the side of his neck and nipped his earlobe. "Tell me what I do to you."

My husky demand got Shade to lift his head and look at me. The searing heat in his eyes threatened to burn me alive. "You turn wild so fast it makes me blind with lust. I want to fuck you until you can't see, either."

His brute honesty ratcheted up my excitement more than any pretty words could. "Do it." I arched into him, the thudding pulse of orgasm already pulling at me from afar. "I want you, Shade. I'm dying to have you inside me."

He exhaled sharply. His forehead dropped to my shoulder, and he ground against me. "You reduce me to instinct. Can't think. Just need. Just want." He palmed my breast, kneading with strong fingers.

I writhed against him. "What do you want?"

"You," he answered instantly.

"What else?" Clenching the empty, aching spot between my legs, I asked, "What do you daydream about?"

Shade went still above me. Then his mouth found my neck, my jaw, my lips. "You," he rasped out, the word a scrape of gravel in his throat. "You touching yourself. And me watching."

The visual struck me fast and in vivid detail. I bit my lip, a cold splash of nerves hitting the inferno inside me. Shade looked down at me, a question in his eyes. He waited, and my own curiosity and desire eventually won out.

"I hardly ever do that," I finally said. "And definitely not with anyone watching."

"You don't have to do anything." He kissed me quickly, as if sealing a promise.

Some of my shyness evaporated, baked away by the heat in his eyes that didn't come with any pressure. "I know. But I asked. And…why not, right?"

His expression turned almost pained. "You're killing me, you know that?"

I loved how thick and gruff his words came out, and I smiled, part nervousness and part sheer happiness. Alone with Shade, I could escape right into him. Into this. Into *us*.

Slowly, Shade slipped off the bed and knelt beside it. The way he watched me, the focus and intensity in his eyes as I sat on the edge of the mattress and faced him, set off a flare of slightly panicked heat in my chest.

"I don't think I'm very good at this," I admitted. In the past, the result had never been particularly satisfying and took a lot of work. Although with Shade's simmering brown eyes practically scorching my naked skin and the feel of his kisses still on my tongue, it might not be so difficult.

He put his hands on my knees and then slid them up my thighs, gently parting my legs. "It's all I can do not to lean forward and lick you."

I shivered from head to toe. "You can."

His lips tilted up at the corners, his eyes anchored straight ahead. "Not yet." With his thumbs teasing the creases of my thighs and his gaze riveted to my sex, I felt craved, maybe even necessary, and it was a powerful aphrodisiac.

Shade brushed the tip of his finger lightly down my seam. Sensation radiated from his skimming touch in heady little zaps that made me clench and twitch. A shiver raced beneath my skin, raising goose bumps. My breasts tightened. The air felt both cool and hot, and just having him look at me this way made my heartbeat pound in my throat. "Don't stop."

"You do it." He guided my hand to replace his. He turned his head and feathered a kiss over the inside of my knee. The flick of his tongue traveled up my leg like a solar flare and burst between my legs.

Hesitant, I slipped a finger through my folds. I was already wet, wound up and sensitive, and arousal swelled inside me with each new stroke.

Shade's hands moved to my hips. "Just do what feels good," he coaxed.

"You feel good."

An amused huff fluttered against my most intimate parts. I got bolder with myself, moving faster. His breathing sped up.

"More," he encouraged, his grip tightening on my hips, almost rocking me. "Faster."

My fingers slipped and slid and circled as he watched. Then my breath hitched.

Shade angled up a smoldering look. "Found something good?"

I leaned back on one elbow, getting more comfortable. "I think so."

"Keep going." Fixing his eyes between my legs again, he reached down and gripped his shaft, giving it a long, hard stroke.

Everything hazed around me, my eyes suddenly as riveted as his. The sight of Shade's powerful, sun-darkened hand slowly pulling on his arousal from base to tip and back again washed me in an explosive heat. My pulse surged, and my breathing came short. I stared at what he was doing, entranced.

"I get the appeal now." I really, really did. A whip of pleasure lashed me, and I jerked.

Shade's eyes flicked to my face. We stared at each other. I could still see his arm and shoulder moving, the muscles flexing and working. A rush of moisture hit my hand. I pinched my clitoris, and my mouth fell open on a quiet moan. I rocked my hips, chasing the sparks I'd found. The ember glowed brighter but wouldn't ignite like the firework I wanted, *needed* now.

"It's not enough," I gasped out. "I can't do it."

Shade spread my legs wider. "Try a finger inside yourself."

I flushed violently, mostly with desire. Dipping lower, I penetrated myself, learning my body in a way I never had before. Shade groaned low in his throat, clasping my hip almost hard enough to hurt. He pumped his cock harder.

"Now move," Shade said. "In and out."

I did, and my head dropped back. This was better. So good. I finally understood what I'd been doing wrong in the past. I hadn't been owning my own pleasure. I'd gone at it occasionally like a half-assed project. Not anymore. With Shade, this felt totally different. Utterly absorbing. I inserted another finger, twisting my hand to go deeper.

Shade made a choking sound. "I could come just watching you."

Gasping, I kept going, the sudden crack of orgasm hovering just out of reach. My legs twitched. My heels dug into the floor. Jolts shot through me, but it wasn't enough. "Shade! I need more. Kiss me."

He pushed my hand aside with his face. "Kiss you? I'm going to eat you alive." His words hit me right before his tongue did, all gritty promise and slick wet heat.

I sprawled on my back as Shade gave me the scorching licks I'd been craving. He sucked, and I writhed like a live wire, barreling toward climax. He gripped my bottom and lifted with both hands, bringing me up to his mouth and feasting. Our gazes crashed together over my bowed body, and I suddenly knew what I wanted more than this.

I reached for his shoulders. "You. Now. Inside me. Don't wait."

Shade rose over me as I drew up my knees. I'd never forget the look on his face in a million years or with brainwashing. He pushed inside me, and I almost shattered. I tried to pull him in deeper, angling my hips up and dragging at his back with my heels. He started to rock, slowly at first and then fast and hard, catapulting me into instant orgasm. Relief hurtled through me. I shouted hoarsely, clinging to him and pulsing in mind-numbing pleasure. Shade shuddered, his breath battering my neck. He gripped me hard, thrusting almost too deep, and then the tension ebbed from his body along with a deep, groaning rasp of sound. He dropped in a boneless heap. Within seconds, he must have realized how heavy he was and rose up enough to kiss me. I kissed him back, a long, euphoric, tender kiss, thinking that breathing was overrated when balanced against Shade's delicious weight.

"Hmmm." The drawn-out, satisfied sigh was all I could manage in terms of speech.

"I wish there was a word for you," Shade murmured against my lips.

I threaded my fingers through his short hair, running them over his scalp to his nape and then back again. "What do you mean?"

"I don't know how to describe you. Or what we just did. It's all just...feelings." He rolled onto his back, gazing up at the ceiling and absently rubbing his chest.

I turned to face him. "Is that a bad thing?" He seemed to be frowning.

"No." Looking at me again, he looped his arm around my shoulders and tugged me flush against him. "Nothing with you is bad."

I grinned, snuggling into him.

A few minutes later, Shade lifted his head and looked at the door. "Did someone feed Bonk? I don't remember seeing much food in his bowl in the kitchen."

"I don't know." I sat up and reached for my shirt, even though it felt as if a lead weight were pinning me to the soft bed and to Shade's warm body. I'd never be able to sleep without making sure Bonk had what he needed.

"Stay here. Relax." Shade got up, pressed a kiss to my forehead, and started to dress. "I'll make sure he's all set for the night."

I sank back down. "Thank you."

He smiled at me as I slid under the covers, helping to tug them up and make me comfortable. Then he turned and slipped out to go check on Bonk. The door closed behind him, and a flash flood of happiness rose inside me, filling me to the brim. My heart tugged, and that was when I knew for sure I was in love with Shade Ganavan. There were men who fell mindlessly into a sex stupor. And there were men who got up and took care of the things that mattered to them.

CHAPTER

12

SHADE

THE NEXT MORNING, THE CREW OF THE *ENDEAVOR* eventually started wandering into the kitchen, Bonk included. Tess got breakfast going while Jax made the coffee. Merrick and I both scanned the news on our tablets, reading titles and snippets out loud if they seemed interesting or pertinent. The GIN Project was everywhere. Logistically, it would be nearly impossible to process everyone in the galaxy in less than the six months the Overseer had given, but he was obviously doing everything he could to scare people into getting their chip and number as quickly as possible.

They'd been fine living their lives yesterday and the day before that, and before then also. Now, suddenly if they didn't get shot up with a GIN, some vague catastrophe was going to befall them, their family, maybe their entire Sector? And people actually bought into this shit. It didn't seem possible.

At the same time, how much would I have questioned the GIN Project a month ago? If I were truly honest with myself, I wasn't sure I liked the answer.

"Fake bacon or fake eggs?" Tess held up two boxes for everyone's inspection.

"What makes it fake?" I asked, looking over the choices.

"Well, I guess I should say reconstituted." She made her this-is-going-to-be-nasty-but-we'll-get-through-it face. The expression was par for the course in the *Endeavor*'s kitchen. "And there's probably some additional mystery stuff thrown into the mix. Adds protein or something. Puts hair on your chest." She squinted to read the ingredients on the egg container and then seemed to think better of it and lowered the box.

An image of my kitchen on Albion 5 flashed in my mind, the cupboards and shelves stocked with the fresh food and the healthy eating choices that came so easily with planet-dwelling life. I blinked the picture out of existence. It wasn't relevant. "I vote for both."

"Me too," Merrick murmured, his nose still buried in his tablet.

"Jax?" Tess asked.

"When have I ever said no to either of those things?" Jax's easy smile was one I'd never seen directed at anyone but Tess. In general, the man redefined the word *tense*.

"Both it is." She poured a small cup of water into a pan, added some brown cubes from both boxes to it, and started mashing it all together. "And toast."

I didn't expect Tess to put the bacon and eggs together in one pan, but they probably both tasted more or less the same, and they ended up in the same place anyway, so why the hell not?

Toast was good. We still had fresh bread and butter from the Aisé Resort.

Fiona arrived, looking saucy in a civilian outfit I'd never

seen on her before. High heels, tight pants, and a black leather top that laced up the back clung to her slim frame, showing me just how tiny she was without her boxy lab coat. Like a corset, her top had no straps and showed a good amount of cleavage. She'd left her hair down, which had to be the most unusual part in a whole lot of different.

I glanced at Jax. His jaw hung slack. His eyes dipped over her and then snapped back to her face, but Fiona had already turned, her dark hair sliding over her bare shoulders as she reached into the cabinet for the daily orange she always made sure the crew ate.

"What happened to your lab coat, Fi?" Tess asked, adjusting the temperature on the cooking surface from high to medium as the food expanded and began to pop.

"I don't need it where I'm going this morning," Fiona answered. She left that hanging in the air and so did Tess.

"And where's that?" Jax eventually asked, sounding as though he'd swallowed rocks and was trying to cough them back up.

Leaning her hip against the counter, Fiona peeled the orange. The small smile she tried hard to hide told me she knew she was affecting Jax. The question was, did *he* know it? Jax was a brick wall in more ways than one.

"Frank's taking me to a new greenhouse one of his friends is running."

"You can't just walk around like that," Jax said.

Fiona arched her brows at him. "I can't?"

"It's ... cold here," Jax grated out.

She shrugged. "I'll take a jacket. I have one that matches my pants."

Jax couldn't help but look at her legs again before dragging his gaze back up. His eyes seemed a little wider than usual, but otherwise, the guy just looked frozen in place and slightly flushed. Fiona watched him coolly, the contrast between her space-pale complexion and nearly black hair more arresting than ever in that surprising outfit. Throw in her vibrant green eyes and petite size, and you got something that was almost ethereal.

"I might end up with some new seeds for the *Endeavor*," Fiona said. "Apparently, they've had good luck with some classic fruits here lately. And I'm not sure I'll get anything from that purple clawberry. It kind of took a beating on the climb out of the elevator."

"Fresh fruit?" Tess's eyes brightened.

My mouth started to water, but that might've been from the smell of trigrain nut bread toasting. I was pretty sure it wasn't the fake eggs and bacon. "Peaches?" I asked hopefully.

Fiona snorted. "Not likely. Besides, I don't think I can grow a tree in the cargo hold unless we cart in a whole lot of dirt from somewhere. I'm good, but I'm not a miracle worker. Most of my stuff is hydroponic."

I grinned, my stomach rumbling. "Worth asking."

Jax finished preparing the coffee, now visibly ignoring the fact that Fiona was gorgeous and dressed like a goddess who wanted to get a little dirty. Merrick didn't seem to notice, and I had eyes, but that didn't mean I was interested. I set aside the news and got up to put our plates on the table.

Fiona doled out the orange, and while I'd set a place for Mwende, who hadn't shown up yet, Fiona gave the extra part to Merrick. We all stared at that double portion, but only Jax, Tess, and Fiona suddenly got very quiet. I knew from something Tess had said that Fiona always gave the extra part to Shiori. The blind woman hadn't known she was getting more than the rest of them, and no one ever told her.

Mwende walked into the kitchen with a clipped stride and a no-nonsense attitude. Despite that, for the first time in our presence, she seemed to hesitate.

"Here's your spot." I pointed to the empty plate next to Tess's. It was where I knew Miko used to sit.

Mwende didn't move. "I can find my food elsewhere when we're not flying."

"Just eat, Sanaa." Tess dumped a heap of vaguely bacon-and-egg-shaped globs onto the lieutenant's plate before doing the same around the table.

Mwende sat. Merrick looked at her, at his plate, and then back at her again. He tossed the extra orange wedge at her. Mwende caught it with whip-fast reflexes and without comment.

Jax filled the mugs and set them on the table. As he leaned over to give Fiona hers, he muttered, "Didn't know that's how gardeners dressed these days."

Fiona sipped, hiding a smile behind her cup of coffee.

Tess had shared some of Jax's story with me. He'd lost his family to a Dark Watch raid on his home planet. Wife, children, visiting sister—all destroyed in mere minutes before the soldiers had trapped him and sent him off to prison. What Jax didn't seem to realize, even seven years later, was that moving forward with his own life didn't mean forgetting or betraying them.

Considering his past, I was surprised he'd gone along with Mwende being on the ship, even temporarily. It was because he trusted Tess implicitly. But Tess could make mistakes, just like anyone. I really hoped putting her faith in her uncle and Mwende wouldn't be one of them.

Fiona's posture at the table was impeccable, which highlighted her bare neck and shoulders. She was clearly on a campaign to shake Jax out of the past and make him *see* her. That hadn't seemed like the case before she'd been shot and Jax had gone nearly catatonic with grief and worry. He obviously loved her. Did he think losing her would devastate him any less just because he wouldn't admit it?

Across from me, Jax took his seat next to Fiona's at the table and plunked his mug down heavily. Was he pissed off and fighting it? Or did he not even understand why he was fuming to begin with? That was always irritating as hell for anyone.

"You look like you're about to turn tricks for vegetables." He glanced at Fiona sideways.

Fiona whipped her head around. Her brows slashed together. "What the fuck, Jax?"

His eyes dipped very pointedly to her chest. This time, he made it obvious he was looking. Fiona didn't have much going on there, but what she had was displayed nicely. The choice of clothing was a little bold for a tour of a greenhouse, but who cared? Too bad Tess didn't have that outfit.

Red slowly crept over Fiona's chest and face. Her eyes flashed, furious. "Do you have any idea how nice it would be to have fresh fruit on a regular basis? The orange is great, and I'm glad we always make sure to stock up, and they store well, thank the Powers, but aren't you sick of it? Vegetables aren't *that* hard to grow, even on a spaceship, but fruit is really delicate. If they have something good here and are willing to share, I want it. And if I have to shake my ass a little to get it for us, then I'll do it!"

Jax's face turned to stone. "What ass? You're as thin as a rail, Fiona."

Fiona stood up so fast her chair fell over. With a sudden howl of rage, she cracked her palm across Jax's cheek. He didn't even budge, probably because he outweighed her by more than twofold. His expression turned even blanker. A statue looked up at her from where he still sat at the breakfast table. His skin turned ruddy on both sides of his face—though more on one side than the other. A handprint gradually became visible. For a few long seconds, they stared at each other.

Fiona turned on her heel and left the kitchen, her breakfast untouched. No one moved, in shock probably. And if I was anything to go by, highly uncomfortable. I looked to Tess for her reaction.

"You're an idiot, Jax." Crossing her arms, she leaned back in her chair and shook her head at him.

"Did you see her?" Jax flapped his hands in the approximate shape of a woman. "That outfit?"

"Yeah. And she looked fantastic," Tess shot back. "Which is what you should've told her."

Jax gaped at her. Then he turned to me. "Back me up here," he demanded.

I shook my head in a firm negative. "You were an asshole."

Tess's gaze jumped to mine, her expression grateful and even a little surprised. Did she not expect me to back her up? Moreover, I agreed with her.

"Looking like that, she could get…" Jax's jaw bulged, a big muscle bouncing. "Someone might…"

"Admire her?" Tess offered.

"Frank—he's always…" Jax scowled, stiffening.

"Always what, Jax?" Tess asked sharply.

Grumbling a curse, Jax turned to Merrick. "Merrick?"

Merrick pursed his lips. "It was a bit different from her usual, but most women don't live in a lab coat, either."

"But her hair…" Jax growled.

"Was loose?" Tess's brows flew up, her eyes screaming like twin meteors ready to crash down in a pit of fury and destruction. "What's the matter with you, Jax? If you're so concerned about what Fiona is doing with her hair and clothes and body, maybe you should make it so that you actually have the right to express an opinion about any of that."

He stared at her, seeming more stunned than angry. He looked completely blindsided, like he'd just gone through a really rough reentry. Jax's usual pallor doubled in seconds.

Pressing her mouth into a thin line, Tess shook her head at him again. She ate quickly, scraping the brown uni-glob off her plate with efficiency and ignoring the bread that was the only part of this anyone really wanted. When she was done, she put her dishes in the sink and turned to kiss me. Our lips met briefly. "You can have my toast," she whispered before pulling away again.

I smiled. "I like toast."

"I know." She squeezed my shoulder.

She left the kitchen, still pissed off enough at Jax to not even look at him. Bonk followed her out like Tess was the comet and he was the tail that trailed behind her.

"What the fuck just happened?" Jax asked no one in particular. He hadn't touched his food and didn't look hungry.

"You were a Neanderthal," Mwende said dryly. "So much for human evolution."

Jax shot her a look that said she wasn't particularly welcome here, especially for her commentary.

The only woman left in the room shrugged and ate her breakfast. As she chewed, she studied Merrick with zero pretense.

As Merrick ate, he studied her back. Neither of them blinked much. Maybe that was another super-soldier power. Eyes open. Always alert and ready. They sat on opposite sides of the table, and I had to wonder if what I saw in their narrowed, burning gazes was animosity, or something else entirely.

CHAPTER

13

TESS

I FOUND FIONA IN HER ROOM ON THE LOWER LEVEL OF the ship, gathering a few things for her morning outing.

"Hey," I called from the open doorway of her sleeping quarters. Her room was the mirror image of mine, which was across the hallway.

Fiona looked up from the pile of stuff on her bed and smiled a little too brightly. "I'm just leaving."

I crossed my legs at the ankles, relaxing against the doorframe. "Have fun. And don't worry about Jax. He forgot to evolve along with the rest of mankind. I'll send him a memo."

A smile cracked her face, disappearing quickly. "That's the thing. He didn't. I don't get it."

I pushed off the door and moved into her room. Bonk bumped against my ankles. I crouched to pat him, amused by his whiskery insistence. "Did you catch the look on Jax's face when he saw you walk into the kitchen? He was stunned speechless and couldn't take his eyes off you. That's the only thing you need to take out of this."

A little color came back into her cheeks, two red flags under eyes that seemed to waver between forlorn and furious. Personally, I'd veer toward spitting mad, and I doubted Fiona would choose differently.

She finally huffed loudly. "I guess it took nearly dying for him to notice me. Maybe if I get shot *twice* next time, I'll get a kiss out of him."

"Okay, first of all, please don't get shot again. That was awful for everyone." I stood back up when Bonk left me to go curl up on a lab coat Fiona had dropped in a corner. He poked and prodded at it, circled, and then settled down right where he wanted. Cats couldn't just plop down, apparently. They had to pick just the right spot and then soften it up or something. Either felines were weird, or they were smarter than most humans and actually thought about what they were going to do before they went ahead and did it. "Second, Jax is all messed up. Give him time to figure things out."

Fiona snorted. "What? Like five years? I've already done that."

"Two weeks ago, if you'd shown up in that outfit, he would've stared at the wall and kept his mouth shut. Today, you got a reaction." Practically an explosion, coming from Jax. "That's progress."

Fiona caught her bottom lip between her teeth and shoved random things into her bag without even looking. "He was mean," she finally said.

"Your ass is adorable, and he knows it."

Her eyes flicked my way, humor sparking in them. "I'm glad you think so."

"That new outfit is amazing. If I wasn't a giant compared to you, I'd totally borrow it. And that slap was epic."

She smiled even as she ruefully shook her head. "I shouldn't have done it."

"Maybe. Probably. But Jax is a tank. One slap in five years isn't going to break him."

"I'm still sorry," she said.

"Was it satisfying?" I asked.

"Hell, yes." She flicked her loose hair over her shoulder. "Until I felt awful for doing it."

"If it's any consolation, I'm pretty sure Jax feels awful, too."

Fiona stared blankly past me. "It's not, actually." Focusing on me again, she slung the strap of her satchel over her shoulder, letting the bulky bag hang against her hip. "How are things with Shade?"

I hummed a satisfied sound, volcanic warmth instantly filling me.

"That good, huh?" She arched her brows, looking eager for details.

I lowered my tone, confidential. "I keep getting these shocks of feeling inside me. Little zaps and jolts when I think about him. And the stuff we do together. It's like I'm all twisted up and on fire, but in a good way, you know?" I felt myself flush. I wasn't used to talking to Fiona this way. To *anyone* this way. Even at the orphanage, I'd never engaged in much girl-talk. I was either shadowing Mareeka, taking care of Coltin, or spending time with Gabe. This was new to me. And I liked it.

Fiona smiled. "Enjoy it. You deserve it." She held up a hand in caution. "As long as you're sure Shade's not going to go back to being part of the evil galactic machine of oppression."

"I don't think he ever wanted to be part of the evil galactic machine of oppression."

"In that case, fuck like flervers," she said.

I cracked up, and Fiona laughed with me.

"You don't even know what a flerver looks like," I said, still laughing.

"I looked them up. Apparently, they're a midsized semiaquatic rodent native to Albion 5 that have an average of fifteen offspring a year, so 'fuck like flervers' seems like a pretty appropriate analogy to me."

"Holy Sky Mother. Fifteen!" I shuddered. "Busy little beasts."

"Busier than I am, that's for sure." Sighing, Fiona asked, "Do you have any idea how long it's been since I've been kissed? Let alone any of the rest of it?"

"Five years?" I guessed.

She nodded, her expression souring.

Fiona had been intimate with her partner on Hourglass Mile. There hadn't been any question of that between Jax and me. He'd been grieving his family, and I'd just lost Gabe. I hadn't looked twice at a man in seven years until Shade came into my life.

"Jax will come around," I said, hoping it was true.

"Do you think he knows how I feel?" Looking down, Fiona scraped at the frayed edge of her bag with her fingernail.

I answered to the best of my knowledge. "I don't know. I think he feels it, though, regardless of knowing whether you reciprocate or not. His fear is holding him back."

She looked back up. "Maybe he wouldn't be afraid if I make it clear I'm interested."

"He's not afraid of rejection."

"Yeah, I know." She looked down again.

A knot formed in my throat. I loved Jax so much. I wanted him to be happy. He'd be forty in a few years. Life was passing him by, and he wasn't *living* it. I loved Fiona, too. "You're the one thing that can drag him out of the past and bring him joy again. Please don't give up. He needs you."

"I'm not sure he wants to be happy." Her voice wavered. She swallowed. "It's like he doesn't think he deserves it. Not when his wife and kids are all dead."

Unfortunately, I agreed, even though I hated it. "But that's only half of it. He's terrified of actually getting what he wants and then losing it—just like he lost them."

Fiona took a deep breath, steadying herself. "It's not as though I can claim a danger-free existence as a push in the right direction."

"No, but keep wearing that corset, and he'll crack. Hell, *I* almost want to kiss you, you look so good."

Fiona laughed, some of her usual confidence coming back. She slung a jacket over her arm and moved past me, stopping just outside the door. "Should I tell them on the *Unholy Stench* that you need the details of their plan ASAP?"

I nodded, although it sounded like a classic get-in-while-there's-confusion and get-out-before-they-notice-you type of heist. "I'll head over to their hangar as soon as the Mooncamp crew clears out our cargo holds. They're due any minute now. Can't do anything until that's done."

"Got it." Fiona started down the corridor, tossing me a sultry look over her shoulder. She put a little extra swing into her hips.

I laughed and wiggled my fingers in goodbye. "Have fun with Frank," I said suggestively.

"You know as well as I do that Frank's gay." She turned back around with a smile.

I chuckled, wondering when Jax would finally figure out that Frank wasn't a rival for Fiona.

***

Raz arrived with only half a crew, promising the other half in about an hour after a gale storm around Mooncamp 3 died down. I hadn't been to any of the other DT moons. The food coordinator redistributed from here, so this was where the *Endeavor* landed. From what I'd heard, the inhabitable moons orbiting Demeter Terre were all pretty similar: mostly empty, largely barren, and incredibly windy.

I hated going outside here and mostly stayed in our designated shed. There wasn't really anything out there besides pieced-together living quarters, sudden squalls, and relatively clean air, the latter of which we could take advantage of from the hangar.

While we'd flown in, Shade had asked me why this had become the principal settlement, probably because it looked so bleak and underdeveloped. I hadn't had much of an answer. As far as I knew, no single moon had been chosen over another for its merits. A few ships had landed here first during the panic to get off Demeter Terre, probably because they were damaged or their crews were dying, and that was that. Mooncamp 1: established.

I helped Raz direct where our haul was going after he gave me half his spreadsheet. Shade, Jax, Merrick, and Sanaa did a lot of the heavy lifting on the *Endeavor* while the food crew filled hover crates according to Raz's and my instructions. The crates were color coded for each of the six refugee cities, with red crates staying here, blue crates going onto a transport vessel destined for Mooncamp 2, yellow crates headed to Mooncamp 3, and so on. Raz's overall distribution was pretty even this time, which meant breaking into sealed containers and manually parceling out the boxes or cans inside to provide similar amounts for everyone.

"For fuck's sake, Raz." Jax wiped sweat from his brow before taking a long drink of water. "Could you have made this any slower?"

Raz gave Jax an owlish blink from behind his round glasses. "Are you in a hurry?"

"I'm always in a hurry." Jax's smile said he was just fooling around. "And you're lucky you didn't kill us with last night's dinner, or your spaghetti arms would be the ones lifting all this food right now."

"My spaghetti arms are perfect for checking off boxes." Raz lowered his clipboard and peered at the contents of the large hover crate Jax and Merrick had just finished loading. After counting off the items, he gave the go-ahead, and his crew began maneuvering the crate off the *Endeavor*. They'd steer it out of the hangar and onto a nearby waiting transport. "See—check, check, check." With extra flair, Raz marked three things off and then flipped the page of his spreadsheet.

Jax chuckled, then groaned when he saw the next hover crate. It was just as big as the previous one and needed the exact same contents. Raz buzzed around like a worker bee, busy and dedicated. I couldn't begin to count the number of times in an hour he went up and down the loading ramp at the back of the *Endeavor*, making sure the supplies we'd brought were headed to the locations he'd chosen with care and intention. His B-Team was unloading the *Unholy Stench* in the next hangar over. We had more food, so we got Raz and his main battalion. The DT Mooncamp food coordinator was one of the only people I knew who refused to use a tablet. He said it was a pen and paper and his own damn writing, or nothing. Seeing how straight the lines were on the spreadsheet he'd given me, I knew he also used a ruler.

We were more than halfway done unloading when the rest of Raz's crew showed up, bringing the remaining transport vessels and hover crates that had been stuck on Mooncamp 3 in the tempest.

"Good. They're here." Jax glanced past me toward the hangar entrance as he helped two women and a man fill a green hover crate with boxes of the dried brown beans we all ate on a regular basis. From the picture, they looked like animal droppings. I had to convince myself they weren't sometimes. "We've almost cleared out the two cargo holds with food in them. Almost everything's in the hangar now and ready to be loaded up again."

"Did you set aside anything for yourselves?" Raz asked.

Jax shook his head.

"You're sure?" Raz turned to me for assurance.

"We stocked up not long ago. We're fine," I answered. If there had been anything fresh, I would have kept it. I was generous but not stupid. Cans, boxes, and other tasteless generic stuff, most of it containing the ubiquitous trigrain *something*, could be had anywhere it was safe to dock. "If we end up starving, we'll come back here. I know you'll feed us something catastrophic." I grinned at Raz, taking the sting from my words.

He scratched his head, pushing his fingers through his buzz cut. "Was it that bad?"

"Worse," I answered, meaning it.

"I'm not entirely sure what it was," he admitted. "I gave it to Frank, too."

"You're lucky I'm more forgiving than Frank. He might never come back here. Ever."

"*I'm* not," Jax called from behind a huge crate. "You're dead to me, Raz," he promised.

Merrick good-naturedly voiced his agreement. Sanaa didn't say anything and worked as hard as anybody else here, even though she really had no reason to.

We continued unloading and organizing. When Shade walked past where I stood at the corner of the lowered ramp to the *Endeavor*, he gave me a hot-as-the-Reaginine-sun look that said he didn't care what he ate, as long as he got his dessert afterward.

His smile set my blood on fire. My breasts tingled, and arousal swam in my belly. All Shade had to do was look at me, and I was ready. I was about to toss him my best you're-so-incredibly-on-for-tonight grin when the voice of a ghost froze me solid.

"Tess? Great Powers. Tess, is that you?"

I turned slowly. *Impossible.* But that voice … I'd know it anywhere.

I lost all sensation in my body as my blood crashed away, leaving me empty, numb, and shaking. It couldn't be. But it was. That was Gabe—running straight at me. Gabe was dead. Wasn't he?

He rushed in and hugged me so powerfully that my feet left the ground and my lungs felt crushed. He swung me around. I landed again, staring past the shell of an ear and longish brown hair that was darker than I remembered. He squeezed me hard, but I couldn't move, couldn't squeeze back. Couldn't breathe. Couldn't talk. My arms hung limp, and all I knew was shock. I opened my mouth, but no sound came out.

"Tess. Tess. Thank the Sky Mother, you got away." Gabe looked at me, a heart and a thousand kisses in his eyes. He gripped my face with shaky hands and covered my mouth with his. Soft. Hard. Urgent. Trembling. He kissed me like we were nineteen again, the center of each other's universes, and looking for a rebel crew to join so we could kick some Dark Watch ass. The two of us. Together. Like we'd always planned.

Gabe flew away from me, a look of total surprise on his face. Shade shoved him another several feet back and stood in front of me.

"Get the hell off my... captain." He glanced at me. His gaze dipped, making sure I was all right.

I touched an unsteady hand to my mouth. I blinked. Blinked again. My lips felt numb and my vision dark.

Gabe recovered his balance quickly. This was no beanstalk of a boy anymore. He rivaled Shade in height and strength. In fact, his new build reminded me more of Jax.

I'd only ever guessed at what happened to Gabe when I got caught and sent to jail. Now, the pieces slammed together like a cell door crashing closed. "You were on Hourglass Mile, weren't you? You were in the mines?" We'd never seen each other. Never crossed paths. The whole place was segmented to reduce the risk of riots. The warden wouldn't have partnered up two people who'd been caught in the same place at the same time, and I'd had no way of knowing who was in a different section of the huge prison, or if Gabe had ended up there at all.

I swallowed, but the tears still rose. He'd been right next to me for two years. He'd been *that* close.

Gabe nodded. He didn't move, wary of Shade now.

In a daze, I bypassed Shade and went to Gabe. I touched his arm. Warm. Solid. *There*. Gabriel was alive. He had been all these years. "I was there, too. From the day we got separated."

"Me too." His eyes searched mine, shining with moisture. Aglow with invitation. That life we'd talked about was still on offer. I saw it, right there for the taking.

My chest ached so deeply it felt as if someone had buried a hatchet in it. Gabe and I had lost so much. Freedom. Each other. *Us.* We were both out of prison, but we hadn't found each other until now. In my heart, I knew that meant he'd been on the Mile this whole time, but I still needed to hear it from him. "I escaped five years ago. When did you get out?"

"Five years? Oh, the explosion. Good." He looked relieved for me. "I just got out. Barely a snap ago." His hazel eyes were just as I recalled, green and brown with flecks of gold. They looked into me and burned my soul. I'd left him. I'd left him there and gone on alone.

"How?" My eyes stung and watered. He blurred in front of me. This man I'd loved. My first friend on Starway 8. Gabe.

"They blamed me for a riot. A DW general picked me up to get me out of their hair while they brought things back under control on the Mile, but I was slated for a lethal injection. He was supposed to make a public spectacle of it from his big scary warship. Instead, the guy, Bridgebane, gave me a choice. The injection, or try my luck in a black hole."

My jaw fell open as I stared at him. I knew this story. "He sent you after me. *I* went through the Black Widow, and Bridgebane wanted to know if I could have survived somehow."

Surprise wiped all expression from Gabe's face, and we were both pretty damn shocked to begin with. "You. I followed you?"

"Well, no." I dropped my hand from his arm, realizing I was still gripping it so hard my fingers hurt. "I ended up in Sector 2, and you went to Sector 17."

Gabe's dark brows drew together under the shaggy fall of hair that tumbled over his forehead. "How do you know that?"

"Bridgebane told me."

His frown deepened. "How did—"

I shook my head. "It doesn't matter. You're alive. I can't believe it. Have you told Mareeka and Surral yet? They've been so worried."

"No." He looked surprised. "I didn't really think about it."

A knife finally pierced my fog, the cold, sharp prick of a dagger. "Didn't *think* about it?" How was that possible?

"Yeah. I made it here. Figured I'd join the DT refugees and earn my keep until a crew had room to take me on with them." He stood up straighter. "Did that guy say 'captain'?"

I nodded, looking at *that guy*. Shade. I touched my lips again, still feeling the press of Gabe's mouth there.

"Fucking Captain Tess Bailey." Gabe grinned at me. "You're living the life we always wanted."

"I guess so," I mumbled, shaken and off-kilter. I glanced at the people around me. Shade wore the wariest expression I'd ever seen on his face. Guarded. Not happy. Jax understood what was happening, and the sympathy written all over his features only rammed home my unexpected and difficult position. No one else knew what the hell was going on, but they were morbidly curious.

"You got a spot for me, Captain?" Gabe's question came out half-teasing and half-unsure but hopeful. The flame in his eyes, the way he smiled, were an encouragement to pick up where we'd left off seven years ago, before the Dark Watch had destroyed the life we'd built together since childhood.

I opened my mouth. Closed it. My heart hurt. My mind blanked. Gabe on the *Endeavor*?

"I…" *I have no idea what to answer.* "I'd have to talk to my crew first. And we're leaving in about"—I glanced at my watch—"ten hours."

"Sure." The word left his lips easily enough, but his face told a different story. I'd always hated disappointing Gabe. Having spent eleven years as close companions, it had definitely happened. The hatchet in my chest twisted, the ache intensifying until I could barely breathe and wanted to blurt out something stupid just to make him feel better.

I didn't.

Gabe took a step away from me. "I'll help finish with this haul you brought in. Gotta make the trip back to Mooncamp 3 with the stuff anyway. I'll come back later."

I nodded, aware of how stiff the quick jerks of my chin must look to everyone around us. Gabe kept his smile, but he knew things weren't what he'd hoped and wanted. He knew something was different when he looked at Shade, still wary, tense, and not far from me, and then back at me again. His hazel eyes changed, questioning.

"Don't leave before I come back, okay?" The smile he'd tried hard to maintain faded. "You know, if you might want me to go with you."

I nodded again, a flood of tears thickening my throat and battering the backs of my eyelids. My breath hitched, and I moved without thinking, launching myself at him. Everything had changed, but I was so happy to see him. Gabe was *alive*. I'd given up, especially recently. I'd buried him in my mind since I didn't have a body.

I gripped him hard, aware of how different he felt. The lanky teenager was gone. My arms barely circled this man's torso, and his arms felt twice as thick when they came around me, folding me into him. "Thank the Powers you're all right, Gabe. I can't believe it."

He cupped the back of my head and gently rocked me. His other arm stayed wrapped around my shoulders, pulling me so close that we touched from top to bottom. I closed my eyes against his neck, just like I used to. The scent of industrial soap, metal, and icy wind filled my nostrils. He didn't smell at all like I remembered.

"I love you, Tess," he said. "No matter what."

"I love you, too." I squeezed my eyes shut and held him, my heart breaking into pieces that fell straight into the dark swirling void losing him seven years ago had left.

CHAPTER

14

SHADE

SHE'D LET HIM COME. GABE WAS ON BOARD THE *ENDEAVOR*. Ex-boyfriend Gabe. Companion of her youth Gabe. First love—and lover—Gabe.

Over the course of the day, I'd ground my teeth so much they hurt. The resulting headache was crawling up the back of my scalp now. I couldn't relax for the life of me and wasn't sure I wanted to. It didn't help that Tess wavered between jumpy as hell and completely shell-shocked. She didn't flee my touch, but she didn't reciprocate it much, either. I backed off, giving her the space she needed. For the first time since we made up, she intentionally closed herself off from me, and it scared the ever-living shit out of me. If I lost her, I lost *everything*.

Fiona came back with the residents of the *Unholy Stench* at lunchtime so that we could all go over the plan Frank and his crew had established based on their intel. They liked to prepare, which made me like them even better. They had a good plan. Simple. Not too many variables. Efficiency would be key, and I liked that.

What I liked less was that by adding Tess to the mix, they'd gone from nabbing one cargo attachment to *four* and dumped the heaviest danger onto Tess.

She had a special way with locks—which I still didn't understand, but she'd promised to explain to me. That meant Tess was going in. She chose Jax and me to accompany her. Frank and Caeryssa would fly in with us on my cruiser. We'd pose as the Dark Watch maintenance team whose security codes Frank had stolen. Once we were inside, we'd go straight to the spine of cargo attachments fastened to the outer wall of the spacedock and get to work.

As Tess overrode the vacuum seals to each of the food holds we planned to take, one of us would get inside the container, close it up again, and use its built-in thrusters to maneuver it away from the spacedock. Either the *Unholy Stench* or the *Endeavor* would pick up the floating unit with a vacuum seal at one of their available exits. Starboard or back door for the *Endeavor*. Portside wasn't equipped with an air lock.

Unfortunately, we couldn't take advantage of having super soldiers. Mwende wanted to keep a low profile and avoid being seen in a potentially compromising position. As for Merrick, his enhanced size made him stand out like a colossal thumb, and he could possibly also be recognized following his time in captivity. We were all wanted. All we could do now was take a calculated risk and send the least recognizable of us onto the spacedock.

It was a gamble—a gamble we didn't really need when we had a bigger mission looming. The priority remained freeing Ahern and Shiori from Starbase 12, and the days were ticking down to when Daniel Ahern's contact would disarm the plasma-shield alarm for us. I'd already come up with and discarded a dozen ideas about how to get in and get out with our targets, but making concrete plans was proving difficult without knowing what Bridgebane might bring to the table.

I'd signed on for sudden gambles when I chose Tess, and now I was seeing the reality of it. One risk after another. Provide for those in need. Further the rebellion. Nightchasers didn't pass up opportunities like this. Reliable intel and relatively easy access to a fully stocked Dark Watch security hub didn't come around that often. I got that—or I was trying to.

During lunch, Tess and Frank decided who would go and who would stay. Neither of their crews argued with their final choices, including me. In silence, I worked to convince myself any of this should be happening in the first place.

For our part, Merrick would fly the ship. Mwende and Gabe would man our two air locks with vacuum-seal capacities and attach the stolen food holds as soon as Merrick lined everything up.

Frank and his crew would do the same, with Macey, Asher, and Nic all staying aboard. One to fly, and two to work the vacuum seals.

Fiona planned to stay out of the way, but she'd have a com, like we all did. Frank had provided coms that hid behind the shell of the ear under a patch of adhesive that looked like skin. They were small and inconspicuous, even if they were outdated. We linked them to a common secure channel and could communicate with barely a mumble once they were activated.

The main problem I had with this whole plan was leaving Tess on the Ewelock station by herself. After Frank, Caeryssa, Jax, and I all floated off in a cargo attachment to be picked up by our ships, Tess would be left alone on the Dark

Watch security hub to make her way back to my cruiser, take off, and meet us again.

For a rendezvous point, we settled on the Sector 2 planet of Nickleback—a place no one wanted to go because of the huge man-eating spiders. We chose coordinates for an uninhabited plateau in the fourth quadrant of the northern hemisphere and memorized the numbers. Once we secured the stolen goods, the acting captains would program in the coordinates and jump.

There was no question of preprogramming in the location. If one ship got captured, the navigation log would lead the Dark Watch straight to the others. On Nickleback, we'd transfer the food into our own cargo holds, ditch the empty military containers, reload my star cruiser through the freed-up back entrance, and bring everything to Mooncamp 1 for unloading. If everything went well, Raz would have his work cut out for him.

Tess and I were going to have to hit four different levels on the spacedock to detach four separate cargo holds. At least the stairs running up the back spine of the station between the inner and outer walls meant we didn't need to go back to the lifts to access each new level. That would speed things up and reduce the risk of running into the-Powers-knew-who as the station repopulated. But then Tess would have to go back into the heart of the security hub to pick up the *Queen Bee* on the landing platform—a scenario that made me break out in a cold sweat every time I thought about it.

Gabe seemed capable of working air locks, and his prison-miner build told me he'd be able to do his part when it came to lifting and transferring the food items. What other skills he had remained to be seen. Turning Tess into a comatose zombie whenever she wasn't fully focused on this heist appeared to be one of them. In his favor, he seemed ready to follow Tess's lead and defer to a crew he hoped to become a part of, probably permanently. He didn't know the crew was in total upheaval anyway, with recent additions and devastating changes all over the place.

Apart from me, Fiona seemed the most reticent about taking him on. The way his presence affected Tess clearly didn't sit well with the scientist. I knew it fucking didn't sit well with me.

A serrated weight plowed into my chest.

"I love you, Tess. No matter what."

"I love you, too," she'd whispered back.

I curled my hands into fists, wanting to grab something and rip it in half. Those should have been *my* words to her. Maybe Tess would've given them back to me as easily as she'd given them to him. They'd passed her lips for Gabe, for the man she'd pined for and hoped to find again for seven years. What did I have on that? On that kind of devotion? A few weeks?

After the plans were final, we went our separate ways for a few hours of downtime. I wanted to spend it with Tess, but she immediately disappeared on me, taking off to one of the food warehouses with Raz instead. I ended up on my own, tinkering with my cruiser and doing a lot of banging and muttering. It didn't help.

Now, I cursed under my breath as I approached the *Endeavor*'s bridge. Everyone had agreed to meet there for final preparations, and I still hadn't managed to get a second of alone time with Tess.

The retracting doors opened with a swipe of my palm. My eyes instantly found Tess even though she barely looked over at my entrance. The others were up front already, including

Fiona. She looked like herself again, her lab coat buttoned up to her neck and her hair scraped away from her face in a tight ponytail that turned her cheekbones into sharp little lines. She looked severe and formidable, and Jax snuck a glance like he was fifteen and fascinated. I gave him a month until he cracked. Maybe less if Fiona wore that outfit from this morning again.

Frank and Caeryssa were also on the bridge. They'd make the jump with us on my cruiser. The *Queen Bee* was ready to go.

The door whooshed shut behind me as I moved toward the captain's chair. Gabe's jaw hardened when I joined Tess at her console. Ignoring his stony stare, I gave her a smile I had to push past the jealousy clawing at my throat. Here I was, and right over there was the man she'd wanted for years. It made me queasy.

"The cruiser's all set." Casually, I rested my arm along the back of her chair without touching her.

Her glance up at me was fleeting. She focused on dials and switches and checking the systems.

I shifted my balance. "All three ships are set to arrive out of sight of the Ewelock station but within sight of one another. We'll fly in together, which'll look normal enough with the influx of new people to the spacedock."

"Thank you, Shade." Tess's voice couldn't have sounded any more impersonal if she'd been a robot.

"The personnel change going on today will mean ships all over the place. No need to worry about them picking us up on their scanners." Frank stood with Caeryssa next to the portside window panel, letting her adjust the gun holster on his stolen Dark Watch uniform. We all wore them, courtesy of Raz. Frank asked and Raz produced. Nightchasers left more than just food at the Mooncamps.

"The hard part won't be getting in this time," Caeryssa said, checking her own uniform. It was a little big on her, and she tucked the shirt in tighter. "It'll be getting out before they realize what we're up to."

Gabe moved closer, hovering on the other side of Tess. He didn't touch her, but my hostility grew as he tried to lay claim to a part of her space, just like I had. She didn't look at either of us and wrapped up her systems check, either not noticing or successfully ignoring the chill in the air between her ex-lover and me.

She turned to Frank. "Asher's flying for you guys, right?"

Frank dipped his chin in confirmation. "The Ewelock coordinates are locked in, and he knows where to meet on Nickleback."

"Good." Tess checked her watch. "We've got about thirty minutes before takeoff."

She looked around, and I followed her gaze. Everyone was organized. Dressed to blend in on the security hub. Knew their roles. We were ready.

So why did I have this enormous knot in my chest?

Tess stood, vacating the chair she'd been occupying and choosing to circle around it on my side rather than Gabe's. It felt like a small victory. "The ship's yours, Merrick."

Merrick took his place at Tess's console, but it was hard to miss the frustration pinching at his features. It must suck to be a super soldier and not get in on the action.

Tess found herself in the center of a whole group that obviously orbited around her. "Gabe and Sanaa, follow Merrick's lead and do whatever he needs. He's in charge of the ship until either Jax or I get back. Fiona knows the drill. If you have to leave without the cargo and without us, you *leave*," she said firmly. "If for some reason Nickleback doesn't work out for one or any of us, the ultimate rendezvous is back here, on Mooncamp 1. Sometime, somehow. For whoever can make it."

Fiona sat heavily on one of the side chairs that folded down from the wall. "I hate this speech."

My nostrils flared. I was pretty sure I hated it, too.

"It's not fun to think about losing, or making mistakes, or getting caught," Tess said. "But they're not out of the realm of possibility. Just do your jobs, stay focused, and watch each other's backs. We'll do our best to move quickly and be out of there in no time."

She looked at her crew one by one, including the two from the *Stench*. Her gaze landed and stayed on Gabe last. It lingered, and my gut tightened with a sharp twist.

Tess finally turned and crouched by Bonk, giving him several long pats. Gently, she tucked Jax's old sweater more firmly around the tabby and then straightened, glancing again at her watch. She set an alarm before looking back up. "Those of us taking Shade's cruiser need to meet there in about twenty-five minutes. Coms go on the second we're all off the ground and stay on. Under no circumstances do we turn them off. These are cheap, old-school generation-12 coms, so our radius is limi—"

"Hey, don't knock my coms," Frank interrupted. "I nearly had to trade Caeryssa for those." He winked at his crewmate.

Tess cracked a smile. "Our radius is limited with these *awesome* coms, but the good news is that they're discreet and small, and they can't be used to locate the positions of other people on the channel, like you can with gen-15 coms and beyond. The bad news is, we can't use them to electronically locate you, either. If something goes wrong and we're still nearby, though, we can hear what's happening and adjust. Hopefully figure things out from there."

Everyone nodded. It was as solid a backup plan as we were getting for this mission. My life had gone from clear, detailed, and strategic to what felt like a free-for-all with pitfalls all over the place. The lack of up-to-date gadgets and a satisfactory security net chafed. I would bring better equipment into the mix as soon as we could dock on a decent rock and shopping came up on the everchanging to-do list. As for the lack of a security net—I'd better get used to it.

Tess finally looked at me. "Shade… Can we talk?"

Fuck. Three little words really could stop a heart.

I nodded. What else could I do? Beg her to look at me like she had last night? Or even just moments before Gabe showed up?

Given the choice, I'd shove him off the ship and lock the doors before we all took off. Leave him on this dirt-patch Mooncamp and pretend I'd never seen the emotion and familiarity fusing Tess to him in that long, tight hug.

He'd kissed her. Tess hadn't kissed him back, but would she have, if I hadn't pulled them apart?

I followed her off the bridge, only a trickle of air finding a pathway into my lungs. I wouldn't be able to breathe again until Tess understood that I'd fight for her with everything I had in me—and then some.

She made her way to her room—*our room?*—waited for me to follow her inside, and then shut the door on the rest of the universe.

Blood slammed through my veins. I turned to her, reluctant and stiff. In front of me, she shifted from foot to foot, making me even more nervous. My heart crawled toward my mouth, choking me. Was this what dread tasted like? A hot burn and a tight knot that wouldn't stop wrenching in my throat?

"So…" She bit down on her lower lip, letting her gaze slide away from me. "Locks."

I stared at her, my pulse rampaging. This was about locks? *Holy Sky Mother*, I hoped so.

"Is this when you tell me about your lock magic?" My voice came out much harsher than usual. I'd been so ready to put my fist through a wall that I hadn't been prepared to talk.

"Yeah, the… 'lock magic.'" Tess looked even more uncomfortable at my gruff tone.

I cleared my throat, more than ready to go with this line of conversation. It sure as hell beat her saying she was leaving me for Gabe. "Does Frank know whatever it is? His crew?"

She shrugged, her uneasy body language starting to worry me for new reasons now. What could make Tess this hesitant? This freaked out?

"They've seen it from afar and asked questions. I've never explained. Just brushed it off as big skills and lots of luck." Her nervous laugh was so unlike her that I scowled.

She bit her lip again, grinding down with her incisor until the flesh turned white. I couldn't even begin to understand what was going on here—and wrong—so I waited.

"Only Jax knows the truth," she finally said. "We're usually a team on these kinds of heists. And soon you—if you're interested."

If I'm interested? Just like that, I was back to wanting to put my fist through a wall. "Of course I'm interested." I forced an even tone, making sure I didn't accidentally growl at her again.

Tess swallowed. "Yeah, but it's…" She paled.

Holy shit. How much bigger a secret could she have than being Quintessa Novalight? A type A1 blood source? The origin of the Overseer's super soldiers and the lost heir to the whole fucking galactic empire?

Not that she wanted it. No, Tess wanted to run an orphanage. And I wanted to do that with her.

"It's all right, baby." I reached for her, brushing my hands down her arms. The high-tech material of her stolen uniform felt strange, lightweight, and too smooth under my palms. I hated seeing Tess in military clothing. It was anathema to everything she loved. "You can tell me anything."

She winced, her nose scrunching up. Her indecision hit me like a punch to the gut. Did she think I would judge her? That didn't feel like trust.

Breaking my loose hold on her arms, Tess turned away, grabbed an elastic from her nightstand, and wrangled her hair into a ponytail. I could've sworn her hands shook as she snapped the hair band into place.

"Tell me or don't." Sincerity erased the last traces of roughness from my voice. "Whatever *you* want. Share the secret or just say *Abracadabra* and pop the locks. We'll be in. I don't need to know how, and you don't need to tell me if you don't want to."

Her hands twitched at her sides. Her fingers curled in. "You're not curious?"

"I'm curious." Who wouldn't be at this point? "But I won't push."

"I just feel like you should know. Especially since we're"—she swept a vague hand between us—"close."

Close? It was all I could do not to flinch. I didn't want *close*. I wanted fucking *combined*.

But the time to talk about that never seemed right. Tess was still uncomfortable with my past and the fortune bounty-hunting had made me. Sometimes her barriers went up, and I knew my second chance hadn't come with complete forgiveness and trust. I still needed to earn those. Now, Gabe had materialized from out of nowhere, exploding into the present from a past everyone thought was dead. We had to take off for the Ewelock heist in mere minutes. We barely had time for this important talk, let alone another one.

"It's an AI. Inside me," she blurted out.

I couldn't help the slow blink that followed her unexpected admission. Magic might've been easier to believe somehow. "It's galactic law that no human can be enhanced by artificial intelligence. It has been for almost three hundred years now."

Her smile held anything but humor. "Yes, well, the Overseer doesn't follow galactic law. He just imposes it on everyone else and adds new ones at the drop of a hat to suit his agenda."

My stomach turned over. The man knew no limits. "Did he do this to you? When you were a kid?"

She shook her head *no* and visibly tensed.

"I don't understand." There were rules about this. People could have mechanical elements inside them as long as they didn't contain programming, things like bionic limbs or other prosthetics, mainly for medical reasons. Robots, especially humanoid ones, were full of AI. Basically, they were walking, talking computers shaped a bit like people and doing a lot of human tasks. Working toward artificial general intelligence in truly humanlike androids had been banned ever since the Wei-Peng experience. That disaster took up a whole semester in every kid's history classes. It had proven once and for all that robots that believed they were smarter, faster, and better than humans would eventually band together to destroy their makers.

Luckily for the human race, the experiment had been contained by a necessary fail-safe: the constantly evolving androids had never once been made aware that anything existed outside of the self-sustaining Wei-Peng station. No entrances. No exits. No outside communications. No visitors on or off, *ever*, from the moment the scientists activated their AGI bots. When the last human heartbeat extinguished on the space station, it blew up. History books told us that Wei-Peng exploded well before the original human crew would've died of old age—and they'd been reproducing. The station log, recovered from the debris, reported that the conquering androids hadn't offered terms of surrender. They chose execution, even for children. It was more efficient.

"How much of you is AI?" I asked, trying to understand. Tess had blood. I'd heard her heart beat against my ear. Touched her everywhere. She was real. I loved her.

"Not much." She turned away from me, fiddling with her hair again. It was sheer nerves, and I wanted to stop her. "But I get it. You're right. I'm not fully ... human anymore. Not everywhere. It's disgusting."

"I didn't say that." I turned her back to me. "I'm just surprised, and no part of you is disgusting. Can you explain? I thought any experiments melding AI with the human body were banned after the Wei-Peng explosion." Scientists and lawmakers had taken a step back from what everyone had assumed was the future, fearing that people could end up dominated by the artificial intelligence inside them. The human mind and body evolved. It stood to reason that an internal AI component connected to that evolving system could also evolve, learning things and behaviors outside of its original programming. That was a risk humans had decided not to take after seeing how quickly Wei-Peng went wrong.

Tess pressed her lips together, a flat line that said she was still afraid to talk.

I cupped her face in my hands and searched her eyes with mine. "You can talk to me. I won't judge."

Her fear gutted me. That lack of trust. *My fault.*

I brushed my thumbs across her cheeks, my heart in a knot. "Every part of you is precious to me."

Tess's eyes softened. Her slight nod came just before she stepped back. "It's not in my brain or anything. I don't think it's connected to me in that way, or if it is, I'm not aware of it." She frowned, probably because that was the whole fear with integrated AI. If it adapted and learned your muscular and nervous systems, making improvements on them, what was to stop it from hijacking your entire body? From getting to the point where the computer ran the show instead of the person?

"Okay." I wanted her to go on. Nothing was clear to me yet.

"The Overseer commissioned the new technology for himself. It was totally off the books and covered by about a thousand smoke screens. A one-of-a-kind deal, just for him. That's why the exchange happened at our house, instead of on Starbase 12, where he did almost everything else. And I have no doubt the scientist who developed it died the day he delivered it to my father." She winced. "I mean, to the Overseer."

I bit down on a curse. *Our house...* He'd kept Tess and her mother prisoners to his scare tactics and tyrannical gloom, strapped Tess down in a basement laboratory and stole her blood, and now this—along with a whole hell of a lot of other abusive and shady things that made me want to fly into a rage. Fuck the wall; my fist needed his face.

"What was it exactly? This new tech?" I was curious, but that was it. Any anger or disgust I felt wasn't directed at Tess.

All I wanted to do was take her in my arms and kiss the crease from between her brows, but she was stiff and didn't particularly look like she wanted to be touched. I hoped she'd relax when she realized I didn't give a damn what was inside her. I just wanted to be a part of it.

She took a deep breath. "From what I understood from a conversation I wasn't supposed to hear, it's a computer system integrated into my hand that recharges based on my own kinetic energy. It's specifically designed to interpret data from electronic locks in close proximity and adjust its own response to disable them. With nothing telling a door to stay closed, it opens."

"Lock magic." *Incredible*. "How did you end up with it?"

Tess backed up a few steps and leaned against the door, staring past my shoulder. "Mom had just died. The person I thought was my father hadn't looked at me or talked to me in days, or offered a word of comfort, although that was no surprise. I was totally alone, with no idea what was going to happen, or what I should do next. I wanted to know why Mom got so sick like that, just out of the blue. I wanted to know what was happening for her funeral. Help. Understand…"

She shook her head. Her eyes dropped to the floor. "I wanted to find Uncle Nate. That was my real reason for sneaking around. He'd been gone for several days and didn't even come back when Mom was just lying there… burning up and turning into this… shell. He missed her last days, last hours. Even if he'd changed, pulling back from us, I couldn't understand him not coming back for Mom and me. Not then. Not when I had no one else." Her voice wavered. Tear-bright eyes lifted to my face. "I thought if I could just send him a message, he'd come. Even if Mom was gone, I thought he'd come back for me. I knew he would."

Pressure banded in hard ribbons around my chest. He'd come back, all right. He'd come back to betray her, terrify her, abandon her to strangers, and tell her she was dead.

"Oh, sweetheart..." Everything in me burned to close the distance between us. "I'm aching to reach for you. Please let me, Tess."

Her eyes brimmed with tears. Suddenly, she moved. She came straight into my open arms, and I wrapped her in a tight hug.

"I'm sorry. You must've been so scared. So alone." Eight years old, on her own in the Overseer's house, not knowing if there was anyone left in the galaxy to love or protect her. It broke my heart.

Tess exhaled with a shudder, softening against me. "I thought maybe I could find some information in the Overseer's office. Figure out where Uncle Nate went. I snuck in two days after Mom died and snooped around, looking for something that might help me send him a message. I didn't find anything, and then I heard him coming—the Overseer, talking with someone else."

Tess put some distance between us again but without the wary stiffness from before. "I was *not* supposed to be in his office unless summoned. I panicked and hid under the desk. He came in with a scientist. I never saw what the man looked like. Didn't recognize his voice. I heard them talking about a fancy new AI—what it did and how to inject it."

"What did they say?" I asked, wishing she hadn't left my arms so fast. But that was Tess. She had two feet and she stood on them.

She held out her left hand, palm up. "To inject it into the center of the hand. It would spread out, merging with everything from wrist to fingertips. The scientist loaded it with programming based on a bazillion different variables that would be able to 'speak' to any modern electronic lock. If I can get my hand within a few centimeters of the control panel, the AI can interface with it and tell it to open up."

I asked the first question that popped into my head. "Why did you stay on Hourglass Mile?"

"The locking mechanism was out of reach when I was in my cell, and the mine exits were always crawling with guards, although they didn't really care what went on in the tunnels. Fights. Sex. Murders." She grimaced. "And even if I somehow managed, I wasn't leaving without Jax."

Right. Jax. He was already broken enough. Losing Tess would've finished him.

"How long does it take to interface?"

She thought about it. "I don't think it's ever taken more than thirty seconds to trigger a lock." She looked at her left hand as though an alien had sprouted from it and was waving tentacles in her face. "That sounds fast, but those have been some of the longest half minutes of my life."

I'd bet. Then again, betting had never gone well for me. "And the door just opens?"

She nodded, looking uneasy again.

Tess needed to understand that I was the last person she should feel uncomfortable with, especially concerning her body. I lifted her hand and kissed the center of her palm. I could see the injection point now—a tiny dot where the skin was whiter. Tess's gaze jumped to mine, a hesitant smile pulling at her lips.

"Let me get this straight." Watching her closely, I kept her hand in mine. "You were eight years old, your mother had just died from a mysterious fever, your father—or the man you thought was your father—was a tyrant who terrorized you and everyone else, and you waltzed into his private office, eavesdropped about a brand-new invention he was going to use to benefit only himself, and took the damn thing before he could?"

She looked at me blankly, clearly not getting where I was going with this. "I guess so."

"Do you understand how incredibly strong and brave you are?"

Denial flashed across her features. "I was scared out of my mind! I just wanted a bargaining chip. I could tell something was happening. Something big. I *knew* he was about to get rid of me. Mom was gone. He already had a basement full of my blood. He'd always been so cold to me, sometimes violent. Not paternal at all." She snatched her hand back and folded her fingers in on the tiny pinprick. "I thought if I took his AI and made it merge with me, he couldn't kill me. He'd still need me for something."

"You wanted to stay with him?"

"No!" The word blew from her with the force of a jet engine. "I was a kid. Alone. I didn't know what to do—besides try to find Uncle Nate. I wanted to run away. Mom and I had wanted to run for years, but we couldn't escape. There was no *out* from him." She snorted in disgust. "No out but death."

Our eyes met. Tess's suddenly widened. "He faked my death."

I slowly nodded. I didn't like the way Bridgebane had done it, with secrets and lies, even from his niece, but he'd given her the only out either of them could conceive of: the death of Quintessa Novalight.

"Fuck." Tess ground the heel of her hand against her forehead, squeezing her eyes shut. "Should I feel guilty for being awful to him? Because I was. Don't deny it."

"Don't even think about that." I clasped her head in my hands, urging her to look at me. "He deserved everything you said to him. But what you can do is move forward from here."

Her eyes glittered with moisture again. She finally nodded and swallowed so hard I could practically hear the tears sinking back down her throat.

Letting her go, I asked, "What made you think the Overseer couldn't just get another AI from the scientist?"

"It was the only one. They said so. A unique piece developed for the Overseer alone. It would give him access to anything, anywhere. No one could hide from him—or hide anything *from* him. He would never allow anyone else to have that kind of power."

"But the knowledge was there. The plans were somewhere. Couldn't this scientist make another?"

A genuine smile ghosted over Tess's lips. "That's the thing most people don't understand about Simon Novalight. He makes long-term plans on a huge scale, but he's somehow criminally shortsighted. I'm confident that scientist died before he ever left the Overseer's house that day, and before the Overseer discovered the AI was missing from his office. The scientist *couldn't* make another. Did someone else create one from his notes? Maybe. Maybe the Overseer has 'lock magic' now after all. I don't know. But if you'd heard his roar that afternoon, you'd know it wasn't easy to replace."

Good for Tess. The man deserved a hefty setback. "He never suspected you?"

"Me?" She shook her head. "I was just a tool he didn't need anymore. He couldn't use me to control Mom now, and he had all the blood he thought he needed. He threw me out the next day. Uncle Nate finally showed up the same day I stole the AI, and the Overseer apparently greeted him with orders to take me away and make my disappearance permanent."

Criminally shortsighted was just the start of it. Arrogance blinded the man. At least that day, his disregard for Tess had worked in her favor.

"He was done with me," she said, "just like he was done with that scientist. He couldn't conceive of a world where his huge supply of base ingredient was destroyed or stolen any more than he could conceive of a world where he left something precious and irreplaceable in his private office and then never saw it again. A blow like that doesn't happen to the Galactic Overseer. Just like the wife he chose couldn't possibly think he was a monster. Mom loathed him, and he hated that he couldn't change her mind, no matter what his tactic. She was the one thing he never managed to control, and his only power over her ended up being me. Suddenly, she was gone, and I was an utterly unnecessary element in his life and household." Tess flicked her hand through the air. "*Boom*—float the girl from the air lock."

I swiped a hand down my face, trying to wipe away the shock, even though nothing that man did should shock anyone anymore. "He loved your mother." Obsessive, abusive, controlling. That wasn't what love looked like to me, but I was beginning to sense the Overseer's version of it.

"I'm not sure 'love' is the right word, but yeah, I think so. In a really warped way. I mean…he killed her." Tess fidgeted with her pants, rolling the side seam between her fingers.

"Why would he think your uncle would comply with an order to murder you?"

"Bridgebane had already been following the Overseer's orders for years, ever since he followed Mom to Sector 12 and somehow got in with Novalight. He was a Dark Watch general, captain of *DW 12*, and someone people feared across the galaxy. Not to mention the Overseer's 'best friend,'" she said with air quotes.

"So, another inveterate asshole?"

Her one-shoulder shrug was noncommittal. "I hoped not, but it looked like he was headed that way fast. The Overseer already thought so—or thought Uncle Nate was the kind of man he wanted for a friend and general. And I think a person like the Overseer, someone with no normal human feelings or compassion, can't conceive of those things in others, especially when those others are careful to hide them."

Tess's watch beeped with a repeated three-toned chime. She switched off the alarm, and I could already see her focus shifting in the way her body angled toward the door. "Time's up. We need to get to the cruiser."

"Wait." I reached out and caught her wrist. "The GIN Project... Once he finds new sources of A1 blood, will he keep going with it?"

"He'll have to. It's not some secret project in his own home that he can sweep into the closet after he gets what he wants. And why wouldn't he? He'll reap the benefits of getting to control people in the most effective way yet without having to do anything. His goons will keep the project in motion with the established *It's all for your own safety* discourse, and he knows that."

Novalight's short-term goal of creating super soldiers would be satisfied, and the long-term repercussions around the galaxy would be all to his benefit. That didn't seem shortsighted to me, but maybe he only lacked foresight with things he kept close to the vest.

Or with things he actually cared about in his sociopathic way, like Tess's mother. Did he regret causing her death?

"Finish the story," I urged. "Before we go, I need to know. That day you took the Overseer's AI... What happened?"

She glanced at her watch again, pursing her lips. "When he left his office with that scientist—likely to murder him—the Overseer left the invention sitting on his desk, all set up with the special injector. Knowing him, he wanted to inject it alone, all gleeful and triumphant with some horrifying plan in mind.

"I'd heard the instructions. The inventor had explained everything in detail, and as soon as I was alone again in the office, I got out from my hiding place and grabbed it. I thought about just taking it—saving it for a rainy day or something—but that didn't seem permanent enough. I also didn't want the Overseer to have it, to use it, the way he used everything and everyone else. I didn't plan on becoming a rebel thief at the time, but even at eight years old, I knew the best way to keep it from him *and* safeguard myself was to appropriate it before he could.

"So, I just picked it up and did it. I injected the AI into my palm before I could think about it too much or frighten myself out of it. My whole hand prickled and then went numb for a while. Long enough to really scare me, actually. I remember shaking so hard my teeth rattled. I knew AI in humans was totally illegal, although I didn't know much about Wei-Peng yet. I was terrified I'd already started turning into a robot. I kept poking at my hand and not even feeling it."

Tess lifted her left hand between us and flipped it back and forth, staring at it like a foreign object. "The numbness spread to my wrist but then stopped. I had to get out of the office before the Overseer came back, so I put the empty injector in my pocket and snuck out. The coast was clear. The house never had many people in it. Mom and I weren't really allowed to see anyone, unless we were involved in something official on Starbase 12 or accompanied somewhere by the Dark Watch. He isolated us as much as possible. I think it was this weird drive to keep Mom to himself—as if that would make her need him. I crept to the kitchen without crossing paths with anyone, dumped the injector into the garbage compactor, and mashed the shit out of it. Repeatedly."

I tried to picture the house where Tess first lived and came up with a big empty tomb, completely lifeless. Totally different from my childhood experience, with happy parents, cats sprawled on laps, music always playing, overflowing bookshelves, and no fear. It never even occurred to me to be scared of life until much later. That kind of naivety doesn't last, but kids should have it. Tess obviously hadn't.

"I thought the lab was in his house. What about those scientists? The ones taking your blood? Or guards?"

"The lab was underground with a separate entrance. The house was guarded, but the soldiers stayed at the doors. They didn't move around the place."

"So, inside it was just... who?" There must've been help. I doubted the Galactic Overseer made his own bed or cooked meals for himself.

"Mom, the Overseer, me, a chef and a housekeeper who didn't live there, the occasional handyman, and Uncle Nate, if he was around."

"No cameras?"

She snorted. "The Overseer was smart enough not to record what he was doing and saying, especially anywhere near his private office or that underground lab where he was illegally experimenting on his own daughter without her consent. His public image is what sustains him now that he can't just blow up planets and blame it on war anymore. Any kind of generalized outrage wouldn't stroke his ego, which is all he really wants from the entire universe."

"He wants to be liked. Needed, even." Shocking as it was, his desire for affirmation came through in a lot of his moves. The paternalistic, overarching control of everything. The constant reminding that he'd brought us peace. Large-scale atrocities would tarnish his image, so he used pinpointed brutality to keep an entire galaxy in line. What better way to get everyone to like you than to get rid of anyone who didn't? That could change a mind fast. Or at least keep most people from expressing their true opinions.

Where did super soldiers fit into his plans? He already had the Dark Watch.

"Have you noticed how most of his galactic broadcasts are from his home office, though? Making them feel nice and personal? For *that*, he brings in a camera." Grimly mocking, Tess said, "He's such a concerned leader. Such a family man, a poor widower who lost his wife and child. *The galaxy is all I have left, and I'll protect it. Don't mind me while I strip away your fundamental rights. Preserve the peace!*" She rolled her eyes.

Hatred lodged deep in my throat with a chemical sharpness. He murdered his wife and thought he'd murdered his child. There were no words for that level of wrongness.

"People buy into it. He can be convincing," I said. Among other things, the Overseer was more of a liar than I'd ever suspected. Maybe he was even lying to himself.

"Believe me, there isn't a nanosecond that goes by when that man isn't acting out of pure self-interest. He pretends well, but he can't see a thing outside of himself."

In that case, it was even more terrifying to think what he might do next "for the good of the galaxy." It seemed impossible to me now that most people across the eighteen Sectors were just going about their daily lives, keeping their heads down, and not worrying about it. Successfully ignoring all the fearful moments, accusations, and announcements that didn't sit right. That had been me, too—before Tess.

Tess glanced at her watch. "Shade, it's time."

"I know, baby, but I want you to listen to me first. I don't give a damn if you've got a computer in your hand. Or *for* a hand. It doesn't matter to me at all."

"Okay." She nodded like she wasn't convinced. "I can try not to touch you with it—if you want."

How could she possibly think I'd reject any part of her? "You unlocked me." I picked up her left hand and placed it flat over my heart. "Just like you open doors, you opened a new life for me. I'd imprisoned myself in a situation I hated more and more every day, but I didn't see any way out of it. *You* broke me out. You freed me, just like you free books, and food, and cure-alls for people who need them and are denied that precious resource."

Tess's fingers pressed against my chest. "You freed yourself, Shade. *You* chose."

"But you gave me the reason and the strength. Because you're the strongest, bravest, most resourceful person I know."

Her gaze dropped to her hand over my heart and then rose again. "I'm pretty sure you're stronger." Her half-hearted joke redirected my words on purpose. She wasn't getting away with that.

"I'm not talking about muscle, Tess. I'm talking about the ability to make difficult decisions and carry through with them. That AI. The Black Widow. Leaving me on the Squirrel Tree when I deserved it. And I'm especially talking about the incredible inner strength it takes to forgive."

She drew in a sharp breath.

"If we didn't have to go, I'd show you exactly where I want your hands on me. *Both* of them. And I'd fucking lick *starshine* onto your skin."

Her eyes flared with interest. "No time. Frank is probably having kittens right now—no offense to Bonk."

I bent my head. I wasn't leaving without a kiss. The moment our lips touched, Tess wrapped her arms around my neck and kissed me back, pressing her body into mine. The contact was fast, but fierce and true, and that was all I needed right now. We were still on the same page of the story I wanted to write together. Tess was mine, I was hers, and *now* I was ready for my first heist.

CHAPTER

15

TESS

ANOTHER HUNDRED METERS AND WE'D BE IN. A MULTI-level plasma-shielded entrance loomed before us, several large platforms beyond the invisible barrier teeming with activity. Vessels, people, crates, and cargo. Personal belongings. We were just another ship in the crowd as the seventy-eight-story station housing about ten thousand soldiers switched crews. Family leave or a different assignment for those headed out. A new post for the ones arriving. Us—breaking and entering.

Unless we bungled the security check.

Shade eased the *Queen Bee* closer, maintaining his spot in line. Two ships to go, and then it was our turn. It was hard not to stare out the clear panel at the massive guns pointed in our direction. Firepower like that could cut this little cruiser in half. Decimate it in just the second it took for one of those high-powered energy beams to hit.

Frank's intel gave us the access code belonging to a maintenance crew arriving sometime today from a Dark

Watch ground facility on Ewelock. That code was the reason we needed to maintain a tight schedule, get here sooner rather than later, and do our work quickly. If that new crew had already checked in, we were screwed. We'd have to run with our tails between our legs and hope a phaser beam didn't blast us into oblivion. If they tried to check in while we were still inside...

Yeah. That would be a problem, too.

The plan was good but not foolproof. As far as heists went, this one balanced out at about medium-high risk, with a few too many variables orbiting the core of the operation for any of us to go into it entirely confident of our success. The payoff for the DT Mooncamps would be huge if we pulled it off. But there were no guarantees in this business, and suddenly, I wondered if I'd made a bad choice when Shiori needed me most.

We moved up one more spot in line, and Frank started rattling off our jobs again. Going over the plan at least eight times before we actually got started was as much a part of Frank as his cheeky smile.

I looked over my shoulder into the back section of the cruiser as he started his final rundown, pointing at Caeryssa first.

"You've got the first unit. As soon as Tess detaches the food hold, use its thrusters to move away from the spacedock. You'll have a monitor showing you nearby objects and distances, but it's not like flying a ship. It's a glorified hover crate, bigger and pressurized. Just avoid whatever's out there and get enough free space around you for the *Unholy Stench* to pick you up."

Caeryssa nodded, just as she had the first several times. Her tightly pulled-back hair and angular features made her look austere and humorless, especially in that Dark Watch uniform. She smiled, ruining the dour vibe. "I got it, Frank. Relax."

Frank didn't relax. If he'd had the room, he would have paced. "Asher?"

"Here, Boss." Asher's voice came to us over the coms. "Like we agreed, I'm staying back until the time's right. Don't want to make anyone suspicious."

"Same." Merrick spoke for the first time since our initial device check. We'd arrived outside of Ewelock together, he'd grunted, and that was that. "I've got the *Stench* on our starboard side. We should still be off the station's close-range monitors."

There was way too much traffic around a big rock like Ewelock for the Dark Watch to worry about ships farther out, especially on a station turnover day with tons of activity. No one would give a second thought to a couple of cargo cruisers hovering in high orbit, probably just recharging.

"Good. Good." I hoped Frank looking like a bobblehead meant he was satisfied, because we were next in line once the ship ahead of us cleared out.

I turned back around and peered through the clear panel. The midsized vessel in front of us didn't go anywhere.

"They usually this slow?" Shade's fingers drummed against the long, strong thigh that filled out his Dark Watch uniform to perfection. I didn't like seeing him in these clothes, though. It was too close to the reality of less than a month ago.

"You tell me." I shrugged. "I don't usually come in through the front door."

His mouth flattened..

Shit, I didn't mean... "Shade—"

He cut me off with a shake of his head. "Don't worry about it."

I took a deep breath, trying not to look at those huge guns

or think about the fact that I'd just thrown Shade's past in his face again. He'd accepted a freaking AI inside my body. Why couldn't I let this go?

We still didn't move up, so I turned back around. Frank had stopped bobbing his blond head up and down in order to nag Caeryssa again.

"Asher will tell you when to reverse thrusters and stop. Hopefully, whoever's monitoring the supply attachments from the station will just think it's a normal pickup. We'll be two cargo cruisers switching out some storage units. By the time they verify the schedule, or even figure out who's supposed to be verifying it today, we should be long gone."

Caeryssa gave a simple thumbs-up, used to Frank's game-day repetition. I pursed my lips. That was one of the variables I didn't like. It seemed like a lot to hope for that organization would be that out of whack, but if we worked fast, we should be all right.

Should. I caught my cheek between my teeth.

"Once the *Stench* is done attaching you, I'll be free of the security hub and ready for pickup. We'll jump to Nickleback and get out of the *Endeavor*'s way. The *Endeavor* picks up Jax first. Same system: thrusters to get loose and make some room for yourself, reverse to stop, Merrick directing you and steering his ship so that everything lines up for the vacuum seal. Shade, welcome to your first galactic heist, by the way"—Frank levered up and reached around Shade's seat to give him a hearty clap on the shoulder—"detaches the fourth cargo hold and does the same as everyone else. The *Endeavor* jumps ASAP, because somebody will've started asking questions by now.

"Tess, you get back to the cruiser. Fucking own that Dark Watch uniform and look like you belong every step of the way. Kick some poor sap while he's down, if you have to.

You'll blend right in. When you're back on board the cruiser, screw waiting in line to leave. Just fly the fuck out as fast as you can and don't get hit."

Turning forward again, I mumbled a confirmation, my mind already filtering through the hundreds of things that could go wrong with this. Teaming up was a little complicated to begin with, and Jax and I were working with a whole new crew now. We'd never been through a heist before with Shade or Merrick, and now Sanaa and Gabe were part of the mix. It felt like a fumble somewhere, from someone, was inevitable.

The midsized vessel in front of us eased forward onto one of the platforms. Second-thought jitters hit me with a vengeance just when it was too late. Our outside com button flashed, and Shade reached forward to open the channel to the security base.

I had to clench my fists in my lap to keep from grabbing his hand and snatching it back. We still had the Bridgebane info drop. Shiori to save. Reena Ahern to break out!

Shade hit the button. A thousand volts of electricity zapped my heart and sent it kicking against my ribs so hard my breath stopped. Adrenaline flared out. This was it. No turning back. Full speed ahead. *Oh great Powers. Crap!*

"Ewelock Security Hub to incoming cruiser," a bored male voice droned over the now-open channel. "State your purpose and code."

"Maintenance crew 32 coming in for duty from down below. Security code 149 354 990 Beta Echo Charlie." Shade severed the sound from our side.

I looked at him, a little wide-eyed. *Wow*, he'd kept his voice really even. I didn't think he was as calm as he sounded, but he'd done a good job at pretending.

A long pause followed. No answer.

Shade glanced at me just as my back started to sweat. I shook my head at his unspoken question. No, I didn't think a response from the station should take this long, either.

My unease building, I swiveled in my seat, turning around to gauge the rest of the crew's reactions. Behind me, Jax sat with his shoulders rolled forward, his forearms braced on his thighs, and his tense back all hunched up over him. His narrowed gaze never left the outside com button. Frank half stood behind Shade's seat, his blue eyes the only color in his face as he watched the station's entrance with a worried scowl. In a third-row pull-down seat behind him, Caeryssa started to twitch. Her legs launched into rapid-fire nervous bounces that made me want to leap into the back and sit on her. I could practically see the perspiration beading on their foreheads.

I swung back around, a ball of dread ballooning in my windpipe. *Holy Sky Mother, what were we thinking?*

Frank was going to hit one food hold during the moving day confusion and take off with it. Now we were stealing *four*? With two unarmed cargo cruisers coming into the line of fire? And five of us going onto the Ewelock hub, with me left there alone?

My breath sawed in and out. Only an idiot wouldn't be scared shitless, right? But didn't big jobs always feel like this? A tangle of sweat and fear and near-regret with the potential reward keeping you too invested in the process to back out? If we pulled this off—*when* we pulled it off—we'd have a whole lot to show for our efforts. Food for the DT Mooncamps for *months*. That was where I needed to focus.

My breathing turned easier, and my pulse started to even out. No one had fired on us. Nothing was technically wrong yet.

"This doesn't feel right." Shade's mouth drew down as he lifted a hand to his controls and got ready to drop us out of line and run.

The outside com flared to life again. One bright flash undid all my calming work. Nerves clanged inside me like cymbals and jarred a hard beat from my heart.

"Crew 32, did you mean Beta Echo *Echo* Charlie?" the same uninterested voice asked.

Shade jerked his hand back from his console like a whip had cracked down on his knuckles.

I gaped at the now-silent communications board. I couldn't believe it. That was some sloppy Dark Watch.

Shade looked shocked also. He glanced at me, then over his shoulder at Frank. "What do you think?"

"It's a trick." Frank sat down and started strapping in. "They're trying to trip us up. We should go. Now."

"No." I shook my head, disagreeing with him. "They're being careless. Just listen to his voice. He's already had it with this shit. He wants moving day to be *over*. Our intel was missing something, and he's giving us an out."

Two blue lasers stared at me from Frank's grim face as he clicked his harness into place. The snick of the latch punched into my raw nerves like a fist. "You can't be sure of that."

"No, but it's a good guess. Vote now," I said, "or they'll get suspicious."

Abruptly, Jax straightened from his turtle hunch. "Let's do it."

Everyone else nodded, Frank just a half second behind.

Shade opened the channel from our end. "Yeah. Echo Echo Charlie. Isn't that what I said?"

I held my breath, not moving a single muscle. Shade's game face was incredible. Or his voice, in this case. Totally convincing. He had even me believing he was utterly calm and exactly where he belonged. I was so glad he was on my team now. I'd thought it before, but this time, the reality of it swamped me in a hot rush that raced through my blood.

The voice came back, as fed-up as ever. "When the light turns green, dock on Platform 9, Slot 28. They're waiting for you on Lower Z Level to repair those phasers that went out."

I slowly exhaled. We were in—but LZL was nearly the polar opposite of where we needed to go on the station. If we had to go to the very bottom level to maintain our cover, it would mean being on the Ewelock hub for longer than any of us wanted.

Good thing I had a mechanic. I glanced at Shade. He could totally fix some phasers.

"Got it." Shade kept his response short and sweet and disconnected from our end.

The signal light on Platform 9 turned green. He eased us through the plasma shield to the landing area.

"When this is over and you're flying out by yourself, you drop the second you can." Shade glanced at me. "If the lower phasers are out, they can't shoot you if you're beneath them."

I nodded. Not getting blown up was high on my to-do list. Right up there with stealing a bunch of stuff without getting caught. If we had to *fix* the phasers, though, this idea didn't help.

I reached for the navigation controls as Shade located Slot 28. "Time for a blank slate." If the Dark Watch somehow got its hands on the *Queen Bee*, we didn't want anyone knowing where we'd been.

"You're one step ahead of everyone, aren't you, sugar?" Shade said with a wink.

"Cupcake, we already knew that." I wiped the memory. *Delete.*

A low chuckle rumbled in his chest. "Not a modest muffin, are you?"

My lips twitched. I wiped the com device next. It looked like a new unit when I put it back in place. "I'm the big one with the nuts on top."

Shade grinned, his eyes laughing when they met mine. I grinned back, and right then, I was *sure* this crazy, ballsy plan could work.

"Are you two talking in code or something?" Caeryssa asked from the back. "Now I'm hungry," she grumbled.

"Seriously. Focus," Frank said.

I settled back in my seat. "Just blowing off steam." It was better than flipping out, which half of me still wanted to do as a traffic controller pointed us toward Landing Pad 28 with a flashing wand, backing up as we approached. Her Dark Watch uniform flapped hard against her body until Shade shut down the propulsion system and powered off. She pushed back her short blonde hair, turning to her next job without sparing us another glance.

I unbuckled my harness and stood. Unlike Frank, I was a firm believer that sometimes the only way to move forward was with a smile. *Now* I would focus.

Shade reached over and gave my wrist a quick squeeze. The faint ink still on my arm with the *Queen Bee*'s ignition codes disappeared under his big hand. I'd memorized the numbers now, along with the Nickleback coordinates. He looked at me hard before letting go. I nodded a silent promise to be careful. He nodded back the same vow and then popped the locks, exhaling a long steadying stream of air.

I did the same and hopped down, trying to release tension and move in the loose, relaxed way of a person who had every right to be here. I wasn't sure I succeeded. The stolen uniform felt slippery and weird, and these boots were heavy and a size too big for my feet. Moreover, I'd never be comfortable with a gun openly strapped to my side. I hoped we wouldn't have to use our Grayhawks, but we sure as hell weren't leaving them behind.

The others poured out after me, but Shade slipped into the back. A moment later, he emerged with a steel-gray oblong toolbox. We really were a Dark Watch maintenance team of five.

I glanced from side to side as Shade closed the cruiser, hoping we could walk straight to the lifts and disappear. My eyes snagged on a woman staring out at us from a glassed-in side office, a frown making her squint through the window. I let my gaze skate away but kept her in my peripheral vision as we started moving.

Uh-oh. She left the office and strode over to intercept us at a rapid, boot-pounding pace.

I tried not to panic as she planted herself in front of us halfway to the elevator block and swept a quick inspection over the whole group. Her stark black uniform matched everyone else's here, including ours, except for the red stripe across her chest pocket. She was a team captain of some sort. Landing dock security? Chief of Platform 9? Her scowl sent a wary vibration tingling up my spine.

"Crew 32?" Blue eyes narrowed under thick blunt bangs that partially hid an amoeba-shaped birthmark sliding down her temple.

"That's right," I answered.

She looked beyond us toward the *Queen Bee.* "Where's

Bob?" Suspicion scrolled across her face like a computerized warning.

Bob? How the hell should I know? "Grounded. Whole crew's in the hospital." I forced a twang into my voice to match the nasally thing I'd heard coming from Sector-7-born kids at the orphanage, some of them from Ewelock. "Food poisoning. Can you believe that? Bad luck. Anyhow, Bob sent us instead. Knew it was urgent to fix those LZL phasers. Gotta keep your bottoms up."

And that was that. We weren't impersonating the maintenance crew anymore; we were replacing them. Adapt. Move forward. Don't get caught.

My fingernails bit into my palm, and I uncurled my fist, letting my hand dangle.

"The phasers went out earlier." She frowned. "No explanation for it."

"We'll figure it out." I gave a short nod, trying to end the conversation and hoping she might not pay attention if we went up the spacedock instead of down.

The Ewelock security hub followed the same architectural pattern as any spacedock the Dark Watch had built during the last twenty-five years. Just more proof that the Overseer had zero imagination and that once he found a system that worked, he poured it in concrete across the galaxy. Or in this case, reinforced metal, huge clear panels, and massive firepower. Upper A to Z. Middle A to Z. Lower A to Z. Seventy-eight levels. Food storage units were always attached to Upper Levels A to O.

I didn't know Bob, but I knew how to pretend to fit in here, thanks to time spent on Starbase 12—the original three-tiered alphabet-model spacedock. The Overseer had required "his daughter" for plenty of official functions and paraded Mom and me out when it was convenient. On the starbase, it was Uncle Nate who'd shown me around, and I'd been granted a certain amount of freedom because of the secure location. Otherwise, Mom and I were only allowed some fancy shopping trips here and there on Alpha Sambian, mainly to show our faces in public—a reminder to the galaxy that the Overseer was a generous family man, a model for everyone.

A model who didn't even let his kid go to school. People assumed I had a home tutor, but I didn't. Mom taught me to read and write, and Uncle Nate brought us books. I didn't set foot in a classroom or interact with other children until Starway 8 became my home.

"But Bob..." The team captain's eyes strayed to the entrance with the long line of waiting ships.

"He'll be up when he's feeling better. Won't be long now."

Her expression cleared somewhat. I must have been convincing.

She glanced at Shade's toolbox and waved us forward. "Follow me." She walked us to the lifts, waited for one to open, and pushed the button to the bottom level herself. "You know the way once you're down there?"

"Yeah. Not our first DWALSH." Hopefully, no one but me noticed the irritation in my voice. No choice now: we were going in the wrong direction first.

She stepped back, letting us go. I couldn't tell if she was still suspicious. I wasn't using a secret language or anything, but most people didn't say things like LZL, keep your bottoms up, or DWALSH if they didn't frequently live or work on Dark Watch alphabet-level security hubs.

The doors closed, leaving us in the silent lift, although it seemed to me that I could hear every single one of our pulses beating frantically.

"We have to go all the way down now, don't we?" Caeryssa muttered.

"It's safest," I answered, hoping there wasn't a microphone in here. Even the all-controlling Dark Watch didn't want to hear everyone's random conversation in an elevator. The little camera in the back corner needed to keep seeing the tops of our heads until we got off where we were supposed to, though. "Bob's friend with the bangs could be monitoring our progress from her office. And we should walk back up. Get between the inner and outer shells of the station." The elevators would be pandemonium today, slow and crowded, but hardly anyone would actually be working or needing access to the cargo attachments.

Frank groaned. "That's a hell of a workout."

"You scared of some stairs, Frank?" I slid him a challenging look.

"Not all of us get a hearty workout running for our lives every day like you do, Bailey." His effort at humor scraped a thin layer off the coating of dread sticking to our group like rotten honey.

Eight levels down and still in the docking areas, the lift opened. A Red Beam zipped past. I forced myself not to flinch, and the drone's searching red eye swiveled toward the guy blocking the lift with an arm and waving his friends over.

We all stood absolutely still, trying not to draw the drone's attention. It locked on to the two young men moving toward the lift at a jog and then zoomed away to scan an incoming vessel.

Time seemed to slow as we waited for them to get in the elevator. A saw buzzed. Sparks showered off a ship being repaired two landing pads over. The roar of the blowtorch scorched my ears as though it were right next to us, but at least it dulled the sound of my hammering heartbeat, the powerful thuds nearly deafening me.

When the two others arrived, we backed up, making room for the trio juggling bags and boxes at the lift entrance. They barreled in together like an asteroid, all energy and impact. Nerves jumped in my throat. How long until another Red Beam flew by? DWALSHs were always crawling with them.

My pulse echoed through all my hollow places and pounded out warnings. *Close the doors. Move now. Finish this.*

One of the new recruits—because they were definitely that, complete with brand-new Dark Watch uniforms and pristine military-issued packs—glanced up at Jax as he balanced his belongings, using one knee to help. "Can you press Middle H for us? No hands." He smiled, his pile of stuff teetering.

Jax reached past the young man's shoulder and pressed MH on his side of the lift. The scar on his cheek stretched as his jaw flexed.

One of the others tilted his head back. Not too tall and a little scrawny, he seemed in awe of Jax. "Man, you're huge. I'm glad I signed up." All three nodded and grinned, as if simply joining the Dark Watch turned you into a badass heap of man like Jax.

I forced even breaths in and out, reminding myself that these were kids, barely out of school and probably not yet understanding that they'd just sold their souls to a demon in a brown suit.

"You guys part of the new crew?" The boy who'd stopped the elevator glanced at us over his shoulder. His open gaze zeroed in on me. I was in the middle. His bone structure and coloring reminded me of Miko's. Instant fury rose up, because she was gone, and he was joining the man who'd killed her. "This is our first assignment."

No kidding. It was hard not to ask why he looked so proud to be a spanking new member of the arm of oppression that reached across the galaxy. Would he wake up one day and wonder why he was doing the dirty work of a totalitarian regime that had replaced democracy? Would he choose a new path and change his life? Or would that easy, boyish smile gradually twist into a sneer as power over others corrupted him?

"Maintenance," I said curtly.

He seemed to expect more, but I didn't feel like chatting.

He turned back around, looking a little cowed and awkward. After a moment, he and his buddies laughed about something they'd done down on Ewelock the night before, a last hurrah before active duty. Apparently, twins were involved, which was frankly too much information for a crowded elevator.

MH flashed on the upper screen, the lift stopped, and the doors opened.

The three new recruits mumbled goodbyes without looking back at us and quickly exited, still laughing and bumping shoulders with each other. Shade was the only one who managed to mumble a goodbye back. I was too busy wanting to bash their heads together.

We hit Lower Z without meeting anyone else, which was a small miracle considering the moving-day bustle.

As the lift stopped, Shade leaned close to my ear and murmured, "You weren't very friendly to those kids."

"They're not my friends," I answered.

The doors opened, and I leaned cautiously forward, checking the corridor up and down for a Red Beam. No security drones in sight. I stepped into the deserted hallway, not surprised that Lower Z was dead. The last level of each alphabet tier was mainly used to house the big systems for that section. I could hear the low hum of the air and water recycling units that took up most of the level, along with the cluster of phasers that protected the bottom of the spacedock.

"But don't you think they might remember the tall grumpy lady in the lift?" Shade asked, following me down the corridor along with the others.

"We're on a DWALSH," I said. "It's better to intimidate than be friendly. Friendly is what stands out. Pretty soon, they'll know to expect to be scared and bullied, and then they'll start doing the same to the next group of kids just so they can stop getting picked on themselves."

"That doesn't sound like you." Shade looked at me as though he suspected possible body snatching. "And that's a pretty grim outlook."

"The galaxy's a pretty grim place." I waved my hand to the right when we came to a choice of corridors. Then—because now guilt was stabbing at me like a tiny little ice pick—I muttered, "They chose this life."

Besides, what did he want me to do? Give them a rousing *Join the rebellion* speech when we were trying to blend in?

"Not everyone has the luxury of choice," Shade said.

"Luxury?" I asked, incredulous. "Is that what I live in? You *always* have a choice."

If my goal was to shut him up, it worked. Shade didn't say another word.

Regret clawed at my chest. I wanted to stop and apologize, but we didn't have time for that.

"You know where you're going, right?" Frank asked. They'd been following me, but we weren't exactly on the level for which we'd studied floor plans and exits. Or they had. I could walk this place blind.

"We're about to come up on the phaser control room. There's no bypassing it if we want to get to this level's cargo spine exit." And from there, the stairs.

Everyone on this crew was used to simply accepting that I knew certain things about military structures, especially security hubs, which all followed the same design pattern. Jax mostly understood why. So did Shade now, but I could still see the questions spinning in his eyes. Sure, I'd spent time on Starbase 12 as a kid, but Shade probably hadn't expected me to be *this* familiar with the inside of a DWALSH.

"Look sharp," I whispered before we turned the next corner. "Bound to be people here."

A series of windows stretched down the corridor on our left, the slightly darkened room behind them filled with floor-to-ceiling monitors that lent a greenish glow to every-thing around us. A row of podlike chairs faced the monitors, and I knew they had built-in directional and firing controls linked to the LZL phasers. The massive weapons pointed out at different angles from the rounded base of the station. The chairs were unoccupied, and the screens all showed error messages. Only four soldiers milled about when there were chairs for a dozen. Another moving day win—plus the guns weren't working. The soldiers spotted us the second we turned the corner, and I'd bet good money that Bangs on Platform 9 told them we were coming.

I hadn't truly thought we'd make it to the stairwell without having to deal with anyone more dangerous than those kids in the elevator. I'd just…hoped. At least we weren't outnumbered.

Having no choice but to forge ahead, I stopped and popped my head into the room when we reached the entrance. "I hear your guns are out."

A woman left the group by the monitors and walked over. "The damn things stopped working a few hours ago. The system just went blank. Never happened before."

"Yeah. Weird," I agreed. Were we really going to have to fix these phasers? That would be counterproductive in *all* ways.

I felt Shade at my elbow. His body heat steadied me. We had two options, as far as I could see. Do the maintenance, if we could, and move on, or incapacitate these people before they were onto us.

"Glad you're finally here." She frowned, peering through the doorway to look more carefully at us. "Wait. Who are you?"

"Bob couldn't make it. He sent us." Caeryssa's easy-breezy voice rang false to my ears. She leaned against the other side of the doorframe.

"But..." The woman's face blanked in confusion. The pervasive green glow lent a waxen and inanimate quality to her features. "I just talked to Bob. He'll be here in a few minutes."

I stared at her. Well, that was bad news. And moved up our timing. As soon as Bob and the real Crew 32 arrived, this whole starbase would be after us.

Oddly, I didn't panic. Cold calm took over. Incapacitate it was—and quickly.

The soldier's hand inched toward her belt. There was a Grayhawk there as well as an emergency button that would alert the whole base to a problem.

The three others glanced over but didn't leave their spot next to the row of pod chairs. From here, it looked as though they were passing around a handheld video game. Dark Watch downtime. It seemed so...normal.

I was still mostly in the hallway and half-hidden by the doorframe. My gun was visible, just like hers. I didn't even twitch in its direction. No need to confirm her suspicions.

I slid a hand into my pocket hidden by the doorway. My fingers curled around the little canister I'd found near a vault of precious books—a bonus I'd held on to when I sold the rest to Susan. I pulled out the small metallic tube. It was barely palm-sized and felt warm from being against my body. I found the trigger with my index finger, whipped the can up, and misted sleeper spray into the woman's face.

Her eyes made a sudden O, just like her mouth. No sound came out. She dropped, her legs folding under her like ribbons. She was down in two seconds flat.

"What the hell?" The other three goons gawked in shock before springing into action. Two men and a woman charged us.

Shade blew past me like a rocket. *Jab. Jab. Cross.* He sent the largest man down with a crash. Right behind him, I bulldozed into another soldier and shoved him straight into Jax. Jax grabbed him around the neck from behind and heaved him out of the way. I swung back to Shade, finding a gun aimed point-blank at his chest.

Shade's hands went up. My heart stopped dead and so did Shade, all motion arrested as the female soldier looked at him, cocking her head. Steady arm. Finger on the trigger. Bloodlust brightened her eyes. She had *cold-blooded killer* stamped across her face in neon lights.

Panic flared inside me, lighting a reckless and furious fuse. I lunged just as Frank shot out the camera in the corner of the room, distracting her. Her gaze flicked away from her target for half a second, and I rammed into her from the side.

She grunted as we slammed together and went down hard with me on top. I grabbed her wrist and cracked her hand into the thin gray carpet. Once. Twice. Harder. I growled and ground down with a twist.

She yelped and her fingers popped open, letting go of the gun. I shifted my balance and smashed my elbow into her skull. Her eyes rolled back. Done.

A gun went off, leaving a smoking hole in the floor by my feet. I snatched my legs in and scrambled back. Shade jumped in front of me, his arms spread out.

"Frank!" Still in the doorway on lookout, Caeryssa ducked as two Red Beams flew in, buzzing over her head. From a crouch, she pivoted and tracked one with her shots. She sent the first drone spinning into the far wall. Frank blew the second one from the air just as it shot back at him with a stun blast. He dove behind a table.

Damn it! Red Beams were a plague. More would come.

The guy struggling with Jax let off another shot. The free-standing console next to me toppled over, a big crack in the top. Electronics bled out like innards. Sparks flew in my face. I lunged away as an electrical fire broke out.

The goon fired again, and I dragged Shade behind a chair with me. Shots banged. Stuffing flew out. I flinched and kept down. I couldn't shoot back without endangering Jax.

Jax roared like the unhinged beast he was and moved his arm into a crushing hold around the guy's neck. He jerked the man to the side, trying to get me out of the line of fire just as the soldier let off a string of crazy shots. The big monitors on the control-room wall shattered and went dark. Jax clamped down hard and shook the man with a snarl. The goon dropped his gun and ripped at Jax's arm, his air cut off. Jax was immovable, a stone wall with death carved into the lines of his face. His scar whitened. His muscles bulged. He squeezed.

I sprang out from behind the chair. "Jax, no!" He went into terrible depressions when he killed someone with his bare hands. It triggered something that firing shots didn't, even if the outcome was the same.

Jax's eyes met mine, feral. I held his gaze. *Easy, partner.*

He shot at you! Jax's silent scream nearly deafened me, low and hollow and wild.

I stood there, unharmed. Not a spot of blood on me. Not a bruise. *I'm fine. I'm here. Let's take another step—together. Like we always do.*

After a long, fraught beat, his grip loosened, and he eased his choke hold enough for the man to breathe.

Jax's eyes dulled to brown again instead of burning, but I didn't move. I kept his focus on me until Frank dove forward and picked up the tiny can of sleeper spray I'd dropped.

"Jax!" Frank shouted, his arm outstretched. He pressed. Jax held his breath, closed his eyes, and shoved the guy straight into the oncoming vapor. The goon fell while Caeryssa reached out and jerked Jax back, hauling him away from the fast-acting mist. Jax's back hit the wall of windows, and she crashed into his chest. They got their balance and sprang toward the doorway. The rest of us followed without a backward glance.

"Red Beam!" Caeryssa warned, swinging right with her gun to cover us as we flew out the door to the left. The security drone zinged back and forth to avoid her shots, ordering us to surrender in a robotic voice. The machine scanned her while it armed itself.

"Caeryssa Clare Owens. Wanted. Halt."

"Not today," she muttered, letting the Red Beam get closer and level out.

I swung around, starting back. "Ryssa!"

"Go!" she shouted and shot. The Red Beam exploded a millisecond after firing off a crimson ray that crackled with volts.

"Ah! Shit!" Caeryssa stumbled against the wall. Her right leg gave out, and she dropped.

Jax hurried back and scooped her up. "I've got you," he said. "Breathe through it."

"Stupid stun blaster." She winced, clinging to his neck. "Twenty minutes before my leg works."

I cursed. I knew from experience that hurt like hell, and now Jax was going to have to climb about sixty-five levels with a woman on his back.

Strike that. We'd never make it to the food holds unless our luck turned fast.

As if reading my mind, Shade said, "We gotta do something else."

I nodded. "Merrick, fly in now. We're going to need you."

"You, too, Asher," Frank said.

Both confirmed over the coms. "Everyone all right?" Asher asked.

"If by *all right*, you mean alive, then yes," I said.

Someone blew out an audible breath. In my gut, I knew it was Gabe.

"Our time just got cut *way* down." Frank pocketed the sleeper spray as we sped down the corridor. "Goons'll be here any second."

They'd flood the level, but they had to organize and get down here first. We'd be dealing with more Red Beams before that. "Go right!" I cried.

We skidded around the corner, our boots squeaking loudly. Shade and I ran fastest and ended up in front.

Another Red Beam zoomed in from ahead. I got ready to duck, but Shade slowed, took aim, and shot it before it got too close.

We leaped over the debris, parts of the drone still whirring and clicking, its crimson eye wide open and searching for us. Frank kicked it hard as he passed, punting it into the wall. It stopped chirping.

I glanced back. Pretty soon, actual people would catch up, and they'd be a lot more dangerous than security drones.

"Come on!" I yelled over my shoulder. Jax was slower than usual because of Caeryssa's weight, and Frank was hanging back to cover them.

"How far, Tess?" Shade asked, his alert gaze scanning for threats both ahead and behind.

"Haven't you ever been on a DWALSH?" I asked between panting breaths.

"I've never been in the basement of one looking for the spine exit with the Dark Watch about to attack!"

Yeah. Fair point.

"I delivered…" He trailed off with a shake of his head. "I didn't hang around memorizing the layout."

No, that was just me, a kid whose only playground was Starbase 12, the original Dark Watch alphabet-level security hub, with all the others modeled after it to the letter—literally. Uncle Nate had written up treasure hunts that encouraged me to search the station from top to bottom for my reward, usually a book. We'd crawled all over that place.

He'd been preparing me from the beginning, hadn't he? Memorizing the security hub floor plans, flying *Dark Watch 12* from his lap, giving me banned books on the sly, idealizing his and Mom's birth Sector of 17 in my head until the rebel bastion felt more like home to me than Sector 12 ever did. He'd been giving me the tools I needed to escape Simon Novalight. To *fight* him. Uncle Nate had shoved me straight into the arms of the resistance via Starway 8.

My chest started to ache in a way that had nothing to do with bolting down the hallway, each breath more labored than the last. Why did he leave us? Just stop showing up in the months before Mom died? And why did he try to capture me on Starway 8 and then threaten people that I love? He wanted to protect me. I *knew* that.

And deep down, I knew why he'd been willing to bring me in. Nathaniel Bridgebane could sacrifice individuals, even me, for the greater good.

Now, the GIN Project was in motion. Uncle Nate had wanted to keep the Overseer from doing something drastic in search of more type A1 blood by handing over some of mine, but he'd been too late. We both had.

"We're close," I finally answered, my thoughts in turmoil, the next turn in sight. There'd be no going back for Shade's cruiser. The *Queen Bee* was lost.

"We're all coming out in a cargo attachment from the bottom," I said for our crews on the ships. A big box with thrusters would have to do for a getaway ship. No clue what was in it. Something useful, I hoped.

Both temporary captains acknowledged that.

"You pick 'em up. I'll run interference," Asher said.

Merrick grunted an affirmative response.

"Go for two if you can," Sanaa said, speaking for the first time.

Was she for real? She wanted us to climb the stairs to Lower Y and take another box? What the hell? Not all of us were super soldiers.

"Damn it!" Frank growled a curse. "All for nothing."

All for nothing was the least of it. We'd be lucky to get out of here alive.

"We're coming in low," Merrick said. "Just push straight off, and we'll attach you as fast as we can."

"I'll catch you, Tess," Gabe whispered right in my ear, his voice low and intimate and a little bit hoarse. "Just come back to me."

I didn't answer. There was way too much in that request for me to deal with right now.

I slanted a look at Shade. He stared fixedly ahead.

We rounded the corner, my heart seizing in fear when shouts to stop and sudden shots chased us around the bend.

I glanced back. At our rear, Frank spun, stuck his arm around the corner, and hammered off several rounds from his Grayhawk. He sprinted to catch up. "They're closing in!"

The last turn loomed ahead. "Left here, then straight to the end!" I took off at a dead sprint, ignoring my aching legs and burning lungs. If I got to the door fast enough, the others might not even have to slow down.

I ran as if death itself chased me. It *did*. My nerves frayed a little more with each step, thinning until the raw bits sawed against each other. I finally came up on the exit door to the cargo spine and slowed just enough not to flatten myself against it. Lifting my hand, I pressed the pad of my right thumb firmly into the center of my left palm and touched all five fingers together like a pointed roof over it. A tingle webbed out from the center of my hand, spidering toward my fingertips.

What I hadn't told Shade was that I had to activate the AI. Someone just holding my hand up to a lock wouldn't get anywhere. Body scans wouldn't pick it up unless it was turned on. The whole thing was disturbingly discreet. A secret weapon—a tool for a spy or a thief. Or a genocidal control freak.

As soon as my hand went completely numb, I positioned it directly in front of the control panel next to the door. I shook, partly from fear and the fatigue of the run and partly because a piece of my body was being controlled by something other than me right now.

"Come on!" Anxiety pumped through me and kept my hair on end. Not even the heat and perspiration of running for our lives could keep the sudden chill from my skin.

I glanced over my shoulder. The others raced down the corridor. Caeryssa clung to Jax's front like a monkey, her arms around his neck, one hand stretched out and firing. Shade and Frank both turned to shoot, loping sideways and trying to cover each other. Bullets pinged around them, but the goons on their tail were taking cover behind the bend and shooting wildly down the hallway without aiming. I'd bet my ship they were waiting for a swarm of Red Beams.

I held my gun in my free hand, shifting nervously. Numbers started flashing across the lock's small screen faster than I could read them.

The lock beeped just seconds after the override started. This type of control panel used simple badge recognition for workers unloading supplies to this level. Nothing fancy, and even quicker than I'd expected.

I pushed through and stepped onto the grated metal platform, holding one side of the double doors open. The cold hit me instantly. I shivered. It was pressurized and livable in the open space between the shells, but it sure as hell wasn't heated like the inner station.

I glanced up, remembering what Sanaa said about nabbing two cargo holds. Zigzagging flights of stairs and a latticework of unloading platforms climbed above me until the curve of the rounded spacedock cut them off from view. There was definitely no making it to the food storage on the upper tier of the station, but one more level might be doable.

I turned back to the others. "Red Beams!" I shouted.

A drone army rounded the corner. Dozens came at us. I could barely see the ceiling. Stun blasts chased my friends down the corridor. They sprinted as though the floor were on fire, and I curved my body around the doorway and shot above their heads. I didn't have to aim. I just fired and hit things.

Goons moved in behind the cover of the drones, masks down and shields up. They weren't taking any chances.

Jax careened past me with Caeryssa, clipping my shoulder. I righted myself and kept shooting. I'd be out of bullets soon.

Shade spun around and faced the Dark Watch as the hallway erupted into a war zone. Drones exploded in the air like bombs, raining down sparks and bits of metal. Frank barreled through the doorway next, and Shade brought up the rear, covering everyone's asses.

He backed toward us, crimson lasers flashing all around him.

"Shade!" I cried. "We're in!"

He turned and sprinted the final steps. I tried to cover him, but a Red Beam swooped down and fired. A stun blast hit him square in the back and he toppled forward, one hand reaching through the doorway.

CHAPTER

16

SHADE

MY BACK IS ON FIRE! I CLAWED AT THE METAL FLOORING under my fingers and tried to haul myself forward.

My shoulder didn't work. The muscles didn't respond. I couldn't feel my upper legs, either.

Tess lunged, grabbed my outstretched arm, and dragged me through the doorway. Where'd she find the strength? I was fucking heavy.

Jax slammed the door on the stun rays blasting into the loading area. One hit my right calf before the barrage cut off. My body erupted in flaming agony. My whole leg went volcanic, and I sucked in a sharp breath. Then I grimaced as a painful loss of control took over. The inability to move chilled me to the bone. Hot. Cold. Fucking terrifying. It felt like most of my body was missing.

Frank plugged the electronic lock on our side with two quick rounds, blowing it to pieces. Sparks flew. It went dead just as the doors rattled.

The heavy thud of bodies pounding against metal

drummed in the loading area. Shouts echoed through to us. I'd never been on the wrong side of this shit before. And here I was, living it every day now.

Someone bellowed. Gunshots rang out on the other side of the door panels. Nothing came through. Were they stupid?

Tess took careful aim above us. With five shots, she destroyed the locks on the next five levels. She tried for six, but her gun clicked, out of bullets.

"Impressive." I looked up at her from the floor, smiling stupidly. My woman thought fast and fought hard. Her hand-to-hand combat was messy and unorthodox, but she could run like the wind and had spectacular aim with a Grayhawk.

"What are you grinning about?" Tess grinned back at me.

"Just happy to be alive, starshine." I was giddy with it.

"This isn't over yet." She crouched next to me and laid her hand on my shoulder. She squeezed, but I didn't feel it. "Can you move?"

Barely. "Parts of me work. Help me up and maybe I can hop somewhere."

She and Jax pulled me up to standing. I balanced on my left foot and grabbed the platform railing.

"This has to be the worst heist ever." My knees knocked together. I only felt one of them. It was like an out-of-body experience—not that I'd ever had one.

Tess pursed her lips. "I don't know about that. We finished the last heist in a black hole. So far, this is better."

"True." It was all relative. But at least they'd had something to show for that one: a lab full of enhancers.

Tess holstered her empty weapon and ground her right thumb into the center of her left hand as she turned toward the vacuum-seal control panel. She mashed her fingers together in a tight triangle and then held her left palm up to the locking mechanism. Within seconds, the control panel beeped, and the doors slid open.

Jax, Frank, Caeryssa, and I were all right there, watching. They had to know, or at least suspect. How could they not? Unless they believed in magic, they had to know there was some kind of illegal tech involved. They simply didn't care. They had Tess's back and kept her secrets—didn't even ask about them. They were family in the way that had been missing from my life for a decade.

But maybe that void was finally filling up again.

An ache shot through my heart. The blazing pain from the two stun blasts had given way to numbness, and that one beating muscle was pretty much all I could feel in my body. I couldn't even lift a hand to rub my chest, so the tightness simply stayed there.

Tess sprang out of the way when the door panel slid open. Frank helped Caeryssa stumble into the accordion-like passageway of the vacuum seal, propelling her toward the other side of the air lock. Jax got a shoulder under my arm and half dragged me through after them. Once we were in, Tess closed the door and changed the code. It was hard to tell, but I thought she typed out *Gabriel* on the number pad, and I scowled.

"We could leave it open," Caeryssa said. "The space between the shells will depressurize when we detach. An emergency like that would distract the whole station. They won't have time to come after us." Her cold pragmatism should've surprised me but didn't. It was a good idea, in fact.

Tess pushed past us to get to the far lock and repeated the process with her hand and fingers. She shook her head as she held up her palm to the control panel. "If I get you guys in this one, I might be able to run up to the next level and snag that one, like Sanaa said. Between both our ships, they can pick us up quickly."

"By yourself?" I frowned at her. "We don't even know what's in the next cargo hold. Not worth it." Goons'd be here any second, despite Tess having shot out the locks on the next five levels. They could still come down the stairs and would—unless they were in danger of being sucked out into space. "Leaving a gaping hole right here sounds like a good plan to me."

Caeryssa nodded.

"We don't know what's in this one, either," Tess said.

"Our escape, for one thing." That was what mattered.

Numbers started scrolling across the small rectangular screen. Tess kept her hand up, watching the blur of combinations go by. "I don't know. We'll see what's in this one. There's usually similar stuff grouped together. *Why* is this taking so long?" She glared at the control panel and shifted from foot to foot, her agitation growing.

This lock was definitely different from the one built into the outer shell of the spacedock. Much more sophisticated. Maybe there was something of real value in this container. Cure-alls? Weapons? I almost hoped not, because Tess wouldn't listen to me then. She'd go for another.

"I'll go with you," Jax said. With his agreement, I sensed a losing battle and bit down on a curse. "Frank can steer this one while Shade and Ryssa recover."

I wanted to howl at the idea of being separated, but Tess just nodded, all business.

"Actually…" Frank lifted his hand from his side. It came away bloody.

"Shit! Frank!" Caeryssa hopped backward on one leg, taking her weight off him.

"I guess a goon got lucky," Frank said through a grimace.

"What's going on?" a female voice asked sharply over the com. Macey? Nic? I couldn't tell. It wasn't Fiona or Mwende.

"Frank has a bullet in his side!" Caeryssa nearly shouted.

"I think it went through," Frank said. "No big deal." The black material of his stolen goon gear clung to his side, now noticeably shiny and wet under his fingers.

No big deal? What was over there? The spleen? I couldn't remember.

"Let me be the judge of that when you get back here," the woman from the *Stench* said.

"Sure, Mace," Frank answered.

"And make it quick, you stupid idiot."

Frank just nodded, even though she couldn't see him.

The lock finally beeped. The door slid open, retracting into the side of the cargo unit. We stared. About a hundred and fifty people stared back at us.

What the hell?

Women, men, and children of all ages and what looked like all walks of life stood crowded against one another in the cargo hold, some in well-made clothing and others in rags and sandals. No matter what they wore, they were rumpled, huddled, and terrified. The place smelled like a filthy prison. Unwashed bodies. Human waste in corners. Fuck, it was disgusting. And inhumane. Who would do this?

"It's her." A middle-aged man at the front of the crowd pointed at Tess. His hand shook from the effort. When had these people last eaten? And why was he pointing at my girlfriend?

Tess pointed back at herself. "Me?"

"He said you'd come for us."

Tess blanched. I lurched closer to her on the leg that still functioned. Focusing on the man who'd spoken, I demanded, "What are you talking about?"

"She's come to save us," he said hollowly. He stared at Tess, everything in his expression half defeated already. "Haven't you?"

"I'll help you," she answered without hesitation. "But I don't know what happened here. Who told you I'd come?"

"The tall man with the dead eyes. He showed up where we were before and said he was moving us to where you'd be. A Dark Watch general. He moved the whole unit... I don't know. Several hours ago." The self-elected spokesperson shook his head, but even that effort seemed to drain him. "I don't know where we were before that, but there were more of us. Another hold like this one. Some of us have been locked up for almost a week now, and they keep adding people."

"A Dark Watch general? Tall, dark hair, blue eyes?" Tess barely breathed as she waited for confirmation.

Several people nodded.

Her nostrils flared, and her eyes turned terrible. She angled away from the crowd a little. "Sanaa? What the fuck is going on here?" Fury cracked through every word she launched at the lieutenant over the com units.

"I might have mentioned you deciding to come here," Mwende answered, a forced blandness almost covering up her accent. "Your uncle was very interested in your arrival on the Ewelock hub, especially after he found some unexpected cargo in the Sambian System. Certain phasers and storage units might have been manipulated in the meantime."

"Oh, really?" Tess spat.

"Yes, really," Mwende answered dryly.

Tess turned back around and swept a concerned gaze over the prisoners. "He could have just told us." All the fury drained from her voice.

"Too many variables. Might not have worked out, and he didn't want you living with that."

Too many variables. That was exactly what Tess had been saying about this whole plan from the start. She and Bridgebane were more alike than they realized.

"Your uncle's a Dark Watch general?" Frank was whiter than a ghost—and I didn't think it was because of the blood he was losing. "And Sanaa? What's she?"

Beside me, Tess took a huge breath, like she was gulping down a new reality. She probably was. General Bridgebane had gone from enemy number two to Uncle Nate in a matter of days, and he'd just sealed the deal with Tess by giving her proof that he was working against the Overseer. These were living, breathing people that needed help, not just empty words or vague promises he might not keep.

On top of that, the man was a mastermind. Mwende revealed our plans to him. To come to the Ewelock station. To pose as a maintenance team. Within hours, he'd organized it all. Taking out the LZL phasers. Forcing us to the bottom level to maintain our cover. Sealing a cargo hold full of prisoners to the exact spot from where we'd probably have to take off in a panic. Had he also contacted Bob, making sure the real maintenance team was on its way so that all hell would break loose and we'd never make it to the upper levels? I wouldn't put it past him, even if it put Tess in danger.

"Frank." Tess finally answered him. "They're trustworthy. Look what they gave us." She spread a hand toward the weakened and terrorized human cargo. *Great Powers,* the looks on their faces as they watched her. Hope and fear. The utter belief that she would save them. I felt their faith in her like a weight in my chest and wondered how Tess could breathe through the sudden pressure.

A swallow moved Frank's throat. He nodded. "Better get moving, Bailey."

"Sanaa, do I need to go to the next level?" Tess asked. "And no half-truths. Just tell me."

"Yes," Mwende answered. "And hurry. Security cruisers are starting to circle the station. *DW 12* is nearby and will undoubtedly be called in for backup."

"Of course it will," I muttered. Bridgebane had planned for that also.

Tess backed into the air lock, her hand rising to the door control that would shut us in here. Without her. "He'll shoot at us, won't he?"

"You know he will, Daraja."

And he'd make it look so real it would be. Tess knew that from experience.

Jax tried to follow her out, but Tess shook her head. "Frank's wounded, Shade can't move, and Ryssa's not back to normal. You fly this one."

He handed her his gun without arguing. "Plenty of rounds left." Jax hadn't been shooting. He'd been carrying Caeryssa.

Tess took it and closed the door, turning away as the panel slid shut.

Her abrupt exit jarred me. Everyone stared after her, maybe feeling as suddenly plunged into uncertainty as I did. This had been Frank's mission to begin with, but every single part of it revolved around Tess, even the unexpected ones. Our center of gravity, the solar to our system, had just left without a backward glance.

"I'm in between the shells again," Tess said softly over the coms, her voice kicking my frozen lungs back into action. "I broke the vacuum seal. You're free to go now."

"Are there goons?" I asked.

"Feet pounding on the staircase. They're coming," she said in a barely audible whisper.

My face twisted, and I swore under my breath, powerless and enraged. The Dark Watch was coming, I couldn't do a damn thing to help her, and we were only partway through a rescue mission we hadn't even known about. We'd been reduced to trying to rescue *ourselves*, and here we were, with hundreds of people counting on us.

I was able to lift a hand enough to scrape it over my scalp. I looked around me, finally getting it now. A day in the life of Tess Bailey. What a Nightchaser really does. I'd better get used to it, embrace it, because I was all in. For Tess. And for this. These people needed help, and it was us.

"Everyone brace yourselves. Jax, let's get this thing outta here." I could barely move, but I was ready to make this happen. We *had* to.

Tess's breath came faster as she raced up the stairs to the next level. Jax moved to the console near the cargo unit door and started waking up the nav system. It was as basic as they come: forward, reverse, and a steering joystick under a large, square monitor showing a bunch of indistinct shapes moving around. It looked like a kid's video game, a challenge to avoid the blobs. Dodge them to get to the next round. Hit one and you explode.

"Engaging thrusters." Jax directed a little power to the rudimentary propulsion system and gave the joystick a delicate push to angle us away from the spacedock. "We're moving out."

Tense as hell, I leaned against the wall where Jax had propped me for balance and prayed I wouldn't fall over as the cargo hold began to rattle and shift. Between not being able to steer this thing myself *or* stand up on my own, my breathing turned tight and shallow, the stale and stinking air leaving a bitter coating on my tongue. The sour bite of people sweating hope and terror from their pores swelled inside the cargo hold. The same mixture rose in me. No Tess. A body I couldn't use. Bridgebane my puppeteer again. No clue as to the outcome of this. I grimaced, clenching my teeth.

After the initial jolt of Jax setting us into motion, the cargo unit steadied as we floated through space on a trajectory toward the *Stench*. Merrick would wait for Tess. There was no question. The nervous silence broke when a man pushed his way forward through the crowd and moved toward us, his eyes on Frank. The blond captain sat slumped against the wall beside me, holding his side, his features stiff with pain. The black uniform made the rest of him look as white as a pristine, snow-capped peak.

"I'm a doctor." The man took in Frank's pale face, tense jaw, and blood-soaked fingers with a worried frown. "Can I help?"

Frank glanced up at him and then lifted his hand from his side, giving unspoken permission for the man to take a look.

As the doctor crouched by Frank and began lifting his shirt, Tess spoke again. "I'm at the Lower Y cargo door," she panted. "Opening it now."

Come on, baby. My lips moved, hardly making a sound. It was torture not having a visual on her, not being able to help. My heart pounded like it wanted to punch through my chest and burst right out. *You'll get through this, starshine. You've made it through worse.*

Silence. Silence. Gunshot!

I jolted off the wall, nearly pitching over. "Tess?"

"They're here! Just above me. Come on, come on!"

"Stop! We've got you now, rebel!" Gunshots cracked over the com, riddling my nerves with bullet holes.

"Tess? Baby!"

No answer, and my chest started to collapse in on itself. *Powers. No. Fuck!*

"Tess!" I bellowed, swiveling frantically to look at Jax.

Jax might've howled louder, covering whatever sounds came from the crews on our ships. He whipped toward me, a crazed gleam spreading through his eyes at the speed of light.

"I'm in!" Tess cried. Another shot went off. She hissed. "Son of a bitch!"

Fear choked me. "What is it?"

Gabe echoed me from the *Endeavor* when he really needed to shut the fuck up.

"Daraja?" Mwende said.

More gunshots roared over the coms, so loud I knew they were point-blank. My world spiraled out of control. No one survived that.

"I'm in the air lock," Tess panted out. "Just blew the station-side control panel."

"Thank the Powers." My leg gave out, and I slid down the wall, landing next to Frank.

The doctor threw me an anxious glance. "Is she all right?" I nodded.

"Are you?" he asked.

"Stun blasts." I flopped my hands and one foot. "Still recovering."

He nodded and went back to examining Frank. It

occurred to me that he might not have been asking about my physical state.

Caeryssa caught my eye and gave me a reassuring nod with her sharp chin. *Things are moving along just fine*, she seemed to say.

I blew out a breath. *A day in the life of a Nightchaser*. I might go gray before my time, but at least I'd go gray with Tess.

She updated us on her progress. "I'm opening the second lock. It's a fancy one again." Her only way out of here now was in that cargo hold. "Someone shot me in the ass," she added, outrage firing up her voice.

"The ass?" I croaked. "Can you walk?"

"Yeah. It hurts like crazy, but I can walk. Or limp," she said.

"Holy shit, Tess. What can I do?" Gabe over the com, sounding panicked.

What can you do? Zip it and man the damn air lock.

"It's fine," Tess ground out, her growing impatience either due to the slow override of the sophisticated lock or to Gabe's stupid question when she had other things to worry about. "Surral will help."

My jaw flexed. That was Tess's solution to everything— Surral will fix it. Well, Surral wasn't here. What happened if Tess couldn't get to Starway 8 before she bled to death?

"Can you fly that hold?" I asked. After she broke the vacuum seal, maybe someone already inside it could pilot the box.

"I can do it." She didn't elaborate, and I waited for the lock to beep over the com. It finally did. The door whooshed open, and her breath hitched. "It's the same. A hundred people, at least."

The door swooshed again as Tess sealed herself inside with the human cargo. "Ignore the uniform," she told the people in the cargo attachment. "I'm here to help. I'm breaking you out of this place."

Soft murmuring and cries of relief came through to us. A shiver rippled over my half-numb body, the discernible reaction of the people trapped in that place painting a sudden wash of goose bumps across my flesh. My blood pumped harder, making me giddy and sick and fearful and alive all at once.

"Lock door and... detach," Tess muttered to herself. "I'm loose, Merrick. Pick me up as soon as I'm far enough out."

"Put pressure on the wound," Merrick answered back.

"I am." She sounded distracted, already on to her next task. "I've got a joystick in one hand and my ass in the other. That sounds like fun, but it really isn't."

Frank snorted and then winced, earning himself a frown from the doctor for jostling himself.

"Grazed rib. No organ damage that I can see." The man gently probed Frank's injury with one hand, keeping the blood-soaked uniform out of the way with the other.

"Stitches?" Caeryssa asked.

He nodded. "Several."

Great. Another patient for Surral—*if* we could get to her.

"Or this." The doc pulled something from his back pocket that made my jaw drop.

A medical laser. It would heal Frank in mere minutes. And Tess, too—as long as we could get the bullet out.

The doctor's smile was a little sad and lopsided. "I never leave home without it. I learned my lesson the day my wife died and I couldn't do a damn thing about it."

"Holy shit, I could kiss you right now," Frank said.

The doctor shrugged, but his smile turned slightly more genuine.

"They let you keep it?" I asked.

"It's not a weapon." He adjusted the little white instrument in his hand, positioning his thumb over the On button. "And I may have given the soldier inspecting me a false prognosis for a flesh-eating skin disease to distract her."

Frank barked a laugh. "Have at me, Doc."

The doctor fired up the laser and began the healing process, one hand on Frank's shoulder to steady him, and what might've been his first smile in a long time tugging at his mouth.

While the doctor worked and I sat there, useless, Jax evaded the dots on the monitor, trying to get away from the security hub and out into open enough space for Asher to pick us up. No windows and shitty visuals made it hard to know who we were avoiding. Dark Watch cruisers trying to block our path? Jax made a couple of abrupt moves that left people clinging to one another for balance and the doctor muttering a curse.

Watching Jax at the console set my teeth on edge. Even though my arms didn't work, I itched to take control.

Jax hissed the second before we collided with something and dipped hard. I toppled over, crashing sideways like gravity came up to eat me. With zero control over my body, I couldn't catch myself, and a resounding thud went through my skull. My vision swam. Blurry figures shouted and fell down. I blinked, but the chaos remained. Limbs and kids and human shit sliding all over the place. I groaned.

"Jax!" Caeryssa yelled.

"I see it!" Jax banked again hard. Everyone slid toward the far wall, screaming. I started to roll away, and the doctor reached out and grabbed me. He jerked me to a stop with one hand, finished with Frank with the other, and turned off the laser. "Everyone okay?" he asked.

Frank gaped at him. "If we live through this, will you join my crew?"

The doctor grinned. Then sobered. "You're serious?"

"You got anywhere else to go?" Was that a hint of flirtatiousness in Frank's voice? I was pretty sure it was—and that Jax could stop worrying about Fiona taking off with the captain of the *Unholy Stench* one of these days.

"I'll think about it," the doctor said. And I could tell he would.

My head still rang, but the shot of adrenaline from that hard hit must've loosened the stun blasts' hold on my limbs. I shook out a leg. A shoulder. Parts of me moved again. I sat back up against the wall next to Frank.

The doctor moved away from us but kept Frank in view, his brow knitting. He snuck another glance.

Had the universe just made a match? It was hard to miss the stars in Frank's eyes as he watched the man who'd just healed him. As for the doctor, he looked more confused than opposed.

Jax kept us on a steady course. The *Stench* moved toward us. Next to Jax, Caeryssa gripped the edge of the console for balance while she pounded her other fist against her numb leg as though trying to wake it up.

"You all right, Tess?" I asked. She'd been awfully quiet.

"For now," she answered. "They're mostly on you guys. You doing okay? Jax?"

Jax grunted, a snarl fixed on his face. There was a lot in his expression that he didn't usually show people, all that blistering hate and rage. It was a good thing he wasn't looking at the cargo. They might try to jump ship.

Jax dodged another something, but more came in fast. He was a damn good pilot, even with this piece-of-shit box. If no one shot at us, we might stand a chance.

A behemoth of a blob suddenly appeared on the radar. I wasn't sure if the sight of it was terrifying or a relief. *DW 12*. The galaxy's fucking premier warship. Because Bridgebane would be the one to mess with this escape *after setting it up*. And I knew he'd shoot the stuffing out of the little guy. I'd seen Tess's ship when the *Endeavor* landed on my doorstep.

Caeryssa gasped, making Frank turn to the monitor.

"Holy fuck, look at that," he said in horror. For the first time, he looked genuinely scared.

What had he gleaned from Tess's conversation with Mwende over the coms? Not enough to know this wasn't catastrophic. A ship like that usually spelled a guaranteed death sentence to a bunch of rebels fumbling through the Dark.

"*Dark Watch 12* just showed up," Asher said in a strangled voice. "What do I do, Boss?"

I leaned toward Frank and quietly told him, "That'll be the uncle."

Frank's blue eyes widened, then narrowed. "You hear that, Ash?"

"Heard," Asher choked out. "Belief hasn't set in yet."

"Don't worry, Asher. I feel the exact same way most of the time," Tess muttered from her cargo hold.

I kept my eyes on the monitor, watching the huge ship close in on what I thought was our cargo box next to the *Unholy Stench*. Everyone in here was watching the same thing, terror a new stink in the room.

"He better not blow us up," Frank muttered. "*Any* of us."

Caeryssa shushed him, her eyes darting to the people in the cargo hold.

"The warship is turning its phasers on us!" Asher hollered. "Tess!"

"Hold steady," Mwende said.

"Keep going, but he'll fire on you. Don't think he won't." Tess's warning came three seconds before an alarm wailed on the *Stench*.

"He grazed us, like a warning." Asher silenced the alert. "Threw me off course, but we're close. I've almost got you."

"Seal off your bottom level," Tess said. "You too, Merrick. Oh no! Bonk! Where is he?"

"I've got him, Tess," Merrick said. "Don't worry."

"He's on the bridge?"

"Yes."

I squeezed my eyes shut. Tess and that cat. I might've been kind of attached to the tabby myself.

"*DW 12*'s sending out warning messages to all cargo cruisers in the area," Asher said. "Evacuate. No attachments allowed."

"Don't back off. Keep coming," Jax said. "Is that you on my doorstep?"

The door we'd come through was the only place on the cargo hold to make the seal. Asher confirmed his position. "Yeah, we swung around. Reverse thrusters. Stop now."

Jax did as Asher directed. The abrupt slowdown jostled our human cargo again. A baby started crying. We were in the home stretch. Where was Tess?

As if I'd asked out loud, she suddenly gave an update. "I'm higher than you and going faster. *DW 12* got between us and the Ewelock phasers. They can't shoot at us now."

Given the choice, I'd rather have Bridgebane firing on us.

But I also remembered the holes in Tess's hull. Her uncle kept up appearances almost too well.

"Don't go too fast or you'll pass me," Merrick warned. "We turned and are backing toward you now."

"Got it," she said. "Who's at the back door?"

"Gabe," Merrick answered.

An image of Tess coming through the vacuum seal and jumping into Gabe's arms was *not* what I needed right now. It slammed into my brain on repeat.

"He's gonna fire!" Asher couldn't hide his panic.

"Just go with it," Tess said.

"*Go with it?*" Asher's what-the-fuck voice almost squeaked.

"I told you! Seal off your bottom level!" Tess obviously had more confidence than I did that Bridgebane wouldn't aim for something vital that could tear apart the ship.

"Okay. I sealed off the living quarters," Asher said. "But I've got Mace and Nic at the doors."

"And we've got Gabe and Sanaa." Tess hissed in pain as if she'd moved wrong and hurt herself. "Fiona, you're on the bridge?"

"Yes," the botanist answered. "And my plants better not be sucked into outer space, or I will personally dismantle *DW 12* and make Bridgebane eat a poison mushroom."

"I like this woman," Mwende said. "She has *fire*."

For some reason, Jax looked at me. He blinked. "Fiona."

"Jax?" Her voice seemed less confident now.

"I'm sorry," he said. "For yesterday. At breakfast."

A slight pause followed his apology. "I forgive you."

He drank down her words with a hard swallow. His eyes haunted, he turned back to the monitor.

For fuck's sake, if he didn't realize *I forgive you* was

actually *I love you,* he needed to have his head examined.
ASAP.

For the next thirty seconds, I watched the monitor along
with everyone else. There wasn't any space between us and
the *Stench* now. Asher was just lining us up at the air lock.

"Almost there..." he said.

Our cargo unit jolted hard as we rubbed up against the
Unholy Stench in a way that wouldn't have happened if we'd
had time to gently drift in. People gasped. The infant wailed
now, a raw scraping in my eardrums.

"He's firing!" Asher's shout got lost in the rumble of an
explosion, the deep roar rolling through the coms. We shook
also. Metal grated as we scraped against the ship. Alarms
blared on the *Stench,* shrieking like that kid.

"We've got damage! Nic? Mace?"

They both answered Asher's frantic call. Jax did his best
to steer us back into position.

"Stay focused," Tess said. "Make the vacuum attachment."

"We're bleeding crap into space. It's all over the place!"

"Crap can be replaced," she snapped. "A hundred and
fifty people and your crew and captain can't. Make. The.
Seal, Asher. Now!"

"Yeah. Yeah, I got it." Asher quieted the alarms and got
back to work. He'd have to line us up with precision again.
Under pressure, that was hard.

I figured I'd see if I could drag myself a dozen feet and
do something useful while our fate hung in the balance. It
was a struggle, but I managed to reach the terrified mother
who could barely breathe, let alone calm down her child. I
sat beside her and held out my arms. She passed the infant
over. I couldn't tell if it was a boy or a girl. It was dressed in
brown. I laid its bald head in the crook of my arm and stuck

my little finger in the kid's mouth. The baby looked up at me and sucked. Blessed silence.

"We're in place," Asher said. "Nic!"

Tension locked my shoulders. I waited.

"Done!" Nic cried in triumph.

"Go!" Tess shouted. "Don't wait for us. We'll meet you on Nickleback."

The imminent reality of leaving Tess behind sent panic blasting through my chest.

"Everyone sit!" Frank bellowed.

These people didn't need to be told twice. They sat.

Boom! Bridgebane hit the *Stench* again. We shook hard along with her. The baby's eyes widened, but it kept sucking. My heart pounded against my ribs like a professional boxer with a speed bag, punch, punch, punching as fast as it could.

"We can't take another hit like that. Gotta jump now," Asher said.

Before I knew it, a yell ripped from my mouth. "Tess!"

"Get ready to take a bullet out of my ass, cupcake."

"I—" Darkness folded in on me. Hyperspace wrapped her arms around us, and everything went weightless, quiet, and blank. I cradled the baby as my stomach started to writhe and tumble, words I didn't get to utter lodged tightly behind clenched teeth.

—love you.

Once again, I was too late. The words burned in my throat, and Tess and I were light-years apart already.

CHAPTER

17

TESS

IT WAS SO FREAKING QUIET ALL OF A SUDDEN. THE *Unholy Stench* was gone, taking Shade, Jax, its crew, and that whole cargo hold away with it. They'd detached first from the DWALSH and had taken the brunt of the chase. I would be the focus now. And the *Endeavor*. We weren't lined up yet. We still had to make the attachment, and I'd never felt so alone in my life. If it weren't for the two big blobs near me on the radar, I'd have panicked.

The *Endeavor* and *Dark Watch 12*.

Who'd ever have thought I'd find *DW 12* looming over me reassuring?

I swallowed, and it tasted like fear in my mouth. "Merrick?"

"Reverse thrusters," he ordered.

"Brace yourselves!" I shouted. I couldn't turn to see if anyone listened. If the yells and flops of people on metal were any indication, I didn't give them enough warning.

My hips rammed into the edge of the console. I gasped, the jolt echoing in my injury. *Who the hell gets shot in the ass?*

Me, apparently.

Just before we started moving backward, I killed the power to the thrusters and waited for Merrick's instructions.

"Stay there, Tess," he said. "I'll do the maneuvering."

I lifted my hands from the console. "What's Bridgebane doing?"

"Sending a lot of threats and warnings."

"And?" That couldn't be all.

"He shot the *Stench* at least twice. They're limping through their jump right now."

"I heard the explosions." I sure hoped the damage wasn't bad enough to ground them on the near-deserted Nickleback. Shade could repair a lot of things, but not without materials.

I rubbed my forehead. "Bridgebane won't do nothing for long. He can't risk it." Even with Sanaa and me in the line of fire, he'd shoot. I knew that.

A jolt went through the cargo unit, throwing me away from the console so hard I fell over. We tilted, and I slid toward the mass of human passengers, slamming into someone sitting on the floor. Two knees hit the back of my rib cage like fists with iron knuckles and drove the air from my lungs. I wheezed in a breath, rolled over, and stared at the woman above me. For a second, she looked just like my mother.

I blinked. A stranger looked back at me.

Lank dark hair curtained forward as she leaned down to help me sit up. Her helpful grip turned into painful clinging when the lights went out in the cargo hold. The darkness was as dense as the Black Widow. Not a single pinpoint of brightness, not a glowing button, not a flashing control panel broke the intense blackness around us.

The woman's nails dug into my shoulders. Her breath came in scared little shudders. People murmured in fear. The whirring of the air filters stopped abruptly. The gravity shut off, eliminating the universal standard. Up I went, my heart in my throat. Pandemonium erupted in the cargo hold.

"Merrick? Can you hear me?" The coms were independent, right? They'd still function.

"I hear you. *DW 12* shot your box with some kind of electrical charge."

"All the systems are off. No new oxygen. No gravity. Can't see!" I tried to keep my voice down, but stress made it rise beyond the whisper I'd started with.

Someone grabbed my ankle. The woman still had one of my arms. Something smacked me in the ear, making the com ring. I tore myself free from grasping hands only to ram into the person floating above me. He grunted and clutched my hair like a lifeline, jerking me sideways and into him. I punched his wrist. He let go with a gasp, and I threw myself away from him.

"Merrick!" A shoe hit my nose. It hurt *and* stank. "I need you!"

We tumbled in the void, spinning, bodies colliding. I hit a wall—or the ceiling—face-first and hissed. Pain flared from my eye to my teeth, my cheekbone throbbing. At least I'd found something solid.

I fumbled for something to hold on to. A cold, smooth surface met my fingers. Children wailed like sirens.

Was it my imagination, or was the temperature in here already dropping? Cold, dark, airless. We were drowning, and there was no up or down or anywhere.

"I've almost got you." Merrick's even, virtually toneless answer didn't satisfy me in the least or calm my rising panic.

Almost didn't get the job done. *Almost* was a mission that went up in smoke. *Almost* was a hundred people dying when you told them you were here to help.

My pulse beat savagely against my skin. I closed my eyes—it seemed better than staring without sight—and touched my hot cheek with cold fingers. I had to count on my team now. That was part of this—relying on others.

"Come on! Hurry up!" Gabe snapped. "Line us up!"

"Shut up!" Fiona snapped back.

"I concur," Sanaa said dryly.

A rough exhale scraped across my lips. There was a smile in there somewhere, buried deep. Nothing was funny, but my people were still mine, and I could count on them to be who I thought. Gabe, impatient, his heart in the right place. Fiona not taking any shit. Merrick only speaking when necessary and always calm when he did.

Shade and Jax only freaking out when someone they cared about was in trouble, especially me. Otherwise, they were rocks, and I missed them.

I pressed a hand to my chest, trying to push back the emotion that was stabbing out.

I couldn't say much about Sanaa yet other than that she impressed the hell out of me, and not only for putting up with my uncle. It was Bridgebane who threw me for a loop. Family. Stranger. Enemy. Friend. I didn't dare speculate about what came next. He'd either blow my expectations out of the water—or sink them without a second thought.

We jolted hard again. People screamed. My eyes flew open, meeting total darkness. "What was that?" I asked.

"Another blast like the first." Merrick muttered a curse. "Knocked you off course. I'll have to readjust."

"Hurry, Merrick." How long would it take a hundred people to breathe through the remaining air in here?

"He's shooting at us!" Fiona sounded more incensed than scared.

Worry gripped my heart in a crushing fist. What if Bridgebane shut them down like he had us?

"Midgrade phaser," Merrick reported through an alarm that blared on the *Endeavor*. He shut it off. "Damage. No hole."

I blew out a tight breath. "Is there room to jump?" Dark Watch fighters could be gathering. Swarming the ship.

"We'll shove our way out. We're bigger," Merrick said.

"But they're armed."

"They're just trying to hold us in place. They're counting on the warship to shoot."

"It *is* shooting!" Fiona said.

"It's not shooting to kill," Sanaa clipped out. "Otherwise, we'd be dead, and we're close enough to take the cargo attachment out with us."

How could Bridgebane get away with this? This was a very public half-assed effort to catch us. There was no way he could cover this up.

Unless…

"Everyone quiet!" I bellowed.

People shut up. Even kids. Everything stopped.

"Why are you in here?" I asked.

A masculine voice drifted through the dark. "It's something about our blood. They won't tell us what. We were part of the early GIN Project. It started almost three weeks ago—before the announcement. They've been taking samples from us ever since. Sometimes a lot."

Almost three weeks ago? Just after I stole the Overseer's lab?

My lungs suddenly felt shallow and tight. Was this my fault? All these people, caged up?

"From talking to each other, we think they covered several big cities across the Sectors," he continued. "Said it was for research. Said they'd pay us. I saw people walking out just fine, but when my turn came, they wouldn't let me back out."

More voices confirmed his story, and my heart sank, rose, jumped all over the place. Had I found the Mornavail? Were they like me? Did they know more than I did?

"Did they inject you with anything?" I asked. "A GIN? Is it already in you?" There was no hiding anywhere in the galaxy if the Dark Watch had already tagged them with that shit.

"N-No. That's why they're holding us—we think. The tech isn't ready yet. But they drew a lot more blood from us, even the kids."

A1 blood. I was sure of it. The Overseer would have super soldiers. But so would the rebellion. Loralie Harris was probably lining them up by the dozen. I'd given her thousands of ready-to-go injections, but the Overseer still had to gather A1 blood and engineer the serum again. We were a step ahead of him for once. Could we strike first?

We hadn't really been at war before. Just…doing what we could. That was all about to change, wasn't it? The clash of our generation was upon us. The surety of that detonated inside me like a bomb blasting out destruction along with tiny unbreakable kernels of hope.

Fear and something close to excitement ignited in my chest as another hit rattled the hold. People screamed. I lost my position against the wall and free floated.

"Calm down!" I said loud enough to be heard. "They

want you alive, which means they won't blow us up." And Uncle Nate had his excuse to use less-than-lethal force— assuming he was even supposed to know about this. He must have just found out. Why else would he have demanded my blood on Reaginine?

"But we were escaping." A sob-heavy female voice rose above the rest. Others followed her straight into her pit of doom. Crying erupted in the cargo hold. *Great Powers, don't these people know anything about morale?*

"*Are* escaping," I said firmly. I was scared, too. I just wouldn't show it.

"They'll blow your people up and take us back." That teary, half-broken voice sounded like a child's. Too young not to believe in happy endings.

"They won't. I have an ace in the hole," I promised. "You'll see."

A softer thud jostled us. It felt like a hip bump from a friend, and I breathed a sigh of relief.

"All lined up," Merrick said.

Thank the Sky Mother.

"Gabe! The vacuum seal!" Merrick barked.

"I'm trying. The accordion won't extend." Anxiety carried Gabe's voice across the com like a poison-coated bullet. "I used the password you gave me. What do I do, Tess?"

Won't extend? I never had trouble with my air locks. "Try again."

"It's not working!" Gabe said.

"Something must have damaged the mechanism, or is blocking the passageway from coming out." It was an awful feeling, free floating in the dark when I wanted to pace or grind my hands into something. I clenched my fists.

"Merrick, try backing off a bit and bumping us again. Maybe it'll jostle the walkway out."

"On it," Merrick said.

A hard thump resonated through the box.

"Gabe?" I asked.

"Shit! No luck."

What the hell is wrong with my air lock? "Swing around and line us up with the starboard door," I said.

An explosion shook the cargo hold. We ground against the *Endeavor*. People freaked out around me, grunting, cursing, crying. I spiraled into someone and shoved off with a gut-reaction push that sent me somersaulting over backward. An alarm shrieked in my com. Fiona made a sound of distress. Purring rolled in my ear like thunder.

My heart flipped over. She had Bonk.

"We don't have time to come around," Sanaa said. "How much bad shooting do you think he can do? Gabe, try again. Daraja, figure it out!"

I hit a wall and stopped spiraling. *Oof.* Blindness was terrifying. No idea where up or down was. Too much noise. I tried to concentrate. "Merrick, is there anything strange on the main console?"

"Other than it blaring about the big hole in your portside storage closet?"

Oh no! There went my tools. Frank better have something. If we got stuck on Nickleback, we'd be spider food!

I shoved that thought out of my head. "It has to be something right at the air lock. The vacuum seal should just pop out and latch on to us when Gabe pushes the button. Bump us again—hard."

I didn't bother telling people to brace themselves. No

one could see. We were all floating around like particles. The shock came about thirty seconds later, and I pinpointed the noise. It was on my left, which meant the door was over there somewhere. My foot was on something—or maybe someone—and I pushed off, flying in the right direction. For a second, I must have forgotten I had a bullet in my ass. Pain shot down my leg, and I winced, pressing a hand to my throbbing cheek. My pants were sticky with blood. Adrenaline wasn't enough to keep me warm anymore. I shivered, cold.

"It's extending!" Gabe shouted.

I hit a wall and clung to the smooth surface, my heart pounding like I'd just run a race.

"We have a lock," Merrick said.

I whooped. I couldn't help it. But how would we get out of the cargo hold? Without any power, it would take a saw to break us out. I didn't have a saw capable of cutting through metal. Did Frank? Would the systems come back on? Oxygen renewal? Gravity? The door panel?

"The seal's airtight," Merrick announced. "Ready to go."

"He's shooting!" Fiona yelled at the same time.

We rattled hard along with the *Endeavor*, an extension of her now and not just alongside her. Merrick shut down the new alarm almost before it started. Super-soldier reflexes. More people started crying.

"Just let us go!" someone pleaded from the darkness. "At least they weren't trying to kill us!"

I turned my head toward the voice, a slow swivel on shocked hinges. No one answered. No one fucking answered. What the hell?

"Well," I ground out, "I invite you to report back to a Dark Watch security hub to be drained of blood and used indefinitely by a homicidal monster *after* I rescue the people who have something better to live for!"

I could practically feel the collective blink in the cargo unit, everyone so taken aback they went silent.

I couldn't feel guilty for my outburst. I *couldn't*. There were sides to choose, and you had to either own yours or get the hell out of the way of the people who had the balls to know where they stood.

"The GIN Project is coming for each and every one of us. We need to stop him, or no one will ever be safe. You think he owns the galaxy now? Imagine when he can find any of you with just the click of a button. No one should have that power. He wants you for a reason. *You* specifically. *Your* blood. He needs you in order to create super soldiers to solidify his control, to enable more terror and destruction. An unbeatable military. Can you imagine? We have to act before it's too late.

"Fight! I don't care who you were before. I don't care how old you are. Fight, before there's nothing left to fight for. Die right here, if you have to. At least you'll deprive the Overseer of something he needs for his dark doings. This is the battle of every man, woman, and child. This is the battle of our lifetime. Resist! Stand up and say *No* before your voice is lost—and all others are crushed also."

The silence was absolute, even from the *Endeavor*.

Then someone started clapping. "I'm with you, Captain!" a man shouted. More people joined in until it was deafening.

I didn't want cheering. I wanted *commitment*.

"*DW 12* cleared a path for us. Made it look like an attack that barely missed us. Guy's a genius," Merrick said.

"Can we be friends now, darling?" Sanaa asked. "Maybe friends with benefits?"

Merrick grunted. "Jumping in ten…nine…eight…"

"Jumping in eight seconds!" I called out. I had no idea what it would feel like to jump with zero gravity. The thought began to terrify me just as the lights came back on, the systems whirred to life, and a hundred people crashed down, screaming.

I managed to twist in the air and landed mostly on my front, smacking down like a pancake. Pain rang through my body, a hot-cold hammering in my bones. I couldn't move a muscle and groaned out the bit of air I had left in me. Breathing in again was a struggle. My lungs didn't want to expand. My ass was killing me.

"Seven…six…five…"

A woman tried to tug her hand out from under my hip, jostling my aching backside. I winced and scooted over. A kid sat on my ponytail, pulling my head tight against the floor. He put his small hand on my forehead and held on with sticky fingers.

Our eyes met. The kid smiled. I smiled back, half grimace.

"Four…three…two…one…"

I closed my eyes. Darkness crashed down on me, both crushing and a huge relief. My bones ached under the pressure, my mind blanked, and I'd never been happier to race headlong into the mysteries of hyperspace.

✳✳✳

"Tess? Tess!" Someone shouted in my ear. I opened my eyes. Lots of people stared at me, but they were all silent. I rubbed my forehead, confused.

Everything flooded back at once. Had I fallen asleep during the jump? Or blacked out? I'd never passed out in my life except due to blood loss—which couldn't be ruled out right now. I sat up and pain shot through my bottom. My head spun.

"Merrick?" I croaked.

"We're here," he told me. "About to touch down on Nickleback. I've got eyes on the *Stench*. She made it but hasn't landed yet. You all right in there?"

Relief squeezed an abrupt breath from my lungs. "Um…" I looked around. Everyone seemed fine. Rumpled and anxious, but okay. "Yeah. Looking forward to getting out of this box." It stank in here. And it was starting to feel small. Really small. Where was the door? I wanted out.

A familiar anxiety gripped me, but I didn't move. I was afraid I wouldn't be very steady on my feet yet, and people blocked me in every direction. The reality of what we'd done started to sink in. We had about two-hundred-and-fifty escaped prisoners to relocate. We couldn't bring them to the Fold. That was too many people to trust with the rebellion's biggest secret. We couldn't leave them here. Humans hadn't completely deserted Nickleback, but they would soon. There were giant spiders eating everyone in sight.

The Mooncamps maybe? That was the safest bet, but that just meant more mouths for Raz to feed, and we hadn't even found him any new food with this totally off-the-rails heist.

Merrick landed. There was no mistaking the soft jolt. The second we touched down and stopped moving, my pulse went haywire, pounding dizziness into my head. I swallowed. A cold sweat broke out. We didn't leave the *Endeavor*'s doors open when we docked in places only to air out. We did it because otherwise, I freaked out.

Phantom restraints cinched around my wrists and ankles. I could practically smell the cold antiseptic environment of the Overseer's basement laboratory and feel the bright glare of the overhead lights in my face. Tension banded tighter and tighter around my chest until breathing felt like a joke.

Not moving. Closed space. Trapped. Get out!

I sprang up and lunged for the door, spots marring my vision. I'd changed the code when I locked myself in here and punched in the simple star pattern that was Jax's and my backup. If I'd been knocked out—or worse—he would have known the code to open the cargo attachment.

The door slid sideways with a whoosh. Gabe was right in front of me, his smile so big. *This is the life!* his excited expression screamed at me while I tried to breathe and convince myself I wasn't a claustrophobic mess. *The life we always talked about! We've got it, Tess!*

I turned away from him, my pulse thundering in my ears. Sanaa was also there, looking like we hadn't just been to hell and back. Not a glimmer of sweat. Not a hair out of place. A small smile tilting up her lips. She looked fresh and relaxed, as if she'd just come from the spa and not from a space battle that had left at least two holes in my ship.

I gulped down a breath.

Merrick turned the corner, jogging toward us from the bridge. Something rose in me, an emotion I had to beat down hard or risk bawling in front of people who needed to think I was a rock.

A rock could still hug, though, right?

I dodged Gabe and threw myself at Big Guy. He caught me, his body and grip huge and strong enough to make me feel safe. I even stopped worrying about the *Endeavor*'s doors still being closed right now—probably a good thing, considering the spiders. Merrick rocked me a little. My feet didn't touch the floor anymore, and I was fine with that. My pulse evened out, and my lungs got back to work. I felt almost normal again when he set me on my feet.

As I stepped back, the look Merrick gave me arrowed straight to my heart. Approving. Affectionate. Almost paternal. The only man who'd ever looked at me that way was Uncle Nate. But unlike my uncle, Merrick hadn't abandoned me. He'd come back for me when I needed him most.

My throat burned with a thousand tears I wouldn't let out. I'd just been scared out of my mind, our original plan had exploded in stardust, and my entire body hurt, but everyone was counting on me to pull it together and make decisions for the whole group.

Static crackled in my ear a second before I heard Shade's voice. "Tess?"

"I'm here! Where are you?" My heartbeat took off like a rocket.

"We just landed. We stayed in orbit until we were sure you guys made it."

"You're on the plateau?"

"Right next to you," he answered. "I'm on my way over."

"Don't get eaten!"

He laughed. "Don't worry, starshine. Nothing's keeping me from you." A soft click sounded, Shade disconnecting from the channel. Several devices clicked off in quick succession.

Giddy with relief, I turned off my com, my fingers shaking. I couldn't wait to see Shade. Going off on my own had been lonely and horrible. We were a team now. I liked it that way.

Fiona stalked down the hallway, Bonk in her arms. She passed him off to me with a sour look even she couldn't pull off. "He scratched me twice."

I gathered Bonk in my arms, a ridiculous smile on my

face. Bonk crawled up my chest and put his paws around my neck. *Holy shit, my cat can hug!* I snuggled against him. He purred in my ear, his stiff whiskers tickling my cheek.

"He doesn't like to be startled." I stroked his back. Little shoulder blades and a spine bumped against my hand. Bonk's purring revved up, his chest vibrating against mine. He wasn't expressing his ire this time, but I hadn't been gone that long. And all the jolts and noises had frightened him. Tiny claws dug into my skin, but I ignored the sting in favor of kitty love.

"Then he needs to get used to it," Fiona muttered, brushing gray and white fur from her shirt. "He's a rebel space cat. Explosions *will* happen."

I grinned. How could I not?

"Tess!" Shade's bellow came from the direction of the starboard door.

I took a few steps toward the sound of his voice but then he was there, barreling down the corridor. He abruptly slowed, readjusting his approach. The embrace that would have been fierce and perfect ended up being gentle and even more perfect as Shade took care not to crush Bonk. It was awkward, both of us bent around the cat between us. It also felt like a family of three.

Shade gripped my face and kissed me. It was fast, but the quick contact breathed new life into me.

"That was fucking terrifying," he whispered against my lips. "How do you do this all the time?"

I understood what scared Shade, because they were the same things that petrified me. Someone I loved getting hurt. Things spiraling out of my control. Being taken out of the game before we finally swept the Overseer and his minions from the board.

I kissed him this time, lifting up to press my lips to his. "It's not *all* the time."

"Thank the Powers for that." Heartfelt conviction punctuated his words as he scratched behind Bonk's ears. Bonk tilted his head back, still hugging me but leaning toward Shade.

Shade and I looked at each other over Bonk's head, and something passed between us when our eyes met. A silent communication. A promise to reach that life at the orphanage we'd talked about.

I nodded. He nodded back.

"We've got a man with a working wand in his hands on the *Unholy Stench*," Shade suddenly said.

I looked at him, taking a second to work that out. "There's so much wrong with that sentence, I don't even know where to start."

He grinned. "How 'bout we start by getting that bullet out of your ass before the giant carnivorous spiders find us?"

I laughed, even though the pulsing pain in my rear end was no joke. "I'm not looking forward to either, to be honest. At least once I'm healed, I can run away from them." Although flying away was the better option. "How fast can we get off this rock?" I asked, worried about the damage to both ships.

"The *Stench* can fly," Shade said. "Asher said the hits were ... well placed. She's good to go as long as we ditch the cargo attachment. No point dragging around extra weight."

"They can make repairs on Mooncamp 1, which is where I think we should bring everyone. Merrick?" I asked. "How's the *Endeavor*?"

"Same," he answered. "Two holes, but in rooms that were sealed off. Nothing that'll ground us. We'll move all these people into the main cargo hold and ditch the attachment."

I nodded. I had no problem abandoning the big cargo holds on Nickleback to become spider houses. "The people on the *Stench* stay there, and these people here—unless Frank doesn't have enough room for them." I was pretty sure he had more people than I did, but we were both empty after unloading at the DT Mooncamps.

Jax walked up behind Shade, giving me a thorough once-over that was strictly about assessing my continued ability to walk. His scowl said a lot about how worried he'd been. A lump rose in my throat.

I lifted Bonk from around my neck and passed him over to Jax. Jax wouldn't take the affection Fiona wanted to offer if only he'd open himself up, but there was no way he would reject snuggles from the cat. Or me. I leaned into him, briefly laying my head on his shoulder.

"I'm fine," I quietly reassured him. *Mostly. Whatever.* I could stand up, so there was that.

He held Bonk in the crook of one burly arm, his other hand lifting to scratch the white fluff under the tabby's chin. Fiona caught his eye, and their gazes locked. She smiled. Jax looked away first.

Sighing, I realized nothing had changed. I just hoped Jax would break this barrier before it was too late and Fiona moved on without him.

I took a deep breath to brace myself. Time for surgery. "Let's do this," I told Shade, moving to his side again. "Can you get the doc and his wand and bring him to our room?"

"Damn, baby. There's so much I can do with that." Innuendo lit his brown eyes, and I laughed.

"This poor doctor. He's going to be terrified of us," I said.

"Nah." Shade smiled. "He's made of sturdy stuff."

"Is that another joke?" I rolled my lips in, picturing things that were totally inappropriate.

"Maybe a little." The warmth in Shade's eyes spread through my whole body. "But it's also the truth."

Smiling, I looked around at the people who had slowly spread out into the main cargo hold of the *Endeavor*. The worst heist ever had turned out pretty well in the end. We had the Overseer's new supply of A1 blood. We still had time to stop the GIN Project. No one had died, although I was fairly certain I couldn't stand up much longer and could really use a nap—preferably with a cat taking up half the pillow.

My gaze landed on Gabe. He stared at me like I was a stranger, and a sharp, unpleasant twist screwed up my stomach. The universe had played a cruel trick on us. Seven years of waiting and then a month too late. Regret didn't grow inside me, though. Not like it used to, and had for so long.

"Can you help get them settled?" I asked Gabe, nodding toward the refugees. "See what they need?" Food, for one thing. Raz was going to have to resupply *us* after this.

Gabe acknowledged my request with a nod that seemed forced and mechanical. His eyes swung back and forth just once between Shade and me. A muscle bunched in his jaw. "Yeah. I got it."

From his tone, I knew he understood more than just my instructions. As much as it kicked me in the heart to disappoint him, I didn't want any gray areas. I wanted Shade.

I turned away, a thousand memories tugging at my soul. First kiss. First heist. First plans for a future together. First pretty much everything. But things were different now. Time didn't stand still or go backwards. Neither did people. I'd changed. Hadn't Gabe? There was no picking up as though nearly a decade hadn't happened.

I'd wanted only two men in my entire life. Gabe had pursued me, and I'd pursued Shade. I had no doubt I'd still be with Gabe if we hadn't been separated and caught. Now I was with Shade, who'd chosen me, too. My heart and my body knew that.

Shade's knuckles brushed mine as we moved away from the rear air lock. "You all right, starshine?"

His softly spoken question spread through me like warm honey, sweet and concerned and just the glue I needed to keep myself together.

I limped a few steps before answering. "I'm glad you're with me."

Shade waited until we rounded the corner before sweeping me into his arms and carrying me to the bedroom.

CHAPTER

18

TESS

WE FINISHED LUNCH TOGETHER, THIS TIME JUST THE CREW of the *Endeavor*. We were a changed landscape that I was finally getting used to. We'd gone from a family of five to a solid crew of seven, and four of us were new here. It had taken a near-deadly mission, but the wariness surrounding Sanaa's and Gabe's arrivals felt far away now. Everyone breathed easier. The next steps seemed less...insurmountable.

We'd spent the last few days helping to settle the escaped prisoners on the DT Mooncamps. It took some convincing to get them to stay put while we figured things out, but in the end, they'd agreed that sitting tight for the time being was better than getting recaptured and forced back into being unwilling blood donors. In most cases, parents were already with their children, having gone in for early GIN testing together. That helped, and when Raz separated and distributed the group around his Mooncamps, he kept families and friends together. Eggs went in different baskets, though, even in this case.

Frank and his crew helped Raz more than we did, moving people around in the *Unholy Stench* and helping clean up unused living spaces and rustle up furniture and other necessary items. All six Mooncamps pulled together to help, and our role tapered off once everything was in motion. We dove into deep planning mode and tried to get the *Endeavor* up to full power and ready for some big jumps before we had to take her out again. Repeatedly leaping through hyperspace with holes in the hull might be doable, but it wasn't intelligent, and we worked frantically on repairs when we weren't working on a plan to break into Starbase 12.

Luckily, I had a strong and handy crew and Raz had a huge supply of space-worthy metal. The day of the massacre, countless ships had taken off from Demeter Terre in a panic, not knowing where to go. Whole families and crews died before they decided, the blood agents already inside them, leaving thousands of ships floating in orbit around their poisoned planet. Demeter Terre still had a ring around it, but it wasn't dust and gases. It was ghost ships. A reminder of what they'd suffered. With the Mooncampers' blessing, Raz collected metal from it for repair projects.

We shared a large hangar with the *Stench* this time, and I hadn't been able to help observing certain interactions while we banged away at repairs on the *Endeavor*. The doctor we'd found had slipped seamlessly into the Nightchaser's life, taking responsibility for things that were spreading Frank too thin. He hadn't decided yet if he was staying on the Mooncamps or taking up Frank's spontaneous offer to join the crew of the *Stench*. It was hard to miss Frank's hungry glances at the man. Or the way the doctor looked baffled and a little pink but kept walking by Frank, even when he didn't need to.

I kept hoping he'd trip and fall into Frank's arms. And that I'd be there to see it.

"Tess?" Shade tilted his head at me in question. I brought my eyes back into focus. Everyone around the kitchen table looked as though they were waiting for me to say something.

"Sorry." I scrubbed my hands over my face. It wasn't like me to zone out on an important conversation, although in my defense, we were bordering on Frank-like repetition, even though we were leaving the *Stench* and her crew out of this.

It was game day in a way, though, wasn't it? Or at least the kickoff. We were about to find out if my uncle had left me anything useful. We had a solid plan for the Starbase 12 rescues now, but it could still be adjusted. Uncle Nate's drop point was in Sector 10, on Galligar Prime. Sanaa had finally coughed up the coordinates, and we'd set them before sitting down to lunch.

"You look a galaxy away," Shade said.

"No, maybe just a few star systems over." I wrapped my hands around my coffee mug and drank some of Jax's brew. He made the best coffee, somewhere between eye-popping and smooth enough to swallow without a grimace. The kitchen had turned into planning central lately, and here we were again, most of us with coffees, our empty lunch dishes piled in the middle of the table.

"Let's recap." I glanced at Shade, hoping he would do the rundown of the plan for me this time. I was sick of my own voice by now.

Shade drank, too, only his mug was filled with some kind of fruit juice Raz had come up with. My scaredy-cat boyfriend had tried to get me to taste it first, but I'd refused. Shade swallowed with difficulty then set the mug down, sliding it away from him.

I tried not to smile. I'd told him that getting a little extra vitamin C wouldn't be worth ingesting whatever that fruit drink was.

He cleared his throat. "Even if Daniel Ahern's contact shuts off the plasma shield alarm on Platform 7, most people can't just fly onto Starbase 12, hop out, and walk around." Shade grimaced, which had less to do with the dubious fruit juice than with the fact we all agreed that Daniel Ahern's "help" was useless. In the end, we'd decided to avoid his upcoming window of opportunity altogether and make our move two days after it. If his plan had leaked, we'd avoid a trap and hopefully lull Dark Watch security into thinking we weren't coming. If it hadn't leaked... Well, ours was a better plan anyway.

"We have the lieutenant," Shade continued. "Mwende has high security clearance and is known, at least to *some* people, as a close associate of Bridgebane's." Shade still seemed a bit salty about never having met Sanaa while he worked for my uncle. He wouldn't admit it, but I thought it was because he actually liked Bridgebane well enough. Or if not liked, then at least respected. With recent revelations, we were all reluctantly moving in that direction. My uncle had truly impressed me lately, even if I hated some of his actions.

"Merrick's cruiser is the type they use for Dark Watch fighters. It could easily be the lieutenant's, or one she's commandeered for herself. She flies in with me, Jax, Merrick, and Tess—all wanted criminals that she's arrested."

That was the other thing Shade was irritated about: me on this mission. But if Sanaa had to stay behind on the starbase to maintain her cover, they'd need my directional capabilities on a DWALSH to get us out of there quickly.

Gabe's chair creaked under his weight as he leaned back

in it. His mouth flattened. I had a second irritated man on board, but I refused to feel guilty. There was a reason he was being left behind again, even though I knew he wanted in on the action.

"We can only do this," I said, "because now we have Gabe to fly the *Endeavor*. There's no way a lot of people didn't have eyes on her outside of Ewelock. Changing the ID stickers and hoping for the best isn't going to cut it anymore. We can't have her anywhere near this, or it'll tip someone off. We can't even have her in the Sambian System. It's too risky." We were taking enough risks here already. I was *not* adding to them. "Gabe takes Fiona and the *Endeavor* to Earth, which is the last place anyone will look for us. None of us have *any* ties there. It's not a rebel bastion. It's barely populated. Assuming we successfully get off Starbase 12, either in Merrick's cruiser or in something else, we'll meet you in New Denver. That's where we'll regroup, hopefully with Shiori and Reena Ahern with us."

We'd all memorized the coordinates. I even made Fiona do it, and Shade had walked her through the navigation system. He'd left notes—numbered and color-coded. Fiona was going to have to pull her weight on the bridge this time. We needed all of Sanaa's and Merrick's smarts, aplomb, sangfroid, and muscle on the starbase, we needed me in case we ended up in unexpected places on the spacedock without Sanaa, and there was no way I was telling Shade to stay back while I took Gabe with me. I doubted Shade would listen, and the *Endeavor* needed a pilot. Possibly even a future captain.

Gabe simply nodded when I looked at him. He knew his role. Get Fiona to safety. Use the *Endeavor* wisely if we never showed up in New Denver. He hadn't liked hearing me say that, but we all knew there was a chance we wouldn't make it to Earth. And if we didn't, then Gabe would have the ship he'd always dreamed of. I wanted him to have something good after all those years in prison.

"Once we're in," Shade continued, "the lieutenant will take us to the prison levels and an interrogation room. Because she doubts our cooperation, she'll bring in known associates of ours—Shiori Takashi and Reena Ahern—to *encourage* us to talk about rebel operations."

He looked at Sanaa in warning, who simply lifted an eyebrow. We all knew she would do what it took to make this look real, but it had better not involve hurting Shiori.

"But she receives fresh intel on a private channel." Shade's tone lowered, turning confidential. "Rebels plotting to break into Starbase 12? Coming for her prized prisoners? The lieutenant immediately decides to move us all to a different, *secret* location where she'll continue her interrogation while Starbase 12 prepares for a break-in that'll never happen."

"It'll have been a break-out," Merrick said, getting up to clear the dishes from the table. He started loading things into the machine with a clatter. "And we'll be in New Denver before Sanaa breaks the bad news to her boss, the general. We gave her the slip. Got away." He smirked. "We were just too smart for her. Nearly killed her."

Sanaa snorted.

"We'll be in New Denver without any dishes after you're through with them," I teased Merrick, getting up to help him slide the plates and mugs more carefully into the dishwasher. He could toss around the forks and knives. They were hard plastic.

Merrick frowned, as if he hadn't realized he was being so forceful. Super-soldier strength probably made it difficult to be delicate. Maybe that was one of the reasons why Sanaa kept looking at Merrick with undisguised interest. She wanted to get a little wild with someone she couldn't accidentally break; that much was obvious. Also, Merrick was awesome.

Once the kitchen was tidied up, I dropped my hands to my hips and looked around, but no excuse to put off leaving came to me. At least, not a plausible one.

"I guess we're ready." I'd been avoiding thinking about our next destination. I had a feeling this location Uncle Nate was sending me to wouldn't be dangerous—except to my emotions. I already felt all squeezed up and twisted around inside just thinking about his *secret-secret* place that he hadn't really wanted me to see, and whatever information or help he might have stashed there.

Jax moved toward the doorway. "I'll power up the *Endeavor*."

"Thanks, partner." My vacant murmur made him toss me a quizzical look over his shoulder. For Jax, I pulled it together. "Check the ventilation in Fiona's lab from your console, will you? It was glitching on mine this morning." Jax nodded as he left the kitchen, but I stayed rooted to the spot like one of Fiona's plants, finding it impossible to put one foot in front of the other.

We'd said goodbye to Frank and his crew earlier. To Raz also. I'd written to Mareeka and Surral. All was well at the orphanage. Coltin had a new interest. He'd decided he needed muscles and was "working out." I wasn't sure what that meant for a severely asthmatic eleven-year-old, but I knew Surral would keep an eye on him.

Exhaling slowly, I slid my hands down my thighs, rubbing jumpy fingers over the suede-like grain of the dark-gray fabric. I'd chosen my favorite pants today for moral support. I'd worn them to the beach with Shade on Albion 5. Discounting that terrifying run-in with a flerver at the edge of the water, nothing bad had ever happened to me in them.

"Let's go, then." Having to mentally propel myself into motion, I headed for the bridge, scooping up Bonk first to have him with us during the jump. The rest of the crew followed. Sanaa had finally convinced me to go into the info-drop location alone with her. I didn't like it. Shade didn't like it. Jax didn't like it, but hell... The way she'd looked at me, I just knew I should. It made me even more skittish about this whole thing.

"Secret-secret," I muttered into the top of Bonk's head. He purred.

The others wouldn't be far—just on the rooftop docking platform of the building we were going to on Galligar Prime. I'd never been to the Sector 10 planet before, but it was supposed to be one of the nicest rocks around.

Shortly after, I stood at my console and flew us out of the hangar. The *Endeavor* rose until Demeter Terre slid out of our clear panel and two of the DT moons were just reddish-brown dots in our periphery. I turned us toward open space and then nodded at Jax to engage the hyperdrive engine.

The long jump used a hefty portion of the *Endeavor*'s power and left my stomach in even tighter knots than before. I nearly dry heaved when we finally slowed and only managed to control my unruly insides by putting all my focus into steering us through the busy spheres over the capital city. The crowded sky distracted me from the bile rising in my throat.

We eventually landed on the rooftop corresponding to Sanaa's coordinates. It was empty, a private platform.

I opened the ship and exited, shading my eyes and willing my stomach to settle. It looked like high noon on Galligar Prime, her sun blazing down. Sanaa followed me onto the platform.

"Ready for a showdown?" I asked.

Sanaa's blade-sharp gaze cut to mine. "Daraja, the general's not here. I guarantee it."

Good. I wasn't ready to face my uncle. Except... I swallowed. I wanted the confrontation. Thoughts and questions flamed inside me, igniting more. I had no outlet for them, and they were starting to burn me up inside.

Shade stood grimly in the doorway with his arms crossed, his steady brown eyes watching me. The rest of the crew came up behind him. I took a few steps away from the *Endeavor*, bouncing on gravity that was less than the universal standard. My steps lighter than the weight in my mind, I followed Sanaa to the rooftop elevator. She used the key card Uncle Nate had printed out and then punched in a code. I trailed her into the lift and turned. Shade's eyes met mine as the doors closed.

We hardly moved before the elevator stopped again. *Top floor?* The doors opened to a security wall that looked as thick as the outside of a spaceship. Sanaa typed in another code, and a machine that wanted a retinal scan emerged. This wasn't your typical home security. What was this place? Double agent central?

"Even if my uncle had given me the key card and the codes, how would I have passed the retinal scan?" I asked.

"You're programmed in."

"What? Why?" *And how?*

As if that wasn't weird enough already, Sanaa looked at me hard before offering up her eye to the security machine. "He's not who you think he is."

Meaning what? That my uncle wasn't the asshole I kept shooting my mouth off at? I already knew that. Two-hundred-and-sixty-seven people were better off, *free*, because he'd messed with our heist and put himself and his own ship in the middle of our escape. Now, assuming he'd placed some information on Galligar Prime, he was helping us rescue Shiori. Because of Sanaa's involvement, he obviously also knew about Reena Ahern. I wasn't sure how they communicated, but they did. Nathaniel Bridgebane was there at every turn.

Knowing those lives meant something to him made emotion grow inside me in a way I couldn't seem to contain anymore. It just pushed and pulled and shoved at everything until I felt insane.

And a little jealous of Sanaa Mwende, who knew my uncle like I never would.

"He really trusts you with everything, doesn't he?" Yes, there was that small prick of envy, but I was mainly glad that Uncle Nate had someone. Everyone needed a friend.

Sanaa shrugged. "With everything except for what I wanted for a long time."

"What's that?" I asked.

"Himself."

I stood there, my jaw slack as she completed the retinal scan.

"But I'm over that. Have been for a long time." Sanaa glanced at me as the security system started to unlock. "I'm ready to stop being lonely just because he is. There's a small chance he might be ready to stop being lonely, too."

"With who?" I asked. "You?" I'd seen Sanaa's interest in Merrick. I hadn't imagined it.

"Oh no, not with me, Daraja. With you."

"Me?" Uncle Nate and I were family, but we hardly knew each other. I'd barely seen him in eighteen years. It seemed a little farfetched to think we might suddenly become best buds. "Why do you call me that? Daraja?"

Just then, the double doors parted, revealing a beautiful and comfortable home. Sanaa swept inside, and I followed, looking around. Curiosity and an odd sharp pinch crunched together in my chest. My throat suddenly thickened, a lump expanding in it fast. Mom would have loved this place.

Most of it was a large living space sprinkled with colorful furniture that had been placed at angles around a low glass table that looked perfect for kicking up your feet at the end of the day with a warm drink and a book. Huge windows let in natural light and offered a spectacular view over the capital city. Rooftop gardens. Spires. Some high traffic. Bookshelves, only half-full, lined the whole wall on my right. There was an open kitchen off to the left. It looked pristine, never used. In fact, everything in here looked brand new.

"Daraja means bridge in my language," Sanaa answered while I stood there in shock. I loved this place. It was welcoming and warm, like the Uncle Nate I used to know. "I call you that because you are what kept him walking between two worlds. Without you, he might have stepped to one side or the other. It would have been easy to embrace the Dark Watch general, to *be* him. It would have been even easier to strip off that uniform and go back to the Fold."

My eyes widened. "The Fold?"

"We'll all die with secrets, Daraja. Even when he didn't know where you were, without proof that you were dead, you lived in his mind. The thought of you kept him walking the line he'd chosen, when there were days, weeks, *years* when it was so tempting to simply step off the bridge."

"Why pretend all this time? Why not just...kill the Overseer?"

"And make that man a martyr? Murdered by his own kin?" Anger boiled in Sanaa's midnight-sky eyes, darkening them further. "The man you knew as your father has many admirers. Mostly people with much in the way of currency and weapons and little in the way of conscience."

Isn't that the truth. "So my uncle's goal was just to"—I shook my head in question—"limit damage?"

"You make that sound easy. On a galactic scale, I assure you, it's not."

"Someone else could kill him." Every now and then, we heard about attacks on the Overseer's life. I was always hoping one of those attempts would succeed and we'd finally be rid of him.

Sanaa cocked her head at me. "You?"

I was thinking of *her*, but yeah, maybe. "If I have the opportunity, I might." Simon Novalight was probably the only person I could kill in cold blood. "And I'd bet Merrick would be willing." A memory sprang to mind—Big Guy charging toward the Overseer's cruiser on Starway 8. "Just seeing Merrick scared the shit out of him the last time they met. Why is that?"

"Merrick got away before the final injection," she said.

"What do you mean?" How many injections were there? I'd only passed over one kind to the rebel leaders. Were they missing something?

"The one that makes you forget," Sanaa answered. "Wiped clean, only knowing what the Overseer says."

I stared at her in horror. "He's rebooting people?" The living room blurred around me. "Oh no! What's in that serum I passed off?"

"Don't worry, Daraja. The final injection is a separate thing. They'll end up like Merrick. It's okay."

"You're sure?" I choked out.

"Yes. He's still him, just enhanced. He was undoubtably sexy and quiet before, but now he can rip a metal spaceship apart with his bare hands and use it for a shield." Her smile turned almost dreamy. "I wish I'd seen that."

A little breath burst from me. I had two super soldiers aboard the *Endeavor*. If they had wild sex, would it…throw us off course or something?

I coughed and glanced around the apartment. "So, where's this info my uncle might've left us?" There had to be a safe somewhere. And it looked as if there were some rooms off a hallway. Bedrooms, no doubt.

It struck me again how the place seemed stocked with everything a family could need to live here; it just didn't look like anyone did.

"What's that?" I asked, a small metallic square snagging my eye before Sanaa could answer my previous question. Curious, I moved toward the picture frame on the kitchen island. It was facing away from the living room, so that someone at the sink might see it.

I turned it, and everything in me stopped. It was a picture of Mom, me, and Uncle Nate. I was…six maybe? I was on his shoulders, and Mom looked up at me, smiling. He looked at her, smiling also, his hands up to hold mine just above his head.

The sudden rush of blood in my veins threw me off-balance. My heart pounding, I set down the picture, suddenly on a vital mission to inspect every single inch of this place. I couldn't articulate why, exactly, but I knew I had to—and that what I found might change everything.

Breathing harder than usual, I entered the first room along the hallway.

A large bed, definitely for two people. Nice colors. Good light. A closet. A dresser with a framed photo on it. A rather feminine writing desk and chair. On the desk, still in the store packaging, sat a sketchpad and set of drawing pencils. Everything about the room screamed *A couple belongs here*, not a bachelor general.

I picked up the photo, seeing Mom when she was younger. Probably a late teen and well before she married the Overseer. Her smile was radiant. I'd never seen her smile like that. It almost hurt to look at.

I put down the picture, a tremble in my fingers. The truth was starting to weave itself into my consciousness, but I wanted more proof before I let myself believe.

I ignored the bathroom off the master suite and opened the closet. It was huge, a walk-in, but not very full. I recognized some of Mom's clothing and reached out to touch a red dress she'd kept from before her marriage but had never worn again, as far as I knew. I bent and sniffed the dress on impulse. The fabric didn't hold her scent. It didn't smell like anything. Or maybe I didn't remember what she smelled like to begin with.

I closed the closet door and left the master bedroom, continuing down the hallway in a sort of trance. Sanaa walked behind me, keeping a slight distance. The next door I opened revealed a large playroom. Toys. A hopscotch rug. A rocking horse. Books and games. I shut the door with a clack.

I opened the final door along the hallway, shaking hard now. This was my room, wasn't it?

I stepped inside and had no doubt. Color everywhere.

Pale-pink walls, bright-raspberry bed, a mound of pillows in every shade of the rainbow piled high against the headboard. A stuffed-animal monkey sat perched on top of the pillows, and I almost lost it. At the last second, I trapped the sob in my throat.

Blinking a hot sheen of tears from my eyes, I went and looked at the picture on the bookshelf. Mom held an infant. Me—I was her only kid. I was fast asleep, a happy little blob in her arms, having no idea what life was really like. The white blanket wrapped around me in the photograph now lay carefully folded at the foot of the bed. I dragged down a hiccupping breath.

Sanaa ducked out of the doorway, saying, "I'll go check the safe."

And then I was alone in this little girl's bedroom, with the life I might have had staring me in the face.

Oddly, the most pounding thought in my head was that I had to tell Shade and Jax. I wished they'd come with me after all. I wanted Shade's warm hand on my back.

I swallowed hard as my gaze landed on the bedside table and the lamp with constellations printed across the shade. Lit up at night, it would throw stars across the bedroom. Another framed photograph sat next to it, angled toward the bed. Stiffly, I sat on the edge of the mattress and stared at the picture while I realigned my life.

Nathaniel Bridgebane held me on his lap as he pointed to illustrations of what looked like old Earth animals in a big glossy-paged book. I wasn't paying attention at all and chewed on a finger while I played with my foot. I was a good judge of age after growing up in an orphanage and knew I was about five months old in that shot.

It was just a flat, 2-D image, but it told a story with almost more depth than I could handle. *That* was what a father looked like.

Tears welled up. I opened the bedside table drawer. A fake ID—what would have been *my* fake ID—stared up at me, the picture of myself at age eight hitting me like a Red Beam's crimson shock. The small document had a Sector 10 citizen matriculation number on it, as if I'd been born here when I hadn't. My hair color wasn't right, which was the only effort at disguising me. It was a dark red that made my freckles stand out. My blue eyes still blazed like beacons in my head.

Margaret Suzanna Walker. The birth date wasn't mine. It was about five months early.

A tarnished silver bracelet for a small wrist circled the Sector 10 ID card. The drawer was otherwise empty apart from a box of red hair dye.

Natural pigments. Two universal months without fading. Safe for children and adults.

I didn't move for a long time. Everything just sort of stopped as an alternate life filled my glazed-over vision and my aching soul reached for it, even though it was far too late for any of the careful things that had been planned here. Eventually, I picked up the silver bracelet. The name *Maggie* scrawled across the top in an engraved script with pretty swirls and dips. My heart jerked sideways. I put the bracelet back and closed the drawer, my lips pressed flat. If I could keep the worst of the tears in, I might not shatter from the inside out.

Sanaa appeared again in the doorway. She carried a bag in her hand.

I met her cautious gaze with watery eyes. "Nathaniel Bridgebane is my father."

Sanaa didn't deny it. I hadn't thought she would. "He was working on getting you out. Both of you." Her low, careful pitch made this place seem like a tomb all of a sudden. Things were buried here, things like love and hope.

Sanaa moved into the bedroom but only barely. "He was putting the finishing touches on this place when your mother passed away. He went back to get you and found her dead."

My heart withered and died a little in my chest. So close? A matter of days, and we might have had all this?

My chin quivered. Why didn't he take me anyway? Without Mom, I wasn't enough?

I swiped a tear from my cheek. "Murdered, you mean."

"Yes. Murdered." Sanaa's voice hardened. True rage stormed into her expression like a desert wind. Harsh. Dry. Ready to flay skin off in strips. "I know what happened. The deadly virus. How the Overseer held the cure over her head."

"She wouldn't tell him who my real father was, so he let her die, just like he said he would. Probably the only person he ever loved, and he killed her," I spat out in disgust.

"There are small blessings, Daraja. At least you haven't lived nearly two decades knowing you could have saved her with just a few drops of your blood."

Sanaa's dark eyes held mine, and my whole world tipped over. Bridgebane was the source of my A1 blood.

I reached out and picked up the picture of my father and me on the bedside table. *My father and me.* Mom's stepbrother. The man who'd gone with her into hell. When had they fallen in love? As teenagers, after their parents' marriage brought them together, these two people who might never have met? Or was it later, when my mother needed the touch of a man who didn't make her skin crawl?

Nathaniel Bridgebane was a little older than Caitrin

Bishop. She'd followed him into all sorts of rebel trouble when they were young, but he'd followed her into something much more destructive, hadn't he? And then…I'd come along.

I stared at the picture. How had no one guessed, even me? Tall, dark hair, blue eyes. I looked just like him. Was the Overseer that blind? Caitrin and Nate—they were the two he just couldn't see past, weren't they? Because they *meant* something to him.

It was hard to understand the Overseer's obsession with my mother. He'd seen her and put her on a weird sort of pedestal that I don't think she'd understood, either, but knew she could use. Their marriage stopped the attacks on the Outer Zones and ended the final Sambian War. She agreed to be his and got him to back off on the bombings and accept negotiations. Like a pawn, she sacrificed herself for the good of the game. The stability it brought consolidated Novalight's power, yes, but it also brought an end to decades of fighting and murder on a mass scale. Caitrin did that. That was her legacy. It wasn't the Overseer who brought peace to the galaxy; it was my mother.

Whatever the Overseer thought love was made no sense to me, but he *desired* in ways that warped his mind. He desired control, power, Caitrin Bishop. But Mom had wielded her own power, even though it was hard to see sometimes, especially from the outside. He only got her on *her* terms, and he'd never been able to control her, not even when death was the alternative.

My parents never gave in to him. They both walked that bridge. I closed my eyes and saw them together. They were a perfect fit.

I opened my eyes to the picture in the frame again. Me

on my father's lap. I set it down before I threw it across the room and ruined the herd of unicorns stenciled on the wall. "How dare he? How dare he let me be poked and prodded and *drained* when he had the same blood!"

"Listen to me carefully." Sanaa took a step closer, her voice snapping with anger at me now. "First of all, your father couldn't have done *anything* for *anyone* if the Overseer had locked him up the way he locked up you and your mother. Second, do you want to know why I'm a better super soldier than Merrick? Why I don't have the bulk and can blend in? Why I can beat ten Merricks in a fight and not even break a sweat?"

"Yeah." I popped off the bed and stood eye to eye with Sanaa, scowling at her tone and at everything else. "I *do* want to know that."

"Because it was the general's blood in my formula. Pure Mornavail. You're a half breed, darling, and the Overseer's enhanced army is based on *you*, not him."

Holy shit. I choked on the acid burn in the back of my mouth. "Does the Overseer know about you?"

She shook her head. "That's a well-kept secret around him. How would we explain the differences? And like I said before, he reboots you otherwise. Reprograms a person to be his."

Were Sanaa and Merrick the only ones who'd escaped the final injection? There would be rebel super soldiers now, too. But the Overseer was searching for more A1 blood as we spoke. There had to be others like Bridgebane—pure Mornavail.

"And the GIN Project?" I asked. "The early test subjects?"

Sanaa spread her hands. "He'll find more pure blood. He already did in that lot we pulled off the Ewelock DWALSH."

"Has he had time to use it? Make more enhancers?" I panicked. I might have given the rebellion super soldiers, but the Overseer would have Sanaa Mwendes. That wasn't a fair fight.

"We don't think so. We didn't know about the GIN Project or the early testing. The Overseer did that all by himself. He's still analyzing, as far as your father can tell. Figuring out the variations in the blood samples and seeing how the differences interact with his formula. They weren't all pures. Most of them weren't. And now, he's lost his supply again."

Well, thank the Powers for that. Turning to pace, I scraped my hands through my hair and pulled it back. "The wider GIN Project is still coming. We have to stop it."

"One thing at a time. Let's worry about Starbase 12 next." Sanaa held up the bag in her hand.

Curiosity about what my father—shit, even *thinking* that was weird—had left us warred with pulse-spiking anxiety over the GIN Project. I couldn't shake the feeling that it was my fault.

The expensive hardwood floor creaked under my feet, like new and unused things did. "The early testing started right after I stole the lab, didn't it? I took the Overseer's whole stash of enhancers, and he realized he'd fucked himself by 'killing' me when I was eight."

"Something like that."

I stabbed a prickly look at Sanaa as I stalked past. "You mean *exactly* like that."

"Don't blame yourself, Daraja. The Overseer is the one dragging people off to laboratory prisons."

I expelled a bitter huff. It felt a little like flying apart at the seams—except everything was finally knitting together.

"The lab or me. That was what Bridgebane said on Starway 8. He didn't get either, so he threatened the orphanage and forced the blood exchange on me instead. He knew he had to scramble to appease that monster with something, *anything*, before the Overseer set something terrible into motion to look for more A1 blood."

But he'd already been too late. He just didn't know it. And the Overseer had tried to capture me even while launching a backup plan. There'd still been time to stop the GIN Project. No public announcement yet. If either of them had caught me or taken the lab back, none of this would be happening right now.

"He'll do it every time, won't he? Sacrifice me for the greater good? I'm expendable to my own father." That hurt so much more now that I knew who my real father was.

At the same time, what was he supposed to do? Sacrifice everyone else?

Sanaa flicked an impatient hand through the air. "You're too smart to say stupid things."

"Okay. Then why this sudden concern for me? After all this time without a word? After being ready to hand me over as a blood dispenser, even if he didn't want to?"

"My opinion?" She lifted her brows.

"Yeah." I was pretty sure it would be spot on.

"The general could live without you before. He was used to it. The longer you're back in his life, the closer he gets to choosing *you*. No matter the cost."

I sat abruptly on the bright berry-red bed again, my legs suddenly weak. That was exactly what I wanted to hear. It filled my chest with hope, and yet... What would choosing me mean? Leaving the galaxy solely in the hands of the Overseer? How could I ever want that?

There were probably days when my father found a way to save hundreds of lives and make it look like some rebel scum had messed with the Dark Watch, just like he had on the Ewelock hub. Nathaniel Bridgebane was essential to the resistance. He had been from the start. "I can't let him do that. He has to stay strong."

And despite my railing at him, he *had* put me in the best possible place. I loved the orphanage. Starway 8 was my dream, past, present, and future.

But did that erase abandonment? And believing the only real family I had left would slit my throat if I ever showed up on his doorstep? Bridgebane was *convincing*. He had to be. How else could he walk this ... bridge for decades?

"Yes," Sanaa agreed. "He has to stay strong."

And right then, I saw the dead eyes in her also. Cold and ruthless couldn't always be an act. It had to be real, along with real atrocities, or it wouldn't fool the Overseer.

What an awful burden, pretending all the time, doing things you hated. Kill ten to save twenty. Those were the kind of choices they made, Sanaa and my father. Maybe his lies had spared me that.

I swallowed, a dry bob of muscle that hurt my throat. "All right, then. On to the next step." They didn't know it yet, but Shiori and Reena Ahern were waiting for a jailbreak.

Without a word, Sanaa led the way out, locking up behind us. I didn't take anything with me. Unless I was dead, I'd be back.

CHAPTER

19

SHADE

I LOOKED IN THE MIRROR. NATHANIEL BRIDGEBANE, Galactic General, *Dark Watch 12*, stared back at me.

Tess had a lot of questions for her real father. Unfortunately, I couldn't answer them. I only wore his face and his uniform. Held his badge in my hand. I couldn't explain his choices, but I hoped Tess got the chance to ask about them. And about the past. I saw the cracks in her, the holes that needed to be filled with information only Bridgebane could give.

The general had left five things for Tess in the safe inside that Galligar Prime apartment.

A pile of trick handcuffs—he'd obviously conferred with Mwende about our plan.

A crimson Dark Watch uniform for a tall man with broad shoulders.

A full Nathaniel Bridgebane head mask, complete with dark-brown hair turning silver at the temples.

Blue contact lenses.

A duplicate of his security badge.

With everything on and pulled into place as it was now, I was General Bridgebane. He was about to walk onto Starbase 12, as usual. The man had provided us with the easiest access imaginable to the most secure location in the galaxy. Bridgebane and Mwende would arrive together with high-profile prisoners. Nothing unusual in that. Not a single person could question our actions except for the Overseer himself. He was the only one who outranked Bridgebane.

If something went wrong, the real Bridgebane could deny all knowledge of the deception and pin the betrayal on Mwende. Not ideal, but someone had to stay the course if we couldn't.

It was our original plan, improved upon by trading prisoner Shade Ganavan for a fake General Bridgebane, a man no one would dare disobey in the entire military, even if his voice sounded a little different. I could mimic well, but it wasn't perfect. I'd speak as little as possible. Bark out orders. We still had Tess, Jax, and Merrick as important captives—our reason for demanding an interrogation room and the presence of "incentives" to make them talk.

It should work. Get Shiori and Ahern in the same place as the rest of us. Get out.

Our biggest concern was the Overseer catching wind of our actions and asking questions before we left the starbase.

I turned to Tess. "You ready, baby?"

She made a face. "Don't call me that when you look like my father."

I sidled closer, amping up the sleaze. "No daddy fetish?"

Tess's full body shiver came with a little giggle. It was the first time she'd cracked a smile in days. "Dressed like that, you're my worst nightmare."

"He's handsome." I glanced in the mirror again. Gave myself a wink. Posed like a muscle man. Growled a little.

"Shade!" Tess laughed outright this time, and it felt like victory. Her next once-over didn't look quite so revolted at the idea of cozying up to me.

"Are you done with that message?" I asked, slipping Bridgebane's security badge into the slot in his uniform designed for it.

She nodded and pressed Send. "Mareeka and Surral will read between the lines and know I'm up to something dangerous."

"They'll want news from you when you return."

She powered off her tablet and set it on the bedside table. Bonk was taking up most of her pillow, and she stopped to pat him before turning back to me. "I said to hug Coltin for me. I told them I'd found Gabe."

"I'm sure they'll be overjoyed." I tried hard to keep any of the stiffness I felt from my voice.

"Yeah." She nodded, sounding distant.

"What is it?" I coaxed her up and settled my hands on her hips. Tess almost leaned into me and then seemed to recoil from the uniform. Or from the illusion of her father. Maybe both.

"Gabe doesn't care about Starway 8 like I do."

My heart thudded, a hard beat that told me this was either a conversation I really wanted or really didn't. "Why do you say that? There hasn't been much time for long talks, or for reminiscing about the past." I forced myself to sound as neutral as possible. Now wasn't the time for jealousy or reverting to a Neanderthal. Jax had that covered for all of us.

"He didn't think about telling them he was alive. It didn't occur to him. It didn't even occur to him that Mareeka and

Surral could get word to *me*. It's as if he left and that was it. Done. Goodbye."

"That's probably the way it is for most everyone," I said. "Thousands of people can't just hang around forever. They'd need more room."

A smile tugged at her mouth again. "Maybe. But for him, it should've been more."

"Because it's more for you." I got where she was coming from with this. When you love someone, what matters to them matters to you. Period. I already respected the hell out of Starway 8, and I had no doubt my feelings for the orphanage would evolve into something probably as obsessive as my devotion to my docks. That was just how I worked when I cared about something. For now, though, I was in it for Tess.

"See? It's not that hard to understand, and you didn't even live there for more than half your life."

I drew her against me, wishing she didn't feel stiff and that I didn't look like a man she was so damn conflicted about. I pressed her head against my neck, hoping she'd just listen to my voice, hear *me*. "You're a gift, Tess. Starway 8 is a gift. I'm the luckiest son of a bitch in the galaxy because you chose me. I swear to care for the orphanage as much as you do, and to protect it and everyone in it, right alongside you, with my life."

"Shade." She sighed my name and melted into me. Her arms came around my waist. The clenching in my chest went from uncomfortable to unbearable as I realized this was it.

"I want to kiss you. I want to make love to you." Splaying my hand wide against the back of her head, I kept her tucked in close. Could she feel my heart beating? It hammered relentlessly against my ribs. "But I look like your asshole-maybe-not-asshole father, and we don't have time for that."

Her breath punched out, something between a huffed-out laugh and a not-quite sob hitting my neck with a sudden rush of warmth. I didn't mean to turn her inside out with this Starway 8 stuff. I just wanted her to know...

"There's something I've been wanting to tell you." I paused and swallowed. "There were all these times I wanted to, but it just never came out."

She glanced up. The second she saw my face, she frowned.

"No, don't look at me wearing this mask. That'll screw everything up." I pressed on her head again, angling it down.

She leaned against my shoulder. "You're freaking me out."

"I'm freaking myself out." My heart was doing backflips now. "I've never done this before."

"What the hell, Shade?" Her grip tightened around my waist, even as she tensed away from me.

I sank my fingers into her hair, not letting her go anywhere. The thick rope of her braid felt strange when I was used to having her long hair down and smooth between my fingers. I pushed deeper to feel *her* under my hand. "I love you, Tess. I'm so fucking in love with you it hurts. And I'll love the orphanage, too, and not only because you do. I promise."

She didn't move. She didn't say a thing, and the worst sort of fear started crawling up my chest.

"You'll have to clean up your language," she finally said, her voice muffled against my jacket.

"What?" I rasped out. Maybe she wasn't there yet, but love grew, right? I could still convince Tess.

"You'll have to clean up your language on Starway 8,"

she said more clearly. "The kids can't hear us talking like that."

"Kids know everything by age eleven. I swear, there are no secrets left."

She looked up at me, catching her lower lip between her teeth. "Well, there are some things *we* don't need to teach them."

A spike of adrenaline hit my veins. "Are you saying what I think you're saying?" The painful knot in my chest started to loosen, but my breath came short, and my hands almost shook.

She smiled. "I love you, too, Shade. And I trust you with Starway 8."

Joy nearly ripped apart my heart. Not caring that I looked like Bridgebane, I lowered my head and kissed her. Tess closed her eyes and kissed me back. She was all there, all in. I could *feel* it. Blood fired through my body. Tess. A future. A place that needed us. It electrified me like nothing had in a decade and unleashed something wild inside.

I clutched her hard and growled like a savage. "I wish we had more time." Before she could respond, I brought her to her toes and devoured every hot, delicious inch of her mouth, consuming her.

"I wish you didn't have that mask and uniform." Her breathless voice went straight to my tightening groin. I ground against her.

"Keep your eyes closed." I swept my tongue into her mouth again, her taste and the feel of her under my hands driving me crazy with need.

Tess hooked her leg around my hip and rocked into me. I lifted her and spun her against the closed door, pinning her with my whole body. She moaned. We lined up perfectly. My erection pressed against the juncture of her thighs, and the heat of her left a permanent imprint on me. I was stamped for life. She softened, but I went rock-hard.

I broke off for a ragged breath before I drowned. Tess opened her eyes. They widened. She stared at me in horror and then burst out laughing.

"That is by far the *weirdest* thing I've ever done." She half choked on another laugh, slamming her eyes closed again.

I reluctantly unglued myself from her and cleared my throat. "I guess it's time to go anyway. You ready for this?" I asked in a hoarse voice.

She opened her eyes, two bright-blue starbursts that glittered with teasing warmth. "Cupcake, I'm ready for anything."

"Cupcake." I shook my head. "I should never have called you 'sugar,' not even once."

"Nope." A smile curved her lips. It expanded, her grin infectious, until we both laughed. "But I love you anyway."

My heart grew ten sizes too big for my chest and squashed everything else aside. I couldn't breathe, but I kissed her again. And then again, because I couldn't help it, and because there was no telling what the next few hours would bring.

We landed on Starbase 12 without incident. Mwende rattled off security codes and personal identification numbers while the rest of us stayed quiet and waited. It was two days after Daniel Ahern's contact was supposed to have lowered the alarm for three hours on Platform 7. Two days after the man probably thought we'd bailed on the mission and abandoned his wife. The rebel leaders in the Fold probably thought so, too. We hadn't informed anyone of the change of plan.

It wouldn't have been smart. We also had no easy way to contact them.

Mwende seemed fully committed to helping us, even though she had a lot to lose if things went wrong here. We could all potentially lose our lives, and she could potentially blow her cover. There was no mask on her face. That was her own dark skin and sweat-free complexion. It was almost a shame to risk her.

She looked over at me from the passenger's seat as I powered down the cruiser. Ten heavily armed Dark Watch guards were already coming forward to greet us. Tess, Jax, and Merrick were out of sight and handcuffed in the back section. They'd need to be careful not to move wrong, or the fake cuffs could pop open.

"Own that uniform," Mwende told me in a low but steely voice. "*Believe* it."

Her words sank deep. *Belief.* That was what it took. Purpose. Convictions that went beyond myself. Hope.

The echo of a thousand revolutions rose inside me to grip me around the throat. Drumbeat heart. Gunshot pulse. My whole body burning up.

I nodded, not trusting my voice. A war cry wanted to fly out.

Squaring my shoulders, I opened the door and stepped down. Today wouldn't be about battling these people. It would be about pretending to be one of them until we got what we came here for.

"General, we're here to escort you." The leading soldier's quick salute was picture perfect. It made me want to kick him in the head.

I nodded again. I could corral my natural drawl into more clipped tones, but there was no reason to tempt fate. I'd speak when necessary.

Mwende gathered the prisoners. We surrounded them along with the ten guards and started toward the lifts.

"We want the Lower H interrogation room. Make sure it's clear," Mwende snapped.

"Yes, Lieutenant." The same soldier who'd greeted me used a pocket-sized tablet to confirm that the room was empty. "I'll bring the usual instruments," he said.

Was there a way that could sound any *more* ominous? My jaw clenched.

"Not necessary." Mwende shoved Merrick forward when he balked at the block of elevators. "Bring prisoners Reena Ahern and Shiori Takashi to the interrogation room. They're all we need to get information from this group."

Tess hissed in a breath and shot Mwende a look so hate-blackened I almost thought she'd missed her calling as an actress.

Jax ground out, "You bitch."

Mwende gave him a cold look. She ignored Tess.

Merrick didn't say anything but growled when the guards pushed him into a lift. He was with Mwende and half the guards. I took a different elevator with Jax, Tess, and the rest of the soldiers who'd met us on the landing dock.

At Lower H, we stepped out first. Mwende wasn't there yet, and I didn't know which direction to take. Tess angled her body to the left. I pretended to have pushed her that way to begin with and headed where she led. The second lift opened, and the others followed us down the corridor.

It was impossible to miss the interrogation room. It was large and labeled, its size being the reason we chose it. Instead of separating the prisoners, we could chain them all in one place. The guards shoved Tess, Jax, and Merrick into seats on the far side of a rectangular table and attached their cuffed wrists to the metal rings in front of them.

Tess jerked her hands away at the last second. The head goon grabbed her joined wrists and slammed them down hard on the table. Pain blazed across her expression, and it was all I could do not to heave the man away from her and teach him a bone-breaking lesson.

Forced to seethe in silence, I watched him clip Tess to the ring, rattling her hands again just because he knew it would hurt and because she was tied down like an animal. She spat in his face.

Oh yeah. I loved her.

"Rebel bitch." He backhanded her, snapping her head to one side with a crack that resounded.

A bomb went off in my brain. Pure rage. I didn't move, didn't make a sound. I stared at the red mark blooming on Tess's pale cheek, my vision on fire.

"Did I say you could harm my prisoners?" Lethally soft, my voice came out a deceptive whisper.

The goon turned to me, his eyes widening. "But, usually…" He backed up a step, my wrath pushing him away from the table. He flinched, looking to the others for support. They kept their heads down. Cowardice hiding behind Dark Watch uniforms.

Mwende slid me a glance that reminded me of who I was right now: a cold-hearted bastard with prisoners.

"Do not take the pleasure of the first hit away from me again," I growled, narrowing my eyes on the soldier who led this unit.

He nodded, fear draining his face of color. The whole unit stepped back as I spread my hands on the table and leaned toward the prisoners, menace in every line of my body.

"Bring the other prisoners we asked for." Without looking at the soldiers again, I slammed my hands down on the cold metal surface. "Now!"

All three of our prisoners jumped, even Merrick. I'd bet the guards jumped higher.

The goons left the room, some to stand outside the door and others to fetch our "motivation." Lieutenant Mwende started perusing the torture devices on the shelf beside us. Shock wands. Hammers. Spikes. Blades. Scalpels. And these weren't even her "usual." I nearly shuddered.

Glancing up, I took stock of the camera in the corner. Was there audio in this room as well as visual? Probably. I waited.

The lieutenant picked up a long-handled prod and fired it up, looking at the shock wand with something close to affection. Electricity crackled at the tip. "Where's the rebel hideout?" Sparks jumped in her dark eyes, a sinister reflection.

Mwende pointed the wand at Merrick. "Talk. You first."

Merrick stared her down, his chin lowered.

"No?" Mwende turned on Jax. "Talk and I might go easy on..."—she jabbed Tess in the fleshy part of her shoulder—"her."

Tess screamed in agony. She bucked and jerked like a live wire, throwing herself backward and nearly toppling over.

I lunged for her, almost blowing my cover before I jerked back. Was Mwende crazy? Jax bellowed. Merrick snarled. I breathed hard, bracing myself against the table. "Enough!" I grated.

Mwende pulled back the stick. The electric buzz of contact faded into a waiting hum that was almost as unnerving. Tess's head lolled before she managed to steady it again on her shoulders. Her gaze found mine, unfocused. My insides flipped over. I swallowed.

"Let's try this again." Mwende slowly paced in front of the table, the shock wand pointed toward the prisoners. It was impossible for their eyes not to follow the crackling tip. Mwende stopped. She looked at Jax but held the stick in Tess's direction, her message unmistakable. "Where's the rebel hideout?"

"We're not that high up in the pecking order," Merrick answered stiffly for everyone. "We don't know anything."

Mwende lunged and jabbed Merrick in the chest with the weapon. He curled inward, grunting. After the initial punch of electricity, he straightened and stared at her while she zapped him. Other than his nostrils flaring, he didn't move a muscle. He watched her, the whites of his eyes blazing.

"Wrong answer." Voice as flat as her expression, Mwende finally broke eye contact with Merrick and threatened Tess again. "Last chance or she gets another shock. Maybe in the face this time."

Jax stared in horror. He looked at Tess, then at me. Was Mwende bluffing? I didn't agree to torture. None of us did. As Bridgebane, I could stop it. Should I?

Own that uniform. Believe *it.*

"Lieutenant." Ice-cold. Ruthless. Dead eyes stared out from me. "I want this room blacked out for interrogation."

"They've seen worse than a shock wand in the monitor room," Mwende said.

I could imagine. "I have special plans for this group." I picked up a hammer. A knuckle-breaking blunt-force primitive basher. Might come in handy. "Do as I ordered."

"Yes, General." Mwende strode to a control panel on the wall and typed out a code I wouldn't have known. It'd been a guess, but it looked like taking down the AV for a messy questioning wasn't that unusual when you were General Bridgebane.

The little red light on the corner camera stopped flashing. The surveillance device retracted into a box. The front panel closed, sealing with a click that would've scared the shit out of me if I'd been chained to the table and about to be tortured. At least now we could talk without riddles and stop electrocuting my girlfriend.

Mwende lowered the zapper. "No wonder you call him cupcake," she muttered to Tess. Her gaze spiked to me. She shook her head.

"You didn't have to torture her," I said, furious.

Mwende scoffed. "That was *one* shock."

"A long one!" I snapped.

"That hurt more than the bullet in my ass." Tess scowled. "Seriously, Sanaa, I didn't agree to that."

"Well, I guarantee your reaction looked real to the people watching from the surveillance deck." Mwende waved a hand toward the now-hidden and turned-off camera while glancing at me again. "But Softy here had a good idea with that."

I huffed. *Softy*. I hoped *that* nickname wouldn't stick.

Someone rapped on the door. "Enter!" I barked.

One of the guards from earlier opened the door. Another two entered, hauling Shiori between them. Her legs dragged on the floor.

My chest jerked at the sight of her. So small and fragile. Head down, gray hair in strings, her wrists bound with old gauze. Rusty stains left a gruesome slash of color across both bandages. The soldiers threw her down on the interrogation room floor. Shiori gasped and barely caught herself on hands and knees that cracked against the hard surface. Her head lifted. Milky eyes stared sightlessly ahead, pointed toward the bottom shelf of the torture cabinet.

"Shiori," Tess whispered.

"No." The old woman's face crumpled. No tears came, just a look of utter anguish as she turned toward the voice she recognized. "I told you not to."

"Shut up, you old dog." The head goon kicked Shiori and sent her crashing into the table leg in front of her. I flinched. Tess yelled. Merrick rattled his chains, growling, and Jax looked fucking terrifying. Even Mwende seemed shocked, although it barely lasted a second.

Blind fury coursed through me. Before I knew what I was doing, I grabbed the goon's neck and slammed him up against the wall. Breathing hard, I squeezed until the man's face turned purple. I was bigger, stronger, and right now, I was fucking General Bridgebane, and this insect was going to piss his pants in terror.

"*What* did I *say* about leaving me the first hit?" I snarled.

"I-I'm sorry, General," he gasped out.

I was about to put the fear of the cosmos into this asshole *and* save my cover. I carried him by the neck and threw him into the hallway. He landed flat out on the floor, wheezing. I stomped hard on his ribs and ground my heel down until I heard a crack. The guy squealed like a piglet. I kicked his broken bone, and he passed out before he finished rolling over.

"Get him out of my sight," I ordered. The other guards left immediately, hauling the unconscious man between them.

So this was power. Unquestioned. To use or abuse in any fashion. No wonder Bridgebane was such a dead-eyed bastard. How could you do this every day and not hate yourself?

Shiori knelt and groped above her, feeling for the tabletop. She found its edge and pulled herself to standing. Calling for her, Tess banged with her chains. Shiori followed the sound. She reached out and wrapped her hands around Tess's, the metal ring between them. Tess's sudden sob broke my heart ten times over.

"Why, child? And now this..." Shiori's trembling voice had half the strength that I remembered. "If I'd died, you wouldn't be here."

"If you'd died, I'd have lost even more of my family," Tess answered.

"We missed you, Shiori," Jax said.

"Jaxon, too?" Shiori squeezed her eyes closed, but even blindness didn't shut out the worst views. "I've failed you."

"No, I failed *you*," Tess said. "You and Miko. This is all my fault."

Shiori spread her hands, showing her bloody bandages. "I tried. I tried to stop you."

"By killing yourself?" Tess's tone hardened. "Then it's a good thing you failed, too. And this... It's not what it seems." Guards trooped outside the door again. Tess lowered her voice. "Now hush and don't move."

Someone knocked. Shiori's face went blank, her paper-thin skin waxen and static. If it weren't for the unhealthy spots and the tremors she couldn't control, she'd have looked like a doll. Still. Small. Powerless. Except she wasn't. With the rest of her face expressionless, her blind eyes held more than I'd ever realized. Love, hate, determination, and a hardness that said anything she'd done in here wasn't about giving up, it was about fighting back. Always.

She froze the second Tess told her to stop moving. Shiori was a damn good soldier.

My breath gusted out. "Enter!" I shouted.

Shiori turned her head a fraction. She cocked an ear and *saw*. In that moment, she knew me, and my insides clenched in a way that said family could be given and taken away, and sometimes, it was found.

Three more goons entered with a woman who must be Reena Ahern. I'd been expecting an older, graying female of Caucasian origin, like her husband. The woman shoved in front of me was the total opposite. Not a day over fifty, compact and hard, with near-black hair, light-brown skin, and dark eyes that incinerated. She turned a scathing look on me and her upper lip curled. "*You.*"

My back stiffened. This was starting off well.

The soldiers pushed her inside the interrogation room but didn't lay a finger on her. It appeared they learned from each other. Mistakes. Corrected behavior. Survival of the fittest was still at work everywhere, especially inside the Dark Watch.

"Leave us," I ordered.

They got the hell out. I closed the door and bolted it. As I turned back around, Reena Ahern kicked me in the face.

Pain rang in my head. I reeled back a step. Mwende grabbed her and pulled her away from me as I hissed in a breath and gingerly touched my nose. Bleeding. A quick check assured me that the mask was still in place. The throbbing intensified.

I glared at Ahern. Even with her hands bound, she'd blindsided me and managed one hell of a kick.

"Keeping in fighting shape inside your cell, I see." I dabbed my nose with my sleeve. Crimson on crimson. It wouldn't stain. The Dark Watch wore black, but the Overseer's generals wore the blood of the galaxy.

Hatred burned from her like radiation from a star. "You evil bastard. I'll never give you what you need."

"And what's that?" I asked.

She snort-huffed like we'd already had this conversation a thousand times. "I'd rather let my beautiful planet stay a poisoned jewel in the heavens than turn her over to the Overseer. The bounty of Demeter Terre will never be yours." She struggled forward, trying to lunge at me.

Mwende jerked her back again. Ahern flung herself from side to side but couldn't break the lieutenant's iron hold. With a bellow, she stopped struggling and looked around, her chest heaving. She swept a fearsome gaze over the prisoners but didn't stop, no recognition flickering in her eyes as she turned back to me.

"Why am I here?" She glared. "You know I won't talk."

I wiped my nose again with Bridgebane's jacket. He probably didn't want it back anyway.

At least we knew Ahern hadn't turned over her formula for cleaning up the DT atmosphere—if she'd even figured it out. As far as we knew, the neutralizing method was still a theory.

"We're here to rescue you." I checked to make sure my nose wasn't broken. The throbbing was settling down—just like Ahern now.

She looked at me and started laughing.

I wasn't in a laughing mood for several reasons. Tess in chains. The Overseer somewhere on this starbase. Us still in the interrogation room instead of leaving. I'd laugh when we were safe, but until then, nothing was funny.

"You're always trying different things. You should know

by now that I. Won't. Crack." Ahern's dark eyes narrowed in promise.

I lowered my chin in acknowledgment. "You and Fiona are gonna get along great." I turned to Mwende. "You have the key to those cuffs?"

The lieutenant took a master key from the shelf and liberated Ahern first.

"What's going on?" Warily, she rubbed her wrists.

"We're freeing you." I reached for Shiori, who wasn't bound, and guided her against my side. The frailty of her body didn't fool me anymore. Her backbone was made of heroic stuff. "Get on board with it," I said to Ahern, "and only kick the bad guys in the face."

The rebel scientist snapped her mouth shut, but suspicion stayed plastered across her face like this damn mask across mine. I already hated looking like Bridgebane, but I suddenly wanted to rip his likeness away and howl my own name for once. For the first time in a decade, I wanted to claim myself.

Shiori leaned against me, light and cool, a ghostly weight. Her trust humbled me, and I wrapped an arm around her, wanting to steady her and warm her up. She trembled. I didn't think it was fear. More like adrenaline and age. As Mwende freed the prisoners from the rings on the table, Shiori lifted her fingers to touch my face.

Gently, I took hold of her hand and lowered it. "That's not my face. I'd rather you touched the real one." She'd never learned my features. She'd obviously learned my voice.

Her smile was so soft I might've imagined it. "Tess forgave you then?"

I nodded, then remembered she couldn't see and scraped a sound of confirmation from my thickening throat.

"I knew your heart before you did." Her gentle murmur

went straight to the organ she was talking about and squeezed out a painful beat.

"Did you?" I asked, my voice rough.

She nodded. "It whispered to me of your choice."

Before I could answer, or even try to understand, Tess spun Shiori from my arms and folded her into a tight hug. Jax joined them, his arms around them both.

"Merrick's here, too." Tess pulled back. She sniffled once. "Big Guy, I mean."

Shiori nodded. To my surprise, she reached for me again. "Is your plan to walk right out?"

"Will *she* let us?" Ahern tilted her head toward Mwende, her hellion hackles going back up. "And what about you?" Swung back on me, her poison-dart eyes were something else. "Is the Dark Watch turning on itself? Finally melting down into a pile of galactic waste?"

"*She* just let you out of your cuffs," Mwende muttered.

"And I may look like him, but I'm not." I handed Ahern a pair of dummy cuffs from deep inside my jacket pocket. The lieutenant stashed the real restraints under the torture cabinet, pushing them out of sight.

"Put those on," I instructed. "They latch, but don't lock. One hard pull, and they'll come apart."

Ahern's nostrils flared once. Slowly, her mouth pinching, she put her hands behind her back and let Mwende cuff her again. She immediately yanked the cuffs open, looking shocked when they gave way. "Just checking," she said stiffly.

Grumbling in her native language, Mwende cuffed her again—not gently. When Jax, Merrick, and Tess also wore the fake restraints again, the lieutenant and I drew our guns. It was time to move some prisoners.

I held Shiori's arm to guide her. "Here's the plan to get

us out of here. We're transferring you because we suddenly have reason to believe that rebel spies might've infiltrated Starbase 12. We're not telling anyone that unless they *ask*. No need to cause a ruckus unless we have to. We're banking on Bridgebane not explaining himself to anyone. If someone wants a reason for the transfer, we're moving you to a secure location for further questioning. That's it. Unfortunately for them, the Dark Watch is going to lose you along the way."

"Lose us?" Ahern questioned.

"That's right. Five prisoners are about to fade like stardust." And it was going to look bad for Bridgebane and Mwende. How much more of Bridgebane's soul was he going to have to give up in order to convince the Overseer he'd played no part in this? The guy couldn't have much soul to spare, and now, he might have to pin this whole thing on Sanaa Mwende, probably his only friend. At least if she wanted it, Mwende had a place with us now.

"Your husband's waiting for you." I gave Ahern a get-with-the-program look. "So is an entire planet."

Her lips parted. She took a startled breath. "Daniel?"

"That's the one." I opened the door, pointing my gun at Merrick. "Now walk."

Most of the guards from earlier waited in the hallway. They snapped to attention. The hardness in my tone helped bring my voice closer to Bridgebane's, but the mimic wasn't perfect. It didn't seem to matter. These goons were too afraid of me to notice. That was what zero hesitation about breaking someone's bones did. If their fear got us out of here without questions, it was a fair trade for that little chunk of *my* soul.

"We're moving these prisoners to a new location," I announced, clipping out the words. Thanks to Mwende, we knew Bridgebane kept a midsized vessel on the starbase—a Ruslan Interceptor 280 with holding cells. She had the ignition codes. "Accompany us to my RI-280."

"Yes, General." They immediately fell into step beside us.

So far, so good. And unless Mwende somehow came out of this with her cover intact and flew it back here, we were gaining a solid ship with firepower. Not bad for a day's work.

Maybe we could give the Interceptor to Gabe and get him off the *Endeavor*.

We went through several sets of doors that were retracted when we'd come by earlier. They were closed now, and Mwende had to use her badge to open them. We avoided using mine. We didn't need to damn Bridgebane any more than we were already doing.

A group of heavily armed goons patrolled the second zone we strode through, the beat of their boots echoing down the long hallway. Doors lined both sides of the corridor, closed, solid, and numbered. Prison cells. No sound came from behind them, but I knew better than to confuse quiet with empty.

Sweat prickled beneath my mask as we made our way toward the elevator block at the center of the starbase. The walk to the interrogation room had seemed long. The walk back out felt interminable, like an endless trek across a desert planet.

Rounding a corner, we nearly collided with a captive shuffling between two soldiers, a bag over his head, his hands bound in front of him, and three fingers missing. They'd been gone for a while now, the wounds healed over. White scars twisted over dark-beige skin, snaking toward his cinched wrists and then up into his shirtsleeves. Red and black tattoos swirled down heavy, flat-boned forearms and met the puckered flesh.

Ahern gasped. "Okano?"

The prisoner's head snapped up. He turned. Harsh breaths chuffed the bag in and out over his mouth.

"Move it!" His guards pulled. He stumbled and kept walking, his head dropping forward.

Mwende gave Ahern a sharp jerk on her elbow, tugging her back into line with us. "All you rebel scum know each other," she muttered, propelling Ahern along with enough force to tell us all to shut up and keep moving. We had a mission, and this Okano wasn't a part of it.

I stared straight ahead and ignored the man's low moan as we walked in the opposite direction. A shudder rose inside me as Okano's limping tread faded down the hallway.

A month ago, I could've brought him in. I hadn't, but I could've. No wonder Tess sometimes pulled back and asked herself what the hell she was doing with me in her bed.

I glanced at Tess, too quick for her to notice. Haunted eyes. Visible sorrow. Her heart bleeding for a stranger who shared her values. I looked dead ahead again, our destination finally in sight. Tess had lived her entire life by unwavering principles. She'd jumped into a black hole for them. She did what she had to, no matter what. And what had I done? I'd floundered with simple decency and nearly cashed her in.

Steeling my spine, I steered my thoughts away from that dark chasm and drove Tess ahead of me with a harshness I had to force. I loved her. She loved me. We had more than a little to build on.

Finally, we stood in front of the elevators, waiting for one of them to open. This nightmare was almost over. No more shock wands nearly sending Tess over backward while

I stood there and watched like her pain didn't matter. This was a heist—a people heist—and there were two things left to accomplish. Up to Platform 5 for the ship we were stealing. Out on Bridgebane's RI-280. We had this. And we had the women we'd come for.

A lift opened. Mwende and I stepped inside with all the prisoners. I jerked my chin toward a Dark Watch soldier. "You're with us. There's no room for the rest of you. Take the next one and meet us on the platform." I didn't want us separated at this point. I'd go crazy if I didn't have eyes on everyone.

The goon followed, keeping a hard eye on Merrick and his hand on his Grayhawk. Flash blasts lined his belt. Nasty little fuckers. The other soldiers stood aside and waited. The doors closed. I pressed the level we needed, and the box started upward.

I squeezed Shiori's arm as we rose in the elevator, a light reassurance that we were on our way now. She shook less and stood taller. My other hand still held my gun at the ready. We'd have to cross a sea of goons on the platform, and I needed to act exactly like Bridgebane. This was a day like any other. I was taking rebel prisoners to my galactic death ship. No problem.

I braced for the walk across the platform. We'd almost reached our exit.

Instead of slowing down, we blew past the floor I'd selected.

I glanced at Tess, sudden unease corroding my stomach like battery acid. The tiny confused shake of her head inflated my worry to nuclear proportions.

I reached out and hit the correct button again. Nothing changed. If anything, we moved faster. Something else controlled the lift—or *someone*. We passed the middle tier and hit the upper section.

The Dark Watch goon shifted nervously. "I don't think I'm supposed to be up here, General."

He shrank under my withering glare. No need to channel Bridgebane for that one.

We'd almost reached the top of the spacedock. "Lieutenant?" *What the hell is happening?*

The look on Mwende's face was chilling, a mix of disappointment, rage, and disgust. She snapped her wrists and knives landed in both hands. She lowered her chin. Her eyes flicked up, and she growled low in her throat. I had my answer.

I pushed Shiori behind me toward Jax and Tess in the corner. The lift stopped, the doors opened, and I stared at the man who was now my very personal enemy.

The Overseer stared back, a dozen guards around him all bristling with weapons. The goons were all Merrick-sized. Our only way forward was through a unit of super soldiers.

"Nathaniel." The Overseer canted his head to one side in question. "What are you doing with my prisoners?"

CHAPTER

20

TESS

No. *No!* This wasn't happening. Not after everything we'd done.

The Overseer wore that smile I hated. Small but gleeful—the one displayed by every fairy-tale villain right before he burned a village to the ground.

Simon Novalight beckoned us out of the lift, and we had no choice but to enter his spacious command center at the apex of Starbase 12. There was no more *up* from here, and down didn't really matter when the Overseer controlled the elevator.

"I just heard about a possible rebel infiltration here. I'm bringing these prisoners to *Dark Watch 12* for further questioning," Shade answered. He knew the man he was impersonating. The intonation, pitch, stiffness—he almost sounded like Bridgebane. *Almost.*

"*Dark Watch 12*?" The Overseer's hard stare bore into Shade, as if trying to peel back the layers of his mask. Behind him, the huge window panels offered an unparalleled view of Alpha Sambian, clouds floating over oceans, green continents, and mountains. "I wasn't aware that either you or your ship were anywhere near here. Or that rebels were running amok on my starbase."

Shade didn't miss a beat. "We only just received the intel. I was about to contact you to verify it. I wanted to lock this lot up somewhere safe in the meantime. I failed to properly deal with Quintessa the last time we met. It's time to rectify that."

The Overseer studied Shade, expressionless. "Is it?"

Shade nodded, a quick military-efficient dip of his chin that fit perfectly with Bridgebane's head.

"And you needed an old blind woman and Reena Ahern for that?" The Overseer didn't even glance at the women he spoke of. He looked my way briefly, his suspicious gaze like a reptile slithering over my body. It was Merrick he focused on.

Sanaa saw his focus, too, and instantly put a knife to Merrick's throat. I worried, though... Was this ruse already up? Handcuffs wouldn't hold a super soldier. Neither would a knife.

"They're leverage," Shade said with the same dead flatness Bridgebane used when he spoke.

Without comment, the Overseer turned and typed out something on the big control panel next to him. I stopped breathing when the elevator doors shut, trapping us at the top of the starbase. There was only one other area up here—the family living quarters. Except, this monster had no family.

The Overseer turned back to us with a Grayhawk in his hand. He leveled the gun on me, his cold brown eyes screaming triumph down the barrel. "Quintessa won't talk, and I don't need her anymore. So, you won't mind if I—"

I dove on instinct, popping open my cuffs to break my fall. The shot hit the goon behind me. I twisted, grabbed his gun as he dropped, and swung it on the Overseer.

"Your turn." I aimed and fired.

The Overseer took a step back, a flash of surprise animating his features. I spun to my knees and hammered off another shot right at his black heart. I'd never aimed to kill before. I didn't regret it for a second. I'd destroy this bastard twice if I could.

His guards took aim at us but didn't return fire without his order. And he just stood there, metal glinting from his chest. No blood seeped out. He smiled again, and this time it wasn't the village he was going to burn, it was the whole damn universe.

Fear contaminated my wrath. I fired again, the deafening bang of useless shots echoing back to me as violently as the recoil pounding up my arm. Like the walls on Starway 8, the Overseer's dark-brown uniform was impenetrable and absorbed the impact.

I stopped shooting but kept my gun up.

"You stupid girl," he sneered. "People try to kill me every day. Do you really think I wouldn't make myself bulletproof?"

My hostile gaze dipped up and down his body. I adjusted and aimed for his head.

His mouth flattened in acknowledgment of a strategy that might work—until he turned his gun on Jax instead. "Throw the gun away from you. *Now*."

Scowling, I set down the gun and sent it spiraling off. With my other hand, I swiped a flash blast from the dead goon's belt and folded the small weapon into my grip as I stood. Whatever happened next, I wouldn't be on my knees for it. If I was going to die, I'd die on my feet and do some damage before I left.

I lifted my chin in a *fuck-you* that I hoped slapped the Overseer right across the face.

His eyes narrowed. Jax, Merrick, and Ahern still appeared to be in cuffs. Was he questioning that?

Sanaa distracted him from his scrutiny by prodding Merrick with her knife. "Knock it off," she growled when Merrick twitched. She shoved him closer to Shade, which forced Shiori farther back.

The Overseer focused on his long-favored general again. "Nathaniel, I suggest you get control of your niece and prove your loyalty, which I've been questioning of late."

Shade's jaw hardened beneath the mask. He modulated his voice, dropping it to a low, clipped tone to try to emulate Bridgebane's. "You have no reason to question my loyalty. I'm with you—as always."

The Overseer pursed his lips. "You didn't kill her when she was eight. You let her go just a few weeks ago. You brought me a paltry amount of her blood as some kind of stall tactic. You disappear for days on end. And now this?"

As his voice rose in fury, something occurred to me: the Overseer had only one friend, one person he trusted. Bridgebane was *it*. And while Bridgebane's capacity for lying and subterfuge was impressive, the Overseer hadn't *wanted* to see what was becoming plain enough.

That faith and trust were crumbling now. I could see it in the Overseer's expression, like rocks tumbling down the side of a cliff, breaking apart as they crashed together, the raw insides exposed to the harsh light. Because of me, in a short amount of time, Bridgebane had taken one too many risks. Now, doubt glared from the darkening flush spreading across the Overseer's face.

"You got the blood you wanted from the early GIN subjects," Shade said briskly.

"And then I *lost* them." The Overseer pounded a fist on the edge of his console. The skin whitened around his mouth. The look he turned on Shade was like cocking a gun—primed and ready to go off. "Do you know anything about that?" Accusation flicked a spark toward the gunpowder in his voice.

Shade stiffened his shoulders. "I attempted to get them back. *DW 12* fired shots on those rebel bandits."

"Useless shots!" the despot spat.

A warning voice in my head grew louder than the speed-of-light pulse in my ears. I needed to distract the Overseer away from our fake Bridgebane. Shade had already slipped a few times with his voice. What was next? The Overseer was bound to hear something that didn't make sense.

"What do you even want? What *more* could you want?" I asked the man who used to be my father in name only. The Overseer loved to hear himself talk—and to give me lessons in how stupid and useless I was while trying to convince me of his own perceived virtue. It had been an endless cycle when I was a kid. He reveled in the sound of his own voice, and right now, he had a literal captive audience. There was no way he could resist.

He focused on me again, his ire sucking at my soul like a black hole that wanted to inhale everyone's happiness and crush it into a dark mass. "What do I want?"

Soundlessly, I breathed in and out. More than air fed my body. I'd seen Shiori again. Jax was with me. Shade and I had said what we needed to. I'd even found my father. Now,

I would draw the Overseer's fire. I hadn't been able to save my mother or Miko, but I'd be damned if I'd let him murder anyone else I loved.

"You control the entire galaxy." I nodded out the clear panel toward the Dark beyond, my home planet still taking up half the panoramic view from the upper deck of the starbase. "Why do you need to hurt people, too?"

"It's not about hurting people." He actually looked shocked—almost believably so. "I've protected them for years."

A hard laugh burst from me, a spasm of disbelief I couldn't control. "What are you talking about?"

"The war your grandparents lived through? I stopped it."

"Yeah, by nuking a planet and poisoning another. And bombing the Outer Zones to pieces. How many innocent lives did galactic harmony cost?" Or had he conveniently forgotten the mass casualties, as dictators do?

"Humanity had been tearing itself apart for generations. It wasn't the Sambian War, Quintessa, it was the Sambian *Wars*. One bled into another, endless. People courted conflict across *planets*, and I didn't invent conquest." The Overseer stood there, bullets in his jacket, armed guards all around him, and something made me stop and listen to him for once. There was a to-hell-with-this tone to his voice that I'd never heard before. It scared the crap out of me. A predictable Overseer I could almost deal with. An unpredictable one was a loose cannon of cosmic proportions.

"Planets' worth of people had already killed one another because they couldn't agree on the most basic of things. One faction had to have power over another. Sycophants had to crawl up the ranks. No one was ever happy with what they had," he spat. "Ever."

"It's called free will, asshole," Merrick ground out. "People argue."

"Argue?" The Overseer aimed a missile-blast look on Merrick. "They mowed each other down in the name of freedom—a concept that can't apply to an entity this big. People tried. And failed. Unified needs and desires could barely work on a planetary level. At a Sector level, they started to unravel. No one could agree on what liberty looked like. What it should be. For whom. One person's utopia was another person's hell. Each wanted their version of peace and happiness to win."

"So you came along to impose yours?" I scoffed.

He shrugged. "Someone had to."

"No, actually, someone didn't. Democratic planetary rule worked in a lot of places."

"Until someone ambitious on Planet A decided he or she should rule longer, or without the consent of the majority. And then why not do the same on the rock next door? Why not the whole Sector? That's how wars start, Quintessa. Don't you know your history?"

Now he was impugning my schooling? Fuck him. "Millions of people annihilated in order for *your* version of perfection to take over?" His version was *my* hell. "Books burned. History erased so people won't understand that revolt *works*. Unfairly distributed resources and medicines. Power abuse rampant across the military." My voice almost shook with disgust. "Not a single vote in my lifetime—for anyone or anything. Existence across the galaxy determined by a dictator with zero sympathy and more firepower than anyone else. How many people did you kill to get what you want?"

"Less, I imagine, than what endless war would have

eliminated." His cold, unfeeling response was a slap in the face after my outburst.

I gaped in shock. "Do you actually believe you're the good guy in all this?"

"I don't really care anymore, Quintessa, because when I'm done, I'll have wiped forty years from existence and can start again—thanks to you and your blood."

I stared at him. He'd just said a bunch of words, but I didn't understand. Confusion and sudden terror choked off my breath. My heartbeat sped up, battering wildly in my chest.

"You're bluffing," Jax growled. "No one can do that."

Sanaa took a sharp step forward to stand next to Shade. "What do you need from us, sir?"

I shot her an angry look on instinct. She was still playing her role, standing tall and straight, seemingly unaffected by anything the Overseer said, no matter how awful or preposterous. Sanaa's ability to adapt and carry on, no matter what, kickstarted mine and got my brain back online. She was a force of nature, and right then, she reminded me of lava hardened into strong black rock and polished smooth by the trials she and my father had been through to try to contain this lunatic. The time would come when she would heat and crack and fucking explode all over. I couldn't wait. The Overseer had no idea what was coming for him in the form of Sanaa Mwende.

Or Tess Bailey.

My fingers curled around the flash blast in my hand. I found the detonator switch and rubbed my thumb across the corrugated knob as my gaze whisked over Jax and Merrick. Wrath. Shock. Revulsion. Dread. The same storm crashed inside me. I needed to understand what the Overseer had planned.

Shade kept quiet at the forefront with me and Sanaa, probably thinking his Bridgebane act was up but not quite certain. Not speaking just condemned him further. His disgust came through the mask. No one could hide that kind of visceral reaction. Behind me, Ahern didn't say a word. Shiori murmured a soft prayer, her lilting whisper a reminder of times and places worth fighting for. I swallowed.

"I don't need anything at this time, Lieutenant," the Overseer answered. "Quintessa's already given me all the answers."

"*What* are you talking about?" I'd never given this man anything. Not affection. Not trust. Not an inch of me or anything else.

"You see ... " The Overseer flipped a switch on his console and lit up a monitor. He swung the screen our way. Explosions popped and burst all over the place. Phaser fire sped across the screen. Unarmed ships and cruisers disintegrated, picked off by blinding flashes as they tried to flee. My eyes widened. There was a war zone somewhere in the galaxy.

Shock stabbed me in the gut. I nearly doubled over. There was no sound on the monitor, just a savage visual bombardment. One whole side of a huge spacedock blew apart, the damage catastrophic. *Great Powers, where is that?*

"Is this happening?" Horror flooded me like a toxin that froze my limbs and stopped my heart. "Right now?"

"The enhanced soldiers I created before you stopped my production had one purpose: to find the rebel hideout. This wasn't their original function, of course, but I revised it as new facts came to light. I began to understand several years ago that the rebel base wasn't simply hidden, it was *elsewhere*, in another dimension—and one not just anyone can get into. You had to be special—or have someone special near you."

Sickness crashed through me in a wave.

The Overseer switched on another monitor. I recognized the shapes on the screen, those connected structures. There was Spacedock 1. That was the Fold going up in flames.

I took a step forward, my heart shattering like the wall that blew outward from the center of the rebel stronghold. Bodies floated like tiny stars in the darkness, lit up by flames and swirling through the void.

"You monster!" Tears blurred my eyes. The Fold wasn't just a home for rebel soldiers. There were thousands of families. Whole communities. *Gone.*

"Then you found the wormhole in Sector 14. The Black Widow isn't a black hole after all, is it? And it didn't take you anywhere you knew. It took you where you *needed* to go. Your ship-fixing lover's basement was filled with several interesting things, including your DNA. He was one of your best hunters, Nathaniel"—the Overseer's questioning gaze settled on Shade—"or so I'm told by the people who are still looking for him on my orders. Yours, apparently, were canceled. Care to explain?"

I gripped the flash blast so hard it dug into bone. "I ditched him," I snarled before Shade could talk. "I hate him almost as much as I hate you."

The Overseer shrugged. "This…pocket in space where you've all been hiding. It isn't a *here* or a *now*. It's a phenomenon the faithful have been whispering about for years. It's why I've indulged them—to learn more. They call it the home of the Second Children. The Mornavail."

My body could barely keep up with my frantic heartbeat, my blood pumping too fast through my veins. Light-headed, I said hoarsely, "I don't know what you're talking about."

"The Mornavail must have come from there, but then

they spread out and integrated into our version of humanity. They forgot who they were and where they came from. Except their differences remained, no matter how diluted. One:"—he ticked off a finger—"their incorruptible blood, preventing them from succumbing to any of our diseases. And two:"—another finger—"their ability to slide into an alternate time and place within the fabric of the universe."

The Overseer flicked on another monitor. There was Loralie Harris—covered in blood and soot and being dragged half-conscious onto a Dark Watch warship.

"The rebel leader is a pure blood. I had others, but you stole them—driving me to *this*." He indicated the death and ruination coming across the monitors. I shuddered, so heartsick my stomach heaved.

"Not too long ago, one of my patrol ships stumbled through a gravitational warp in Sector 17 and found what you've been hiding all these years. How rebels can disappear so completely. Only the enhanced soldiers survived, though. Two came back to report while a small unit hovered on the edge of the hideaway, following it. It moved, but they were able to keep up. Like a living thing, it tried to shake them. It couldn't. I'm emptying it now, as you can see."

Oh, I saw. The destruction of something irreplaceable and unique. Something I cherished. Explosions and murder. People I didn't know. Friends. Comrades. So many dead. I thanked the Powers the *Unholy Stench* was at the Mooncamps and not anywhere near this.

I couldn't watch anymore and looked at the Overseer through a haze of burning hate. This man *took*. He took with no conscience. "Why? What do you want from this?"

"I want to start over, and thanks to you, I can. With a few tweaks, I can have everything I have now *and* the love of the people. I'll be a god to them when I'm finished. And Caitrin will love me. She'll see me settle the war peacefully and worship me like everyone else. I'll have her. Our children." His disdain scraped over me like a rash. "Not whatever you are."

My brain short-circuited again. "The war's over. Mom's dead. You're insane, and she would hate this!"

The Overseer's smile didn't need to stretch wide for his triumph to be huge in it. A little upward tug to his lips was all it took to terrify me into believing he truly had a plan. "She'll never know. It'll all be different."

"How? You killed Mom. You can't get her back now."

"I've been doing experiments. And do you know what I've learned, thanks to you mostly?"

I shook my head, the ache inside me so raw and heavy I knew the weight of it would pin me to this man's atrocities forever.

"If I jump into the Black Widow at warp speed with Loralie Harris's blood in my veins, thinking not only about wanting to end up in what I believe you call the Fold, but *when*, I can arrive where I want, at the time I want, and create a new future from there."

Wait. *When?* Was that something he'd discovered on his own? Was that even possible? We never lost time in the Fold. But I'd also never entered it via the Black Widow while thinking about a date forty years ago.

"And your army of super soldiers can go through with you," I said, sickened and devastated. They were the only invaders who could survive the Fold. No wonder he'd been trying to churn them out in a hurry. He'd put the final pieces together and was ready. For this.

"Precisely. I quell unrest in the galaxy through firm but ..."

less destructive means and rise again less military dictator and more benevolent savior. Caitrin will be pleased."

He talked about Mom as though she were alive. Or would be again. "You'll still be you. Mom will see that, and she'll hate you just as much as the first time."

"She didn't always hate me. We were happy until whoever spawned you corrupted her and turned her against me."

Did he really believe that? Did he suspect Bridgebane? He didn't act like it. Not really. He'd barely looked at his friend and general in minutes. He was too gleefully destroying me.

I wanted to tell him this whole thing was impossible, but I couldn't. The Fold was a mystery. It had taken him years and liters of my blood, but he'd figured it out, or at least the potential of it. A potential that a twisted, selfish mind could think up.

"I'll never exist." So many people would never exist.

Others might live, though.

"No." The Overseer clicked off the monitors again. "And she'll love me like she said she did."

"She didn't." Fury shook my voice. "She didn't then, and she *won't*. You bought her. She sold herself for peace."

"That's the delightful thing about a do-over, girl. You can change how everything looks."

Abruptly, he turned to our fake General Bridgebane. "So quiet, Nathaniel? Afraid I'll notice that's not your voice? I'm assuming it's the bounty-hunter boyfriend beneath the mask. But Lieutenant Mwende"—he shook his head—"I'm very disappointed in you. You had the potential to accompany me on this groundbreaking journey, with the help of an injection or two."

All thought stopped, all fear and questions and dread. I acted. *Reacted*. I pressed the detonator switch, jumped in front of Shade, and hurled the flash blast at the Overseer's head. "Catch!"

He automatically lifted his hands. When someone throws something at you and yells *Catch*, you do.

The flash blast went off in the Overseer's face. I closed my eyes at the last second and hoped my head shielded Shade from the blinding flare of light. The percussion part hit, and I gasped as my heart slammed back against my spine and stopped. I couldn't draw a breath. *No air! Can't see!*

I stood still and waited for my lungs to recover. The shock to my body wouldn't last, and I had to be ready first. The Dark Watch used flash blasts to keep people back, usually in prisons where mob situations cropped up, throwing them from a distance to avoid the detonation effects themselves. We'd only been ten feet from the center of the blast. The Overseer and his super soldiers absorbed the worst of it, but my body still felt hollowed-out and crushed.

I dragged in a breath and opened my eyes. My lids hadn't shielded me entirely. A spotted landscape swam before me, but at least it wasn't total temporary blindness.

The Overseer stumbled, groping sightlessly for his console. He gripped it for balance. "Kill them!" he gasped out, his lungs still crippled by the blast.

Enhanced soldiers charged forward. The residual punch of the weapon hardly slowed them down. Their attack was swift and terrifying, and I reeled back from the onslaught.

"Sanaa! Merrick!" We had super soldiers, too, and they were *better*. Free will and pure blood. Fuck those goons. We'd beat them, even with the odds against us.

I spun and propelled Shade toward Jax, Shiori, and Ahern while Merrick and Sanaa sprang into action. Shiori stood still, blind already. Ahern had her hands up for protection and swayed a little. Shade's eyes watered, but they were open. He blinked and squinted. Had the blue eye lenses protected him?

"Tess?" He reached for me, missing by a few inches.

I stuck Shiori's hand in Jax's and Ahern's in Shade's. The fake cuffs were gone. They must have popped them open after the blast.

"Go!" I pointed Shade toward the living quarters. "There's an escape cruiser off the Overseer's bedroom. There's an air lock. Bring them!"

"I'm not leaving you!" He reached for me with his free hand.

"I'll be there!" I cried, breaking his hold. "Just bring them!"

He hesitated. Whatever he saw in my face convinced him. "Don't let me down, Tess Bailey."

I nodded, leaned forward, and kissed him. The electric connection between us zapped my lungs into working again. Shade's eyes met mine. Then he wheeled around, gathered his blind flock, and herded them toward the living quarters.

I turned in time to see Sanaa use a downed goon as a vault as she kicked two others into oblivion. She landed on her feet and attacked the next one.

Merrick grappled with two soldiers. They both dodged bullets. Sanaa threw a knife. Blood spurted. Merrick cracked a neck, and the sound snapped me into action. I sprang toward the Overseer, darting between Dark Watch soldiers.

Someone grabbed the back of my jacket, yanking me to a stop so hard my arms ripped back in their sockets. I shouted. Merrick seized the soldier by the neck and threw her into the window panel. A shot went off. I ducked. Merrick grunted but hardly moved, a hole in the meaty flesh of his shoulder. His lips pulled back in a snarl. His eyes lit with such boiling hatred that I almost pitied anyone in his path as he lunged forward.

Merrick ducked, spun, kicked—kept fighting as though he didn't even feel the second bullet that hit him. His blood splattered across my forehead. I jerked back, blinking.

Sanaa threw another knife and followed it with rapid bullets. Three goons fell, and my ears rang with the sound of gunshots. She moved so fast I hardly saw her. She and Merrick got back to back and fought together.

I saw a clear path to the Overseer and sprinted, ramming into him. We both toppled over. His eyes moved wildly in an effort to see me. He started to flail and hit, and I kneeled on his arms, straddling him.

"It'll never work," I growled, gripping him by the throat and forcing his head back at a hard angle.

"Why's that?" He laughed in my face, the bastard. I squeezed harder.

"Because you'll be an old man, and she'll be fourteen. She'll look at you and be disgusted."

"I'm working on that. Pure Mornavail blood is astoundingly regenerative. Experiments are going well. You can be a test subject."

"Never!"

He wrestled an arm free and jabbed me in the thigh with something. I looked down and saw him finish emptying a syringe into me. Pain flared out from the quick injection.

"What is that?" Alarm tore through me. A burn hit my veins from whatever he'd dumped through the needle.

He smiled—wicked. "The final injection."

Horror crashed over me. "The one that reboots people?"

"It was meant for Merrick Maddox, but you're the one who jumped on me. I'm not sure what it'll do to someone who hasn't had the previous enhancements." His eyes focused again, the pupils returning to almost normal. "I guess you're still my guinea pig."

Snarling, I lifted the Overseer's head by the neck and slammed his skull against the floor. His mouth slackened and his eyes lost focus. I started choking him. "I'll float myself before I ever let you control me." The dark vow settled into me as I gripped his neck harder than I'd ever gripped anything.

His mouth opened, gasping for air. He couldn't breathe. I wouldn't let him.

The lift doors opened. I glanced over my shoulder. Goons poured out, a deluge of Dark Watch. They started firing.

I threw myself to the side, taking cover behind the large console. Wheezing and choking down air, the Overseer rolled in the other direction.

Merrick lifted a huge table and threw it at the incoming soldiers. Sanaa grabbed me and carried me under her arm as she dodged bullets. Merrick spun and followed.

I screamed. I wasn't done! Was there an antidote?

We barreled into the living quarters. Sanaa swung around and closed the doors. She blew the lock with a punch that went halfway through the wall, but I doubted even that would stop super soldiers.

She tossed me to my feet. I landed running, and we crossed rooms that hadn't changed in decades. Despite the overall drabness, I could see Mom's touch everywhere, making plain things special. That was my mother. Subversive. A survivor. She'd walked the same bridge as my father.

We reached the master bedroom. Shade stood at the door to the air lock, tense, armed, and looking ready to come back for me. His eyes widened, relief flaring in them. "Come on!" He waved us toward the tunnel.

"You got it open." I pushed him ahead of me and followed him down the accordion-like passageway. It was a long one, twenty-five feet maybe. I'd thought I'd need my lock magic, but someone had guessed the password.

"It wasn't hard. 'Caitrin' was the code. The man's obsessed. The others are already on board. Jax is powering up the ship. It turned on to 'Caitrin' also."

I shuddered. My poor mother.

Shouts reached us from somewhere in the living quarters. Goons were catching up to us. We raced onto the escape cruiser. It wasn't the one I remembered, although it was similar and could probably house a dozen people. We entered through an antechamber stocked with weapons, several of which I recognized.

"Jax!" Shade hollered into the main body of the ship. "They're on!"

The ship hummed as Jax kicked up the power. Sanaa raced down the hallway and disappeared, but Merrick stumbled. Shade grabbed him. A fat bead of blood fell toward the metal floor between them. My eyes tracked it, seeing details that seemed impossible. Too red. Too slow. Too shattered on impact. The globule hit the floor like a thunderclap, and I stumbled backward.

My heart pounded. I squeezed the sore spot on my thigh where the Overseer injected me, shook my head, and forced away the tunnel vision. My senses widened, and I whipped back into action.

Shelves. Loaded with weapons. I bypassed the guns, pulled a Keeler hand bomb from the rack on the wall, and flicked on the detonator. I turned back to the passageway, counting down the seconds before the weapon exploded.

As the first goons stepped into view, I launched the

bomb down the air-lock tunnel. This wasn't a blinding flash and concussive blast designed for crowd control. This was deadly fire. This was holes in walls with only the vacuum of space outside. This was body parts to pick up, not bodies.

With ice in my veins, I slapped my palm down on the door control. The panels whooshed shut, cutting us off just before the bomb detonated.

We rattled, and I flattened my hand against the wall for balance. Jax would know the second I sealed the ship. The information would flash across the pilot's console.

We moved almost instantly, banking hard to the side. I scrambled to stay upright. Shade and Merrick slammed into a rack of weapons. Shade winced. Merrick hissed, his pain obvious. Even from inside the ship, the rip of metal was deafening as we tore ourselves from the vacuum seal instead of closing off the tunnel and releasing it. Jax accelerated fast, zooming away from the starbase. He'd jump as soon as he set the coordinates.

Sanaa rounded the corner again at a sprint, looking a little wild until she spotted Merrick. She took him from Shade, lifting him in her arms as though the biggest man I'd ever seen weighed nothing. Merrick looked at her, sheer incredulity flashing across his face before his head lolled, and he lost consciousness.

Next to them, Shade straightened and pulled off the Bridgebane mask, his temporarily blue eyes guarded as he watched me from across the antechamber of the getaway ship. Sanaa did the same, her dark gaze questioning.

I'd just crossed a line. We could have escaped without those deaths. I could have closed the air lock.

Whatever twisted in my chest wasn't exactly regret. It felt

more like loss, mourning for a part of myself I could never get back.

Daraja, Sanaa had called me from the day we met. My bridge was different from hers, from Nathaniel Bridgebane's, and Caitrin Bishop's. I didn't play two sides or pretend, but I had one foot in murder now and one foot in my own good reasons for it. The name fit.

I'd just left a hole in Starbase 12.

The vacuum of space was claiming goons, alive and dead.

Would tomorrow dawn better for it? *I hope so.*

I lifted my chin and looked back at Shade and Sanaa. "With any luck, the Dark is sucking out the Galactic Overseer right now and turning him into a chunk of frozen space trash."

Because he was garbage. I was done letting that man have power over me. I refused to take the blame any longer for the things he'd pinned on me, or the things I'd pinned on myself because of him. I didn't make that psychopath hunt down A1 blood, or start the GIN Project, or obliterate the Fold. I didn't help him find a way to destroy life as we know it, or maybe get a second chance to destroy Mom's.

I did, however, try to shoot him, strangle him, and hopefully end his life with that Keeler blast. And I was fine with that.

EPILOGUE

SHADE

I STOOD BEHIND TESS, HOLDING HER AROUND THE WAIST and watching the rocky peaks get closer through the clear panel as Jax steered the Overseer's escape cruiser toward New Denver. She'd finally stopped shaking. The long jump to Earth without sitting down or strapping in was an experience neither of us wanted to repeat. We'd both collapsed in the antechamber, our hands clasped. When we came out of warp speed, we picked ourselves up and joined the others, finding Mwende still wrapped protectively around Merrick.

Now, Merrick lay on the floor of the bridge, Shiori, Mwende, and Ahern each applying pressure to a different gunshot wound. Despite three bullet holes, he was holding up okay. He kept saying he'd been through worse, but when Mwende finally rolled her eyes, said, "Fine, then," and got up to leave him, he groaned low and long, getting her to come back to him with a worried frown.

"It's a shame we can't stay." I breathed against the back of Tess's head, soaking in her scent, her solidness, *her*. She was still with me. Terror had a new face for me—Tess in a battle for her life without me. It would never happen again, no matter what she wanted or thought was best.

"Hmm?" She sounded tired. The adrenaline drop was hard on everyone.

"Now that we're here, I kind of want to explore Earth."
These mountains looked like they held secrets. We'd passed
lakes the size of oceans. There was so much *nothing*, but
instead of feeling lonely and intimidating, it burst with
potential. A clean slate. New Denver was tiny, hardly a
speck on the horizon. Staying and helping to build it up held
sudden appeal. Maybe it was the engineer in me. Or maybe
it was just the man who wanted to make something.

"If the Overseer survived my hole in his box, I give him ten
minutes to swear his head off, kill some people out of rage,
and then track this ship to wherever we are." Tess leaned
against me. "The second we touch down next to the *Endeavor*,
we transfer everyone onto her, and get the hell out of here."

She sighed, reluctance in the little gust of air she let out
as she watched the landscape slide by. Did she like these
purple-hued peaks as much as I did? There was magic in the
sunset colors. A sky on fire.

I gripped her a little tighter. "We'll come back."

"We'll come back." Tess's parroted answer seemed oddly
robotic. I turned her toward me, worry worming into my
chest at her glazed-over expression. I knew what happened
in the control room. The injection. Was it doing something
to her already?

"Careful," Mwende said softly from the floor next to
Merrick. "She's very susceptible to suggestion."

I nodded, acknowledging the lieutenant's caution.

"So if I tell her to bark like a dog, she will?" Reena Ahern
asked.

Tess instantly barked like a dog.

I gaped at her. My heart banged against my ribs. Reena
Ahern's jaw dropped, an *Oh shit!* look freezing on her face.

Tess cracked up. "Just kidding. But yeah, that was

weird before." She sobered. Her gaze dropped to the floor, the picturesque world outside not holding her attention anymore.

I wrapped her in my arms again from behind, my chin beside her ear and my eyes on the painted landscape. A dusk-hued brushstroke swept across the mountains.

"I can't help Merrick if he needs a transfusion," Tess said, folding her hands on top of mine. "I can't risk contaminating him with the final injection."

"It'll work out of your bloodstream," Mwende said, glancing up from her patient. "There are no chemicals for it to bind to."

"You're sure about that?" Tess asked. We both turned to Mwende. Beside her, Merrick blinked heavily, barely keeping his eyes open.

"It's an educated guess," the lieutenant answered.

Tess bit her lip, nodding. Her eyes stayed focused on Merrick.

"You'll be okay, partner," Jax said, decelerating as New Denver got closer. "Merrick, too."

Tess relaxed against me, as if Jax's voice or words gave her solace no one else's could. Jealousy wasn't an issue. I was glad she had him. He could give her anything I couldn't, and between us, we'd get her through this.

"Merrick, you holding up okay?" Tess asked. I felt her tense as she waited for his answer.

"Been better." Merrick breathed for a moment. "Been worse," he said philosophically.

"Surral will fix you up," Tess said with absolute certainty.

Of course she would. As soon as we boarded the *Endeavor*, we'd head to Starway 8 for the best and most trustworthy doctor the galaxy had to offer. This Dark Watch cruiser would draw pursuers here while we skipped across three Sectors—sorry, New Denver.

Mwende had already contacted Bridgebane. He'd meet us at the orphanage.

If the Overseer still lived, we had a lot to plan for. Or plan *against*.

If the bastard was dead, the Dark Watch would turn to Bridgebane for guidance. At the end of the day, maybe Nathaniel Bridgebane wouldn't make a bad Galactic Overseer.

Tess turned in my arms and kissed me. I kissed her back, my heart expanding. Despite so much weighing on us, just like when I looked at New Denver, all I felt was potential. I couldn't wait to set foot on Starway 8 with new eyes as I looked at the orphanage. I'd stand there beside Tess and see my future.

And then I'd make it happen.

HAVE YOU DISCOVERED
THE KINGMAKER CHRONICLES?

*Read on for an extract from the first book in
Amanda Bouchet's bestselling series...*

A
PROMISE
❧ OF FIRE ❧

I PLUCK AT MY CRIMSON TUNIC, TENTING THE lightweight linen away from my sticky skin. The southern Sintan climate isn't my worst nightmare, but it sometimes ranks pretty high, right along with the stifling layers of cosmetics masking my face, my leather pants, and my knee-high boots.

Heat and leather and heels don't mix, but at least looking like a brigand means blending into the circus. Here, discreet only gets you noticed.

Craning my neck for a breath of fresh air, I navigate my way through the beehive of tables already set up for the circus fair. The performers on the center stage are the main attraction. The rest of us surround them, carving out places for ourselves amid the crowd. Tonight, hemmed in on all sides in an amphitheater lit by hundreds of torches and filled to capacity, I feel like a Cyclops is sitting on my chest—suffocated.

Damp curls cling to my neck. I peel them off and tuck them back into my braid, scanning the crowd as I walk. I recognize some of the regulars. Others I don't know. My eyes trip over a man and get stuck. He's looking at me, and it's hard not to look back. He's striking in a dark, magnetic way, his size, weapons, and bearing all telling me he's a tribal warlord. His build is strong and masculine, his gait perfectly balanced and fluid. He walks with predatory confidence, unhurried, and yet there's no mistaking his potential for swift, explosive violence. It's not latent or hidden, just leashed.

Watchful, alert, he's aware of everything in his vicinity. Especially me.

Our gazes collide, and something in me freezes. His eyes remind me of Poseidon's wrath—stormy, gray, *intense*—the kind of eyes that draw you in, hold you there, and might not let you go.

Adrenaline surges through me, ratcheting up my pulse. My heart thumping, I blink and take in the rest of him. Intelligent brow. Strong jaw. Wide mouth. Hawkish nose. Black hair brushes a corded neck atop broad shoulders that have no doubt been swinging a sword since before he could walk. Body toned to perfection, skin darkened by a lifetime in the sun, he's battle-chiseled and hard, the type of man who can cleave an enemy in two with little effort and even less consequence to his conscience.

He keeps staring at me, and a shiver prickles my spine. *Is this man my enemy?*

There's no reason to think so, but I didn't stay alive this long without the help of a healthy dose of paranoia.

Wary, I sit at my table, keeping an eye on him as he weaves a bold path through an array of potions, trinkets, and charms. He's flanked by four similar men. Their coloring varies, but they all have the same sure look about them, although they pale in comparison to the warlord in both authority and allure. The man with the gray eyes is a born leader, and only an idiot would mistake him for anything else.

He stares for so long that I start to wonder if he can somehow bore through my layers of face paint and unmask me, but I've never seen him before, and he can't possibly know the person underneath. I'm from the north of Fisa, where magic is might. He's from the south of Sinta, where muscle and cunning decide who lives or dies. Our paths would never have crossed in the past, and warlords don't usually frequent the circus.

I look away, hoping he'll do the same. There are plenty of reasons a man stares at a woman. An exotic face and generous figure attract as much attention as a good mystery, if not more, and the warlord's intense scrutiny feels more appreciative than alarming.

Ignoring the flush now creeping into my cheeks, I smooth the wrinkles from the coarse wool blanket covering my table and arrange my paraphernalia like usual. My glittering, gold-lettered sign advertises *Cat the Magnificent—Soothsayer Extraordinaire*, even though flashes of the future only come here and there, usually in dreams. Luckily, it only takes a few questions for truths to reveal themselves like flowers opening for the sun. I read people's body language and glean who they are, what they want, and maybe even what they're capable of. It's about knowledge and illusion. I get a copper for it, which is more than a fair deal for me. I won't peddle futures. I have an idea of my own, and that's more than enough.

My leg starts a nervous bounce. Prophecies can be interpreted loosely, right?

The audience gasps, and I turn to see what's happening on the stage. Vasili is throwing knives at his wife. She's strapped to the flat side of a vertical, rotating wheel, and he's blindfolded. He's never hit her, but my heart still comes to a complete standstill every time they perform. Tonight is no exception, and I hold my breath, both riveted and terrified, until he runs out of knives.

The crowd is too caught up in the circus to take advantage of the fair, so I get up again and head to the performers' gate to watch the end of the show and put some distance between the warlord and me. He's still looking when he shouldn't be.

The air coming through the gate is fresher, bringing with it the sound of Cerberus's chuffing breaths and the scent of sweaty dog. He's Hades's pet, so I doubt the heat bothers him. I toss him a wave, and two of his three upper lips curl in a snarl of acknowledgment. One of these days, I'll get all three, although in eight years I never have. I think his middle head just doesn't like me.

Finished with his performance, Vasili unstraps his wife while Aetos launches himself onto the stage with a triple flip and lands in a fighter's crouch that shakes the platform. The solid wood creaks under his colossal weight, and the rapt crowd murmurs in awe. Aetos straightens, pounds his chest, tears the horse pelt off his giant back, and catches fire. His roar shakes the amphitheater. No one can roar like Aetos. I've seen him perform hundreds of times, and I still get chills.

Seven and a half feet tall, muscle-bound, and tattooed blue from head to toe with Tarvan tribal swirls, he moves his hands in an impossibly fast dance, weaving fire until he's encased in a sphere of living flame. He bursts through the crackling barrier with another roar. The explosion blasts the hair away from my face and dries out the inside of my nose. I'm forty feet away but feel like I'm in the furnaces of the Underworld. Fanning myself is useless. I'll never get used to the southern heat, and with Aetos performing, it's even worse.

The Sintan Hoi Polloi can barely contain themselves. It's like doing tricks for children—everything enchants.

For them, the circus is a whirlwind of power and impossible magical delights. Everywhere from the hard-packed dirt floor surrounding the fair tables and stage to the high, far reaches of the circular stone seating, people jump up and down, hooting and stomping their feet.

My feet tap along with the crowd's, my eyes following Aetos around the stage. What a relief to be back in Sinta, even with all the dust and heat. I do whatever I can to stay on the west side of Thalyria. Our recent sojourn in the middle realm of Tarva made my lungs tight and my fingers itch for a knife. I'd probably start jumping at shadows if the circus ever went all the way east to Fisa. Just the thought of my home realm makes my sweat turn cold.

Sinta. Tarva. Fisa. West to east. Here to … Nothing I'm going to think about.

The audience whoops in approval of Aetos's fiery moves. Hoi Polloi in the amphitheater are ecstatic—and not only with the show. They've been celebrating ever since a warlord from the tribal south hacked his way north to Castle Sinta to put his own sister on the throne. You'd think Dionysus had dumped a three-month supply of wine over the entire realm. Temples have been overflowing with Sintans offering prayers of gratitude, their holy men overcome with gifts to help clothe and feed the poor. Statues of Athena, who is apparently well loved by the conquering warlord, are being spontaneously erected in towns and villages from here to the Ice Plains in Sinta's north. Happiness and generosity abound, and I don't even want to think about how many sheep have been slaughtered for celebratory feasts.

For the first time *ever*, the magicless majority is in charge, and Hoi Polloi are literally dancing in the streets—but only when they're not throwing themselves in abject loyalty at the feet of the new royal family. Or so I've heard. I haven't actually seen the new royals, but news spreads fast when there's something to say. After the warlord and his southern army secured the Sintan throne during the spring, his family took weeks just to move north. Not because they're slow, but because of the sheer number of adoring people in their way.

It's no secret the northern-born Magoi royals here in Sinta were despots, just like everywhere else in Thalyria. Hoi Polloi know they're better off with one of their own in charge.

But royals without magic? My cynical snort is lost in the boisterousness of the crowd. *It'll never last.*

Sweeping the horsehide back over his shoulders, Aetos takes a mighty leap into the air and doesn't come back down. He hovers well above the open-air seating and shoots flames into the darkening sky. They drizzle down in a shower of sparks that char the raised wooden stage and add to the oppressive heat. He lands with the last of them, tramples a budding fire under his huge boot, roars, of course, and then takes a solemn bow.

I cover my ears, grinning. I might go deaf from the applause.

Aetos stomps to the exit in a swirl of black cape and red flame, nodding to me as Desma takes the stage for her Dance of a Thousand Colors.

She moves to the melody of a kithara, starting out slowly and building speed until she's whirling around the stage in a kaleidoscope of color. Her feet barely touch the ground. A rainbow shines from every pore, from every strand of hair and eyelash, illuminating summer's twilight with an impossibly complex brightness. Her eyes glow with more shades of color than even the Gods have names for. Inconceivably beautiful, Desma is the grand finale, and the crowd worships her.

I'm as spellbound by Desma's dance as everyone else, and Vasili startles a squeak out of me when he nudges me in the ribs with the blunt end of a knife.

"You should be out there with her, Cat. Make a new act and call it the Fantastical Fisan Twins."

I whip the knife out of his hand, flip it, and nudge him back. "Twins look alike."

He looks back and forth between Desma and me. "Short. Long, dark hair. Bright-green eyes. Fisan."

Okay. He has a point. We're even the same age—twenty-three.

I sweep a hand down, indicating my curvaceous figure, and then point to Desma's much straighter frame.

Vasili grins, and his wide mustache spreads out, nearly meeting his bushy eyebrows on either side. "There is that. Desma should eat more."

I snort. "Or I should eat less."

"You're a woman, Cat. That's how you're supposed to look."

I make a face at him. Vasili has treated me like family since the day I showed up—fifteen years old, emaciated and dirty, with blisters all over my feet. "There's nothing like starving to make a person appreciate food," I say, my eyes roaming the place where I first saw Selena's traveling circus in action. Eight years have passed, but this southern Sintan dust heap is still my favorite venue.

Vasili grabs his knife back and twirls the base of the hilt on his palm, spinning it on an imaginary axis.

I watch the whirling blade. "You know I wish I could do that."

Smiling, he increases the speed until the knife is nothing but a blur.

"Show-off," I grumble.

He chuckles, backing up so that Desma can make her way through the gate. She keeps moving, swaying rhythmically, and I turn to follow. We all know from experience that she can't just stop, or the colors will build up inside her, the pressure unbearable. She takes my hands and spins me into her dance, our feet stirring dust into the shimmering air. We pass Cerberus on our way out, and one head pops up, ears twitching.

Desma's colors skitter over me with tiny teeth, nipping at my skin. Her rainbows jump to me, eager, and I absorb them so fast the magic leaves me breathless and floating.

"You soothe me, Cat." She guides us along the rough stone wall as we travel down the back side of the amphitheater. "You're a balm to my soul."

"I'm a bucket of water to your torch."

She laughs at my tart response, colors pouring from her throat and sinking into me.

It doesn't take long for Desma to stop glowing, and her power leaves me energized enough to forget the stifling heat. Rainbows fly from my fingertips, painting the evening shadows with splashes of color. I draw a picture of the Minotaur on the wall and then aim harmless ribbons of magic at friends who pass. Tadd and Alyssa launch into tumbling runs over the burned-out grass to avoid the beams. Zosimo and Yannis take my colorful volley head-on before staggering to the ground with imaginary wounds.

"Cat! You're a menace!" Aetos booms from behind me.

Laughing, I whirl and hit him with everything I've got left. The magic can't do more than tickle, but he acts like he's on the glaciers again, pitting himself against the man-eating Mare of Thrace.

His face contorts, turning more menacing with every step. I eye his hulking form and the giant horsehide flapping behind him like dark wings and wish I'd braved the Ice Plains, defeated a monster, and made an offering like that mare's head to the Gods.

What did I do to deserve my magic, apart from survive?

Aetos wades through the color-thick air and then grabs me, crushing me in a bear hug. "Who's laughing now?" he rumbles somewhere above my head.

"Too tight." I gasp, the magic fizzling as my bones shift.

"Sorry." He lets go, and I breathe again. His eyes, glacial blue like the Ice Plains, narrow when he gets a good look at me. "Zeus! You look like you're forty." He taps a finger against my cosmetic-layered nose. "Your face paints are so thick I can hardly see what's under there."

"That's the idea," I say with a cagey grin.

His expression sobers. "Who are you hiding from, Cat? Who are you?"

I clam up, humor draining from me like someone else's magic. Aetos hasn't looked at me like this in years. Not since he stopped asking where I ran from and why I scream at night.

I force a cocky smile. "I'm Cat the Magnificent. Soothsayer Extraordinaire."

He doesn't smile back, only letting me off the hook once he gives me a look that says he's not done fishing. "Time to dazzle some Sintans, Cat the Magnificent. Soothsayer Extraordinaire."

The tension I hate so much breaks when Desma pats my rump. "Either those pants shrank or you're eating too many spice cakes again."

I make a sound of disgust. "Why is everyone ganging up on me?"

She grins. "Because you're weird, and nobody knows who you are."

"My pants are fine." Actually, they're verging on truly uncomfortable, but I'm not about to admit it now.

Aetos crosses his arms, frowning. "They *are* too tight. If I see anyone looking at you for more than five seconds, I'll tear his bloody head off his bloody body."

My right eyebrow creeps up. "Then everything will be very bloody."

"Laugh all you want," he growls. "Just don't get splashed."

I make a sign to the Gods on Olympus. "Grant me patience."

"Seriously, Cat." Desma grabs my arm, unexpected urgency in her grip. "Those face paints and that outfit make you look a lot older and more experienced than you are. Tread carefully in the crowd tonight."

I roll my eyes. "I have done this before."

"I know." She releases me as abruptly as she grabbed me. "But things are different in Sinta now, especially in the south. These people have realized that muscle *can* overcome magic. Hoi Polloi have been feeling feisty all spring and summer, and you wouldn't want to kill anyone by accident."

Everything in me stills. "What makes you think I can do that?"

Desma shrugs. Aetos looks way too interested, so I shift the focus to him.

"You can kill with fire."

"I can kill with one finger," he scoffs, snapping for good measure. "Fast, too."

Desma's small hands land on her narrow hips. "We're talking about magic, not obscenely overmuscled Giants."

"Who are you calling obscene, rainbow woman?" Aetos's barrel chest heaves with indignation, thunderclouds gathering in his eyes.

"Stop!" I cut off their bickering before they have a chance to warm up. The Fates got everything backward with these two—a huge, tattooed southerner with fire and flight and a tiny Demigoddess with nothing to show for her Olympian heritage except rare beauty and a colorful glow. What a pair. I wish they would finally sleep together and get all the repressed emotion out in the open. "I have to go. My table's up."

Aetos winks. "Careful out there."

I shove him. It's like ramming my hand into a marble statue. "Why does everyone suddenly think I need protection? Didn't you just decide *I'm* the menace who can kill by accident?"

"So you can?" Desma asks.

I shake my head. "Of course not." I hate lying to my friends.

ACKNOWLEDGMENTS

Books come together with the help and support of so many dedicated and talented people. Huge thanks to my agent, Jill Marsal, and to my editor, Cat Clyne. Without them, I would be nowhere. The entire team at Sourcebooks Casablanca has my heartfelt gratitude for putting their skills and expertise to work to turn my words into books, make them look stunning, and get them into the hands of readers. Thank you!

I'm also so happy and grateful to be a part of the Piatkus family with these same books. The UK team is a joy to work with.

I'm lucky to have the support of a fabulous group of women writers who I'm privileged to know and call friends. Even shut away behind my computer, I never feel isolated in this crazy and sometimes difficult business because friends going through the same ups and downs as I am are only an instant message or email away. Thank you to my writing tribe: Adriana Anders, Callie Burdette, Chelsea Mueller, Maria Vale, Jennifer Estep, Jeffe Kennedy, Grace Draven, Mel Sterling, and Darynda Jones. I'm always looking forward to the next time I'll get to see any of you in person, even if I have to cross an ocean to do it!

Many thanks also to my neighbor, Sheila, who's always there for a laugh, a chat, a medical emergency, or a playdate. I'll miss you terribly when you move!

LaQuette, thank you so much for your last-minute help and guidance. I appreciate your generosity with your time and advice immensely.

As always, I'm so grateful for the love and support of my family. I wish we were closer and saw each other more often. Thank goodness for Facetime!

And finally, thank you to all my readers. I'm humbled and overjoyed that you take the time to read my stories. I hope you'll enjoy the continued adventures of Tess, Shade, and the crew of the *Endeavor*. I appreciate your support so much!